M.G. HERRON

THE ALIEN ELEMENT

TRANSLOCATOR TRILOGY BOOK 2

THE ALIEN ELEMENT

A YEAR-LONG PEACE

Rakulo trudged through the ancient forest with low spirits and limbs so tired and heavy it seemed a miracle that his feet continued to obey his commands. He walked on through the grey, sunless day, clenching his teeth each time the cold, biting wind sliced down through the trees to prickle his sweat-soaked skin.

He held his head high despite his exhaustion. Thirty young warriors trailed in a ragged line behind him, their clumsy footsteps occasionally catching on concealed tree roots or vines buried among the deep leaf-covered forest floor.

Even though Rakulo felt as tired as they did, he couldn't let them see any signs of weakness. A good leader never showed weakness, no matter how used up he felt.

About an hour outside the village, Rakulo held an

open hand up, signaling to the warriors following him that it was time to stop and rest. Most of the weary men and women sank wordlessly to the ground with their backs against the nearest tree, not even bothering to seek out the most comfortable spot. When you're that exhausted, anything that supports your weight feels like the softest feather bed.

"We'll be home soon," Rakulo said. "You'll have two days with your families before we set out again, so make good use of the time. And it goes without saying, but not a word, not even among family, about what we were doing at the Wall."

They nodded, but none spoke, for no one had the energy. A few heads lolled back to rest against moss-covered trunks. One or two warriors took deep breaths and blew out their cheeks as they sighed.

Citlali stood from where she had been squatting and walked over to Rakulo. Of all his warriors, Citlali was among the fiercest. Where some of the younger men were still scrawny, lean cords of muscle stood out beneath Citlali's tawny skin. Where others tired after half a day of hard walking, Citlali could run from one end of the Wall to the other in a single day, and have energy to spare. Even now, the only sign of her fatigue was the quick rise of her chest while she breathed, and her puffy eyelids, which betrayed a lack of sleep.

She leaned close to him and spoke in a low voice so the others wouldn't overhear their conversation.

"Don't you think you're pushing them too hard?" Citlali asked. "We've been in the forest for a score of days now."

"They need to be in fighting shape," Rakulo said.

"They also need time to recover," she said. "And time to spend with their children. You're too hard on them. They need strengthening, not breaking."

"No one knows what dangers wait for us beyond the Wall. They need to be ready—for anything."

She bobbed her head from side to side considering this. Rakulo said nothing about the fruitless journey from which they were now returning. They had searched along the Wall for days and days, looking for a way around or through, and found nothing. She finally nodded, turned, and sauntered casually back to where she had been resting a moment ago, making sure not to let her agitation show in her movement or on her face.

Citlali might disagree with Rakulo's methods, but even if she was opposed to him, she would be careful not show any sign of open dissent. Rakulo was their chief now and had been for twelve cycles of the two moons.

Rakulo turned his back on the group of weary warriors and gazed off into the distance, where he knew the stone city called *Uchben Na*—Ancient Mother—stood empty in the jungle. His ancestors had lived there once, but not for many generations. For as long as anyone could remember, and long before that, his people had lived in Kakul, the village on the edge of the sea.

Citlali was right, of course. He was too hard on them. But he had to be. There was no other option.

They hadn't found a way through the Wall this time, but one day they would. He needed them all to be ready when that happened, when the day came to fight for their freedom. Rakulo directed them to prepare in other ways. Together, they had learned to carve canoes from sturdy tree trunks. Together, they made flint-tipped arrows, and knives of obsidian, and spears with tips of obsidian and flint. All of it was training and preparation. All of it was to ready them for the future and whatever may lie ahead.

When his warriors had caught their breath, Rakulo motioned them to their feet and moved onward, setting a slightly slower pace this time. They skirted around *Uchben Na*, crossed the river, and soon were padding into the farmland around the village, past the rows of corn and beans, toward the thatched-roofed huts that made up the village.

Men and women came out of the field and village to greet them. As soon as word spread about their return, more people emerged from between the mud daub walls. Children cried out happily, weaving between their parents' legs on bare feet.

Rakulo exchanged polite greetings, and smiled as

his warriors were reunited with their families and led home by their husbands, wives, brothers, and mothers. The children ran circles around them, whooping and laughing. Rakulo breathed deeply of the tangy sea-smelling air, carried to him by another cool breeze. Despite his discontent at a year of searching and no results, it sure felt good to be home, especially now while the weather seemed to be giving them a reprieve.

A plump figure draped with seashell necklaces, her shoulders thick with tattoos that showed her seniority and elevated social status, turned a corner. Spotting Rakulo, Ixchel walked quickly toward him. He could tell by her posture that something was bothering his mother.

"Chief Rakulo," Ixchel said, loud enough for those still lingering nearby to hear. "I'm glad to see you've returned home safely again, my son."

Rakulo hugged her close to him and whispered, "Is everything okay, mother?"

"We must speak in private," she replied softly.

He followed her back to the house they shared near the center of the village. It was one of the oldest homes, with a fired clay foundation, sturdy wooden walls, and a thick roof that kept the house dry during even the fiercest monsoons. As chief, Rakulo could have commandeered a new house for himself, but he wasn't home that often and didn't want to isolate his mother, who had lost her husband and her youngest son in quick succession last year. Although there was no door to close the hut—all the houses in the village were open to the air—once inside, they had some privacy and could speak more openly.

"Did something happen while I was gone?" Rakulo asked.

"Ekel, the fisherman, has gone missing," Ixchel said without preamble.

"What?" Rakulo swore, his hands clenching into hard fists. "When? Who else knows?"

"Word has certainly spread by now, although no one is talking about it where they can be heard."

So that explained the obvious relief on the faces of his warriors' families when they came to greet their loved ones. It was no shock that no one was talking about it. Everyone knew what it meant when an old man or woman went missing.

"Could he have just gone off on his own for a while? Down the coast, or into the forest? Has anyone checked the caves?"

Ixchel gave him a condescending look. "Old Ekel, the homebody? The man who's gone fishing in the same spot every day for the last ten years?" She shook her head firmly. "No."

Strange, indeed, Rakulo thought.

It had been over a year since Xucha had shown his face—the God had been absent since the death of Chief Dambu, Rakulo's father. Had Xucha taken

Ekel in retribution for what he'd done? And if so, why had it taken so long?

In direct contravention to tradition, Rakulo's first order when he became chief was to immediately cease the human sacrifices that Xucha had demanded, and which had been reinforced by Chief Dambu and the endless line of shamans and chiefs that came before him—often unwillingly. Chief Dambu had been punished for his resistance, and eventually offered as a sacrifice himself.

When Rakulo became chief, he decreed that Chief Dambu was to be the last sacrifice.

The next few cycles of the moons were tense as everyone braced for retaliation from their God. None came. Xucha stayed away, no one fell ill, and eventually people began to relax. Many new babies were born in the last year, and—this was unprecedented—one elderly woman even died a perfectly natural death in her sleep. Rakulo had her buried next to the grave of Ixchel's youngest son, Rakulo's little brother, Tilak, who had been struck ill by Xucha in punishment for Dambu's disobedience.

Since Rakulo took over as chief and refused to continue the tradition of sacrifice, their village had experienced a year-long peace.

Until now. Until Ekel's disappearance. He knew what people would think. The whole situation stank of Xucha's influence. The black-clad God was known to be deceptive, to work in secret and under cover of night.

Or was there another explanation?

"Why Ekel?" Rakulo asked. "Why now?"

"He stopped fishing while you were gone because the journey to the beach had become too hard on his knees. At least, that's what he told everyone." She was silent for a moment, considering the source of the information. "Your father would have said he was the sensible choice."

"There are other things Ekel can do! And father's not with us anymore. I'm Chief now."

"I know that." His mother scowled at him, and for a moment he felt like a child again—and doubly guilty for reminding his mother that her husband was gone. "Why do you think I'm telling you these things? But there's something else."

Rakulo took a deep breath. "What is it?"

"I think Maatiaak had something to do with it."

"Elder Maatiaak?"

"The two of them barely spoke to each other before a few days ago."

Rakulo nodded. "They both wanted to marry Dea, Citlali's mother, and have been rivals ever since. But why does that matter?"

"They were never kind to each other. But after you departed a few weeks ago, that changed. Maatiaak began spending a lot of time with Ekel. They suddenly acted like old friends. I thought it was odd, but paid it no mind at first. I was happy to see that they had finally found common ground after all these years." She pursed her lips and paused.

Rakulo finished her thought for her. "And then Ekel disappeared," he said. "All of a sudden."

"Something's wrong, Rakulo. I can feel it."

A dread twisted his stomach. She was right. Something was very wrong.

"I better pay Citlali's father a visit."

2

FIRST FLIGHT BACK

Eliana hurried across the University of Texas campus, sweat gathering at the collar of her blouse and under her arms. Today was to see her give her final guest lecture of the term, and she was late for her own class.

The leather messenger bag she purchased when she had been offered the guest lecturer position at her alma mater earlier that year swung at her side, rubbing against the bare skin of her legs below her shorts. After a single semester, it was still not broken in, and the edges were sharp.

The spring air was fresh and she couldn't help but slow her steps and bend to admire the bright bluebonnets spilling out of every patch of grass edging the sidewalk. Seeing the bluebonnets bloom wild and free in the spring always made Eliana long to be outdoors, in the sun, and the sight of them today made her check in with herself.

Yes, she thought, *I have been outdoors lately—quite a lot*.

Eliana rose from sniffing the bed of wildflowers and continued her walk across the campus, this time forcing herself to walk more slowly. What did it matter if she was late? It was her last lecture.

After a grueling nine-month application and permission process, the research team she now led had just spent three weeks exploring the Calakmul Biosphere Reserve, a jungle in Mexico's Yucatan Peninsula that extended into Belize and Guatemala. Their goal, at least on paper, was to map uncharted Mayan ruins, of which there were a great many in the dense 13 million acre forest.

She considered, for a moment, the path that led her here. After she returned from Kakul a year ago, Eliana had begun to digest her harrowing experience. She wrote down everything she'd seen and learned, from the moment she was zapped across the galaxy by a glitch in Amon's Translocator, to the last time she saw the two moons in the night sky of that other world.

Even if she had possessed pen and paper while she was in Kakul, she didn't know if she would have had the presence of mind to keep notes. The first weeks had been so incredibly disorienting. She had been so intent on avoiding becoming a sacrifice to their ancient god, and then learning the language and working for her food, that nothing else had mattered. And then she had been brutally attacked. Who has time to keep a journal when your very survival is at stake?

Once Amon brought her home, she wrote down what she did remember. It went slowly at first, but once she had the facts down—how people lived there, what they ate, all the words she knew (spelled out phonetically), the people's religious customs—she finally began to ask the other questions that had been nagging at her mind.

How had the Kakuli people gotten to that planet in the first place? And when? The archaeologist in her demanded an explanation. Eliana consulted with Renee Shaw, her mentor and former advisor at University. Renee was a linguist who specialized in ancient Mesoamerican cultures, and she confirmed that the language Eliana learned was, indeed, a dialect of Yucatec Mayan. Given all the words she didn't recognize, she suspected that it would make sense that it was an unknown dialect or one that had diverged some time ago and had developed in isolation.

Later, much later, Eliana would admit to herself that she thought about going back to Kakul at that moment, and rejected the idea outright. Not only did she have absolutely zero desire to be translocated anywhere again, but Amon's work was under more scrutiny now than ever. The US government had insisted, to Amon's annoyance, on increasing security. She couldn't use a billion-dollar molecular reassembly device under high security for her research without a lot of hassle.

Eliana turned, instead, to the other place she was likely to get answers. Though she still felt scarred from the experience, her recent exposure in the press was a boon. Eliana Fisk wasn't just an archaeologist anymore—she was the woman who survived the world's first and only Translocator accident.

She managed to secure funding from an archaeological society associated with her alma mater, put together a competent exploration team from her old contacts in the field, and go through the nine-month application process with the Mexican government. After today, she could continue the search for answers to her burning questions about the Kakuli people in the Yucatan Peninsula, the ancestral homeland of the Mayan people.

She finally reached the building where the small lecture hall was located, dashed up the steps, and yanked on a polished brass handle. As the door opened on smoothly oiled hinges, a murmur of voices filled the air.

She may have been late for her lecture, but that only enhanced her entrance. A hush fell over the crowded room. Judging by attendance, word had spread that she wouldn't be continuing these guest lectures next year, as originally rumored.

Eliana stopped a few feet from the open door to catch her breath. After composing herself, she strode purposefully into the room. The sound of the door latching echoed across the quiet room.

Eliana heard only the sound of her footsteps as she crossed the floor to the lectern in the center. She took a second to carefully stow her messenger bag on a low shelf, fix her hair, and adjust the microphone down to her height.

"Good afternoon," she said. "I see that there are far more of you here than have been attending class for most of the semester. Many new faces. Thank you for coming. I'm sure we're breaking all the fire code regulations."

Gazing up at the gathering of students, Eliana noticed that not a single seat sat empty. In fact, students even sat side-by-side on the two columns of steps leading up through the theater-style seats. They stood behind the back row and gathered at the doorways.

No pressure, she thought. A vibration came from her messenger bag, where her phone was stored. She ignored it.

"Since you're already here, and this is my last lecture, you are welcome to stay. I won't tell if you won't."

The tension in the room eased visibly, and Eliana

saw a few guilty grins light up the young faces at the back of the room. Laptops opened, the backlit logos of the computer companies shining down at her.

She rested her forearms beside the microphone and began the speech she had prepared. "Our topic today is a continuation of the theme of this series—how Mayan art and architecture has influenced the modern world. Specifically, in this lecture we'll be examining what we can learn about complex societies and economics by studying the decline and abandonment of many major cities in the southern Maya Lowlands during the ninth century CE."

The lecture progressed from there, and Eliana fell into her groove. This was a topic she had been fascinated with since she began her career in archaeology, so it was easy to talk passionately about the details, from when the Maya entered the cultural consciousness of Western civilization in the early 20th century to the restoration of the pyramid at Chichen Itza. She showed them the jade mask of Palenque, evidence of the advanced mathematics of the Maya astronomers, photos of the codices and ancient scripts that, to this day, no one had been able to decipher or catalog in full.

It was a topic that had recently taken on more personal color, but she kept her own theories out of it. So far she had only told Amon and a few people close to her what she'd *really* experienced on Kakul. She couldn't lay her theories on her students—not without more concrete evidence—without coming off as a kook and losing any shred of credibility she had.

An hour passed in the space of a breath. As she began to wrap up the lecture, one young woman who had been typing furiously on a laptop the entire time began to fidget restlessly. Eliana knew her.

"Now—questions?" Eliana said.

The fidgety girl's hand shot into the air. Eliana tried to keep her face relaxed in a neutral smile. So much rested on a teacher's expression. She'd been this girl once, and it wouldn't be kind to embarrass her for her enthusiasm, even unintentionally.

"Is the research you're doing in Mexico connected to your disappearance last year?"

The question stole the breath from her lungs. Eliana blinked and felt her face flush. She closed her mouth and inhaled slowly through her nose.

"I'm sorry, Mrs. Fisk," the girl said. "It's just—I had to ask. The newspapers last year said you came back wearing jade and shell jewelry and dressed in coarse-woven cloth, and I've heard rumors that—"

A door opened and shut. The girl hesitated. Someone cleared their throat.

Eliana held up a hand. "It's okay, Margaret," she finally said. "I suppose someone had to ask eventually. The research my team is doing in Mexico is exploratory in nature. We're trying to map the undocumented ruins in the more remote regions of the Calakmul Reserve. That's all. Those jungles are incredibly dense, and we believe they still may contain some interesting discoveries about the Mayans."

The girl's face dropped, obviously disappointed. But she smiled and nodded, apparently satisfied with that explanation.

It wasn't a lie—more like an evasion. How had this young woman put the pieces together? Not even her research team had the full sense of Eliana's suspicious about the Kakuli people. She had kept those cards close to her chest. Eliana would have to tell Renee about this student. A girl with that kind of intuition—not to mention her passion—showed promise.

"That's all for today," Eliana said. "Thank you all for coming. Be sure you register in advance for the next guest lecture you attend."

With a rustle of bags and papers, the students all rose at once and filed toward the exit. The shy girl, Margaret, averted her face and hurried for the exit. Eliana turned to try to catch her attention, but when she turned around, she looked straight into a familiar face.

"Renee!" she said. "I thought we were meeting later for lunch."

Her former mentor and current president of the University proudly wore a trim red pantsuit that reminded Eliana more of a politician than a linguist.

Renee probably felt that her new position demanded she dresses the part.

"I hope you don't mind. I snuck in at the end," Renee said. "I didn't want to miss your last appearance. The students are completely enamored with you, you know."

Eliana couldn't conceal the blush that crept up her neck. She changed the subject. "That girl who asked me about my research, do you know her?"

Renee inclined her head. "Margaret Jaffray. Yes, she's an excellent student. Made the dean's list three years in a row."

"Oh, good," Eliana said. "She's a bright one. Might have to recruit her for my research team after she graduates."

Eliana grabbed her messenger bag and slung it across her body, then reached in and grabbed her phone. She had two voicemail messages, several missed calls, and half a dozen text messages. She scrolled through the texts as she distractedly followed Renee out of the lecture hall.

"So where would you like to eat?" Renee asked.

Eliana didn't answer her. She wasn't trying to be rude, it was just that the text messages absorbed her whole attention.

We found something. Take the first flight back. You have to see this with your own eyes.

Eliana swallowed against the dryness in her mouth. Her heart slammed against her ribcage. She looked up at her former mentor. "I'm sorry, Renee, I'd love to catch up with you but I think—I have to go. Let's reschedule. I'll let you know when I'm back in town."

Renee stopped, her hands falling loosely at her sides. "Back in town?"

"Yes," Eliana said, walking backward toward the door. "I'll call you!" She turned, not waiting for an answer.

Eliana booked a flight on her phone on the way to the airport. As the plane left the runway, she forced the hope down inside her chest, trying to keep it contained until she'd seen the evidence for herself.

3

NOT QUITE RIGHT

"Reuben!" Amon shouted over the electric thrum of the Translocator.

The clamor of a forklift offloading boxes with a metallic clatter swallowed his voice even through his earplugs. The boxes crashed and clanked as two engineers wrestled them onto the platform, through the gap in the concentric sphere of blue-green alloy rings. Filled with steel arms, screws, nuts, rubber wheels, and other tools, the parts would be used to assemble the last of the fabricators for the lunar base.

Ignoring Amon's call, Reuben focused on the holodeck, where the controls for the great machine —and the particle accelerator which powered it— were located. Two floor-mounted holographic projectors cast dozens of images and models and graphs of real-time energy readouts around him like a cockpit.

Reuben reached out to the broad glass touchscreen at the center of the control unit and tapped a button. The concentric sphere of alloy rings that stabilized the molecular disassembly and reassembly process began to spin, gathering speed until they shifted into a semi-transparent blur.

Simultaneously, a two-hundred-foot-tall, arch-shaped array of silicone and metal nodes that extended to the vaulted ceiling crackled with energy. The noise heightened, filling the vast underground laboratory.

"Reuben, I'm stepping out!" Amon shouted again.

The lead engineer turned his body slightly, but his wild white hair and a holographic image of the inventory blocked him from seeing Amon in his peripheral vision. His attention was pulled back to the controls.

Amon rubbed at his temples, frustrated. Reuben had been more distracted than usual lately. It was a private matter that he didn't talk much about, but everyone knew that his husband had been diagnosed with Alzheimer's over two years ago. Lately, he'd taken a turn for the worse, and Reuben was once again showing signs of sleep deprivation and forgetfulness that were uncharacteristic.

But wasn't Amon the same? Maybe they could all

use a break. Now that the MegaPower nuclear fission reactor was online, the pace of research and construction had nearly doubled. The last few months had been consumed with the construction and shipping of supplies—heavy machinery, mostly, but also the nuclear reactors. Now, the real work began—doing the research the Lunar Terraform Alliance had been formed to do, and figuring out if it's actually possible to sustain life up there.

A headache was new, though. That had come that morning while he was double-checking inventory on the fabricator parts. The fabricators were too big to fit in the Translocator, so they had to be shipped in pieces and he didn't want anything to be forgotten.

With a practiced swipe of his hand, Reuben locked onto the platform in Dome 2 and pressed another button. A sudden absence that Amon would never fully grow accustomed to came next as the pile of boxes seemed to energize, giving off a blinding brightness. When the light faded, the boxes were gone and the platform was empty.

A monitor against the left wall showed that the payload had been successfully reassembled on an identical platform—minus the arch—which Dome 2 had been built atop.

He opened his mouth to call out again but stopped himself. "Forget it," Amon muttered.

Pinching the bridge of his nose, he turned and walked out of the room, nodding at two guards in camouflage fatigues who stood on either side of the wide doorway. They nodded back and continued to stand, looking bored with automatic rifles slung casually over their shoulders. Theirs wasn't the most exciting job, but it was a necessary one. The Lunar Terraform Alliance and their international backers had a lot invested in this project.

Amon went past the stairwell, opting for the elevator to take him up the four flights to ground level.

At ground level, Amon passed through the main security checkpoint manned by two more security guards, a replica of the security checkpoints you had to go through at most airports. A conveyor belt fed through an X-Ray detector. There was also a metal detector and full-body scanner.

"Afternoon, Mr. Fisk," Roger said, nodding and tipping the brim of a Rangers ball cap at Amon, who nodded back.

Afternoon already?

A long hall led him to the lobby of Fisk Industries. His phone showed cell signal again and he checked for a response from Eliana. Although he'd texted her to let her know he'd be at work late, she hadn't responded.

Looking up from the phone, Amon realized the

lobby was filled with people. The traffic and noise had increased until it was nearly as bad as it had been in the Translocator lab. He groaned. It must be lunch hour already. The only thing Amon had ingested all day was coffee, so much of it that his hands had a slight tremor when he held them out, and he felt a little nauseous.

Scientists and other Fisk Industries employees gathered in the glass and steel lobby. In addition to the Translocator project, Fisk Industries made solar panels and conducted other photovoltaic and energy research. The particle accelerator that powered the Translocator was the bridge between the two ends of the company, and they were all housed in this building—and the other buildings across the campus. They had production facilities around the world, but this was the headquarters.

People lingered around the waterfall adjacent to the entrance, sitting on the benches there and at the tables by the café, talking amongst themselves. A woman's high-pitched laughter bounced sharply across the lobby and wormed its way into his ear. He squinted in the sunlight. All of it grated on Amon's last nerve.

Seeing his people happy normally made him happy, but he was getting a headache and needed to find a quiet place to relax and maybe lie down for a few minutes.

It suddenly occurred to him that he hadn't visited

Audrey in several weeks. She wasn't prone to chatter, which he appreciated more than usual right now. Audrey's office was located in a quiet back corner of the first floor, also behind the security checkpoint. He decided to go back and say hi to her, and then sneak in a quick nap in his own office around the corner. Amon turned and hurried back to the security checkpoint, putting his phone and wallet through the X-Ray scanner.

After Eliana returned home last year, the Lunar Terraform Alliance and NASA had agreed that it was everyone's best interests to move the carbonados to a more secure facility. Fisk Industries was an obvious choice. The building had ample office space. Amon had tried to hire Audrey once, and had admired her work ever since, so it seemed fitting that she would work in his building not as an employee, but as a colleague and friend.

In the back halls of the sprawling headquarters building, the lobby's ruckus receded to a dim buzz, and the pounding ache behind his eyes eased. Amon shoved his hands in his pockets to still the caffeine shakes as he walked slowly toward her lab. The walls here were salt and pepper tile, with geometric green and blue designs running around the corner to Audrey's office. He was tracing the designs with his eyes, thinking about calling the cafeteria to order lunch, when he caught sight of a small stream of red liquid in a puddle on the floor.

His stomach clenched, and he gripped the soft cloth on the inside of his pockets with both hands. Ducking low and pressing close to the wall, Amon crept closer and slowly peered around the corner.

The two guards that were always stationed in front of Audrey's lab were sprawled out awkwardly on the floor. One lay on top of his rifle, his elbow bent oddly. They each had a hole in the back of their head from which the blood seeped. The wall across the hall was stained with two distinct red splatter marks. Amon laid his hand on the nearest rifle. The barrel was cold.

A crash of glass came from inside the lab.

Audrey!

Amon unbuttoned the pistol holster on the thigh of one dead guard and withdrew the man's sidearm, a black Glock. He released the magazine and glanced down—it was fully loaded. Amon replaced the magazine with a snap and racked the slide of the gun. The adrenaline now surging through his veins made his hands shake even more. He paused momentarily, considering whether or not to use the guard's radio to call for backup.

The thirty seconds that would take could be the difference maker. Audrey was a friend. Amon made his decision. He tapped his hip—where his ID was clipped—against the card reader to unlock the door, and gently turned the handle, cracking the door a quarter inch. He peered in.

In the middle of the lab, on a rectangular island with cabinets on all sides, the glass cage of a large glove box isolator had been shattered by a heavy chunk of meteorite—not the large, midnight-black carbonado sample, but a different chunky brown rock the size of a large melon which lay among the mess of shattered glass.

On the floor, sprinkled with glass pebbles, another form lay sprawled. It was Audrey, fair skinned with a neat red braid trailing along the floor.

Amon hurried to her side and knelt down, fearing the worst. As he reached her, she twitched and groaned, but there was no blood. Her eyes opened, flicked to the gun, and a flash of fear contorted her face.

"It's just me," he said.

She stared at him for a long moment, obviously disoriented. Then she tensed as the sound of glass crunching underfoot startled them both. They scurried behind the rectangular base of the island.

"If I didn't tell him where the carbonado was, he would have hurt me," Audrey whispered.

"Who?" Amon mouthed.

She pointed back toward the other end of the lab where the sound had come from, patted her pocket, and gave him a weak smile. "But I didn't give him the key."

Amon glanced around the island, and sure

enough, a large man in black with short-cropped hair was limping around near the storage shelving at the back, where the meteorite samples were kept. The carbonado was kept in a special locked safe not twenty yards away. The man looked vaguely familiar, but Amon couldn't place him.

The man cursed when he saw Amon, his hand darting to his waist. Amon ducked back behind the island. Wood splinters flew into the air near his eyes.

Gasping, Amon held the gun to his chest and rose to a squat on the balls of his feet. He only had the element of surprise. Go where he least expects.

He held the gun around the corner and shot blindly twice, then dove the other way. He jumped up and squeezed the trigger once, twice, three times.

All of the bullets went wide. Amon's throat clenched. The man raised his own gun, training it on Amon, but the gun wavered. Amon tucked, and his shot went wide, too.

Amon screamed, raising his gun and firing rapidly.

One of the bullets finally struck the man in the gut. Another squeeze, and another. The man jerked back and his gun slipped from his fingers. Amon lowered the Glock, breathing heavily.

He waited for a long minute, his own ragged breathing settling as the ringing in his ears receded. Amon crept carefully across the room.

When he kicked the dead man's gun back away

from the body, the doors were shoved open—it was the two guards from the security checkpoint down the hall. Amon held his hands high over his head. Roger, recognizing Amon, lowered his weapon and waved for the other man to do the same.

As he waited for them to approach, Amon looked back down at the dead man's booted feet. Something was off. He wore cowboy boots of nice brown leather, but one of them was facing the wrong direction. Had that happened when he fell? Amon's eyes swept up the man's clothes. There was an awkward bulge in the area of his ribs that was not quite right either.

His face was normal. And it was a face that Amon recognized. It was Montoya, the Hawkwood mercenary who had impersonated an FBI agent after Eliana disappeared last year.

As if that wasn't worrisome enough, Amon knew with a rising terror that there was only one way Montoya could have snuck behind the two guards shot them in the back of the head without raising any alarms. And that this method was also responsible for his backward foot and the bulge in his side.

The guards approached and peered over his shoulder, as Amon used one shoe to lift the man's shirt, exposing the bulge near his ribs.

Roger hissed a breath inward. "What in the hell?"

The other man cursed and turned away. Audrey

came up behind Amon, one hand on her head. "Oh, my."

Amon grimaced when the shirt was drawn up to reveal a complete knee joint sticking out of the Montoya's abdomen.

4

NO SMALL ACTION

His mother didn't need to tell him to be careful. Rakulo was always on his guard now. But while he was filled with a low smoldering rage at the thought of one of his people being kidnapped in the night, he remained hesitant at the thought of confronting Maatiaak.

And this made him even angrier. Rakulo never remembered a single instance of his father hesitating as chief. Hesitation showed weakness. His father would have *acted*—immediately.

With that in mind, Rakulo stormed out of his house and strode purposefully toward Maatiaak's place. But as he got close, he thought of something else and circled back toward the field, angrier at himself with every step that carried him away from the conflict.

Maatiaak had been close to Rakulo's father. *Elder* Maatiaak. This man had known him since he was a bare-assed child. He'd watched Rakulo grow up playing games with the other boys, and with his daughter, Citlali, who was faster and stronger than most of them. Maatiaak and his wife were close with Rakulo's parents. They farmed together and took care of each other's kids.

But more than that, Maatiaak's standing within the village meant that confronting him would cause a ripple effect. Rakulo was not daft enough to believe it was a coincidence that most of the warriors who he'd been training were *young* men and women. None of the older warriors—Maatiaak's peers—the downtrodden, conservative men of his father's generation, took orders from Rakulo. And he knew that those same men had been suspicious of his plan to defy Xucha, and were now doubly dubious about why it seemed to be working.

Who can know the mind of a god? What did it matter if the ancient god hadn't retaliated yet? The retaliation would come again because it always had.

Among these conservative men of his father's generation, Maatiaak was the most respected. Standing up to him was no small thing.

And then there was the issue of Citlali. Maatiaak was her father. Before he confronted the elder, Rakulo must warn her. She knew nothing of what his mother had told Rakulo. Would she have found out from Maatiaak? A schism between him and Citlali could lead to a divide among the warriors loyal to him. If he went to Citlali first, he was pretty sure he could get her on his side.

All these thoughts and more raced through Rakulo's head as he paced the outskirts of the village, fuming.

He finally stopped when he came across the old hut that Eliana had occupied when she'd been here. Rakulo squatted before the open doorway. In the year since her departure, the hut had returned to its former state of disrepair. The roof sagged in the middle. The dirt floor had been reshaped and muddied by rivulets of water that ran through it when it rained. No one else needed this hut. There were more dwellings than people in the village. This hut and many like it stood empty. One day, Rakulo hoped, there would be more families to fill the huts. One day, he hoped, they would need to build more.

But not if people continued to vanish in the night.

Maatiaak either knew something or he didn't. He was either involved, or he wasn't. It seemed clear enough. Rakulo stoked his courage, stood up straight and tall, and walked quickly back into the heart of the village.

Rakulo first made his way to Ekel's hut, to see for

himself whether he was truly gone. The old man was a widower and lived alone. Rakulo knew him to be a messy man since his wife passed—he was a good fisherman, but a poor homemaker. Yet the inside of his hut was clean. A bed of straw in the far corner had been straightened and trimmed, with a woven blanket was folded at its foot. The bare clay floor had been swept clean of dust. A pot of water stood dry and empty by the door, and on the other side, several fishing poles leaned against the wall in a neat row. Rakulo had known Ekel all his life. He was not a neat man. This was not the house of the living man Rakulo had known. This was the house of a man who had prepared to die, a man who had confronted his fate and accepted it.

His mind made up, Rakulo turned and marched on. He didn't pause to think about what he was planning to do next until Maatiaak's house loomed into view. Citlali, who was helping her little brother clean corn in the shade of the porch, set down a half-shucked cob and rose lithely to her feet.

"Easy, Rakulo." She placed a gentle hand firmly against his torso, cold fingers bringing him back to himself for a moment. "What's happened? You look like you've seen a ghost."

"Ekel disappeared while we were gone," he said. "And my mother told me your father had something to do with it."

Citlali made a face like she'd just tasted spoiled fish. "What does that mean?"

Maatiaak emerged from the house then, his face expressionless and unreadable.

"If you have something to say, boy, say it to my face."

Rakulo stepped around Citlali and strode up to Maatiaak. In his memory, Maatiaak had loomed as tall as his father, high above him. He actually stood a handspan below him now, so that Rakulo could look down at the older man. He stepped so close that he could smell Maatiaak's breath, like grass and sea salt and smoke leaf, and discern the individual dark pinpricks of the pattern that made up the intertwined tattoos on his upper shoulders and neck.

"Where did Ekel go?" Rakulo said.

"How should I know?" Maatiaak said. "I am not his keeper. Ah, but you know old Ekel, he is probably fishing. The best fish come at dusk, he always said."

Maatiaak neither stepped back nor pushed Rakulo away. He simply tilted his chin up and returned the younger man's accusing gaze with apparent indifference.

"Then why are all his fishing poles lined up in his hut?"

"Perhaps he acquired a new one."

Rakulo clenched his jaw and bumped his bare chest into the older man, forcing him back. Due to the year of training and preparation, Rakulo was not only bigger than the old man, he was stronger, too. "As your chief, I demand you tell me what happened to him." Rakulo clamped his lips shut, but it was too late.

"Your mother put a bug in your ear," Maatiaak sneered. "What did she say? Eh?"

"She told me you and Ekel were seen together."

"Did she, now?"

"You hated him. What were you talking about?"

"Well, you'd know if you were here, wouldn't you?"

Maatiaak stepped away, turning his back to Rakulo and addressing the crowd that had begun to gather during the argument. Looking out at the worried faces of the villagers, Rakulo felt suddenly very silly and fought down the shame that rose like a tide to his cheeks.

"It seems that our *Chief*," Maatiaak said, his deep voice carrying, "has been listening too closely to the rumors of his *mother*. If you want to accuse me of something, say it in front of everyone."

"You didn't deny it. Tell me she's wrong."

"What is there to deny? She is wrong, boy. I don't know where old Ekel is, but I have no doubt he will surface sooner or later. He was never very reliable as a man, but you can't say he's not a survivor, can you?"

Rakulo felt himself clench his fists. The crowd

had grown thicker. If Rakulo backed down now, he would look like the biggest fool that had ever lived. Certainly, the biggest fool ever to call himself Chief.

Maatiaak stepped closer to him again. A smirk played at his lips. Was the old man *enjoying* this?

"Your mother always was a bit of a gossip," Maatiaak said as he passed him.

Rakulo pounced on his back. The older man spilled to the dirt, his forehead cracking against a stone bordering the garden of his house. Rakulo's fists sank into the old man's soft sides, but the punches were ineffective. He was too close to get the leverage he needed for a solid blow. Maatiaak snarled, wrenched his body around, and spat in Rakulo's face, momentarily blinding him. The older man managed to draw his knees to his chest. He kicked Rakulo off with powerful legs.

Strong arms wrapped around Rakulo's frame and hauled him away while he tried to retaliate. Citlali spun and pushed him so hard he stumbled. He caught himself on a corner beam holding up the roof of a nearby hut.

"Go!" she yelled at him, making shooing motions. "Get out of here." She glared at him, the anger evident, but her eyes pleading.

Rakulo hesitated. He glanced around him, but the faces of the other villagers were stony and unforgiving. When he met their eyes, they looked away or wrinkled their noses at him. An older warrior was helping Maatiaak up off the ground now, brushing him off. Several others stood at his back.

Rakulo turned and stalked off toward the safe shadows of the forest as the sun sank into the treetops.

5

MAYAN MONOLITH

The plane had barely finishing taxiing when Eliana was out of her seat and collecting her bags to deplane.

She rented a car like she always did, and was driving on the highway, headed southeast across the Mexican state of Campeche before she dug her phone out of her purse. Remembering that she meant to call Amon at the airport—before she got sidetracked by the photos her team sent her—she decided to fork up the international calling fees and dialed his phone.

His voicemail picked up. "Amon here. Leave a message at the beep."

She shook her head at the familiar voicemail greeting. *Never one to mince words, is he?*

"Hey hun, it's me. I'm sorry I missed you at home, and also bummed that we didn't get to spend more time together while I was there…but I saw you'd be working late, and so when I got an interesting call from my team, I decided to fly straight back to Mexico. We finally found something, and it's incredible. Just amazing. I'll try you again tonight. Hopefully, I'll know more details then. Love you, talk soon."

Well, that was annoying, but it was her fault. She should have called him, but she had been absorbed by the photos her team sent to her email, and she lost track of time. All of a sudden they had been calling her name through the overhead speakers because she'd missed boarding.

She wasn't herself with an imminent discovery at her fingertips. In this state of mind, she understood Amon's tunnel vision when he was working through a sticky problem with the Translocator. Everything outside of her work was no more than a dim reflection, a distant voice, a vague sense of unease. Amon would be sad he missed her, but he would understand.

After an hour of driving, Eliana came upon a military checkpoint where she had to show her ID and visa to get through—these were common in Mexico, but always intimidating, although her paperwork was up to date, the guns still made her uncomfortable. Another few hours of driving, and she finally turned off the broad two-sided highway and reduced her speed as she bumped onto the cracked pavement of the old back roads. Then she slowed again as she turned onto a familiar, pothole-ridden rough dirt trail.

It was getting dark when, ahead of her, parked near a small cluster of buildings and a gas station around which a little village had grown up, she spotted the dark green Land Rover. A few locals came out of the taqueria inside the gas station to gawk and stare as Eliana parked and got out of the rental car. They cradled beer bottles in their hands and leaned against the building as they whispered to each other about what the *gringa* might be doing here. Eliana grabbed her suitcase from the trunk and wheeled it over to deposit it in the rear of the Land Rover, which opened automatically and then closed again. The halogen lights snapped on, and the engine rumbled to life as Eliana climbed into the passenger seat.

"Hello, Lakshmi," Eliana said after the door snapped shut.

"Hello, yourself," said the long-limbed brown woman as she shifted the SUV into gear. She wore a pixie cut, tan-colored pants, and a collared shirt with two buttons open at the neck. "You got down here fast. Didn't you have a class to teach?"

"I didn't want to miss a thing. I left immediately after the lecture ended."

"Was Austin any cooler than it is here?" Lakshmi asked. "I feel like I've been sweating for weeks."

"I thought you were used to the hot weather," Eliana teased her.

"Heat doesn't bother me. But I was wrong, El," she sighed dramatically. "*No one* gets used to this humidity."

"You could wear shorts, you know."

"Are you kidding me? And let the mosquitoes feast on my legs? My legs are far too marvelous to let those hungry little bastards have a single bite."

Eliana laughed, and Lakshmi joined in with her deep-throated chuckle. Not that it was a hysterical joke, but they both felt giddy with the secret knowledge of the discovery shared between them.

When the giggles receded, and she had caught her breath, Eliana turned in the seat to look directly at Lakshmi while she drove.

"Tell me everything about this monolith you found."

The others were asleep when they reached the camp after ten o' clock, and Eliana had to satisfy herself with Lakshmi's story and the photos because it was a several-hour hike into the jungle to see the monolith in person. Not a fun or advisable trip in the dark. More than one person had been lost and swallowed by this jungle. It would have to wait until morning.

She ate chicken leftover from dinner, stretched out on a simple bedroll with mosquito netting draped atop her, and fell asleep in her tent.

Eliana was awakened by a brown hand holding a steaming mug of coffee through the opening of her tent.

"Rise and shine," Lakshmi said in her sing-song voice. Eliana could see her long legs through the door flap of her tent.

Grinning, Eliana tossed aside the mosquito netting and took the warm ceramic mug into her hands. She didn't need the caffeine to wake her this morning, but she inhaled the rich earth and chocolate scent gratefully, appreciating the good camping mattress and the slippery feel of the tent fabric under her bare feet as she stood and took a careful sip of the hot coffee.

Her small team of archaeologists was sitting around a freshly stoked campfire when she emerged. Lakshmi was scrambling eggs on a grate over the hot coals.

"Morning, boss," said Ross in his low baritone without looking up from the mystery novel cradled in his big hands. Despite the camouflage pants he'd purchased at the army navy store—for the many pockets, he said—he was a bookworm at heart.

"Hey there."

"Hi," said Talia in a smaller voice.

"Hello!" said Turner, boisterous as always.

Talia and Turner were twins. They were her study buddies in graduate school and had worked for her company before they lost funding a couple of years back. They had been working caretaker jobs at museums in Philadelphia and New York City, respectively, when she had offered them this job several months ago.

In fact, they had all quit to come work with her.

"When are we leaving?" Eliana asked.

"Breakfast first," Lakshmi said, handing Eliana a plate of scrambled eggs and bacon and baked beans. "It's quite the hike."

"Oh?"

"Yes, indeed," Turner said. "We never would have found the place if Talia didn't have a terrible sense of direction."

Talia gave her brother a disgusted look. "It was raining!"

"Yes, but why would you go *up* the hill?"

Ross snorted and glanced up, then went back to reading his book.

"Anyway," Eliana said, "you found the monolith. So I, for one, am glad you got lost."

"See?" Talia said.

Lakshmi turned off the stove and disconnected the gas canister, then stowed the gear in her tent.

They finished eating in silence. Ross put his book away, and the twins produced two light daypacks. Eliana took the camera case, Ross took a machete, and Lakshmi grabbed the maps and compasses. They were packed and ready to move out in less than ten minutes.

The enthusiasm bubbling inside of Eliana waned a couple of hours into the hike as Ross used his machete to cut through thick vines.

"I would have sworn I hacked those away yesterday," Turner said. "It's incredible how fast they regrow."

Soon they were moving uphill, taking five-minute breaks every twenty minutes to rest on the steep incline. The damp soil clung to her boots. Eliana didn't say anything out loud but thought more than once how improbable it was that Talia hadn't realized this was clearly the wrong direction. But she was a smart girl. Perhaps she knew it was the wrong direction and had hiked bullishly ahead just to annoy her brother or force him to walk uphill for a while. When they walked uphill, his constant chatter ground to a halt.

Eliana had sweated through her clothes by the time the ground leveled out. Her shirt and shorts clung to her skin. And, unlike Lakshmi, she had dozens of bug bites on her legs below her shorts. She forced herself not to scratch, knowing that would only make it worse.

"Here we are," Lakshmi said. The twins set down their packs and took long drinks of water. Talia passed her bottle to Eliana, who shot a spout of water into her mouth. After the exertion of that hike in the heat, it seemed like the best water she'd ever tasted.

Ahead of her, Ross grunted as he hacked at a wall of leaves with a machete.

Eliana glanced around, looking for any sign of the gray limestone used by the Mayan people to construct their temples and pyramids. She let out a soft, "Ahhh," when she realized that the wall of leaves that Ross was hacking at *was* the stone monolith. Like the photos they'd sent her, it was so grown over with green lichen and pressed back into the foliage that only a trained eye would have picked it out as stone.

"Good eye, Talia," Eliana said, handing her back the water bottle. "How did you spot it?"

"Truth be told, Turner was the one who noticed it was a stone. I just forced his whiney ass to hike up here and look around."

Turner squinted at his sister, but the smirk on his face betrayed the good nature of his expression. They shared smiles among each other, each of them giddy with the excitement of the discovery.

A moment later, Ross finished hacking away the vines and leaves that had folded over the stone in the two nights since they found it.

Lakshmi stepped up to examine the stone and with a small knife peeled back a bit of lichen to expose the carving.

Eliana reached out and brushed her fingers across the distinctive outline of two overlapping circles.

The photos hadn't done it justice. It was clearer in person, as the noonday sun cast shallow lines into relief. A small circle overlapped a larger circle. An irregular chunk had been cut out of the upper left quadrant of the larger circle.

Could this be a coincidence? Would the others see it, too?

To Eliana, the carving looked like a perfect representation of the two moons that hung in the night sky over that other planet she had visited—the moons the Kakuli natives called Ky and Kal.

6

STRANGE SIGHTINGS

"You knew this man, Mr. Fisk?" the stocky, blonde FBI agent said over her shoulder as she squatted beside Montoya's body.

The badge she showed Amon when she arrived said her name was Agent Monica Wiley. Amon was suspicious of anyone with a badge, based purely on past experience, but she seemed legit.

Agent Wiley wore her shoulder-length hair pulled back in a ponytail so tight it seemed to stretch the skin of her forehead taut. Her blazer was tailored so that it wouldn't hinder her movements, and she wore light boots that were well broken-in but still polished. She acted professional and seemed very confident.

Her partner, an equally serious man she called Agent Moreno, was interviewing the security guards in the hallway outside Audrey's meteorite research lab. Audrey herself sat in a wheeled office chair nearby, holding an icepack to her cheekbone. A greenish-brown bruise had begun to form where Montoya had struck her. Audrey observed Amon's conversation with Agent Wiley with pursed lips. She fidgeted but stayed put so as not to get in the way of the crime scene investigators as they bustled about, snapping photos of the bodies and making notes on tablets.

"I did," Amon said. "He was one of the Hawkwood mercenaries who impersonated FBI agents after Eliana disappeared. That was over a year ago."

Amon watched a brief twinge of disgust flash across the woman's impassive face at the mention of the impersonators. She turned away and knelt over the body. Her expressions were more contained with dead bodies—she barely showed any emotion as she prodded at the kneecap in Montoya's chest with her finger. She tapped on her tablet, then stood again.

"How do you think he got in here? Do you have any theories?"

Amon glanced at Montoya's body and let out a sigh. *That* question could be answered many ways. The mechanism through which Montoya had arrived was obvious. But how was it even possible? Amon had been racking his brain since he'd gunned the man down, and the only answers he could come up with were highly unsettling.

"I'm not sure," he said at last. It was the most

honest thing he could think of.

"Humor me," Agent Wiley said. "I already told you, we're not interested in charging you with anything. It was clearly self-defense. The most you'll have to do is a little paperwork."

It was best, to be honest with her. That's what Eliana would have encouraged him to do.

"He translocated in here," Amon said. "That's the only way he would have gotten in, behind the guards. You saw the camera feeds of the lobby and the security checkpoint. He didn't come through there."

She nodded, and a worried expression clouded her stoic face.

Amon shook his head. "What kind of maniac would use a Translocator without a stabilization platform?" But in the back of his mind, he knew. He didn't understand why. But who else could it be?

"Maybe he thought it was worth the risk," Agent Wiley said.

"As far as I know—and believe me, I would be the first to know—the Translocator in this building is the only one in existence. And clearly, I didn't send him in here."

"Obviously, someone else has a Translocator."

"Even if someone did manage to build another one," Amon went on, "where would they get a particle accelerator to power it? There are only a handful in existence. One here in Austin, one in

Switzerland, another in Japan. And they're almost exclusively used for particle physics research—never as a power source, except for ours, which was built specifically for that purpose. If someone were using another one as a power source, people would know. That's not the kind of thing that can be kept hidden for long."

Amon shook his head. It didn't add up. What would he want with his own Translocator?

"What was the man looking for in the lab?"

Amon felt his face pull into a deep frown. "The carbonado."

"That's the meteorite that was responsible for the incident with your wife, wasn't it?"

"What? No."

"I read the file."

He stared at her. The details of that incident were kept strictly confidential. It wasn't safe for the public to know *why* the Translocator had malfunctioned. Amon and Audrey had both continued to study the meteorite in the year since Eliana's return, but they still didn't understand the material or how it worked. Amon glanced at Audrey, who shrugged and continued to pick at her nails.

Agent Wiley was silent for a beat. She seemed to struggle for a moment, and then reached some kind of decision. "We were going to tell you eventually, but until now you were a suspect. I don't think it was you."

"What do you mean *I* was a suspect?" Amon snapped. "What's going on here?" He clenched his teeth so tight a twinge of pain shot into his cheek.

Audrey came to her feet beside him.

Agent Wiley held up one finger and waved to get her partner's attention through the doorway. When Agent Moreno arrived, Agent Wiley took a deep breath and began again.

"We've been investigating strange sightings across the United States," she said. "Interpol has reported another few in Europe as well. There may be others, but inter-agency communication isn't always effective or transparent."

"What sightings?"

Agent Moreno made a placating gesture with an open hand. "Mr. Fisk, I understand you're upset, but we didn't have any idea what it could be until recently. Let her explain."

"We thought we were chasing a serial killer for the first several months," Agent Wiley said, "until Agent Moreno rewatched the speech you gave last year at the unveiling of the Translocator. Right before your wife disappeared."

Amon's eyes widened. Most of the world had seen that speech by now, but he didn't know the FBI had been mining it for clues to some sort of serial killer mystery. He glanced from Agent Wiley to Agent Moreno and back again.

"Some of the most gruesome crime scenes I've

ever seen," Agent Moreno said. "The first few victims had their limbs scattered through the woods or across the roofs of buildings—blood everywhere, disfigured limbs, several body parts. Horrible stuff. But then we started finding the body parts closer together, and then grotesque but mostly whole. That's when we first suspected a serial killer. Didn't know how he was doing it, but his methods had a sort of pattern that we began to recognize."

Agent Wiley leaned close and lowered her voice. "But not like a hand had been removed and reattached. Not sewn together like Frankenstein. It looked like they were grown that way. We found one guy with some of his digestive organs outside of his body. He died in horrible agony. Our CSIs were completely baffled."

It felt like the breath had been sucked out of Amon's chest with a vacuum. He knew exactly where this was going. They all saw him working his mouth, and waited.

"My speech," he finally managed to say. "Where I was talking about the work the ESA did after the Nazi fringe science documents were first declassified."

"Yes!" Agent Wiley said, excited now. "You mentioned the lab mice being reassembled with missing limbs and the animal activists that got the project shut down. Well, I found old photos of that project that the activists posted online back in the day. It's almost exactly the same thing as what we've been chasing. So, our first suspect was you."

Audrey licked her lips and glanced at Amon. Amon looked away. One of his worst nightmares was coming true, but it was someone else doing it. His work had fallen into the wrong hands.

"Why didn't you say anything? Why not come talk to me?"

"We were watching you but…you're a hard man to watch."

He grunted. He supposed that made a certain kind of sense.

"Apart from your speech, Mr. Fisk, over time the bodies that we were sent to investigate were less and less disfigured. Two weeks ago, a woman arrived, and according to witnesses, walked about two miles to a nearby farmhouse before she died."

"Really," Amon said. That was actually kind of impressive. Amon's research with the Translocator was based on the stabilization platform he had developed to mitigate this issue with the molecular reassembly. Proving that worked on a small scale was what got his foot in the door at the LTA.

"So when we got the call about a security incident at Fisk Industries and heard the description of the body, Moreno and I came to see for ourselves."

They stopped talking. The sounds of investigators moving around the lab, clicking their cameras and typing on their phones, came back into focus. Someone coughed in the hallway outside.

Amon put a hand to his forehead. A migraine thudded dully on the inside of his skull. He needed time alone to think about the implications. "Are we done here?"

"One more question," Agent Wiley said. "I don't understand why he wanted the carbonado. If I'm going to find who's behind this, I need to understand that part of it."

Should he tell them? Amon supposed it was the best thing. They were on his side, and he had been taken off their suspect list. He should help them. It was the right thing to do. He glanced at Audrey, who nodded eagerly.

"We don't know exactly how it works yet," Amon said. "But the meteorite he was looking for is some kind of…superconductor."

"It may even be a power source of its own," Audrey added. "If we can just figure out—"

"Like I said, we don't know yet," Amon interrupted her. He was fine with cooperating, but there was no reason to tell them *everything*. "We're still trying to work it out. What I can tell you is this: if you use the Translocator to move matter over a distance—in other words, disassemble at one end, and reassemble in another location—you need a stabilization platform to control the reassembly. It takes a lot of power, and that power has to come from somewhere. Inorganic matter is less complicated—it doesn't move and live and breathe. Even a leaf has a fairly simple organic structure and can tolerate some...flux. But living beings, with a heart that beats and blood that flows? That is more complex. We have a *very* small margin for error. What the meteorite Audrey is studying enables us to do is short-circuit some of that complexity. Like I said, we don't fully understand it yet, but it enables us to send matter over greater distances with less power and more precision. Essentially, our theory is that by using the carbonado we may not even need the stabilization platform at the receiving end."

In fact, I'd bet Eliana's life on it. She and Amon had both translocated that way. Amon and Audrey had both been trying to understand why that had worked ever since.

Agent Moreno let out a heavy breath filled with discontent. "So whoever is translocating those maimed bodies around the country is doing experiments? Trying to get around this limitation?"

"That's exactly what I'm saying. I don't know if it's a good thing or a bad thing they didn't get that rock."

"Do you have any idea who could be behind this?" Agent Wiley said. "Montoya isn't the first one they've killed, and he won't be the last."

Amon glanced at his feet. Should he tell them? He had to go talk to Reuben and tell him what had happened. They would have to upgrade the security protocols on the Hopper. He hated the idea of more guards and more guns, but that was probably a good idea, too.

Amon sighed. They had the best chance of catching the bastard. "Lucas Lamotte," Amon said. "It has to be him."

The two FBI agents nodded. "He was on the top of our list, too," Agent Wiley said. "Do you have any idea where we might be able to find him?"

"I don't have a clue."

"Is it possible that he had access to the Translocator designs?"

"He ran the company in my absence last year, while I was searching for Eliana. He had access to everything."

The two agents exchanged a look.

"I hate to do it, but I'm going to have to increase security. Can the FBI pitch in if this is an important case?" Amon said.

Agent Moreno nodded. "I'll call it in, see what they say."

"Great," Amon said, already moving away. "That will help. I have to go now."

Without waiting for a response, Amon was out the door and walking down to the Translocator lab, using the four flights of stairs this time. It was quiet down there when he arrived. Blessed quiet, for a change.

But people were still there. When Amon passed by the security guards, he spotted his scientists. They were all crowded in a group around the holodeck. Was something wrong with the Hopper?

Amon was about to call out when the crowd parted and he saw Reuben's tear-streaked face lift from where he had been sobbing into Jeanine's shoulder.

Amon caught Reuben's gaze. There was a deep well of pain in his friend's watery eyes.

"Oh, no," Amon said, realizing what had happened.

"He's gone, Amon," Reuben said in a cracked voice. "Charlie passed away this afternoon."

"Oh, Reuben, I'm so sorry." The crowd parted and he embraced his friend.

Amon felt a terrible sorrow, and also a knot of worry in his stomach that had nothing to do with his friend's sudden and terrible loss.

As he held Reuben, who grieved for his dead partner, he thought of Eliana. When he lost her in the Translocator, it felt like being torn apart. Surely that's how Reuben felt now. Shredded. Ripped. Flayed open.

Amon had come down here to tell Reuben about Lucas, but now he couldn't. He couldn't bring himself to burden his friend.

"I'm sorry, Reuben. I'm so, so sorry."

7

THE CAVE DWELLER

The cave dweller will know what to do.

That thought ran through Rakulo's head as he retreated through the leaf-strewn forest. He startled a wild turkey, and it squawked as it flapped its fat, feathered body out of his path. The creatures weren't very good at flying, but they lifted into the air briefly when they were caught by surprise before powering into the woods on scrawny legs.

The cave dweller will know what to do.

A bruise on his chest where he'd come down on Maatiaak's knee hurt when he breathed, but Rakulo ignored it like he did most physical pains. It would pass in its own time. There were many things he resented his father for, but he was thankful for how Chief Dambu had taught him to bear the pain.

The furious storm of anger and shame battering

his brain, however, hurt more than any physical pain he'd ever experienced. How had he been such a fool? Maatiaak must have known Rakulo would confront him—maybe he had even counted on it. Had Maatiaak known that his mother had been spying on him as he spent time with Ekel? Had Maatiaak orchestrated the whole thing simply to shame him?

Rakulo should have seen it coming. Now, if Citlali didn't hate him, the rest of his warriors would certainly think less of him. He couldn't even beat an old man in a fight. The older warriors never trusted Rakulo's plan—they had seen too much, watched too many of their kin die at Xucha's hand, struck down by sickness or taken in the night.

His foolish mistake would render useless a year of hard work. Rakulo couldn't face Xucha alone. He needed the whole village to be behind him, united as a people. They would have been, once he'd finally found a way around or through the wall. That would have convinced the ones who remained skeptical. But now, even if he did find a way around the wall, Maatiaak and those that took his side would never support him.

They had been divided the whole time. Gods, how had he not seen it? He'd been an utter, ignorant fool. The pretender as the chief.

The cave dweller will know what to do.

Without his father around, the cave dweller was the only one Rakulo trusted to give him good advice.

Rakulo slowed as he approached the caves. The ground was treacherous here—pockmarked limestone hidden beneath the ever-present scattering of leaves made for uneven, slippery footing. He could break an ankle if he wasn't careful.

What is breaking an ankle to this shame? Twigs. A light rain. A dead turkey running around with his head cut off. He laughed at the thought, a kind of hysterical burble that began in his chest and shook his whole body.

He stopped walking so he wouldn't laugh himself right into a hidden hole. Ahead of him, the ground rose slightly to a low limestone wall the height of a medium tree. Along this wall, several low overhangs had been cut out over time by the wash of rainwater. Rakulo had often escaped here as a kid to get away from life in the village—the cutouts provided good, quiet hiding spots.

And that was also how he'd met the cave dweller. The old man had lived out here for as long as Rakulo had been alive, not in a cutout but in one of the several caves carved into the deeper sections at the far end of the limestone outcropping.

Rakulo moved parallel to the wall until he came upon the deeply shadowed cave he was looking for. As he was searching the dark mouth of rock for the old man, he heard a noise behind him and spun.

"What are you doing sneaking around out here?"

He flashed Rakulo a mischievous smile. The old

man was short, stocky, and barefoot. He wore an old dirt-stained tunic with more holes than fabric wrapped around his waist and one shoulder. He held a thick walking stick polished smooth by the oil of his hands over years of regular use.

"Gehro!" Rakulo said, exasperated. To the cave dweller, he must have looked just like that turkey he startled earlier. Rakulo scowled. "You scared me. How do you move so silently?"

"Many years of practice, my boy. Come inside, come." He rattled a pouch at his waist. "I found some good mushrooms today."

Rakulo wrinkled his nose. "You know I don't like mushrooms." But he followed the old man silently into the darkness of the cave.

Gehro stoked a fire back to life in the middle of a ring of stones. The fire cast shadows that hid the back of the cave, which curved around into the darkness. Mushrooms came out of his pack—meaty things with broad hats and thick stems—and the old man nestled them down between the rocks ringing the fire and the hot coals. His callused fingers arranged the coals with a few deft swipes.

They sat in silence for a while. Rakulo brooded over his failures. Gehro focused on cooking the mushrooms and said nothing.

It was funny—his father would have done the same thing, and somehow his silence would have been judgmental and made Rakulo feel even worse about himself. Gehro's silence made him feel comfortable and safe.

Rakulo lifted a hand and rubbed the bruise on his chest, took a deep breath, and let it out. "I think I messed up, Gehro."

"I can see you chewing on something heavy. Want to talk about it?"

"Ekel disappeared from the village. My mother thinks Maatiaak had something to do with it, so I confronted him."

"What did Maatiaak have to say about that?"

"He denied it."

"What did you accuse him of?"

"Well, I…nothing exactly."

Gehro picked a mushroom out of the fire and rolled it from one hand to the other while it cooled. "And then what happened?"

Rakulo pushed a pile of dirt around with the toe of his wooden sandals. His feet were tough, but, unlike Gehro, he didn't have decade's worth of calluses built up to protect him. Even if he did, the sandals provided more protection if he were to accidentally step on a sharp rock or a pointed stick while running.

"We fought, in front of everyone."

"Did you win?"

Rakulo shrugged, not looking up to meet the old

man's eyes. "I guess. I'm stronger than him, and a better fighter, but it didn't matter if I won because I couldn't prove that he had anything to do with Ekel's disappearance."

Gehro nodded. "You're learning, at least."

"Learning what? How to make a fool of myself in front of the whole village?"

"Do you think the others believed Maatiaak when he said he didn't know anything about Ekel?"

Rakulo snorted. "No. Some might have, but anyone who has a head of their own would know it was suspicious."

"Then what are you so worried about?"

"I never should have confronted him without proof."

"Sometimes you learn more by losing a fight than by winning one."

The old man said no more, and Rakulo looked up to demand what that meant but came eye level with a steaming mushroom. Gehro blew on it to cool it off, then handed it to Rakulo.

He took it because refusing would have been impolite. He didn't really like mushrooms but had to admit he was hungry enough to eat anything right now. Rakulo had been so angry hearing about Maatiaak from his mother that he'd forgotten to eat after the long journey home.

He took a careful bite. It was warm and rich. The earthy flavor made his nose wrinkle, but he had to admit that the mushrooms were good—for mushrooms.

"Good, right?" Gehro said.

"Palatable."

The old man chuckled. He tossed another mushroom between his hands and popped it into his mouth whole. Gehro moaned with pleasure as he chewed.

Rakulo had another, and then a third. He refused a fourth. He was no longer hungry enough to tolerate them. Gehro poured water into a wooden cup and handed it to Rakulo, who took it gratefully, swishing the water in his mouth to wash the taste of mushrooms away. He swallowed and handed the cup back to Gehro.

"Not even Maatiaak will go against me when I find a way around the wall," Rakulo said.

"That is not the way to win their hearts."

"You just wait."

Gehro reached over and smacked him upside the head.

"Ow!" Rakulo said, rubbing the spot where it smarted. "What was that for?"

"A good leader is not measured by his deeds, but by how much compassion he has for his people. They will not care if you walk straight through the wall if you do not show them that you care about them. You must put your people first."

"I'm trying to free them! Isn't that good enough?"

"No. Besides, you'll never make it in those flimsy wooden canoes."

Rakulo felt the blood drain from his face. "What are you talking about?" he said.

"Don't play coy with me. You think you can hide what you are doing in my forest from me? Trees don't just go missing, boy! Same as people."

A moment of silence passed. "The only way around the wall is by water," Rakulo said.

"It has been tried. It is not possible."

"Why not?"

"It is not possible."

"That's not an answer, old man."

"Many have tried. How many have returned?"

"None. But what happened to them? Maybe they got away and decided not to come back since they were free."

"Maybe. Maybe not."

Rakulo huffed a breath out.

"You know what else good leaders do?" Gehro asked.

"What?"

"They keep their people alive."

"I'm going to get on the other side of that wall," Rakulo said, inhaling air from the fire, which smoldered low and hot now.

Gehro nodded. "I hope you do. But I don't get many visitors. And if you die, who will be chief then? Maatiaak?"

Rakulo stared into the red hot coals as the flames danced. A vivid memory of Maatiaak's smug expression stared back.

8

THE KAKULI CARVING

"Incredible," Eliana whispered, her face close to the carving of two moons. Stone had a distinctive scent, even covered with foliage—it was the smell of dust and sand, nearly smothered by the wet humid smell of lichen and mud. But sharp, as if the scent of cut stone had lingered for all this time.

"Is that what you were looking for?" Lakshmi asked, apprehension evident in her voice. Eliana glanced around and noticed the twins and Ross were all watching her expression closely.

"It's more than I ever thought we'd find," Eliana admitted. She could see them all light up. "Let's take core samples in the topsoil all around this area. Be on the lookout for potsherds or anything else we can carbon-date. We need to figure out exactly how old this carving is."

The twins began digging in their backpacks for

gloves and sample bags and the coring drill, which came apart in several pieces and had to be assembled. Eliana fished out the camera from her bag and began to snap more photos.

"I gotta ask," Tanner said. "How did you know we would find something here?"

"I didn't. I hoped. I saw one very similar to this in Kakul, on the inside of a stone archway among other carvings. Maybe when we clear this monolith we'll find more of the story."

Her fingers traced the two overlapping circles. Time and rain and the growing plant matter had worn the edges of the carving smooth, but not erased them. Had the person who made this carving been to Kakul and come back to document what they had seen? Surely the sight of those two moons in the sky had made as much—if not more—of an impression on the ancient artist as they had on Eliana. Or had someone else told them what to carve? And if so, who?

"What does it mean?" Ross asked.

"I think it's a depiction of the two moons over Kakul. Ky and Kal, the natives called them."

"How come we've never heard about this other world before? In all my studies of the ancient Mayans, I've never seen anything even remotely close to this symbol."

"So many Maya tribes died off or were lost. It could be that any evidence of these symbols was destroyed by the conquistadors. Their influence was devastating to the cultural artifacts of the Maya. They burned records and destroyed many sacred buildings."

"We're not your students anymore, El," Lakshmi reminded her. "That canned answer doesn't convince me. In fact, it doesn't even sound like *you* really believe it."

Eliana blushed. She knew immediately that she had reverted to professor-mode to hide her real opinions. If she spoke honestly in academic circles—where she had spent years earning her education and where she had recently been fortunate enough to spend more time—she would have sounded like a lunatic. Before she admitted anything, her first instinct was to gather as much hard evidence as possible to back up her claims.

More evidence than normal, considering how outrageous this theory would seem. The whole world knew Eliana had gone *somewhere* exotic when she had disappeared. But only those closest to her knew the details, and Eliana had been close-lipped with the press. Amon, the FBI, and Dr. Badeux from the LTA had all warned her to be careful about what claims she made—not that she had needed the warning. It was hard enough for people to accept that Amon's Translocator had worked. How would they react to finding human beings living on another *planet?*

But this was her team she was talking to—not just her colleagues, but also her friends. They were out here stomping around this humid jungle, wearing mosquito netting and lugging heavy packs full of archaeology equipment because of her crazy theories. She owed them the truth—at least the truth about what had been troubling her, and what would keep her up at night even more with the first piece of evidence in hand.

"I suppose I don't believe it," Eliana said. "But I can't fit the pieces together. If this carving shows the two moons in Kakul, that means those people came from here. I knew they were of Mayan descent because of their language, which brought us to Mexico in the first place. But how did they get from here to there? Or, an even wilder idea, did they come from Kakul first?" She gestured out toward the dense jungle surrounding them. "They didn't have rocket ships, let alone Translocators, back then. So how did they do it? It just doesn't make any sense. I was hoping that what we found here would tell me more of the story, but..." She glanced at the lichen, like a thick coat of fur, on the monolith. "I guess we'll have to find out the old fashioned way."

Lakshmi scuffed at the dirt with a boot. Ross swung the machete casually at a stray leaf that extended down from a low-hanging branch, slicing it in half. The twins busied themselves collecting samples of dirt. Turner exposed a piece of rotting wood and shoved it aside to get at a spot of soft earth where they might be able to dig down.

Eliana shrugged, and they all set to work carefully clearing the monolith and the surrounding area of plant matter and collecting more samples. They celebrated by dancing and cheering when Lakshmi dug up a potsherds nearby—scrapings went into separate sample containers, as the paint would have contained organic matter that could be radiocarbon dated. They found what might have been a bone, but it wasn't buried very deep and didn't seem human. They bagged it anyway.

Night eventually fell and they were forced to abandon the search after taking a single core sample six feet deep. They began the hike back, the weight of their packs which had been filled with food and water now doubly stacked with dirt and other samples. It was slow going. The sky was dark and they were all exhausted when they finally reached the camp.

Eliana washed her face and brushed her teeth and wearily climbed into the tent. She stretched her sore body out on her narrow bedroll to sleep, only to remember that she hadn't remembered to call Amon today, or checked to see if he'd tried to call her. She pulled her phone out of the back, and sure enough, there were several missed calls and practically an essay's worth of text messages.

Her blood went cold as she read the words on the

screen, and she immediately called him back. The phone only rang once before he picked it up.

"Hey baby," he said. The sound of weariness mingled with relief in his voice had a calming sensation on her. She practically melted into her bedroll.

"It's good to hear your voice," she said.

"Yours, too. I was so worried about you."

"What happened? I mean, I read your texts, but..."

He told her about his day, from the morning's work with the Translocator to finding the guards dead outside Audrey's lab, to his conversations with the FBI agents. Last, he talked about Reuben, how heartbroken he was for his friend, and how painful it was to see him in that state, having just found out that his husband had died.

As he spoke, Eliana came to a slow realization.

"I'll fly back tomorrow," she said. "I should be there for the funeral."

Amon let out a breathy sigh. "I hate that you have to leave after you just got there, but I can't say I'm not going to be glad to have you home."

"Is that sympathy pains?"

"That's definitely a part of it," he said. "I don't know what I'd do without you, love. And I don't have to imagine what it feels like to lose you—I already know that, and it hurts just to think about it. But now there's some other lunatic out there with a dysfunctional Translocator, and I'm worried."

Eliana chuckled.

"What's funny?" Amon demanded.

Her chuckles turned into deep belly laughs. Amon brooded silently on the other end of the line. When she regained control of herself, she said, "Dysfunctional Translocator? You don't think that's funny, after everything that's happened?"

"What happened to *you* was an accident. Whoever has this Translocator is maiming people *intentionally*. They're using people as test subjects. It's irresponsible. It's immoral."

"I understand. It's Lucas, isn't it?"

"I don't know how, but yes. Who else could it be?"

"Don't worry. I need to bring some soil samples back for testing anyway," Eliana said. "Which reminds me…"

She launched into her own story about the carving.

"Eliana, that's incredible," Amon said. "Now, I feel guilty asking you to come home."

"Don't. I'll fly back tomorrow. I want to be there. Besides, we took some samples today, and this is a good excuse to get them dated."

"Okay. It's not technically allowed, but you know I could just come get you…no one would know."

"Not a chance in hell am I going through that thing again."

"Okay. I get it. No worries. I'll see you at home."

"Goodnight," Eliana said. "And Amon? I love you."

"Love you, too, babe. Sleep well."

She hung up the phone. Eliana lay awake for a while, thinking about poor Reuben and how it must feel to watch your soulmate die slowly like that. Was it worse to have it happen slowly, or all of a sudden? If it were her, she would choose all of a sudden. She definitely wanted to be there for the funeral.

But in the back of her mind, she was already thinking about how to fit the samples they had taken today into her suitcase and considering who would be able to carbon-date them the fastest—and with the utmost confidence. A few days in Austin and she could be back here to continue her work.

9

SUNK COST FALLACY

After he got off the phone with Eliana, Amon swung aside the landscape photo of the lunar surface—a barren, dusty gray plain with only an American flag and a spacecraft for decoration—and unlocked the safe hidden behind it. He took out a sealed metal canister containing the carbonado solution before locking the safe and returning the picture to its original position.

Amon cradled the canister in the crook of one arm as he walked through the quiet halls of the building down to the Translocator lab. He didn't have to go through security because, like Audrey's lab, his office was behind the checkpoint.

After the excitement, Amon figured people could use a break. He sent everyone home so the FBI could finish their work undisturbed. The crime scene investigators carted out the bodies and departed several hours later, and Amon was left with an empty campus. Apart from a few security guards, he finally had the peace and quiet he'd been looking for earlier that day.

The Translocator scientists needed the break more than the rest. Reuben's reaction to Charlie's death had shaken them all. He'd been so good at keeping his private life to himself that to see him break down like that, as if the weight of the past two years had come crashing in all at once, reminded them all of their own fragility.

He figured they all needed some time to process. Himself included.

The heavy metal door protecting the Translocator lab was closed and sealed now. Amon approached down a long hall. The two men standing guard were fresh-faced and alert. They had been swapped out at the shift change that evening and briefed on the day's events. Amon greeted them with a nod, showed his ID card, and used the retinal scanner at the door to let himself in. The door spiraled open, he stepped inside and sealed it behind him.

Time alone with the Hopper had been in short supply since the main reactor at the lunar base had come online. His experiments with the carbonado solution came to a complete halt. The constant parade of engineers and materials, astronauts, and

LTA officials bound for the lunar surface made it difficult to do much of anything else.

The original carbonado solution he and Reuben had devised out of desperation to rescue Eliana had done its job, but it had been a quick and sloppy job. His only goal at the time was to replicate the transfer that had catapulted his wife across the galaxy and follow her through to wherever it had taken her. The results hadn't been pretty—going through had short-circuited the breathing apparatus on the spacesuit he'd been wearing, and Amon had nearly suffocated as a result.

However, his understanding had slowly progressed. With Audrey's help, they refined the solution and the physical interface that connected it to the Hopper. Now, all he had to do was plug it into the power cables, run tests, then remove it and return the Hopper to its normal operations so that work could resume the next day. He slid the canister into place now and lit up the holodeck controls with a hand gesture. A vast array of hologram controls and measurements and outputs arrayed themselves in the air around his body.

Amon ran a few bootup tests. No more sparks shot from the nodes of the arch like they once had. Nor did sending electronics through the super-charged Translocator cause them to short circuit any longer.

He spun up the machine, hearing the familiar

high-pitched noise, like the keening of a camera flash charging. Amon transferred a small chunk of iron across the room. Playing back the recording, he compared the molecular structure of the iron before and after the translocation, searching for flaws and unexpected changes. All seemed normal to him. The distance was off by a few inches. There was still an irregular result when it came to distance. It was almost like some other variable was interfering that he couldn't track. He had a suspicion it was a side effect of the arch pulling power through itself. But he couldn't track it.

Not being able to set aside more time for his experiments was frustrating. Progress went ahead at a snail's pace. He was still trying to find the best ratio of carbonado shavings to silicone, and learn to target the amplified translocation with more accuracy, all while looking for errors—after what happened to Eliana, he couldn't be too careful.

Apart from not needing a stabilizer at the receiving end, the carbonado solution amplified the Translocator's power, increasing its range and allowing him to send heavier objects through while pulling a tenth of the power from the particle accelerator that they normally saw.

The moon had been the edge of his range before. With the carbonado, Amon had yet to find the new distance limit.

If he wanted to, Amon could send this little

chunk of iron into the sun. Or back to that strange planet where Eliana had ended up.

That was something else he hadn't figured out—why *had* Eliana ended up there in, what did she call it, Kakul? Of all places in the galaxy, why *there*? And if that place existed, what other worlds were out there waiting to be explored? What threats did they harbor? What wonders did they hold?

But he had to concern himself with Earth-bound problems for now. If Lucas got ahold of the carbonado and managed to harness its power, as Amon had done, he would be able to cause incredible damage. The trail of mangled bodies he'd left strewn across the world proved that he was obviously not bound by merely moral considerations.

Amon paced away from the holodeck as his mind found a new groove in this train of thought. Another Translocator out there certainly changed things. He would have to be more careful. Lucas had tried to take the carbonado once. No way would he give up after a single failure.

The hollow quiet in the lab felt suddenly ominous. To fill the silence, Amon walked over to Reuben's desk and removed the radio his friend kept in the top drawer. It was the standalone, battery-powered kind of radio, boxy and black with chunky dial knobs. A thin red line on the front marked the station. Amon turned the knob so the radio cycled through static until it found a clear frequency. He didn't know why Reuben kept the old piece of junk. But then he felt guilty when he thought that it might have been a sentimental gift. Maybe Charlie had gotten it for him.

Amon turned up the volume and heard the voice of the conservative radio talk show host, Reagan Gruber, bray through the speakers.

"Look, John, it's just like one of those science fiction comedy films from the early aughts—*Honey, I Lost My Wife in the Translocator.*"

"Don't give me these weird pop culture references, Reagan, just say what you mean!"

"I always say what I mean. Listen, you know how these things go. When you're watching the movie, it's kind of funny, and wacky, but in the back of your mind, you're wondering, what in the world is this guy thinking? What an idiot! Doesn't he realize he's just making things worse? Doesn't he know he's the cause of all this trouble? The main character is usually a goofy dad type in the films, too, some clumsy nerd who never had the social skills to make it in the real world, so he does his experiments at home, where he endangers his own family instead of his coworkers. Well, that's good—don't bring your crazy to work, right? So there he is tinkering with this incredibly dangerous machinery in his attic. It's funny until you realize he literally has no conception of what kind of danger he poses to society."

Amon had reached for the knob to change the

channel but stopped halfway through the story. He didn't want to listen to this idiot—and yet the danger of the Translocator project being shut down was ever-present. Amon needed to know what he was up against in the press.

"So what do you think the LTA should do, Reagan? They invested billions of dollars into The Auriga Project. They can't just pull the plug. And there's still the problem of getting supplies to the lunar base safely and cheaply."

"That's a sunk cost fallacy, and you know it. They should cut their losses now before it's too late and something truly disastrous happens. What if they screw something up on the moon that messes with the tides or the weather? What if that mining operation they've got going up there collapses a tunnel and skews the orbit by a degree or two? That could cause an ecological disaster that makes this whole global warming hoax look like—"

Amon switched off the radio with an irritated groan. Talk about absurd. There was no mining operation—they were just using moon rocks in the fabricators. Amon knew that what happened when Eliana went through the Translocator was a mistake —and he took full responsibility for it. But to think that a bad translocation would affect the tides was completely ridiculous.

Or was it? He hadn't discovered all of the

carbonado's limitations or abilities yet. Maybe Reagan Gruber was right.

Amon shook his head to banish the horrifying thought of Reagan Gruber being right about *anything*. The man was a loud-mouth conspiracy-theorist. Nothing more.

Still, he couldn't prevent that gnawing sensation in his gut. Gazing up at great arch flying up over the sphere of concentric alloy rings, and the array of hologram controls floating in the air nearby, Amon wondered about the other Translocator. What was Lucas up to? How was he powering that thing?

What am I missing?

10

BY SEA

After sleeping fitfully on the hard stone of Gehro's cave, Rakulo rose early and walked back to the village. He greeted everyone he saw warmly as if nothing had happened, and the shame he carried with him in his heart did not sink the corners of his smile like a stone in deep water.

He played with their children, weeded their gardens, and helped them grind corn masa from sunrise to sunset. He did not have to pretend care for these people—his feelings were genuine. He cared deeply, and with authentic affection, about every person in Kakul. But still, the milk they gave him in return for his labor seemed to curdle on his tongue. It was hard to let go of that shame, though he did his best not to let it show.

It was not until Citlali stepped into his path at

dusk, a shy smile lighting her face, that his inner turmoil began to settle.

"Hello," he said carefully.

She smirked. "I heard you were busy today."

"Is that right?" Rakulo asked. Citlali fell into step beside him and they walked together, brushing shoulders.

"Watiya came over to my house and would not stop talking about how you helped her weed her garden. She kept going on and on about what a nice man you are." Citlali rolled her eyes. "I know how much of a pain you can be, so I was not taken in by her words. Still, you would have loved to see the expression on my father's face." She grinned. "He was furious. Not even my strong-willed father can stop old Watiya from speaking her mind."

Rakulo chuckled under his breath. He had no trouble picturing the scene. Watiya told stories until everyone in the village had heard them three or four times. She was a kind woman, but she was also discerning. Rakulo had no doubt that her appearance at Maatiaak's hut was a strategic move on her part.

If pressed, Rakulo would deny that he had sought her out for that purpose. But Citlali knew the truth of things and seemed to approve. He could see the admiration in her eyes.

They walked in silence for a moment, toward

Rakulo's hut where his mother would now be preparing dinner.

"So you're not mad at me then?" Rakulo asked.

She shook her head ruefully. "I'm not *not* mad. Still, even I must admit that my father has been acting strangely. I noticed it before we left the village last time. I don't know what he did or what your mother told you, but either way, we've been through a lot together, and I trust you, Rakulo. You believe what you're doing is the right thing. You tend to get worked up over it, but I believe in you all the same."

"I hope the others feel that way."

"They will. And now that they've had a chance to spend some time with their families, the rest of your warriors will be ready to go out again soon."

"Good. Spread the word—we'll meet at the cliff's edge in the morning." He bared his teeth. "It is time."

The next morning dawned clear and cloudless and beautiful. He could not have asked for a more perfect day.

Rakulo shivered as he splashed his face with the cold water he had carried from the river the previous night. He left his mother enough water in the clay pot to last her another day or two—the length of time he expected to be gone, assuming his plan failed.

If it didn't, well, she would have to get water on her own for a while. His mother was a strong woman. She would be fine.

He kissed Ixchel's brown cheek, then went to the roof and quietly removed the loop of twine holding Eliana's ring of black stone from where it was hidden, tucked into the thatch ceiling of his mother's hut.

The stone was a beautiful, bottomless black. Even in pale light of the morning, its depths seemed to throw stars back at him. It was the most lovely stone Rakulo had ever seen. After Eliana had given it to him, he had spent hours staring into it. Then he had hidden it, for fear of what Xucha would do to him if it was discovered.

Rakulo had seen the power the black stone emitted—how it had blasted men to the ground with a sudden, invisible force when Xucha's demons were near enough and able to control it. It had never hurt Eliana, who wore it when those things happened. The person who wore it seemed to be protected somehow. But he didn't want to take any chances—and definitely didn't want it to fall into Xucha's hands. So he had kept it out of sight and told no one, not even Citlali, where he had hidden it.

Rakulo wrapped the twine around the stone and tucked the ring into the turkey-skin pouch at his waist that held his flint and the obsidian knife he had inherited from his father.

He met Citlali at the cliff's edge as the orb of the sun separated from the sea. Overhead, the two pale circles of the moons faded and disappeared in the brightening sky as his warriors gathered, one by one.

Once they had all arrived, fresh-faced and well-slept, Rakulo, maintaining a stoic expression, slammed his fist to his chest in salute.

In perfect harmony, they all returned the gesture, adding a booming "Hua!" greeting that probably woke any late risers from their restful slumber. It sounded like the single beat of a deep drum and echoed over the cliffs and across the lavender sea.

"Fine weather today for a swim," Rakulo said. "Don't you think?"

He broke his stoic expression with a sharp grin. His warriors returned his smile, silent and strong.

Then he turned and jogged down the switch-backing cliffs to the beach, and they followed, pounding the ground behind him like a rapid drum-roll. The trip down to the beach was a good warm up, and nothing made Rakulo happier than to be on the move again. He always felt like he was in control when he was on the move. That was part of the reason he had always dreamed of leaving the village, of traveling out on his own. That dream had not gone but had grown up with him.

They reached the beach and passed out of the shadow of the white cliff, cutting down to the wet, packed sand at the ocean's edge. Cold water splashed up onto Rakulo's legs as he ran. To his right, a pristine white beach littered only by the occasional piece of driftwood curved gently toward the horizon. Beyond and above the beach ran an undulating row of sand dunes, and beyond the dunes lay the deep, shadowed jungle of the forest.

They jogged for another little while as the sun rose, until Rakulo raised his fist and brought the column of warriors to a halt.

Their chests rose and fell with the exertion, but they were not tired like they had been two days before. A run like that was just enough to get the blood pumping when they were fresh.

One of the younger warriors, Tolen, stepped forward eagerly. "Are we finally going around the Wall?"

Rakulo bobbed his head from side to side noncommittally. "I had planned on taking us back through the forest to search the Wall again."

The warriors shifted uneasily. They didn't voice any protest, but Rakulo could see that they all thought that was a fruitless mission. He agreed. They had scoured the Wall three or four times, from end to end, and found no holes, no cracks, no flaws at all. There was no way through the Wall except over or around it. The Wall was nothing but a massive curved sheet of smooth, polished stone—if it was stone—from end to end, a hundred feet high, encircling the village entirely. In fact, though it was out of sight right now, one end of the Wall jutted out into the sea just a few miles down the beach.

"Gehro says that going around the Wall by sea is a fool's errand," Rakulo said. "You all know the stories."

"What does that old hermit know about the sea? He hasn't left his cave in years," said Pojuti, a lean, tall woman with short dark hair. She excelled at making the others laugh, and they all chuckled darkly now.

"You've heard the same stories I have. Men have tried to swim around the Wall for generations. None of them ever returned."

"Maybe they got away," said Tolen eagerly. "Maybe they found a way out and never came back."

"Maybe," Rakulo said, carefully watching the expressions of his warriors as he agreed. "Shall we find out, then?"

"Hua!" came the cry of agreement.

Tolen and Pojuti led the way up the beach toward the forest. The warriors scrambled over the row of high sand dunes and disappeared into the shaded jungle. Rakulo waited patiently as they returned, dragging four canoes with them through the sand.

Tolen dropped his canoe at Rakulo's feet, and Rakulo knelt down and ran his hand across the smooth surface. Between trips to the Wall, his warriors had spent months finding the perfect trees, felling them, and shaping them into these four canoes. They discarded many faulty first attempts, wanting only the best seafaring vessels for their journey. Rakulo told them, at first, that carving the canoes was good discipline and strength training, but he'd always had this end goal in mind.

"We only have four canoes, which means that only eight of us can go. I'll take one canoe in the lead, and Citlali will lead another. As for the rest…"

He could see the eagerness in their faces. How could he be fair? "The rest of you will draw sticks."

Pojuti nodded, her broad face solemn and serious for a change. Tolen ran back to the forest and returned a few moments later with a thin branch, and using a flint knife he had made himself, cut it into twigs of various sizes. Rakulo hid the sticks in his fist and made each person draw until he had narrowed down who would be going and who was staying behind. Since they were all eager to go with him, whoever got the short stick in each round won a seat.

A large man named Quen drew the shortest twig the first round. Then it was Yeli, a light-skinned woman with jet-black hair, followed by Pojuti, who shrieked with delight and lorded it over the others. Next was Hopolix, a slight, serious man, followed by Thevanah, a beautiful woman who had a crush on Tolen. Her face lit up when Tolen won the last round and whooped with delight, his youthful exuberance making even those left behind smile.

"The rest of you follow us down the beach until we reach the Wall. And then keep an eye out until we return. This first trip, our only goal is to reach the shore on the other side of the Wall and then come right back, just to prove that it can be done. Simple enough. Got it?"

They nodded their agreement.

Rakulo climbed into the first canoe, with Yeli in front of him, and pushed out into the water. In the next canoe came Citlali paired with Tolen. Quen and Hopolix occupied the third canoe, and finally, Thevanah pushed the fourth canoe into the water, jumping in behind Pojuti.

Rakulo used his paddle to turn the canoe so it was parallel to the shore, and he and Yeli began to paddle in sync like they had practiced, toward the far end of the beach.

The other warriors jogged along the beach as the canoes picked up speed. There was a tailwind today, so they moved along at a good pace, and Rakulo was grateful not to have to paddle into the wind.

As they approached the end of the beach, the sun glinted off the shining sheer face of the massive Wall. It was as high as the cliff face at the other end of the beach, except smooth as polished flint, bronze-silver in color depending on the light, and completely seamless. It was also pretty thin, Rakulo realized as they approached. The Wall cut like a knife through the sand and jutted out into the water, where it tapered down slowly until it sank into the sea.

"Take a break," he told Yeli in front of him. She pulled her paddle into the boat, breathing hard. Rakulo realized his breath was coming quick, too. He reached out his paddle and turned the canoe so it was facing out toward the sea. "And forward again."

The other canoes followed in Rakulo's wake. They approached the edge of the Wall. When they reached it, Rakulo and Yeli both stopped paddling. They rounded the knife's edge of the Wall, and it became thin in their perspective, thinner than a man.

And then they were around it.

Yeli glanced back at Rakulo, her eyes sparkling. He nodded at her, his expression controlled and neutral despite his excitement. "Keep paddling."

Glancing back, he saw the others close behind. Tolen dug his paddle deep into the water, pulling he and Citlali ahead of the others. Quen and Hopolix stared at the Wall where it dipped into the sea. Through the clear lavender water, Rakulo could see how it sliced down to the ocean floor in a smooth line. A school of fish swam beneath his canoe, shadows flitting through the translucent depths.

"Goodbye, Kakul!" cried Pojuti as she and Thevanah crossed the threshold of the Wall. "Hello, new world!"

Rakulo held his breath as they advanced. Tolen pulled ahead of him slightly. Rakulo and Yeli, despite his order, had stopped paddling. They were both bracing for an impact of some kind. The other men had never returned. Why? What happened to them? Rakulo felt his whole body tense.

Glancing at the distant shore on the other side of the Wall, where it was just a tiny sliver of white sand at the edge of his vision, he saw that there was no forest beyond the Wall. It was sparse grass and shrub, and dry red earth with deep cracks—just like he had seen through the Wall when he had watched Xucha come through to retrieve his demon.

Glancing behind him, Rakulo saw only the back of the smooth Wall. It looked just the same as it did on the other side, only it was dull and tarnished, and the sun did not shine on this side so there was no glint. He was cut off from the sight of the rest of his warriors.

"We made it!" Tolen cried as he continued to paddle hard, pulling ahead by several yards and steering their canoe toward the shore. Rakulo did the same, angling to follow them to the beach. Citlali's smile filled her whole face as she looked back, catching Rakulo's eyes. He grinned back at her, feeling less like a leader and more like the child of the forest, son of the open sky, as which he had been raised. She cried out, a long exultant yell inspired by their sudden freedom.

Something drew Rakulo's eyes down—the flitting shadows of the fish underwater all darted away at once, vanishing into the depths.

Ahead of him, near the base and slightly to the left of Tolen and Citlali's canoe, ripples disturbed the surface of the water. Ripples that couldn't have come from Tolen's paddle or the wake of the boat.

More fish? No…Rakulo's whole body broke out in a cold sweat as he realized that something was deeply, terribly wrong.

A brown thing about the width of a thick branch, with a row of small circles extending along its mottled length, rose out of the water. It whipped forward.

"Look out!" Rakulo cried.

11

TURTLETOWN

When they crawled out of their tents in the morning, her team was disconcerted to discover that Eliana had once again packed to leave. She was cooking breakfast, however, so they were careful not to complain—at least until she had dished out the bacon and eggs. Lakshmi was the first one to inquire why Eliana's suitcase was standing outside her tent.

"We haven't even finished exploring the area around the monolith," Lakshmi said, her mouth half-full of bacon, "and you just got here."

"I know," Eliana said, "and I'm really sorry, but it can't be helped. I have to go home to attend a funeral."

Eliana decided she wouldn't blame them if they were a little upset about it. If *her* team leader kept running off when there was work to be done, she would be irritated, too. But this was out of her control, so she stayed cool and composed through the disappointing discussion.

When she told them about Reuben, her explorers began to show a little more sympathy. It wasn't until Eliana explained what she planned to do with the samples they had collected yesterday that they started to be genuinely supportive.

"I'll find someone we can trust to start the radio-carbon dating process," she told them. "Your job while I'm gone is to keep looking for carvings and any other stone structures hidden in that part of the jungle."

"You got it, boss," Tanner said.

Talia bobbed her head enthusiastically.

"Anything you need," Ross chimed in.

Lakshmi finally nodded, too.

Lakshmi drove Eliana back to her rental car and they said goodbye. Half a day later, Eliana walked through the Austin airport and located her own car in the airport parking lot.

It was late afternoon. She was anxious to see Amon. Yet she knew that if she went straight to Fisk Industries it would be days before she could get back out to the university campus to apologize to Renee for bailing on her. She also wanted to pick Renee's brain about what they had found, and would rather not wait.

As she merged onto the highway that curved back into the city, Eliana dialed Fisk Industries' front desk on her cell phone and put the sound through the car speakers. They told her that Audrey wasn't there, but agreed to transfer her through to Audrey's cell phone. A few rings later, Audrey came on the line.

"Mrs. Fisk," Audrey said. "What a pleasant surprise."

"Audrey, how many times do I have to ask you to *please* call me Eliana? Mrs. Fisk is Amon's mother."

She laughed. Audrey's laugh was a pleasant sound, but it came out a little frantic and forced. "Sorry. I know I keep forgetting. To be honest, I'm still a little shaken up right now."

"Amon told me about what happened. I am so relieved to hear you're okay."

"Being a scientist was never supposed to be this exciting. I just want to be left alone with my meteorites and microscopes. Is that so much to ask?"

"I know the feeling, believe me."

Audrey took a breath, chuckled nervously. "How did you handle it, after you went through the Translocator? You seemed so *normal* when you came back. And you went back to work almost immediately! I'm terrified of going back to my lab now. That guy just materialized next to me and pulled me to the ground. I thought he was going to kill me. I didn't know what to do."

"You're a damn sight braver than most," Eliana said, even though she could tell by the way Audrey's words tripped over each other on the way off her tongue that she had still not fully come down from the adrenaline-fueled experience yet. "And I don't think I was normal, really. I'm still terrified of that machine. Not that Amon wants me anywhere near the Translocator, but I've made a point of steering clear since I came back. Being so involved in my work, and the guest lecture position I took, that all helps a lot. It makes me *feel* normal to be busy, you know what I mean?"

Audrey sighed. "I think I do. Maybe. I don't know."

"Well," Eliana said, "if you feel that way—and I'll understand if you're not up to it right now—but here's a proposition that might help cheer you. Do you know how to radiocarbon date organic samples?"

"Of course," Audrey said. "It's pretty straightforward, really, just a process of measuring the amount of carbon-14 in a given sample, and then doing some basic math with the half-life of carbon as a benchmark to extrapolate the age of the thing."

"I brought several samples back with me from Mexico. Are you interested in carbon dating them for me? If my suspicions are correct...actually, I don't want to bias you before you check them out. I'll reserve my theories for an objective, data-driven conclusion."

"Oh, how intriguing. But...wouldn't you rather

send them to a professional lab? Many reputable companies offer carbon dating as a service, and their rates are really affordable. The boyfriend of my old college roommate, Kate, works at a good place in Dallas, actually—"

Eliana cut her off. "I'm sure your friend's boyfriend is great, but the samples are of a some-what...sensitive nature. I don't feel comfortable giving them to a stranger."

She thought about Reagan Gruber, the radio talkshow host who seemed to have some kind of grudge against Amon. Whenever she had listened to him on the radio—which was not often, thank God —he sounded like he was scolding a disobedient child he hated.

"With how much Amon and I have been in the news lately," Eliana said, "it's too much of a risk that some curious lab tech might be tempted to sell the information to an enterprising journalist."

"Oh," Audrey said. "I see."

"You know what, forget I asked," Eliana said. "I don't want to put that kind of pressure on you right now."

"I'll do it."

Eliana blinked. "Really?"

"No problem. Can you bring the samples to my lab this afternoon? It should be clean by now, and I want to go check on things for myself anyhow. That will give me a good reason to get back there today."

"That would be amazing, Audrey. I'd be happy to pay you for your time, of course."

"Oh no, absolutely not. I am quite well compensated, I assure you."

Eliana smiled, bemused at Audrey's brisk and sudden change of heart.

Meeting Audrey at the lab also gave Eliana a reason to go to Fisk Industries, which meant she could stop by and see Amon—he would be working late, of course. She knew without having to ask him that he would be there.

"Thank you, Audrey. I owe you big time. It's three o'clock now, can we meet at six?"

The usual amount of traffic slowed her slightly as she merged onto I-35 and cruised north toward the University of Texas. This gave her an opportunity to safely dial Renee's cell phone and put the call through the car speakers.

"You're back already?" Renee said when Eliana greeted her.

"It's a long story, but yes. Do you have time to catch up?"

They agreed to meet at Turtletown, so they could walk and talk outside. Eliana found Renee squatting on the crushed sandstone path at the edge of the pond, watching three intrepid green turtles clamber over each other to reach the best sunning spot at the end of a log that jutted out of the turtle pond.

"I'm really sorry for ditching you the other day," Eliana said.

"No apologies necessary." Renee stood, brushed her hands off, and shrugged. "The students who attend your lectures really admire you. I ended up having a good conversation with your student, Margaret. She's an incredibly hard worker, and mature for her age. Reminds me of you, actually. I think she's dating an older guy from the engineering program, too." A smirk touched the corner of Renee's mouth.

Eliana cleared her throat and looked away. She and Amon had started dating while she was in college. He started his solar energy company out of a tiny rented warehouse space at the edge of town that year, and had met Eliana at a dinner party with mutual friends. She remembered how anxious she was to leave him in Austin after only dating a few months. She had to go out to Utah to finish her field work, but she couldn't afford a plane ticket then, so Amon lent her his car even though he had meetings all over town that week. He took her unreliable, beat down, turd-colored old Mazda to meet millionaire investors all month without a single complaint. And driving his Jeep Grand Cherokee out to Utah was nice. It didn't smell like him after a week in the desert, but having the jeep was like having a little piece of him with her at all times.

"That was a long time ago," Eliana said.

"Margaret seems like a bright girl, and is very interested in doing fieldwork of her own as her capstone project."

Even if she is a bit nosy, Eliana thought, remembering the question that had caught her off guard during the last lecture.

Renee turned and they began to walk slowly around the edge of the pond. Ahead of them, blue wildflowers grew out of gardens that lined the foundation of nearby greenhouses.

"Speaking of research," Renee prodded gently, "you received some good news? Does that mean you're getting closer to publishing what you've been working on for the past year?"

For some reason, Eliana hesitated. "I'm not sure yet. It's definitely a good start. I'd like to wait until I have something more concrete."

What could be more concrete than a carving of two moons that look like the satellites orbiting the planet where she found Kakul? It seemed so clear to Eliana. But would others see it that way? It would be easier if they found more carvings.

"You can always publish another piece, you know. You have the resources of the university at your disposal. Whatever you need, just ask."

You mean you're happy to have the university's name on the news every time they mention me or Amon. Renee might have been Eliana's professor in college—her mentor, once—but she was an administrator now, which came with a different view of things. Still, Eliana couldn't argue that it had been to her benefit, at least so far.

"I don't want to rush you," Renee said, mistaking the expression of distaste on Eliana's face for nervousness about her research, "but the archaeology department is holding me accountable. The kind of part-time position we offered you is unique, and part of the arrangement was that you'd publish something with us in return."

"I don't remember being tied to a specific timeframe," Eliana said with more bitterness than she had intended.

Renee smiled. It was the same smile she used to use on students who tested her patience in the Culture and Communication 307 class that Eliana took as an anthropology student the year she met Amon.

"It's not that," Renee said. "I understand wanting to be sure. Maybe, if not a full academic paper, I could appease the board if you did a guest column at *Nature* or *National Geographic*? I know the editors there, and—"

A colleague of Renee's hurried past them in the opposite direction, a briefcase in his hand. "Lovely day for a stroll," he said. Renee exchanged greetings and smiles with him.

After he had passed, Eliana said, "I just need a bit

more time. I need to confirm the facts. We're still gathering evidence."

"Have you considered going back?" Renee asked abruptly. "To that other place?"

"I already told you, I can't," Eliana said.

"Can't, or won't?"

"I'd need a security clearance, first of all. No one is allowed near the Translocator anymore without one. Especially not me." She laughed, and her own voice sounded like Audrey's had over the phone less than an hour ago—forced, and a little shrill. She closed her lips, worked her dry mouth, swallowed.

"We'll support you if you want to pursue it," Renee said. "Whatever you need. I only know what you told me, but my interest is piqued, Eliana. What would people with an uncanny similarity to the Preclassic Maya—if I guess right based on what you've told me, and I don't think you've told me the whole story—what would they be doing on that other planet? How did they get there? Where did they come from? Or were they there *first*?"

Eliana had no words. Her mentor had plucked these questions right out of her brain. "I don't know."

"You have to publish something, Eliana. The anthropology community deserves to know what you've found. At least the beginning of it. You can publish theories without drawing any specific conclusions—just pose the question. Normally, without more evidence, I'd say wait. But you're in an extremely unique situation."

"I know, I know."

"Do you?"

Eliana stuffed her hands in the shallow pockets of her jeans and opened her mouth to speak, but cleared her throat against the rapid thud of her heart against her chest. A trickle of sweat chilled the back of her neck despite the heat of the late-spring sun overhead. In her mind, she heard the horrible cracking sound of the Translocator powering up, remembered the feeling like knives lacerating her skin as she had been pulled through, the terrible power of the machine latched onto the black diamond in her ring like a vice grip.

They had walked a full lap around the pond by now. Eliana looked over at the log, now crowded with turtles. They jostled each other until the small green one at the end fell off and plopped into the water.

Renee smiled, but Eliana's expression remained grim.

12

A POWERFUL MOTIVATOR

Amon rubbed his heavy eyelids as he trailed behind Wes McManis and Dr. Enzo Badeux. They were currently on the moon base, walking through a long, upward-sloping zigzag tunnel that connected Dome 2 to the SOLARPulse-1 detection array at the upper lip of the Tycho crater.

The observation room and telescopes had been placed up there purposefully, Amon knew. If the telescopes were installed lower, the crater walls would have blocked part of the sky. But did it have to be so damned high up? Maybe he could ship them one of those moving walkways you find in airports. Or he could have a new Translocator platform installed up here just to avoid the hike.

Amon snorted. When would he find the time?

Walking slightly ahead of them, Stanis, the LTA

engineer in charge of the lunar base's construction, gave them the rundown as they hiked.

"Things have progressed much faster over the past month. The new fabricators are all operational now. The biology and chemistry domes were completed last week. We've got enough generators to keep the fabricators running in two six hour shifts. Best of all, the SOLARPulse-1 detection array should be online in the next few days. We just need to get the final satellites into position, run a few basic drills…"

He trailed off and stopped talking when the ground leveled off and the floor swept out into a broad cement landing.

To one side, stairs led up to an airlock that Amon presumed would take them to the observation deck of SOLARPulse-1. On the other side, in place of an opaque tunnel wall, was a startlingly clear floor-to-ceiling window. Three layers of temperature-regulating and radiation-filtering glass looked out over the Tycho crater and the entire lunar base constructed in its sheltering walls below.

His exhaustion forgotten, Amon gazed across the fifty-three mile-wide crater with a feeling of awe, the kind of experience you only get in the presence of natural beauty. Then he turned his gaze below and felt a warm glow of pride in the work he had been a part of.

Below them, grey domes filled the shelves carved

into the wall of the crater—of many different shapes and sizes, each built to suit a different purpose. One was a biology lab, another equipment storage, and yet another Dome 2, where the Translocator platform was located, and where they had begun their walk. Each dome was connected to the adjacent structures by tunnels and airlocks, so that if one was breached, it wouldn't take the whole system down.

"What's in that one?" Amon asked, pointing to a large dome just below them.

"That's the dormitory and kitchen," Stanis said. "One day we'll be able to house two hundred scientists there."

About halfway down the curve of the crater, a tunnel veered off to the left of the main grouping of domes. It could only be one thing.

"And that one all the way over there?" Amon asked, though he was nearly certain of the answer.

"The nuclear fission reactor," Stanis said. "As you know, that's why we were able to increase the pace of construction. Once the reactor came online, it freed up several of the smaller radioisotope reactors we were using to power individual domes, so those could be used to run additional fabricators. We have to be efficient up here, even with your Translocator."

A dozen clouds of amorphous dust each indicated a fabricator working two shelves below them. These were the newest sections of the base. Each fabricator churned moon rock into the cellular walls of the domes. The hard stone-like shells protected the inhabitants from radiation and the solar winds that pounded the lunar surface, and also made a sturdy shield against small meteorite impact. The interiors were made of inflatables, like a plastic bubble.

He stared, taken aback by the sight, and silently paid homage to the many strokes of luck and twists of fate that had put him in a position to experience this—man's first attempt to colonize the moon.

"Being able to see your progress is a powerful motivator," Dr. Badeux said.

"I figured this window was your idea," Amon said. "Worth the expense?"

"Without a doubt."

Amon nodded and turned to look at Stanis. "I'm glad to see it all coming together."

"We're getting there," Stanis said. "It's still several years before we're able to sustain anything more than the twenty-five scientists we have on rotation now."

"And when did you say your NEO research will begin?" Dr. Badeux inquired.

"A few days. Once the satellites are in place, we'll be able to monitor any small bodies moving around the solar system, with particular attention to NEOs." Stanis turned to Wes, the least technical among the three of them, to explain the acronym. While Amon had been looking out the window, Wes was typing an email on his phone, apparently disinterested in the tour. But he looked up when Stanis began addressing him directly.

"NEOs are Near Earth Objects, such as asteroids that present a potential existential threat to Earth. Anything larger than 2 kilometers across gets monitored closely from Earth already, but telescopes and satellites installed here will give us a bigger view frame. The latest predictive modeling and hologram controls let us manipulate the view, too, so that we can interact with and examine the solar system in new ways. We'll soon be able to explore beyond the solar system, to other parts of the galaxy we could never reach before."

"You fellas deserve a reward for all your hard work," Wes said, sliding his phone into his pocket. "Have you planned a celebration for the big launch? I bet we could requisition you some comforts if you have any particular requests. Whiskey? Women? What do you say, Enzo?"

He chuckled and jostled Dr. Badeux's arm, who smiled uncomfortably.

Amon gritted his teeth. Wes's oily used car salesman attitude grated on his nerves more than usual today.

In the vacuum of Lucas's absence, the board of Fisk Industries had forced Amon to take Wes McManis on as the Chief Operations Officer. He hadn't liked it, but Wes ran a smooth enough ship, and he knew the business. He wasn't the right personality fit, in Amon's opinion, but he made the board happy because he was numbers and profits-oriented. Every day that passed made it more difficult for Amon to replace him. It didn't help that Wes was on the board himself as an early investor, a mistake of Amon's ambitious past that he continued to pay for in stomach ulcers and awkward conversations like these.

"Ah, um," stammered Stanis. "No, thank you. We'll have a small celebration of our own. Nothing big."

"Ah, come on now, I know you Russians like your vodka. Listen…" Wes wrapped an arm around Stanis's neck and pulled him ahead of the other two to whisper in his ear. They went up the stairs toward the airlock that led to the dome housing SOLARPulse-1.

Amon pressed his tongue forcefully against his bottom teeth and shook his head. "I'd get rid of him if I could."

"Don't let him get to you," Dr. Badeux said. "He means well. He's just a little abrasive."

Amon gazed back out the window.

"It's amazing what we've been able to accomplish in a year," Enzo said. "And it's all thanks to you."

"You and Stanis and the engineers building these domes have done all the hard work."

"We did it together."

Amon normally kept his nose out of politics, but a question he'd been wondering about came back into his head now. He felt it was safe to broach the subject alone with Enzo. "The Lunar Terraform Alliance has more nations in it than the UN does," Amon said. "Off the record, have you ever thought about installing something here for planetary defense?"

"Defense against what?"

"Well, large asteroids for one. But who knows? Military operations certainly aren't my specialty, but what if Stanis and his team do find something else out there, and it's not friendly?"

Enzo adjusted his glasses and squinted at Amon. "Is there something you're not telling me? You and Eliana both said that the people she found on that other planet were using stone age tools. And we haven't sent anyone back there because we don't want to interfere with their culture, whoever they are. Live and let live, that's what you said. Right?"

"Right. Of course. But what if something *else* is out there?" *Something we don't understand.* Amon shuddered as he thought of the strange, floating orb the natives had destroyed on his last visit, and the hologram of the man dressed all in black. They'd left that part out of their interviews with the press. Only those closest to them, and ranking officials at the LTA, knew what really happened to Eliana.

Dr. Badeux sighed. "The truth is that even if we

wanted to put some kind of defenses here, the other countries in the alliance wouldn't allow it. Especially the smaller ones. They worry that if things went awry—if tensions ramped up on Earth for some reason—the weapon would be turned against them. They'd threaten to pull their funding and participation if we even so much as broach the subject, guaranteed."

"I suppose I can understand their hesitation," Amon said. You could only trust people until you couldn't anymore. He wondered what Lucas was doing right now…

"We're just starting to make real progress here," Enzo said. "I don't want to derail it with a pissing contest."

Apart from the SOLARPulse-1, the rest of the tour was uneventful. When they got back to the Translocator platform, Amon signaled with his transponder, and he, Wes, and Enzo were reassembled in the lab. Wes went back to work, and Enzo excused himself as well.

Amon was pleased to discover that he didn't experience any of the mild nausea that had once been a hallmark of a successful translocation, even as late in their work as a year ago. Out of habit, Amon walked over to where one of his engineers was manning the holodeck and checked the readout of their translocation.

"Sir," Jeanine said. After Amon and Reuben,

Jeanine was in charge. She had stepped into Reuben's shoes quite naturally. "The lobby phoned down. Eliana is waiting for you."

"Oh thank goodness," he said, checking the time on his phone. They had plans to go see Reuben's family at the wake later this evening, and Amon didn't want to be late.

On his phone, Amon saw that while he was on the lunar base, he'd missed a text from Eliana that said she went to the university, then another that said, "I'm on my way!"

Amon hurried up the stairs.

He caught up with Wes as he was exiting through the door beside the security checkpoint.

"Mr. McManis," Roger the guard said.

"Hey, champ," Wes said, slapping Roger on the shoulder. Then, as Amon was passing through the door, Wes said, "Hey sweetie, long time no see!"

"Hi, Wes," Eliana said. "Just waiting for Amon."

"Yes, ma'am. Have a great night."

Down the hall, Eliana was pacing back and forth, biting her fingernails and generally making the guards flanking the metal detector nervous and restless.

Watching her pace made him anxious, too, but he couldn't help the wide smile that filled half his face at the sight of her.

As she turned to face him, her sun-tanned face smoothed and she smiled back. He embraced his wife, settling his hands on her hips and pulling her warm body close. She wrapped her arms around his neck and they kissed.

"Hello to you, too," she said when their lips finally parted.

"You came just as I was getting ready to leave."

"Really?"

He smiled helplessly. "No. But I don't want to be late for the wake. I'll be ready in fifteen minutes."

She nodded, and her eyes wandered, gazing past him into the lab, a quizzical expression on her face that Amon couldn't quite place.

"Do you want to come in?"

"Would that be okay?"

"Just for a minute."

He nodded to the two guards, and guided Eliana through the checkpoint. As they exited the elevator and walked down the hall to the Translocator lab, her whole body slowly tensed under his arm.

"Are you okay?" Amon said.

As they stepped past the two guards with automatic rifles, she relaxed a little bit. She glanced at the door to the lounge, just left of the entrance.

"I'm fine. It's just that I haven't been back here since…you know."

"Oh," Amon said. It had slipped his mind. He was down here every day. "That's right."

"Go ahead. I'll wait in your fancy new lounge,

maybe make myself something to drink. I'm a bit jetlagged."

Eliana broke away from him and went into the cozy lounge, past the recliners, to the new kitchen, where she filled a kettle and put it on the stove to boil for tea.

Amon had improved the lounge after his stint living out of the tiny and uncomfortable kitchenette that was there before. The old one had sustained him for two months while he was bunkered down in the Translocator lab. He never wished to repeat the experience, so he'd remodeled to make it much nicer.

The Translocator lab had also been expanded on the other side. On the right wall, a partition with a broad doorway led into a five thousand square foot warehouse space. It was toward the warehouse that Amon now walked, leaving Eliana to her tea.

In fifteen minutes, he had checked the inventory and helped Jeanine power down and secure the Hopper. They had installed a biometric security system earlier that day. Even if someone did manage to get into the locked lab, they wouldn't be able to power up or use the Hopper without a retinal scan of an authorized person and thumb prints with two-step password authentication from different engineers.

Someone might call his precaution paranoia.

That person hadn't shot and killed a man with a kneecap in his ribcage.

Amon had kept that sordid detail from Eliana on the phone last night. He decided then that he wouldn't tell her about it at all. Some things are better left unsaid.

Eliana watched from the doorway of the lounge and sipped her tea. When he was ready, she washed her mug and they all left the room together, he, Jeanine, and Eliana. Amon put his hand against a touchscreen on the way out and the massive metal door lowered into place behind him, locking down the lab.

"Amon," Eliana said when they were back in the car and driving home. She stared out the window as they stopped at a red light.

"Yeah?" he said when she didn't go on.

She licked her lips. "I don't know how to say this so I'm just going to say it. I need to go back to Kakul."

He blinked. The light turned green and he didn't move. The person driving the car behind him leaned on their horn.

"All right, damn," he said, accelerating again. He glanced at Eliana as he drove. "Why do you want to go back?"

"We found something in Mexico. I need to verify what I saw in Kakul, to make sure it's what I think it is."

"I thought you said you never wanted to go back there again."

"I didn't. I mean, I did say that. I don't want to go back, not really. Your machine scares the bejeesus out of me now. But I have to."

"Why?"

"I told you, I need to verify something."

"What is it?"

"A carving we found. It's a carving of two moons. I was hoping I could find a similar carving there."

Amon pinched the bridge of his nose. "It's not going to be easy to get you security clearance."

"You brought me in there tonight."

"To send you back to that other planet. It's dangerous."

"Send me through at night," Eliana said. "I know you work late doing experiments with that meteorite. It will only take a few hours. No one will know."

"How did you know I was still doing experiments?" Amon said, blushing. He hadn't told her about that.

"Audrey told me. But don't change the subject."

"It's not safe," Amon said.

"Of course, that's why I wanted you to stop doing the experiments."

"That's not what I mean, and you know it."

"What I *know* is that you told me the meteorites

were dangerous and you weren't going to mess around with them anymore."

"I have to!"

"Why?" Eliana said, mocking him. "It's not safe."

"Because I need to know what it is, and how it works. Because it might help us. And because now someone else has a Translocator, too, and I have to stop them."

"Even better reason to get rid of it."

"What if it falls into the wrong hands?"

"Destroy it, so it doesn't."

"If I did, then you wouldn't be able to go back to Kakul."

She stared at him, considering. "You won't do it. You want to know how it works that badly. Which is even more reason to send me back. I'll be your guinea pig."

She lifted her chin and stared at him. The challenge hung in the air between them.

Amon felt a shudder wash through him. Did he really want to use her as a guinea pig? He considered it...

And immediately rejected the idea. The idea of her going back through again made him want to vomit. No way. He'd seen guinea pigs. They had kneecaps in their chest. They had their organs on the outside. The LTA would say it was irresponsible, though they couldn't stop him. What would someone like Reagan Gruber say if he got ahold of it?

No way. No how. Not going to happen.

Amon could face any danger as long as Eliana was safe. The possibility of something going wrong and endangering her again was just too much for him to handle.

He gripped the steering wheel with both hands and watched the road. They finally pulled into the driveway of their house.

"It's not safe," Amon said. "I'm not sending you back there." He got out of the car and went inside without another word.

They ignored each other while they got ready for the wake. Eliana's chill silence made Amon feel guilty. But he couldn't engage her about it any more. She could be mad at him if she wanted to be. All he cared about was keeping her safe.

An hour later, wearing somber expressions that matched their clothes but had nothing to do with the way they were dressed, Amon knocked on the door of Reuben's house. Instead of being greeted by a house full of quiet, crying people, as he expected, the door opened on smiling faces and bright colors. The house was decorated in a garish *Mardi Gras* theme. Reuben spotted them through the open door, hollered a greeting, and ran across the room to drape a dozen bright-plastic bead necklaces over Eliana's head. She was pulled into the house. A margarita was pressed into her hand. Amon suddenly felt very self-conscious in a dark grey suit with polished black wingtips on his feet.

Reuben returned from delivering Eliana to the party and pulled Amon into a bear hug.

"Thanks for coming, it means a lot."

"I wouldn't miss it for the world," Amon said. "But dude, I thought this was going to be a wake. Look at me!"

Reuben laughed. "It is a wake. And you look fine, don't worry. Charlie's younger sister organized the party. I was skeptical, but you know what, she was right. Charlie loved New Orleans. This is very fitting. Did I ever tell you we met there?"

Amon shook his head slowly, his mouth half-open in a helpless smile as he listened to the story of how Reuben met his late husband. To Amon, his friend seemed to have lost years overnight. Even though his eyes were shimmering with tears and red-rimmed, it was salve for the soul for Reuben to be able to return to these fond memories, and put the more recent past of Charlie's sickness to rest. The wake was an end for Charlie, but a new beginning for Reuben. And both Charlie's life and Reuben's new beginning were worth celebrating.

"Well that was unexpected," Eliana said, coming back to sit next to Amon when she saw that Reuben had been pulled away to greet someone else at the door.

"Tell me about it."

Eliana took a deep breath. "I have to go back to Kakul, Amon."

He stared at her, wide-eyed. "Eliana, I can't."

"Don't look at me like I'm crazy."

"It's too dangerous."

And I don't understand how the carbonados really work. What if I kill you? What if the madman with the other Translocator steals the carbonado from the lab and I can't get you back again? It was too close last time. If I hadn't gone to see Audrey, they would have had them.

"I can't lose you again," Amon said.

"I'm going to lose my job if I don't."

All Amon could do was shake his head.

"Damnit, Amon! This is my life's work. And there are huge opportunities in this for me. You have to see that! Haven't I made sacrifices for you and your projects? All I'm asking for is a few hours. Just to look around and take a few samples and photos, since I couldn't last time. I can barely remember what it looks like!" The frustration was clearly evident in her voice.

Amon shoved down the dark feeling of guilt that threatened to overwhelm him. She was right. She had done so much for him. But he still couldn't let her go back there.

His phone vibrated in his pocket. He pulled it out and saw a 10 digit number he didn't recognize. He never would have answered an unknown number normally, but things had been strange the last few days, and he didn't want to argue with Eliana any more.

"Amon," the inflection of her voice rising, "don't you dare answer that."

"I should get it."

"This conversation is not over. You don't get to tell me what I can or can't do when it comes to my career."

"I do when it's my machine. You're not going back through the Hopper. End of discussion."

"Amon, please."

Strangers they didn't know, family and friends of Reuben and Charlie, were watching them argue out of the corners of their eyes now.

"Not here," Amon said.

"Amon."

"No!" he said, louder than he'd intended. "I forbid it."

"Forbid it? How dare you—"

He slid his thumb across the phone to answer the call and turned his body away from his wife. "Hello?"

Eliana's jaw clenched and her dark eyes flared with a rock-hard anger.

"Mr. Fisk, this is Agent Wiley with the FBI. I think we found something. We should meet in person. It's important."

Amon's stomach dropped into a cold pit as his wife turned and walked away from him.

13

BETTER TO KNOW

The giant tentacle whipped across the canoe between Tolen and Citlali, the thin end plunging back into the water on the other side and drawing its length taut across the middle of the boat.

Rakulo dug his paddle into the water and pulled his canoe forward with all the might he could muster. Yeli sat cross-legged with her mouth hanging open in front of him, her paddle poised in the air. She glanced between the tentacle and Rakulo, terror plainly written on her face.

"Paddle!"

Yeli jerked into motion, digging her paddle deep into the purple seawater.

Shouts of outrage and surprise came from the others behind him. Rakulo kept his gaze fixed on Citlali and Tolen, as if with intensity he might pull himself through the water faster.

Citlali and Tolen kicked and yanked at the slimy length of tentacle, but it was as thick as a man's arm and they couldn't get a good grip. Citlali tried to use her knife to cut at it. Before the stone came into contact with the tentacle, their canoe jostled and jerked down into the water. Tolen braced himself on the side of the boat. Citlali caught her balance with her knife hand, crouching. A great creaking, rending sound came from the wood of the canoe.

Yeli reached forward, but they were still several handspans out of reach.

"Citlali!" Rakulo shouted as he dug his paddle back into the turbulent waters. Bubbles came up around his paddle. "Jump!"

His fiercest warrior sprang into action. Citlali seized Tolen under one arm and pitched him into the water toward Rakulo just as the wood of the canoe buckled under the tension of the tentacle. A rending crunch split the air. Citlali braced herself against the back half of the boat as it rose up out of the water, and kicked off it, launching herself toward Rakulo and the others that gained distance behind him. She went hands first into the water between two additional tentacles that were just now questing up into the air, searching for prey. She disappeared beneath the turbulent surface.

Tolen had crashed awkwardly into the foamy water. Now he turned and scrabbled frantically toward Rakulo, swallowing a lungful of water, spitting, coughing, and windmilling his arms, and spraying water all over. The two tentacles questing above the surface seemed to sense Tolen's struggle. One slapped down over his right arm, while the other darted underwater to curl around his waist. Tolen's screams were smothered by his choking coughs as the tentacles began to pull him down. His open mouth quested upward for air.

Rakulo reached out a hand and locked his fingers around Tolen's forearm, the one not hooked by the tentacle. The boat beneath him turned as he hauled back on the young man's arm, trying to pull him away from the grabbing, slimy things and into the boat.

"Hang on, Tolen!" Rakulo said through gritted teeth. His grip was firm, but Tolen's arm was slippery with water and the force of the tentacle's pull was too strong. It was like hauling back on a tree root whose other end was embedded deep into the earth. Rakulo glanced into the water as he leaned out of his canoe, following the length of tentacle down to where it seemed to be at attached to a dark bar of vegetation or coral on the ocean floor. Cords bulged from Rakulo's neck as he grunted and hauled back with all his might.

His fingers slipped on Tolen's slick skin, and the young warrior fell from his grasp. His choking scream was vanished under the foamy surface.

Rakulo stared at the water, his mouth hanging

open as he breathed heavily. Bubbles rose to the surface where Tolen had gone under. Rakulo must go in after him. Where was Citlali? Did she get away or was she down there, too? Rakulo drew the obsidian knife from his sheath and was leaning over the water, staring at where the bubbles rose to the surface and gathering a deep breath, when Yeli screamed.

Rakulo twisted around and looked at the girl in the front of his canoe. A new tentacle was wrapped three times around her shoulders, creeping up her neck and tightening with a steady throb like a snake suffocating its prey. Her mouth hung open, her face drawn and pale, and her scream pierced his ears.

Rakulo reacted. He jumped forward, slashing down with the obsidian knife at the tentacle near her shoulder. A gash opened in the length, but only a small one. The hide was as thick and tough as anything Rakulo had ever seen. Thick as his own arm, the cut on the tentacle gushed with a white pus. Was that blood? It looked more like plant sap. Rakulo didn't give himself time to consider it. He kept slashing, cutting, until the slimy brown length was flayed open, the inside layered with striated muscle. As he sliced away the last bit of flesh, the tentacle slithered back down and disappeared under water, as silent as it had come.

Rakulo pulled the still-pulsing length of tentacle away from Yeli's body. The tentacle kicked and twisted in his hand like a live fish. Rakulo yanked and cut and pulled until it had released Yeli, and she coughed as the air rushed back into her lungs. Then he tossed it back into the water. Wasting no time, Rakulo grabbed his paddle where it had fallen at the bottom of the boat, and rapidly retreated from the dark shadow under the water, moving away from where the tentacles seemed to originate.

Rakulo glanced at the spot where Tolen had gone under. Was that it? There were no more bubbles. He was gone.

Guilt choked him, and Rakulo blinked back tears. It wouldn't do for the others to see him like this. He rubbed at his eyes with the back of his hand.

"Yeli," he said in the most confident voice he could muster. He cleared his throat. "Are you okay? Can you help me paddle?" The girl, still pale, nodded and picked up her paddle. They focused on pivoting the canoe and paddling back toward the Wall and the others.

Citlali was being pulled into a canoe by Thevanah and Pojuti. Rakulo let loose a shaky sigh of relief at the sight of her. At least she had made it. She must have swam away beneath the surface while Rakulo had cut the tentacle from Yeli.

The others had been lucky they hadn't charged ahead. As they caught their breath, Rakulo took stock. His canoe continued to rock on troubled waters, although the waves were diminishing.

Wooden shards from Tolen and Citlali's splintered canoe bobbed across the surface of the water toward them. Quen was rubbing one arm, which was red and raw. Rakulo saw some of the white pus on the side of Quen's canoe where he had managed to cut a length of tentacle. Unlike Rakulo, he hadn't thrown it back in the water out of disgust.

"Quen, let me see that."

The big man handed it over. The tentacle tapered to a thin end, where a claw-like incisor protruded from it. That must have been what cut Quen's arm, and the only reason it hadn't cut Yeli was because it had been too busy squeezing. Running up the length was a neat row of little mouth-like circles. Rakulo had never seen anything like it in his life. What *was* this monster?

"Now we know why the others who ventured around the Wall by sea never returned," Rakulo said.

The others nodded somberly, their mouths pressed into grim lines.

"I opened my eyes while I was under water," Citlali said.

"What did you see?" Rakulo asked.

"The arms come out of a plant on the bottom of the sea. Dozens of them. It's huge."

Rakulo nodded. This made sense based on what he had seen through the waters, too.

"It seemed to curve out that way."

Rakulo looked up at the massive, shining knife

edge of Wall next to him. Then over to where the tentacles had risen up. He pointed out and drew his arm along the length of the horizon in an arc. Sounds of understanding came from the others.

"A barrier on land, and another in the sea," Rakulo said. "It's another Wall, hidden under the surface of the water."

"This Wall has an appetite," Quen said.

"I'd be willing to bet that there's one at the other end, too," Pojuti said.

"I agree," Rakulo said. "But we've already lost one life today. We better get back to the village now and let the others know what happened." Rakulo tossed the limp tentacle back into Quen's boat. "You're in charge of that. Keep it as your trophy. We need to show it to the others as proof."

Quen nodded seriously, then cupped a handful of water and washed some of the remaining blood off his arm.

They paddled back and were met by the others, who stopped cheering at the sight of their return when they realized that only three of the four canoes had returned. Rakulo and the other seafarers paddled back down the beach to the place from which they had embarked. The rest of the warriors tracked with them along the coast, and greeted them somberly when they finally beached the boats.

"We lost Tolen," Rakulo said.

He explained what had happened, then helped

stash the canoes in the jungle once more, piling them over with brush and leaves. They walked back to the village, where they were greeted by their families once more. It was a more reserved greeting, as the timing was unexpected—Rakulo's warriors were usually gone for weeks at a time. Rakulo kept his face a blank mask. People seemed to sense from a distance that this was not a joyous reunion. Maatiaak was there, scowling. Quen showed everyone the severed tentacle, and the frightened villagers made the sign of protection, touching to their thumb to their forefinger and raising it to their heart.

When Tolen's mother couldn't control her sobs any more, Ixchel pulled the woman into her arms and walked her away from the others so she could grieve more privately.

"You fool," Maatiaak said at last. As he'd watched their explanation, his scowl had deepened. "What did you think was going to happen?"

"If you knew about the sea monster, why didn't you tell us?" Rakulo said. "Why keep it from us?"

"I didn't know!" Maatiaak said. "None of us knew why it was not safe. We only knew that the warriors who have tried to swim around the wall in the past never returned. Of course it was unsafe!"

"Well, now we have proof," Rakulo said, pointing to the severed tentacle. "For all I know, this is the first time we've ever made the discovery.

Isn't it better to know for ourselves? To know the truth?"

"It would be better if that boy were alive," Maatiaak said.

He spat in the sand and walked away, drawing several of the older warriors, who had been silent through Rakulo's explanation, with him in his wake. The area around them suddenly seemed very empty, and the rest of those gathered slowly dispersed, wives and husbands pulling Rakulo's warriors with them back to their homes. Rakulo let them go. Finally, only Citlali remained by his side.

"I should go, too," Citlali said.

"I understand."

"I'm sorry they reacted that way, Rakulo."

"They have every right to be angry."

Rakulo cooked dinner for himself, Ixchel, and Tolen's mother. The women didn't eat, and Rakulo could only stomach a few bites. Then he lay down on the bed he barely used in his mother's house. When he couldn't sleep, he walked outside, took Eliana's deep black stone out of the skin pouch on his belt, and gazed at it under the light of the two moons, half-full. Twinkling stars reflected out of the diamond's depths. But otherwise it seemed just a stone. No powerful magic accessible to him in times of great need. Rakulo was just a reluctant leader who saw one of his people pulled under the water. In his memory, Tolen's grin would be forever replaced by the look of abject terror that washed over his face in the moment before Rakulo let him slip under.

Rakulo put the stone back in the pouch and sighed. He needed to talk to someone. He moved his feet, with no direction in mind, and they took him back into the forest.

Gehro's cave was on the other side of *Uchben Na*. Normally he would have skirted around the place at night for the memories it contained, but tonight he was feeling particularly grim, and he was impatient, so he cut straight through the stone city.

He went under the vast arch, and was halfway across the great courtyard of cracked and weed-grown paving stones when a humming sound came out of the jungle. Rakulo gasped, and began to run. Then a pain erupted in his head.

He stumbled. He fell. He was pulled roughly to his feet by strong, callused hands. Hands of working men, of farmers and warriors of a certain age. Maatiaak was there. Maatiaak ordered his men to search Rakulo.

One of them found Eliana's ring. Maatiaak took it, turning it to observe it.

Of course, Rakulo thought. *That's what Xucha wants. I should have known Maatiaak had people watching me!*

Behind him, the shining orb of Xucha's demon floated in the moonlight, the tall figure clad in a single seamless garment of form-fitting black. On the smooth reflective face of his mask, a snake whipped its tongue out and hissed. When Xucha raised his hand, a blue light searched out from the demon and Eliana's ring rose out of Maatiaak's hand of its own volition.

"No!" Rakulo shouted, swiping his hand at it. "You can't have it!"

Maatiaak's men pulled Rakulo's arms back to his sides and pinned them there. The ring floated up and away, sparkling brightly as it moved through the air like a shooting star. A small hole opened in the smooth armor of Xucha's demon, and the ring disappeared inside.

14

CLEARLY INCOMPLETE

From the moment at the wake when Amon turned his back on her, until she walked out of the artificial cool of the airport in Campeche, Eliana felt like a giant boa constrictor kept squeezing ever tighter around the hollow cavity of her chest where he heart used to be.

Eliana didn't have a heart now. Amon was her heart once, but he was dead to her.

The constricting feeling began to ease as she stepped into the dense humid heat of Campeche at noon, like stepping through a waterfall or entering a steam-filled sauna. She checked her phone—ten missed calls from Amon, and a dozen text messages —locked it without looking at them, and dropped the phone into her purse with a grim satisfaction.

The guilt didn't begin to set in until she was halfway back to the campsite. She had stayed in

Austin for two days after the wake, bought a ticket back to Campeche in secret, and left before Amon woke on Saturday morning. At the time, she had known without a shred of doubt that the bastard deserved the cold treatment. Who was he to dictate the direction of her career?

She had been nothing but encouraging, even when The Auriga Project had been plagued by a grim outlook and everyone thought it would fail. She had been nothing but supportive, even as her career began to burn like a rancid dumpster fire. And she had asked for nothing in return. She had not made demands on him, she had not complained when he worked late night after night after night.

And when she asks him for one thing, what does he do?

He *forbids* her from doing it.

That arrogant bastard.

But the guilt came anyway, creeping in under her anger like a slinky dog with its ears tucked back. *To hell with the guilt*, she thought as she passed through the security checkpoint on the highway. *I can live with it and he can stew for a while. I might even forget about it if my team located another carving while I was gone.*

Two hours and a vehicle swap later she was drinking warm wine and sharing stories over the campfire with her team. And she had been right. She forgot all about her disagreement with Amon when

Lakshmi, Tanner, Ross, and Talia told her what they'd accomplished since she left.

"We found several other monoliths in the area," Talia said. "They seem to be in a square arrangement, almost like they were the stone pillars of a building or something. The walls between the monoliths, made of smaller stones, have rotted away or crumbled, but the larger stones held up."

"Have you found any other petroglyphs?" Eliana asked.

"Not yet. The moss has grown so thick and the foliage is so dense that other carvings could be right under our nose and we wouldn't be able to tell they were there until after we clear the plant matter away. Tanner and Ross spent the last two days just cutting back the jungle. It's *thick*."

"Okay," Eliana said. "Sounds like there's still a lot to do. We should move camp so that we're closer to the work, now that we know it's there."

"You want to lug all this stuff up that hill?" Tanner asked.

"Better than having to wake up even earlier every morning to hike up there. The day will last longer, too, since we won't have to walk as long to get back to camp at night."

"I can't argue with that," said Lakshmi. "Okay then. We'll break camp in the morning and spend tomorrow moving and setting back up. Then we can get to work again."

Eliana was up first, her eagerness to get started pulling her out of bed well before dawn. She made breakfast and disassembled her tent while the others woke. Eliana did more than her fair share in breaking down and hauling supplies, but it was Lakshmi who naturally took charge of the operation. The long-legged, dark-skinned woman was the most organized person Eliana had ever met, and it was thanks to her foresight that they had enough supplies to last for two more weeks—if they were careful—before they would be forced to send someone back to town to restock on food and water.

Lakshmi and Eliana agreed on a new campsite, on an outcropping of limestone about halfway up the steep incline to where the monolith was located. It was well shaded, with a magnificent view of the bowl of dense forest that curved down beneath them. The jungle extended in all directions. The mosquitoes here were thick as clouds, except out on the edge of the rock, in the hot sun, where they were only as thick as a wispy cloud.

"This will do," Eliana said.

Over the next two weeks, they worked from sun up till sundown cutting back the thick foliage of the jungle, trimming vines, and carefully cutting moss off the monoliths with exacto knives, horse-hair brushes, and delicate wire bristles that wouldn't damage the ancient limestone which lay beneath. After two more days spent excavating the cornerstones—for that's how she came to think of the four stones arranged in a clearly defined square exactly twenty feet apart—there was no doubt in her mind that the stones had been placed deliberately. They may once have formed the base of a temple or business, or perhaps a functional government outpost. The walls between them had either crumbled or never been completed. Was it a new project, abandoned before it really got underway? Or perhaps it marked consecrated ground. Was this a burial site? If so, who was buried here?

She didn't have any of those answers.

After a week, the faces of all four cornerstones had been cleared. None of their keen eyes spotted any carvings except the original.

"I don't understand it," Eliana finally said after they stashed their gear for the night. They sat around the fire, each of them sweaty, miserable, and huddling under the dubious shield of mosquito netting. "Why only one carving?"

"It's clearly incomplete," Tanner said. "Maybe they didn't get a chance to finish the job."

"But why carve something so detailed as that petroglyph before the rest of the walls were laid in?"

"It doesn't make much sense, I'll admit," Talia said, shaking her head under her mosquito netting. "Not to mention that, as far as we can tell, this is the only structure nearby."

Ross bobbed his head wearily. While Tanner,

Lakshmi, and Eliana had been clearing plants and scrubbing clean the sides of the monoliths, Ross and Talia had been tromping through the jungle in every direction, searching for other signs of civilization.

"Nothing that we've *found* yet," Ross said.

"Ever the optimist."

Eliana took a deep breath, stood, and turned her back to the fire. She still hadn't spoken with Amon. It was easy as long as she kept busy, and she had been quite busy. Memories of their last conversation came back to her early in the mornings and late at night, though. This deep in the jungle, only the single satellite phone they kept in case of emergencies got service, so she hadn't been distracted by further missed calls or text messages.

The flames of the bonfire lit the treetops below the outcropping with a dancing orange light. Once her eyes adjusted, she could see the starlit bowl of jungle beyond, extending to the horizon. Eventually, the land curved up again.

It was almost as if a giant scoop had been taken out of this ten mile section of land by the hand of God. Whatever had stood here once, nature had long since reclaimed it.

15

LEECHES SHOULD DRINK HIM DRY

Amon thought about Eliana constantly. Her ignoring him was like a ghost limb that constantly itched. But he was able to forget about his heartache the day Reuben swaggered through the door into the Translocator lab again for the first time since Charlie's funeral.

An enthusiastic applause rose from his team of scientists, engineers, and security guards, who had gathered to greet him.

"Welcome back, my friend," Amon said, embracing Reuben in a brotherly hug. He was surprised to feel some of the bones in Reuben's shoulders were more pronounced than he expected, and held him back at arm's length to get a better look at the man.

How a couple weeks can change a man.

Reuben had never been thin, but he had put on

weight when Charlie first got sick. It seemed to have come off all at once since the funeral. The lines of his cheeks were sharper and his strong chin more pronounced. The once round bulge of his gut had receded under his shirt. He even had a fresh haircut, and his normally wild, unkempt white hair was slicked back in a way that made him look ten years younger. It would be wild again in an hour, with hair as thick as his, but it looked good on him.

"You look great," Jeanine said, taking the thoughts right out of Amon's head. "How are you holding up?"

"Better, yeah. Thanks for asking. It's great to see you guys again. I missed this place."

"It's good to have you back, my friend," Amon said. "But if you need more time, just say the word."

"No," Reuben said, shaking his head once, emphatically. "Being back at work is exactly what I need right now."

Reuben embraced Jeanine warmly, and then the others. Amon shook his head. It was truly remarkable to see Reuben so healthy.

Selfishly, he was glad to have Reuben back, too. He trusted all of his people—they wouldn't be in the Translocator lab if he didn't—but Reuben was his right hand. He had put his life in his hands before, and would do it again without hesitation. Reuben once took a bullet for him.

Jeanine led Reuben to the holodeck. He looked

even more like the veteran conductor he was when he raised his arms and the array of hologram controls flickered to life. He grinned from ear to ear as he powered up the Hopper with a practiced motion.

"It feels good to be back!" he shouted over the keening noise of the Translocator's boot-up procedure. They all cheered him again, and then they went back to work.

Agent Wiley and Agent Moreno arrived later that day. Amon pulled Reuben into the lounge to talk, and they all caught him up on what they had discovered in his absence. With everything that had happened in his personal life, Reuben had been informed about the break-in and killings in Audrey's lab, but he had not been filled in on the suspicious activity the FBI was chasing around the country.

Agent Wiley caught Reuben up to speed in just a few minutes.

"Another Translocator?" Reuben said. "Damn. That's not good."

"I'm sorry to lay this on you," Amon said. "I meant what I said earlier. If you need more time, it's yours. But if you're back, I think it's important that you know exactly what's going on. You saw the additional security measures Jeanine and I installed on the Hopper. This is why."

"And you're sure it's Lucas?"

"We always suspected that he stole the blueprints

to the Translocator. We just didn't know what we planned to do with it. I'm still not sure of his endgame, but we can see he's been running…experiments."

"Humph. *Trinkn zoln im piavkes,*" Reuben mumbled.

Agent Wiley and Agent Moreno blinked.

"What's that, German?" Wiley said.

Reuben shook his head ruefully. "It's Yiddish. Something my mother used to say when she was angry at my uncle, who was a real pain in the *toches*. It means, 'leeches should drink him dry.'"

"I concur," Agent Wiley said.

Amon laughed. It was good to see the serious agent joking around. Reuben always brought out the humorous side in people. "It's good to have you back old friend."

A companionable silence fell between them for a moment. Amon pursed his lips and met Agent Wiley's eyes. She raised her eyebrows.

"What is it?" Reuben said. "There's something else I need to know on top of maimed bodies, and a faulty Translocator run by our back-stabbing, embezzling, on-the-run former executive?"

"Well, I never thought about this until Agent Wiley brought it up, but she makes a good case," Amon said. "Montoya translocated directly into Audrey's lab, and took down the two guards outside first, right? How did he know to take out the guards, or even that they were there? And how did he know where the carbonado was kept? They didn't know exactly where in the lab it was located—because no one goes in there except for Audrey. But they certainly knew which lab it was in."

"What are you saying?"

"You have a mole somewhere," Agent Moreno said.

"That's why the others have only been told as much as they need to know to do their jobs," Amon said.

"Don't take this the wrong way," Reuben said. "I appreciate your trust. But why are you telling me this? How do you know *I'm* not the spy?"

Agent Wiley's nostrils flared and she inhaled through her nose, but otherwise she maintained a neutral expression.

"That's exactly why we're telling you," Amon rushed to say. "I *know* you're not the spy. I trust you with my life, Reuben. "

"And we did a thorough background check," Agent Moreno said. Agent Wiley nodded reluctantly. Suspicion of everything and everyone was her natural state. Amon couldn't blame her for that. He would be paranoid, too, if it was his job to fly around the country inspecting dead bodies.

"There's another reason we're telling you," Amon said. "Now that you're back, we need your help.

We have to get to Switzerland, and we need someone to man the Hopper while we're gone."

"Man the—you don't mean…"

Amon shrugged. "That's right. I've sent Wiley and Moreno through a few times already, but I want to go with them this time."

"The LTA won't like this, Amon," Reuben said.

"They don't know. Since we can't figure out who the mole is, we can't send any kind of official request to Dr. Badeux. That would leave a paper trail. It's just a little hop to Switzerland. They'll never know we were gone."

Reuben chewed his lip as he considered this. Then his eyes widened. "You're going to visit the Large Hadron Collider. But Amon, you've said yourself that you don't fully understand how the machine works with the carbonados."

"I don't, but it seems safe enough. And it's the fastest way to get there. The longer we wait, the more people get killed."

Agent Wiley and Agent Moreno exchanged a thoughtful glance. Amon had already gone through the dangers with them, and they agreed that it was worth the risk. He *may* have sounded more confident when he explained it to the FBI agents. Reuben, however, knew about the carbonado and the concerns Amon had about how it affected the molecular reassembly…and the dubious margin of error.

Reuben pushed his tongue against the inside of his cheek while he considered. Finally, he nodded.

Later that night—early morning Switzerland time—after the day's transport to the lunar base was complete and everyone else had gone home, Amon unlocked the lab and let Reuben, Agent Wiley, and Agent Moreno back in. The guards at the doorway were off duty from midnight to six AM, so only the security cameras saw them enter.

Amon snapped the carbonado solution into its slot at the base of the holodeck.

Without preamble, Reuben took his position at the control unit and brought the Translocator to life. The trio of travelers walked into the stabilization sphere on the Translocator platform. The transponder that would bring them home again was on Amon's wrist—it looked like a watch. Instead of telling the time, the device had a blank face set with two LED bulbs and a single button. If Amon held the button for five seconds, the first light would blink red. When it changed to a blinking green light, the transponder signal had been received, and when both bulbs went blue, the translocation was being initiated. Whoever was being translocated with Amon needed to stand close. The machine took everything within a radius of about five feet around him. He also needed to be careful, because the machine didn't discriminate between, for instance, a piece of an object, and the object itself, if it was outside of the acceptable range.

"We're ready," Amon said. Reuben nodded, a blue-white flash of light engulfed the three of them, and then they were standing in the middle of an empty field with the Jura mountain range visible in the distance beyond. Amon's ears popped due to the sudden altitude adjustment.

"I'll never get used to that," Agent Moreno said.

His pale face told Amon he might be sick. Amon mentally checked his own body and was pleased to detect none of the usual side-effects of the translocation. Taking atoms apart and putting them back together was a complex process, but it seemed that Moreno was ill at the *idea* of what just happened to him, rather than the actual translocation itself. A positive sign.

Agent Wiley didn't seem to be so affected. Her lips set in determination. "This way," she said in a commanding voice. He and Moreno both hurried to catch up with her short but purposeful stride.

Not five minutes later, they were in the tiled lobby of the CERN building speaking to a receptionist. She asked them to sit and wait, made a phone call, and soon a half dozen Interpol agents walked in the front door.

Moreno cursed under his breath.

"Agent Monica Wiley?" said the nearest agent, a tall Swiss man, in a heavy accent.

"Yes," she said, standing and shooting an evil glance at the receptionist. The receptionist shrugged. Agent Wiley's brow wrinkled.

"Would you come with us please?"

The Interpol agents took them to two unmarked white cars outside, and Agent Wiley and Agent Moreno spent the next hour arguing with them about inter-agency courtesy and jurisdiction. They were clearly upset that the FBI had not gone through proper channels. Agent Wiley told them to contact Dr. Badeux with the LTA, but they were being stubborn and wanted to put them on a flight back home immediately.

When Amon's phone buzzed in his pocket, he walked a little ways off and checked it, hoping it was finally some word from Eliana. He didn't even care if she was mad at him, he just wanted to know she was okay.

Instead, Reuben was calling.

"Yeah?" he said, glancing back at the Interpol agents, who were watching him carefully. He turned his body away slightly.

"Amon," Reuben said. "I thought you should know…there's been a power failure on the moon base. Dome 2 has fallen back to life-support systems only."

"What happened?"

"I don't know. Some hiccup at the nuclear fission reactor. Power is down in Dome 2 and the rest of the primary structures have fallen back to life support. I heard chatter about buried electric cables being severed. I think they sent men to investigate."

"Is this some kind of drill?" Amon said.

Reuben swallowed. "Not from what I heard."

"I'm on my way."

Amon ended the call and pocketed his phone. Without asking permission, he strode away from the Interpol agents and back inside the CERN building. An agent followed him.

"Bathroom?" he said. The receptionist pointed, and Amon hurried down the hall.

He shut himself in the bathroom as he held the button on the transponder. The lights blinked from flashing red to green to solid blue. He looked at himself in the mirror until the brightness grew, then closed his eyes as he was translocated back to the lab.

16

CLEVER THINKING

When Rakulo woke, his left cheek was wet and swollen. Drool spilled out of his mouth onto a cold, rough floor. Voices rose up and fell outside. They sounded distant, faint.

Feeling with his hands, Rakulo found stone beneath him and pushed up, or what seemed to be the direction he knew as up. The wall tilted, showing him a stone door with no handle, and he fought to hold himself steady. His stomach lurched, he choked, and more liquid splashed from his mouth to the floor.

His fingers came away from his mouth dark and sticky. *Blood.* Then he remembered what had happened.

Three men had rushed him, Maatiaak snarling at their center. A heavy club smashed into his face and down he went. Then they were on top of him. Fists pummeled into the small of his back. His hair caught and ripped on a cracked stone as they dragged him to one of these low stone dugouts, a place for crazy people and criminals, and where the sacrifices were kept while they went through the dreamwalking experience.

Was this the same room that had held Eliana?

Something in the air seemed to rupture, and a wetness seeped out and down the left side of his neck.

That can't be good, he thought, reaching up to touch the warm blood. But his equilibrium had returned after his ear popped, and the nausea faded away.

A distant humming cut through the faint voices outside. Rakulo started, thinking it was Xucha's demon in the cell with him. But the room was black and bare. No shining orbs like deadly moons, only stone walls carved up with drawings and claw marks from generations of prisoners past.

No demon. Only himself in a low stone room. When he stood, his thick, tangled black hair brushed the low ceiling.

Rakulo turned his mind inward and realized the humming came from inside him, from his injured ear, and it wasn't the same sound as the demon made. But there was something else beyond that noise. If he focused, he could make it out. Something loud and angry. He approached the door and put his right ear, the one that hadn't ruptured, close to the door.

He made out thumping, shouts, the sound of a club against flesh. A cry, a heavy thud, some noise that Rakulo imagined like ripping cloth. He felt queasy again, and not because the dizziness had returned.

And then there was a great war cry, a vibrating ululation followed by a hail that pattered against the wall. Something heavy struck the other side of the door, which shuddered in its frame. Another volley came, dozens of strikes of stone against stone within the space of two seconds. Then a pause. Silence. Rakulo stepped back from the door, crouching with his back to the corner. He tensed, ready to spring.

The door opened.

A slight, athletic figure called to him from outside, and he recognized her shadowed shape and two others.

"Are you okay?" Citlali asked.

"Yes," Rakulo said. "At least, I think so. I can walk.

"Can you run? We've got to move fast."

Rakulo stepped into the moonlight. Citlali was one part of the triad and stood back to back with Quen and Thevanah. Both women held a bow nocked with an arrow, and empty quivers at their sides.

"I only have one arrow left," Thevanah growled.

"I'm all out after this one," Citlali said.

"We have to make it to the treeline before your father's men find out it's a distraction." Quen hefted a spear in his thick paws. "Let's go."

Citlali took off at a run, and Rakulo jogged after them. Thevanah reached back and raked him with her long fingernails to adjust his course, like a mom adjusts a toddler finding its walking legs. He realized he was wobbling as he ran.

Eventually, Rakulo caught his stride. They weaved between stone buildings, some of which had caved in years ago and left stones scattered across the path. Rakulo recognized the way, and placed himself mentally at the northeastern end of the courtyard, hidden behind the Temple of the Warriors. Beyond that, a short field stretched to the foot of the great pyramid. The north road led to the Well of Sacrifices. They turned the other way, southeast, where a gate with a low stone arch led into the jungle, back toward the caves. Soon they passed through the gate, and Rakulo swept a familiar hand along the ivy that seemed to coat the whole structure like a net.

His ear ached worse with each breath he took. Rakulo kicked his toe on a jutting floor stone, and stumbled. Thevanah caught him, pushing him upright and away as one of the older warriors, a man loyal to Maatiaak, came around the corner and barreled into Citlali, sending her sprawling.

Quen roared and brought the shaft of his spear

down on the man's neck. The attacker crumpled and fell, and lay still. They all braced for another attack, but none came. They stood for a moment, breathing hard.

He didn't blame Quen for his reaction, but Rakulo didn't want to hurt anyone. These were his people. They had locked him up, but they had been misled by Maatiaak and under Xucha's power—they couldn't help what they were doing. It wasn't their fault.

And in that moment, Rakulo realized he had some empathy for Maatiaak, even though the man had betrayed him. Why had Rakulo tried to fight the inevitable? As he bent at Citlali's side to help her up —to help Maatiaak's only daughter, who had defied her father to free him—the answer came to him in a flash. He fought Maatiaak because he had not known Xucha was behind the deception. Now that Rakulo knew, it made all the difference in the world. His enmity for Maatiaak washed out like a tide. Maatiaak was just a shadow being controlled by the vengeful god, casting his darkness in the direction Xucha pointed.

It could have been anyone. That it happened to be Maatiaak was only a coincidence. He was not the enemy.

"I'm fine," Citlali said as she regained her feet. She was breathless and favoring her ankle, but otherwise intact. There was a rally of cries from the southwest road now. Citlali gestured, and Quen and Thevanah walked on into the forest, away from the stone city, peering around trees and carefully ahead, searching for unpleasant surprises.

"What was that noise?" Rakulo asked, when the ululating cry sounded from a new location in the jungle behind him.

"A distraction."

The noises faded behind and the forest swallowed them. They found shelter among its folded leaves. It was another hour hike to the caves. The tiny flying bugs were thick here, but Rakulo was tired enough not to mind except they kept sticking to the blood on his neck. His ear still throbbed, and his face began to ache as the adrenaline faded. They finally reached the limestone ridge, and Citlali limped on ahead of him.

His bare feet kicked aside some leaves and he explored the pockmarked stone underfoot with his toes, familiar as a field he'd tilled with his own hands. He counted the caves, then turned left, walking carefully along the uneven stone path. A shadow separated itself from the forest, and a concealing coat of leaves revealed itself to be a man.

"Gehro!" The rest of his warriors emerged from behind the trees all around him, and for a moment Rakulo was filled with a shining pride. They had been so silent even he had not heard them.

His hand went to his ear and he rephrased that.

He had not heard them because it was not easy for him to hear. A cold panic took him. He fought to regain control. Gehro approached and lay his hand on Rakulo's neck.

"It's nothing." Rakulo pulled away from Gehro.

"Come inside, you're bleeding. Let me look at you."

"In a minute," he said. He turned back to his people. They were true warriors now. Despite the pain in his ear, Rakulo embraced and exchanged low words with each of them in turn. His heart grew heavy as he made his way around. Three comrades were missing. Apart from Tolen, who would never smile again, Pojuti and Hopolix were also absent. After he'd congratulated each of the survivors on their first battle—reminding them that it was no honor to fight their own people—he asked Quen and Citlali what happened to his two missing warriors.

"Pojuti was already upset about Tolen," Citlali said.

"When she found out you were missing, she insisted we go to the stash and get the bows and arrows," Quen said. "She cornered Maatiaak at the cliff's edge, and shot him."

"By herself?"

Quen averted his gaze. Citlali met his eyes in a challenge. "No. She had help."

"Her arrow went into Maatiaak's shoulder, but then he charged at us anyway. I pushed a few of them away, but Maatiaak hid behind one of them. He dodged me and hit Pojuti while she was pulling drawing back the bowstring. She fell."

Rakulo paled. "Dead?"

"She went bravely."

That meant she didn't scream. Rakulo nodded. If the gods were kind, she would have died on impact. If they were not, she would merely be severely injured by the fall and drown slowly as the waves washed her over rock breakers and into the cliff face.

Gehro put his hands over Rakulo's shoulders and led him toward the fire. Rakulo began to lower himself where several others were gathered, faces soft-seeming and comforting in the light of the flames. Gehro tugged him along, prevented him from sitting down.

"You should wash off, first." The old man led him all the way into the darkness at the back of the cave.

"No, no," Rakulo balked, suddenly afraid of what might be hidden back there.

The old man shushed him, slowing his step. "There's a small stream of water back here. I'm just giving you a chance to wash the blood off your face. You look gruesome."

Gehro let Rakulo scrub his hands and neck clean. He set to the task vigorously. Gehro left him and came back with torch a moment later. Rakulo's mouth dropped open at the sight of all his blood coloring the clear, slow-flowing water.

The flame also lit the rest of the area. The stream itself was about five feet across, but deep. It flowed under the wall at the far end of the deep cave with about an arm span of clearance. The water flowed slowly, at its own pace, affected by the thrust of the current beyond but not swept up in it.

The pool would have been accessible by a person were it not for the low-hanging stalactites, many of whose delicately formed tapers bent nearly to the water, casting geometric shadows from the torch onto the light-dappled eddy.

Gehro set the torch into a pile of stones arranged to hold it. The old man used his hands to administer a stinking salve that smelled of garlic to the cuts on Rakulo's face, and his swollen upper lip.

"Where does this go, Gehro?" Rakulo asked

"Did you not know there was a stream back here?."

"I knew there was water, I just thought it was a pool. But look, it's moving. So where is it going?"

"Don't know. I tried asking a few times, but the stream is reluctant to speak with me."

"Did I tell you that in our explorations we found other wells in the forest?" Rakulo leaned forward, excited again despite his wounds, for the salve Gehro applied had a numbing effect. "I swam in two of them to the northwest. The other one I found in the southwest corner near the wall, is very deep and only accessible by a long fall. We dipped a vine into the water to see how far it was, but we couldn't reach it."

Gehro regarded the low hanging stalactites with sardonic amusement, as if their existence was a practical joke the gods were playing on human transience. "That's a long fall."

Rakulo dipped his hand in the cool water, and tasted it. It was fresh, not salty like the ocean. Fresh like the other sinkholes they had discovered. Fresh like spring water.

He drew a line between the sinkholes on the map of the area he kept in his memory. There were no creeks or canyons deep enough to obstruct the flow of water. It was a long hike between the two points, through hilly and dense forest. But like the canoes, if the current went with him it would go smooth and fast.

Could this be what they were looking for? Did it connect to the ocean, perhaps on the other side of the sea monster?

And then he remembered thick tentacles convulsing around Yeli's small shoulders. He jerked his hand up out of the water and laid it on his waist where his knife should be. The knife was gone. Maatiaak must have taken that, too.

Gehro sighed. "I'm sorry, Raku. Citlali told me

what happened. I didn't know what was out there, just that it was dangerous."

Thanks for not saying I told you so. "It's I who owe you thanks, Gehro. Thanks for providing the distraction. You saved my life."

Gehro grinned, and made that yodeling sound in his throat, but softly, a reminder of its power that night. Trickery had freed him. Perhaps, sometimes, clever thinking was better than resorting to force. The shame of his first encounter with Maatiaak felt somehow tempered by that lesson.

Rakulo glanced back one last time at the quiet current of the underground stream, before walking back to the fire to be among his warriors.

17

WITHOUT FOUNDATION

Eliana stood on the thick, lichen-coated trunk of an uprooted tree and surveyed the cleared stretch of ground between the cornerstones.

The storm that knocked over the trunk took place an indiscriminate number of years before her tiny party of explorers arrived. Yet, because of the way the water plunged down this little hillock on which the cornerstones were situated, and how the trunk was held six inches above the ground by two agave plants crushed beneath it, the trunk itself had been partially preserved. The wood was squishy under her boots.

A straight line that ran between cornerstones A and B—the two exposed monoliths closest to her position. Eliana now thought of that as "the front side."

She had lettered the cornerstones, too. Oh, yes. And this side was the front because it would have faced out over the tree-crowded valley below.

Dozens of colorful birds flitted through the treetops of the thick jungle, soaring through the area Ross had painstakingly cleared with his machete, then on down into the valley, circling and darting through the air in search of the juiciest insects.

Lakshmi paced territorially around the perimeter of the monoliths through a tunnel of wild tamarind trees and tight-packed strangler figs. She stopped when a snake slithered by her feet, darting between a pair of bushes on the side of the dirt path they had worn with their repeated circumnavigation of the site.

"The cornerstones are well preserved," Eliana said. "But what good is a building without a foundation?"

"And why here?" Lakshmi added. "Stone buildings weren't easy to build a thousand years ago. What's the significance of this spot?"

Eliana had no doubt that whatever this structure was intended to be, the stones had been carved and placed by the hands of a skilled mason. It was hard to imagine someone—or even several people—hauling the limestone blocks, weighing a ton each, this high into the dense jungle. Unless the forest had been less thick when this structure was built? Had the valley below them sunk in the last thousand years?

It had taken them a week to excavate the four monoliths and the broken limestone pieces from the encroaching jungle. Each piece of stone was labeled with a plastic orange triangle and numbered 1 through 237, down to the smallest fragment, a chip the size of her pinky nail.

Lakshmi stopped pacing. She bent down, picked up an orange triangle, and wrote 238 on it with a sharpie.

She turned to Eliana. Ross, Talia, and Tanner lounged on camp chairs nearby and regarded Eliana silently, waiting for her verdict.

"What are you thinking, boss?" Lakshmi finally said.

"It's a job well done," Eliana said, making eye contact with each of them. "Truly."

Lakshmi snorted. "Shortest lecture you've ever given. What else?"

Eliana raised her hands and let them fall to her sides. She blew her cheeks out. "Why aren't there any more carvings?"

The carving of the two moons was located on the inside of cornerstone A, on the wall facing cornerstone D. The carving was nothing more than two overlapping circles, but they were perfectly proportioned to the size of the moons that hung in the night sky over Kakul. One circle was incomplete, like it had a chunk taken out of its shoulder. Eliana was certain of it now. Would others see the moons as clearly as she did?

Not if they had never seen the moons. She must get back there, if just to convince them.

After cleaning off the moss around the carving, Eliana found two more shallow lines, like an arrow pointing up to the moons—drawing attention to them, she assumed. The two lines were far too simplistic to glean any other meaning from them.

Strangely, no carvings were found on any of the other stones despite much searching. No petroglyphs, no symbols, no lines, no art, no paint chips, indeed no markings at all to be found.

Foliage still stood in the middle of the rectangle made by the cornerstones—not because Eliana didn't want to cut it down, but because it was impractical to do so. Three fan-shaped Guadalupe Palms grew in an isosceles triangle formation between the cornerstones. The rest of the area was thickly packed with ferns and low prickly agaves. She had combed through it herself a dozen times, wearing her boots and two pairs of jeans to protect herself from agave thorns and startled snakes while she hunted for stones. She was nearly certain they had found them all. The stones provided scant few clues to what this structure might have been used for.

"You've seen the other ruins at Lagunita and

Tamchen. They were all intricately decorated, carved. Do you see any facades or reliefs here? Apart from the one carving of the moons, these are plain unadorned limestone blocks with a wall connecting them. And there aren't as many as I thought there would be, either…"

They all stared at the line of stones in front of them, at the uneven row of orange triangles that extended around the perimeter.

"What if it was dismantled?" Lakshmi said.

Eliana cocked her head at her. "Explain."

"Only this wall seems to have enough stones to connect the corners. The southern, eastern, and western walls all have big gaps. Maybe someone moved the stones, or took them and repurposed them elsewhere?"

"It's possible. But Talia and Tanner scouted the area for five miles in every direction while we've been working on this." Eliana swept her hands out toward the sloped land below and around them.

"What if it was a fort or something?" Tanner said. "The walls were knocked down in some kind of attack."

"Wouldn't we find more fragments, and maybe some weapons, if that were the case? Flint arrowheads? Sharpened obsidian? It doesn't add up. Besides, evidence indicates the cities in this area being abandoned, not destroyed. Not to mention, this structure looks so different from the other Mayan ruins that have been discovered…"

"How do you know the people who built it were Maya at all?" Talia said.

"They had to have been," she said. "You heard what Audrey told me when I called her earlier today. She dated the samples we gave her between 200 AD to 1000 AD. That's close enough to the Late Classic Maya in this area to be part of the same culture as Lagunita and Tamchen. They had to have been Maya."

The others shifted their weight and cleared their throats.

"What if," Ross said, "it just wasn't finished?"

Eliana considered this for a long moment. "That's an interesting theory. So not just the carving, but the whole structure is incomplete. It would explain why there aren't as many stones as you'd expect, why it's so far away from any other structures, and why there are no reliefs, if those were done last. The cornerstones were just to mark the place. The foundation of something…tall."

Ross nodded.

"But why so far up here? And how did they even get the stones up here?"

He shrugged. "Don't know. Maybe the carving was done by someone else, later, after the structure was built."

A rustling sound came from the bushes to their

left. Ross drew his machete from its sheath with a metallic hiss, and turned, holding the blade before him and stepping in front of Lakshmi.

Two low fan-shaped palm leaves burst apart as a brown tapir galloped onto the path. It snorted with irritation and tossed its head as it charged toward Ross.

He brought his machete around instinctively, but halfway through his swing he recognized the animal and redirected the arc of the blade, jumping aside awkwardly as he fought his reactive momentum. The sharp edge of the machete thunked into the trunk of the tree near Eliana's feet.

She pulled her foot back just in the nick of time as the blade sank into the soft wood. The tapir snorted, continued down the path, and trotted out of sight.

Ross cursed. "Sorry," he said sheepishly. "It surprised me."

Eliana blew out the breath she'd been holding. Then they all broke out into laughter, the tension burned away by the sudden, harmless surprise.

She squatted down to stabilize herself and steady her trembling limbs. She was overcome with a helpless laughter. As she laughed, the worry and fear bled out of her, and she lay on the log and let her sweat-soaked body be supported by the old tree.

Bugs buzzed over her, but that didn't bother her. She hardly noticed the perpetual insects any more.

Even Lakshmi didn't seem bothered. She sat down next to Eliana, still chuckling, and rolled up the legs of her pants. Lakshmi took off her boots, and wiggled her toes in the air.

"Really well done, you guys," Eliana said. "I mean it. Let's take some photos, and then call it a day."

After a long, lazy dinner, Eliana dug her phone out of her tent and hiked up to high ground, where the signal was better, and stared at the screen while she thought about calling Amon.

Her anger had faded, but not her sense of injustice. Yet she found that she wanted to share the accomplishments of her team with him. Celebrating among themselves was fine, but telling Amon would be better. Plus, she missed his voice.

She scrolled to his name in her contacts. She pressed the call button. And hung up before the first ring had finished.

What was she thinking? She couldn't talk to him. For a minute, she considered calling Renee and talking to her old mentor instead. *She* would appreciate her team's work. She was an anthropologist herself. Renee had left a voicemail two days ago, actually, though Eliana didn't call her back. She re-listened to it now.

"Hey Eliana, I know you're probably out in the field again now, but I wanted to invite you to the faculty luncheon next Sunday. The editor of *National*

Geographic, Bryce Varley, will be there, and he said he's very interested in meeting you…"

Eliana looked at her calendar. Sunday was tomorrow. She would have to pack now and leave first thing in the morning to make a flight back work. The very idea exhausted her.

Forget it. She deleted the message and drove back to camp. After locating the nice bottle of smoky mezcal she'd saved for a special occasion, Eliana crouched outside the flap of Lakshmi's tent.

"Lakshmi? Can I come in?"

"Oh my," she said, "have you been hiding that from us?"

Lakshmi was lounging on her back, reading a book by the light of an electric lantern. Eliana handed her the bottle, and she took a small sip without sitting up. "Mmmm. I love the taste of mezcal. It's like tequila, but drinkable." Lakshmi glanced down at the cell phone, which Eliana was now twirling through her thumb and forefinger. "Did you talk to Amon?"

"I can't."

"Why not?"

"I just can't right now."

They drank together for a bit in silence.

"What's on your mind?" Lakshmi finally asked.

"I'm trying to figure out our next move. What should we do now?"

"You're in charge, you tell me."

"I didn't just hire you for your organizational ability," Eliana said. "Or your legs, though they are lovely. I'm asking you for your opinion."

"We could call it off for a while, take a break. We'll be able to publish preliminary findings based on what we found here."

"You think that's a good idea?" Eliana said.

"Sure. Why not?"

"I'm just worried what people will think."

"We all have to face that eventually," Lakshmi said. "You're not usually one to hold back if you believe in something."

"I am this time. I need to know more."

"We're mapping out the area. Every building block counts. They'll take the preliminary findings."

"Maybe that's for the best. You guys deserve a break."

Lakshmi stared at Eliana for a second, then shrugged. "Or we can keep looking. It's not so bad out here. Kind of peaceful."

Eliana took another drink. The mezcal burned her throat. She passed the liquor back to Lakshmi.

"There's a lot of jungle here," Lakshmi said. "Lagunita and Temchen were lost until 2014. And now this place. Who knows what else is in this jungle?"

"Yeah," Eliana said. "We'll need more supplies. But I don't know."

"Are you scared of what we'll find or what you'll have to do with it?"

"Both, I guess." Eliana took back the mezcal, and cradled it in her arm. "I've never been one to worry so much. I hate feeling this way all the time."

"You were the one who taught me what lay on the other side of fear."

"Folly," Eliana said. She raised the bottle to her mouth, but Lakshmi snatched it out of her hand before she could take a sip.

"No," Lakshmi said. "You told me that all the best things in life are on the other side of fear. We learn as much from our successes as our failures. Remember?"

Eliana smiled sadly. "The speech I used on you on the way out to do our field work in Utah. A lot has happened since then." She didn't tell Lakshmi that she'd cribbed the lines from one of the science fiction novels she was reading by lantern in her tent in the field, like Lakshmi was doing now. The words had impressed Renee, her mentor, so she thought it might also impress her friend. She was young and foolish back then.

"The stakes are higher now." Lakshmi tilted the neck of the bottle back at Eliana, who took it from her gently. "But that doesn't really change anything, does it?"

Eliana took another swig, then stoppered the mezcal bottle with the cork. Her body buzzed with a low level of intoxication. She felt calm, and braver than she had a moment ago. It was always good to talk to Lakshmi about these things—it had a way of clarifying her thoughts.

"You're right. I want to push on. Keep looking. Let's talk to the others about it in the morning."

18

RUPTURE AT THE AIRLOCK

Amon sprinted off the Translocator platform before his eyes had fully adjusted, and bumped into Wes McManis. Wes stumbled back against a railing by the loading ramp, cussing. He had bleary, bloodshot eyes and wore jeans bunched up at the tops of his cowboy boots. Clearly, he'd been awakened after a long night and it wasn't pretty. His hairy stomach spilled out from under a rumpled button-up flannel shirt, and he stank of a woman's cloying perfume.

"What in the hell is going on?" Wes demanded.

"What are you doing here?" Amon said.

"I told Roger, the security guard up at the 24-hour checkpoint, to call me if anything suspicious was going on. He said he heard a suspicious commotion, an alarm or something."

Amon narrowed his eyes. "Who else does Roger talk to? Do you have someone spying on me?"

"What? I—" Wes's face flushed. "How dare you accuse me of spying on you. If anyone is acting suspicious, it's you. You've been here three nights this week. Did you clear any of this with the LTA?"

Amon grunted and shoved past Wes. He joined Reuben, who was still watching the wide monitor of the holodeck. Amon leaned in close with Reuben and spoke in a low voice.

"What was the alarm for?"

"It's programmed to sound an alarm if we lost connection to the platform. Scared the crap out of me—we've never had that happen except in trials before, and that was intentionally. Something is going on up there."

"Do you mind?"

Reuben nodded and let Amon step in to the middle of the holodeck.

Amon opened the camera feed at the Dome 2 platform and projected it onto the screen—it was black, offline. He pinged the platform, but it didn't respond either. The connection indicator was an uncharacteristic red color.

He split the big glass screen into four quadrants and brought up more camera feeds. One showed the door of the SOLARPulse-1 and the broad overlook window in one shot, although the glare from the overhead light at this angle didn't afford them much of the view. Another camera showed the inside of Dome 3, the pressurized area for repair and maintenance of the fabricators. Only five or six of the twenty-five scientists were there, and they were all huddled at the airlock window, gazing out.

"Is that the direction of the reactor?" Reuben asked.

Amon nodded.

In the last quadrant, bottom right, Amon brought up the exterior camera on top of Dome 2. It was filled with dust from the fabricators. Men ran in the distance, their strides comically elongated due to the low gravity. A couple of blocky fabricators, their outlines similar to Zambonis or huge riding lawn-mowers, stood still in silhouette—they'd all been turned off.

He looked for a camera feed at the nuclear reactor, but that was offline as well.

"What the hell happened?" Wes said.

"Reuben," Amon said, breaking their concentration and pulling their eyes to him. "I want you to put me inside the tunnel near the nuclear reactor."

"No way."

"Yes. You can do it."

"Too risky. I don't trust it. It's one thing to move somewhere on earth because the planetary body's relative velocity stays the same, and the distance is shorter. Without the platform—"

"You have to. I'll get a suit." Amon began walking toward the storage side of the lab.

"Remember what happened last time?" Reuben called after him.

"What happened last time?" Wes asked.

Reuben grunted. "The electronics fried and cut off life support systems."

"Oh. Right."

Their voices cut out when Amon passed through the plastic curtain into the small warehouse space, where the spare high-mobility space suits were kept—light, thin models with a wide range of motion and made of lightweight but durable fabric, weighing only fifteen pounds.

The suits were difficult to squeeze into in the best of times. Now it felt like getting dressed took ages, although he knew it was only a few minutes. They had many clasps, seals, and zippers, and it took agonizing long moments for Amon to shed his clothes, climb into the suit, and check the oxygen tanks. He sealed the helmet, a plastic bubble that gave him about three inches of clearance around his face, and full use of his peripheral vision. He turned the oxygen on as well as the electronics so he could speak to Reuben, albeit with a slight delay.

When Amon ambled back into the Translocator room wearing the suit, Wes and Reuben were both watching one of the external camera feeds. The dust was static as it hung in the atmosphereless firma-ment. They seemed to be working next to the tunnel. Wes turned his cell phone over in his hand nervously. Then he flicked it open, sent a quick text to someone, and returned to flipping it over and over and over.

"Who are you texting?" Amon asked.

"Enzo," Wes said. "I'm telling him what's happening."

"Let's do this, Reuben," Amon said.

"No way."

"I've resolved the electrical issues."

"How many times have you sent yourself through in a space suit since the first time?"

"Well, I haven't yet, but—"

"But nothing."

Amon walked onto the Translocator platform and gave Reuben a thumbs up. "You can do this. Right inside the tunnel—the air is the same pressure as here, remember."

"Yes, yes," Reuben grumbled, "and adjust for the gravity differential and relative velocity…"

The rings around him spun and a second later Amon was looking straight down a tunnel on the lunar surface. A klaxon blared inside the building. He took a hesitant breath. Everything seemed fine with the life support systems. He tapped the computer at his wrist that controlled them. When it lit up, he grinned.

"Well done, Reuben!" he said over the noise of the klaxon.

"What?"

"I said well done!"

"Amon, we can't hear you. Huh, well that's strange, I—"

"Reuben? Hello?" Amon's body broke out in cold sweats inside the suit. He'd been removed from the communication channels. "Damnit!"

Amon looked around him in the silence. Well, he came up here to help, so he might as well see what happened and if he could actually be of assistance. One thing at a time.

Still unsettled, Amon made himself walk forward. This tunnel was quite long, as the nuclear fission reactor was buried apart from the main site due to the possible radiation contamination it would emit in the event it was breached. For safety reasons, it was broken into sections about a hundred yards in length.

Amon walked until he reached the airlock at the end of this section. He slapped the button to open it, entered, and waited till the door closed behind him. When it had, he pressed the next button and the door opened to let him into a connected section of tunnel identical to the one through which he had just passed.

The tunnels had no windows. The interior walls were a stark white. Inset lighting ran lengthwise through the ceiling. Amon passed through three identical sections, curious as to why no one was in these tunnels. Was he even headed in the right direction?

At the next airlock, he pressed the button, but the door wouldn't open. Gazing through the clear window, he saw an identical section of tunnel. Except this one was filled with smoke.

No, not smoke. Dust.

Moon dust from the fabricators had drifted in to the tunnel. Which meant that the atmosphere has been voided. No wonder they hadn't come through this tunnel. The airlocks shut down in the event of a breach.

Another man in a space suit approached through the dust. Amon waved, and the man walked toward him. It wasn't until he was on the other side of the airlock that Amon recognized him. It was Stanis. He said something, but Amon couldn't hear him. He shook his head.

Stanis held fingers in the air in a pattern. One finger, two fingers, and then one. Followed by one finger, two fingers, and then five.

Amon switched his frequency to that channel.

"Amon!" Stanis's voice came through his headset. "What are you doing up here? The platform went offline."

"I'll explain later. What can I do to help?"

"We could use the extra hands! Let's get you through this airlock."

Producing a tablet, Stanis manually overrode the

airlock to let Amon into the dusty tunnel, where he clapped him on the shoulder.

"What happened?"

"A rupture in the tunnel near the reactor. Took out the power, but didn't touch the reactor, thankfully."

"The cause?"

"Don't know yet. It just blew. Happened to take out a main power line when it did. We'll be on life support only until we can replace that. I thought we were beyond these sorts of accidents..."

Over the course of the next several hours, Amon held tools, carried plastic material, and drove a rover back and forth between Dome 3 and the rupture at the airlock to bring Stanis's team extra supplies. They eventually repaired the two-foot rupture in the cellular wall with a freshly printed section from a fabricator, sealing it with the old tunnel by cold welding aluminum and titanium alloys. Not trained for any of this work, Amon stood nearby and watched, fascinated with the procedure.

After a while, he switched frequencies back to the one Reuben was on, to see if the connection had been reestablished.

"Reuben, are you there?"

"Amon! Finally." His voice was shaky.

"Sorry, I found Stanis and switched frequencies. Is everything okay?"

"Amon, it's...Agent Wiley. I think you need to

see," Reuben said. "You aren't gonna like this, I'll tell ya. Brace yourself."

"Hang on."

Amon swallowed once, said his goodbye to Stanis, and went back into Dome 2 so he wouldn't frighten the astronauts.

"Ok, I'm ready," Amon said, and closed his eyes for the sudden shift.

19

TIME ITSELF

Here he was again, as he'd been so many times before.

Rakulo stared up as the smooth, sheer, slightly concave face of the Wall. A short run up a slight hill of soft piled earth and he could touch the sleek surface that was always slightly colder than the air, and often wet. It gathered moisture to its smooth, hard surface like leaves on humid days, big beaded water droplets that dripped down the face and gathered in the damp earth at the Wall's base.

Rakulo had run up the small hill to touch the Wall many times. Only once had he ever seen a way through the Wall, however—a small hole about twice his height where Xucha had come through to retrieve one of his damaged demons. The opening had simply appeared in the Wall while Rakulo was watching from the cover of a nearby ash tree's canopy.

No trees grew close enough to the Wall to climb and peer over. They were kept pruned back. The nearest tree remained at a distance of several dozen long strides, so he'd never been able to see over.

Rakulo knew this jungle. It was his home. Had these trees not been pruned back, they would have climbed up the Wall on their own by now. It was not until months had passed in their patrols along the Wall that Rakulo began to mark skinny young stumps where saplings had been cut down when they grew too tall. First he found one, then another, then dozens when he got better at spotting them. They were severed at the base somehow, the cut perfectly smooth and the trunk's exposed edge charred black. As if by fire. What kind of fire cut trees and carted off the trunks? Rakulo had cut down plenty of trees in their efforts to make canoes. They used flint axes and hand-tools and chipped away at the base. No axe of his could have made a cut as smooth as the trunks of these saplings that had the misfortune to grow too close to the Wall.

Gods' fire. The work of Xucha himself.

Faint footsteps approach from behind, the noise louder in his right ear than his bad left. It was Citlali. Though it had been two days since his warriors rescued him from the cell, and the blood in his ear had dried, his hearing remained faint on the left side.

He'd nearly driven his knife into Thevanah's exposed ribcage when she had startled him in the cave the night before. Rakulo had been checking the knots of the vines they had gathered and tied tightly for today's mission.

Citlali stopped at his shoulder.

"Are they ready, then?" Rakulo asked.

"They are," she said. "Are you?"

Rakulo rubbed his ear. "As I'll ever be."

Citlali shook her head. "It's too dangerous. Send me instead, Raku."

"No," Rakulo said immediately, in a tone that came out harsher than he intended.

Her shoulders slumped, and Rakulo walked away, towards the large tree they had chosen. What Citlali said made sense. She was just as strong as he was, and lighter. She would be the next obvious choice to climb up the tree with the limber Thevanah if Rakulo was not fit for the journey. But this had been the plan all along. He had trained for it. Besides…

"You don't know what to look for," Rakulo said. "I'm the only one that's seen it."

"That strange tree you told me about?"

"It was a different shape than a tree. Tall, and dark, like a knife stabbed into the Earth." He frowned. Rakulo had only glimpsed what was on the other side of the Wall once before. Twelve moon cycles had come and gone since then, but the image was burned in his mind. It was like a tree. A massive, charred tree.

A sharp pain stabbed at his left ear. His hand rose to his head and he rubbed at his ear with his palm until the pain faded away. He squinted with his left eye.

"Look at the kind of pain you're in," Citlali said. "I know what to look for. I can do this."

Rakulo stopped at the base of the large mossy oak with the thickest, oldest-looking trunk in the area, among the rest of his warriors.

Citlali had not kept her voice down. Thevanah hefted the thick vine in her hand and regarded them with a concerned expression. Quen took a deep breath and crossed his meaty biceps across his broad chest. Yeli smiled wanly. The others watched with similar, impatient poses.

"You agree with her?" he asked them, incredulous.

He met Thevanah's eyes. She shrugged as if to say, *sorry, it's my life, too.* Quen pursed his lips and nodded once. The others all agreed, one by one, with small gestures or a brief meeting of his eyes and a mumbled apology.

"All right," Rakulo said. "If that's how you all feel, then Citlali can climb in my place."

Rakulo took Citlali and Thevanah aside and described to them the structure in more detail. "It sounds so odd, but I remember the earth looking dry and cracked around the base of the thing. It was thin and tall like a tree, not broad and square like the buildings and temples in *Uchben Na*. And it was dark color, almost like obsidian. That's all I know."

"What do you want to know about it?" Citlali asked.

"And what do you want us to do when we get up there?" Thevanah said.

"First, see if there's a way we can get over the Wall. Maybe we can anchor a rope on the far side? I don't know. If this tree isn't tall enough to see, look for another. And look for the black tree. I tried to look for it when we went around the Wall in the canoes. Now, though, I think we were probably too far away to see it from the water."

"And you think I'll be able to see it up there?"

"If you get high enough, you should be able to."

Thevanah took a deep, calming breath, and shook out her wrists and ankles. Citlali swallowed and tilted her head back to gaze at the massive, ancient tree. It dwarfed the other trees nearby, jutting straight up into the thick canopy. Judging by its girth and his previous exploratory climbs up the trunk, its top rose high above the other trees in the nearby canopy.

This tree is older than time itself, Rakulo thought. And then an odd idea appeared in his brain, fully formed. He licked his lips nervously.

"Do you think this ancient tree was here first...or

was the Wall?"

"I don't know, Rakulo," Citlali said, rolling her eyes. "What does it matter?"

"You sound like Gehro," Thevanah said. "Maybe that blow to your head knocked something loose."

Rakulo chuckled softly. "I've been spending too much time with the old kook. He's probably just rubbing off on me."

"I think so."

He watched as the girls stood on one side of the ancient tree and pulled the thick, woven cords of rope around their waist. The rope was made of dead plants, agave, vines, and the young saplings they'd found near the cut trunks. Collecting the material needed for such thick ropes, and making them, had been another part of Rakulo's training program.

The girls stretched their limbs. Thevanah's rope harness had come a little loose, so Quen tightened one of the knots under her left thigh. Rakulo double-checked the knot on Citlali's rope as well. The girls tested the tension of the vines again.

"One, two..." Citlali began.

"Three!" they both said.

Jumping up, Citlali caught a low branch, and hauled herself up. Gripping the massive trunk of the tree, she worked her way higher. Thevanah followed.

Although he'd done this twice with Thevanah, Rakulo's pulse pounded in his injured ear as he watched the two women climb. He was way more nervous than he would have been if he were up there himself, focusing on putting one foot in front of the other. Now he just worried that one of them would slip on a loose piece of bark.

After about five minutes, they climbed past the highest point Rakulo had reached. They were tiny now, miniscule. Quen let out a low, strangled noise in his throat as he gazed up at the women.

Rakulo's neck began to ache, and he looked down and rubbed his ear, which was the only reason he spotted a low-crouching man covered in a brown tunic tiptoeing through the trees a spear's-throw away.

"Quen!" Rakulo whispered. "We've got company."

As Rakulo turned, he instinctively looked at the Wall and a cold sweat washed over his body. A large doorway had silently appeared at the base of the Wall. On the other side, the black tree-like thing was there, its base partially visible through the doorway. It was a lot like a tree—big black roots with a thick bark like nothing he'd ever seen before parted and plunged into the red earth. Rakulo spotted something else, a glint of greenish glow, just a shimmer in the crack before it was gone again.

Then a shining little orb darted through the doorway and shot straight for him. Rakulo lifted his two fingers to his mouth and managed a shrill whistle before the demon barreled into his chest and knocked him off his feet.

20

LIKE WARNING
SIGNS

The team responded enthusiastically to Eliana's suggestion to move on. She was secretly relieved, as she harbored the suspicion that at any moment they would question her theories, just as she had done many times during moments of severe self-doubt that crept up on her after midnight as she lay awake in her tent.

Still, Talia, Turner, Ross, and Lakshmi packed to leave without any objections. Eliana took a final set of photos documenting the site while Tanner and Ross hiked back to the first camp site and took the Land Rover to town to grab extra supplies. Lakshmi, with Talia's help, packed the rest of their gear and loaded it into backpacks. The stones were left on the ground where they had lain for almost 1500 years, and the markers removed. The only evidence they would take with them were the photographs.

When the men returned with provisions—food, water, and a few other essentials—they added that to the packs and belted their loads onto their backs.

Eliana adjusted the straps of her pack so it sat off her shoulders by half an inch, distributing the load to her waist, and looked one last time at the carving, trying to burn it into her mind. The two overlapping circles and the simplistic arrow carved below it, nothing more than two angled lines. The rest of the monolith was smooth, if slightly worn and pock-marked stone. She couldn't help feeling like she was missing a piece of the puzzle.

"Which way, boss?" Lakshmi asked.

Eliana shifted her gaze out across the deep bowl of the dense jungle that sloped away below them, falling hundreds of feet and spreading like a lush green blanket to the north. At the far end of the low section, barely visible through haze, another incline rose on the opposite side.

"Did you make it to those hills on the other end of this valley?"

Talia shook her head. "That mountain you see there is about ten miles off. We went maybe halfway."

"The other end of this valley seems like as good a destination as any. How about it?"

The others nodded, and they set off down the slope. The way immediately became difficult, and Eliana soon realized why Talia and Ross hadn't been able to make it to the opposite side in a day. The bugs and trees were so thick they were practically a thicket in the shade-darkened jungle at the bottom of the bowl-shaped valley. Eliana led the way for a time, until she sank up to her knees in a puddle of water and Tanner had to pull her out. They were forced to backtrack to find a way around the bog.

The sun began to fall around the three mile mark. They found a slight rise with a low wall of white stone on which to pitch a couple of tents. Ross gathered firewood but it turned out to be far too wet to burn. Talia distributed a dinner of beef jerky, dehydrated mangos, and fresh coconut milk. They all tried to sleep as soon as it was dark, exhausted from the slow journey and wanting to make better use of the daylight the next day. But sleep wouldn't come for Eliana, even after she had changed into dry clothes. The noises of a restless group of howler monkeys not a hundred yards away kept them all up, tossing fitfully. She knew it wasn't possible, but the cackles and cries of the monkeys gave Eliana the distinct impression that they were laughing at her.

They were awake and moving away from the troop of monkeys at dawn the next morning, as the gray light filtered through the thick canopy. They ate breakfast as they walked. Eliana was gnawing on a piece of jerky with no joy when they came to another low bog-like area, so filled in with rainwater that it was more a lake than a bog.

"Which way now?" Eliana said.

Not once did they pass near any cut stones. A few limestone boulders, half-buried, but no monoliths or decorated structures or facades of any kind that she had seen.

Were more ruins here, buried beneath the lake, or sunk beneath centuries of growth? She might never find them even if she spent years searching. How were they ever going to corroborate enough evidence to prove anything about the carving? If only Amon would let her go back to Kakul…

She shook her head and trudged on, pushing vines and fan-shaped tree boughs aside with tired arms. They camped without a fire again that night.

On the third day, their exhausted party reached the base of the hills rising on the opposite end of the bowl. The walls here were striated, showing centuries of layer after layer of sediment and rock building up on it. After scouting a mile in either direction, Talia and Ross reported back.

"There's a game trail a mile west," Ross said.

"And another one half a mile northeast along this ridge," Talia reported. "Game trail is generous, actually, but there's something resembling a path and it seems to be moving upwards."

Eliana considered their options. "Let's split into two groups and follow each one to see what we find. Ross, show me the trail you found. Lakshmi and Tanner, you go with Talia. Let's meet back here two hours before nightfall so we have time to set up camp."

Eliana followed Ross as he hacked his way back to the west with the machete. Eventually they located a thin trail that led north, up the slope of the mountain. The foliage on the slope was a bit thinner, and the trail zigzagged, showing how animals had picked their way uphill, finding the easiest way to the sun through the local flora. Eliana watched the striation of the earth as they climbed, noting different layers. What did it mean? Had a glacier come through here, slicing into the land and forming this valley some millions of years ago? She wondered if there had always been a lake at the bottom. Or perhaps this whole valley had been filled with water, and the "lake" at the bottom was only a small remnant of an ancient inland sea.

Eliana swung her pack off and set it against a nearby tree. "We'll make better time without the extra weight," she explained when Ross looked at her sideways. They had several hours to explore before they had to meet the others back at the base of the mountain, and Eliana wanted to make the most of it.

Ross grunted a wordless agreement. Eliana took her camera and a water bottle from her pack, and waited while Ross belted his machete at his waist, then put a rope through the straps of both their packs, and hoisted them across a thick branch so that the packs hung suspended in the air, keeping the food away from any creatures who happened to wander by and smell it, like the wild boars and wolves known to inhabit this region. Once the rope was tied around the tree trunk, they began to climb again.

Eliana felt light without the burden of her pack, and they made good time. After two hours, the trees thinned out and the wind picked up, drying the damp skin of her neck and cooling her. Though the wind was still too hot, it felt glorious just to be in the moving air after the humid, stagnant heat of the jungle below. Even Ross, who never complained, sighed with audible relief when he felt the wind on his face.

The game trail wound back and forth, and then suddenly lead her and Ross through a ring of pine trees. Eliana gasped as she stepped inside the ring—for there stood another stone structure in the same rectangular arrangement as the one they had found on the other side of the valley.

One of the stone monoliths lay on its side and was slowly being swallowed by the earth beneath it. But on the other end two low stone walls connected the other three cornerstones, which remained standing. These stones had a ring of reliefs carved around their top—a ring, Eliana realized, of skulls.

A chill raced down her spine. Skulls were a big part of Mayan mythology—skull carvings decorated graveyards and tombs, and many Mesoamerican cultures displayed the skulls of defeated or captured warriors in a *tzompantli,* or skull rack. A particularly famous *tzompantli* relief could be found near the ball court at Chichen Itza—the depictions nearby suggesting quite clearly that the losers of the royal games were beheaded.

But this was no ball court on the top of this mountain. It was more like…a warning sign. Much like the *tzompantli* were a warning to the attendant teams of warrior players that death lay within the walls of the ball court, she couldn't help but feel that the skulls carved on this monolith were a warning that death lay beyond.

"Looks like you may have been right, boss."

She nodded. "The other ruin was never finished. This one was."

Eliana took out her camera and began thumbing back through the photos of the first site, comparing the two. The cornerstones were located in the same position, and they seemed to be the same size. The carved skulls were missing from the first site, but she could see where they would have gone had it been finished.

Her heartbeat quickened when the picture of the carving came up on the screen.

Eliana walked into the shadow of the monolith that would have matched cornerstone A, and turned around so that she was facing out over the front side —this time looking south, again in the direction of the bowl of forest that swept back toward the first site.

"It's almost like…"

She gazed up and spotted the two moon carving, just where she expected it.

This time, she saw the whole sign clearly.

The overlapping circles that represented the two moons of Kakul on top. Beneath them, the arrow pointing up—but in full detail this time. It was not just an arrow, but a clear depiction of a pyramid. Stairs were even drawn down the middle of this one.

Below that was the head of a feathered serpent known to the Maya as Kukulkan. His tongue hung from his open mouth between two big fangs, and a ring of feathers fanned around his serpent head like the petals of a flower.

And finally, below that was a skull.

Eliana reached out a hand and ran her fingers along the carvings.

"Moons, temple, God, death."

"What does that mean?" Ross asked.

"Moons over the temple bring the Gods and cause death?" she said with a rising inflection, uncertainty edging her voice. "Is that too big of a leap?"

Ross whistled. "Maybe…maybe not."

"That's the truth."

Eliana scanned the horizon through the ring of pines and saw how the bowl of land swept down and away, toward the other site they had been at not three days ago—on the high ground on the opposite side.

If Ross had traveled to that other planet with her and met those people, maybe he would see the connection as clearly as she did. Why else would they have a carving of double moons here? Or was she misinterpreting it? Was it something else entirely?

She couldn't help it—Eliana pictured in her mind the ancient city of *Uchben Na* where she had seen a man sacrificed by the light of two moons, where she had seen the god they called Xucha, and had nearly been sacrificed herself.

Was it really a coincidence that they had found no other ruins in this area, apart from these low stone buildings like warning signs, cautioning travelers to be wary of whatever lay beyond them, below them, or between them? She stared into the valley and imagined a Maya city where that lake used to be.

"It's almost like these structures were put here like outposts," Eliana said. "Like warning signs. They say, in pictures, don't go into the valley or you risk bringing death upon yourself."

Ross grunted in agreement.

The people of Kakul told a kind of exodus story while she'd been living among them. It had been hard to follow, since she still had only a rudimentary command of their language. She remembered a man in a snake mask telling the story in the light of a bonfire…what had he said…

When the world was complete, Xucha wrapped his sinuous body around the world and squeezed the sky shut. But he squeezed too tight, and the sky turned a bruised purple as a result. The sky was broken, and even the gods were stuck here, and no one could go back through again.

Back through? Back through to where?

Eliana gazed into the low bowl of the forest. The land looked like a God had reached down and taken a big scoop out of the forest with his powerful hands.

Back through to here.

Eliana turned away from the ruin and began snapping photos of the carving and the positions of the monolith.

She was not certain what these carvings meant. Nor was she certain of her recollection of the Kakuli mythology. But she was sure that *someone* had occupied this area during several millennia when Mayan civilization reigned.

And she was certain of one other thing—no matter what Amon thought or said or wanted her to do, no matter what he might do to try to forbid her from going back through the Translocator, it was her duty as an archaeologist and researcher, as an explorer and seeker of truth, to return to Kakul.

If anything could corroborate what she had found here today, lying hidden in plain sight for over a thousand years, it was whatever was depicted on the walls of the stone city of *Uchben Na*, and the stories preserved and passed down by Rakulo's people.

She had to go back. She just had to.

21

MARGIN OF ERROR

As the light faded, alloy rings swung, rotating around the platform and casting crisscrossing shadows in a geometric pattern around him. Amon ducked under the rings before they had fully come to rest and walked down the ramp, bracing himself for the worst.

When he saw her, he grimaced and felt his gorge rise. His whole body tensed up painfully, and his mouth filled with bile before he managed to swallowed it back down.

His first reaction after the terror was a feeling of immense relief—relief that the body twisted impossibly in the middle of the floor had blonde hair. It was not his wife—not Eliana. That was all that mattered. A sudden trembling lightness shook him.

It's not Eliana, he repeated to himself. Eliana was

alive and well—as far as he knew. She sent him a brief text message a few days ago. *God, why hasn't she called me back? What is she doing? Is she safe?*

The second emotion that struck him was intense guilt mingled with sadness, for the woman on the floor was wearing a suit and practical black shoes whose soles had been worn, he knew, from a lot of recent travel. Her body was maimed and twisted horribly, her limbs scrambled and wrenched into an unnatural arrangement. The fabric of her suit had been blended with her skin in places. She had a blonde ponytail, but her face was placed elsewhere, and Amon didn't dare turn her over to look for it. The cavity of her chest had also been cracked open, exposing a grotesque arrangement of organs that a biologist would barely recognize as human. The pockets of her blazer were still intact somehow. Amon reached down and took the FBI badge out of Agent Monica Wiley's inside coat pocket.

The most he could hope for was that she had died quickly and painlessly. There would be time for an autopsy, whatever good that would do, but first he had to play investigator in Agent Wiley's place. Amon had to find out who did this to her.

Footsteps shuffled up beside him on the right.

"Fucked up, right?" Wes said.

Amon ignored him. "How long ago did her body appear?"

"A few minutes after you went to the moon," Reuben said. "We got an incoming transmission—looked like it was you, but you had stopped answering me. I thought it was because the electronics on the suit cut out after all."

"The electronics on the suit are fine."

"Anyway, I initiated the translocation, and she showed up in the platform like that. Scared the hell out of me." Reuben swallowed. "I thought it was you at first."

They shared a glance. Amon glared at Wes, but Wes didn't seem to notice. He was pale and seemed genuinely distraught at the sight of Agent Wiley.

Amon made himself look back at the grotesque body. As he did, he felt the anger bubble up from his toes and fill his body with a hot rage. He twisted the helmet and began unzipping the cumbersome space suit.

"She didn't deserve this," Reuben said.

Agent Wiley had been with the Interpol agents less than a few hours ago. What had happened after Amon left? It must be connected to the lunar base.

"He's showing off now," Amon said.

Amon had to find and stop Lucas. Not even the early molecular reassembly tests run by the Nazis during world war two had been so horrific—at least they were still dealing with the power source issues.

Even the next generation of Translocator disasters that occurred during the European Space Agency's early experiments were overseen by careful, intelligent men. At least their mistakes were limited to lab mice. Not *people*.

What had been done to Agent Wiley was another strata of cruelty entirely.

Amon gritted his teeth and tightened his fists as he swore that he would put an end to this. For Agent Wiley.

Where was Agent Moreno? Amon ran to the warehouse, quickly shed the suit, pulled his jeans and polo shirt back on, and found his phone. It told him he had one missed call. From the same ten-digit number Agent Wiley had called from.

He dialed the number, hoping it was Agent Moreno simply looking for his missing partner and a ride home. But somehow, he didn't think that was likely. The call rang three times before being answered.

"Hello, Amon," said a voice on the other end of the line.

Amon froze. He knew that voice. It was neat, precise, and…dangerous. Was that new? Or had the faint edge of steel under the dulcet baritone always been there?

"Lucas," Amon said, his tone as flat and even as he could keep it in his rage. "Tell me you're not behind this. Tell me you didn't murder Agent Wiley."

"You murdered her, Amon."

"I did not!" he shouted. Then, collecting himself, Amon lowered his voice again. "What the hell's the matter with you? Why are you doing this? If you didn't run across the border, this could all have blown over by now. You know I never would have pressed charges. We could be working together again, Lucas. Instead, you're murdering innocent people, not to mention federal agents. You—"

Lucas's voice went flat. "We were never working *together*," he said. "You made it very clear that *I* was always working for *you*."

"We were a team," Amon said, disbelief coloring his voice and constricting his throat. Were they really having this conversation right now? "I always said that Fisk Industries belongs to all of us."

Lucas chuckled softly. "You always said that, but you never meant it. Still, it's a good thing I was there in the early days, or you'd have been too distracted by your visions of grandeur to keep the company afloat long enough for you to build anything."

"I was never—"

"I don't have time for personal chatter, Amon," Lucas said, interrupting him.

That put Amon back on his heels. He clamped his mouth shut, fearing for Agent Moreno's life. What about the CERN physicists? What if Lucas somehow managed to get ahold of Eliana? Damnit, but where was his wife right now?

"Think of this like a business transaction," Lucas said. "It will go smoother for you that way—and for Agent Moreno and these other poor bastards—if you shut up and do as I say."

Amon and Reuben exchanged quick, worried looks. Glancing over at Wes, Amon was momentarily pleased to see that even the old cowboy, who normally had a gung ho, "fuck you, come and take it" attitude about everything, seemed frightened.

At least now Amon knew the FBI agents' suspicions were true. He could face a problem he knew. And he knew Lucas. They had been close for twenty years. After college, they met while working for an electronics manufacturing company. They both had engineering degrees, but Amon worked in the R&D department, while Lucas had taken a job as a sales rep. A year later, Amon was making his own panels in his small garage, and he and Lucas combined their skills by making cold calls during their lunch hours to get the business started.

"Okay, Lucas," Amon said in a reasonable tone. "Let's talk about this. What do you want?"

"Isn't it obvious? I want that carbonado. And don't get any ideas, Amon. I know your noble instincts get you into trouble sometimes. If you call the cops or the FBI, or try to surprise us with those security guards you've got now, Agent Moreno and this pretty CERN secretary will suffer slow, agonizing deaths."

"You can do that? You can determine how much they suffer?"

"Within a certain margin of error."

What you're doing is wrong—that's what Amon wanted to say. Instead, he tried to keep a reasonable tone of voice. "Maybe I can help. If you just tell me what you're trying to do, I'll help you iron out the errors—"

"Enough," Lucas said. "Quit stalling. I don't need your help. Bring us in or I'll send another body your way. I've just sent our coordinates to your machine. Bring in the first group, and then send again for myself and your other FBI agent friend."

Amon bent over and rested his hands on his knees. *Damnit. Damnit! Who told him about the carbonado experiments? Who told him where Amon was going with the FBI agents?*

"Okay," he said. "Just one question. Are you using the CERN particle accelerator to power your Translocator?"

"No. Please. Don't be ridiculous."

"How long did it take to build?" Amon was grasping at straws now.

"Enough questions. Translocate us in."

Amon muffled the receiver of the cell phone against his shirt and mouthed silently to Reuben and Wes. "Alert the guards."

"Do it now," Lucas's shouting voice could be

heard through his hand, which was clutched over the receiver. "And keep those security guards out of it, or you'll have more blood on your hands."

Amon ended the call. Lucas must already have known exactly how many guards were on shift at night, and what Amon would try to do. Was Roger the mole, or was it someone else? Who had known about his work with the FBI agents except for Agent Wiley, Agent Moreno, and Reuben. He'd have to figure that out later.

"You can't be serious," Wes said.

"What choice do we have?" Amon gestured to Agent Wiley's body. "He's clearly not bluffing."

"Amon," Reuben said, "we have a responsibility to protect the Translocator."

"You don't think I know that? We also had a responsibility to keep the blueprints out of the hands of dangerous people. It's my fault this happened. I don't want anyone else to get hurt."

Reuben stared at him, obviously battling his conscience. "That's what Lucas is expecting."

"We don't have a choice," Amon said. "You don't have to do it. I will."

Amon stepped up to the holodeck, locked in on the coordinates Lucas had sent originally—somewhere in Switzerland, but too far from CERN to use their particle accelerator as a power source, he noted—and initiated the translocation.

A familiar cry cut the air. The rings of the stabilization sphere began to spin. When the rings wound down and the light faded, six soldiers armed with AK-47 rifles were arranged in two rows on the platform. All tall, blond men. Were they Russian mercenaries? Did they work for Hawkwood, the security company that had colluded with Lucas before to help him steal the plans and drain Fisk Industries' bank accounts? Amon couldn't be sure. Their shirts were bulky and black—probably wearing body armor underneath—with no markings. They all wore matching camouflage pants and combat boots. They looked well trained and deadly as they jogged down the ramp and efficiently took up positions surrounding Wes, Reuben, and Amon. Two of the men remained close to the platform.

Gazing around at the men boxing them in, Amon finally recognized one of them. It was the Interpol agent who had followed Amon toward the bathroom. He met Amon's stare, and smiled.

"Activate it again," the man said. He had a square nutcracker jaw and no glint of humor in his flat blue eyes.

Amon complied, and the CERN secretary and two other scientists in lab coats, all with their hands and wrists bound tightly with heavy-duty plastic zip ties, appeared on the platform, along with two more mercenaries. The mercenaries herded the captives down the ramp into the middle of the room. The captives' eyes went wide as they approached Agent Wiley's grotesque form. The secretary gave a high-pitched whimpering cry as she sidestepped away from the body. A few of the others paled and looked like they might be sick.

"One more time, Mr. Fisk," the square-jawed leader of the mercenaries said.

How polite, Amon thought as he activated the Translocator once more. This time, a tall, well-groomed man in a charcoal suit and shiny black shoes appeared on the platform. In one hand he held a gun pointed between the shoulder blades of Agent Moreno. In the other, he held a clear plastic cube by a handle, like a transparent toolbox. Moreno was more heavily bound than the others, with his arms and hands held tight to his side. Lucas smiled broadly as he walked down the platform, prodding Moreno ahead of him with the gun.

"Amon, Reuben, and Wes," Lucas said expansively. "So good to see you all again."

"Let him go, Lucas," Amon said. "This is between you and me."

Lucas shoved Agent Moreno toward the other captives, then stepped blithely over Agent Wiley's body. He waved his gun. The armed squadron of mercenaries surrounding Amon, Wes, and Reuben shoved them away from the holodeck with their rifles. Lucas set the plastic cube down at his feet, then searched for something on the monitor. He pulled out a manual keyboard and typed in a console window that Amon couldn't read from where he stood. Then he closed the console, returned the keyboard to its hidden tray, and withdrew the canister of carbonado solution.

"I see you've made some modifications," Lucas said. "Nothing I can't figure out, I assure you."

"You're a real bastard, you know that?" Pain exploded in Amon's face as the square-jawed mercenary slammed the butt of his rifle into his cheekbone. He fell to his knees.

"Fine," Lucas said, his voice coming faintly through a ringing. "Have it your way."

Amon glanced up as Lucas gestured to one of the mercenaries. The big man walked over and grabbed a scientist from the group of hostages, pushed him out away from the others, and shot him in the head. His body collapsed next to Agent Wiley's, blood pooling at his feet.

"No!" Amon shouted. But he couldn't move out of the ring of soldiers. Wes's face had turned into a grim mask. Reuben looked away.

Amon pushed himself back to his feet as a pounding came at the blast door. "Mr. Fisk?" one of the guards said on the other side. "Is everything okay in there?"

Two large mercenaries grabbed Amon. Still dazed from the blow to his head, and half their size, he was unable to resist as they brought him to the door and made him open it. They shoved him into the middle of the doorway. As the blast door drew open, the mercenaries shot the guards while they were looking at Amon with a puzzled expression, before they could even make sense of the scene or take aim with their own guns.

Amon felt helpless as their bodies crumpled to the floor. He was yanked back and thrown to the ground where Reuben and Wes had both been forced to a sitting position. Two mercenaries stood guard over them. Lucas took the plastic cube and strode through the blast door and down the long hall.

If Wes is the mole, why is he being treated this way? The man's face was unreadable. Amon's conviction that it was Wes who ratted them out faded. He didn't know who it was anymore. Reuben? Enzo Badeux? Could it be?

Lucas returned not ten minutes later with the large carbonado held in the plastic cube. Amon had managed to recover some of his wits by this point, and through the throbbing in his head finally realized that the cube was a containment device. A glimmering liquid filled a thin space between the plastic walls.

"Where did you get that?" Amon asked from his position on the floor. He needed to get some more information out of Lucas before he disappeared through the Translocator again.

"I made it," Lucas said.

"Really?" Amon said, as brightly as he could manage. "Does it isolate the cube and the carbonado completely from electrical interference? How does it work exactly?"

Lucas glared at him, but couldn't help the glow of pride that parted his lips. "If you must know, it's a non-conductive gel suspension. Any charge that comes into contact with the cube is moved away and around the cube by the gel and the electrical currents running from these nodes set into the sides." He pointed to two small metal discs and the lines that connected them.

"Impressive," Amon said, and was surprised to find he meant it. He had always known that Lucas had a certain facility running the operations of the company. He also knew he had an engineering background. But seeing something he built came as a bit of a shock. Lucas had never shown an interest in physical engineering, being too busy managing the rapid growth of the company to devote the time.

Without another word, Lucas stepped back up to the holodeck. He keyed a new set of coordinates into it, then exchanged a whispered word with the square-jawed mercenary leader. When the man nodded affirmation, Lucas turned, crossed the room, and began to walk up the ramp when the sphere of rings began to spin.

"I said—" Lucas turned back to the man, his face

angry. But Amon had been watching the man, and he hadn't touched the controls. Lucas must have realized it, too, because he began backing away down the ramp.

"Oh God," Reuben said.

"What in the hell?" Wes gasped.

Amon said nothing, but his eyes widened, darting between Lucas's shocked face, the holodeck, and the sphere of rings. They spun so fast they became a shapeless blur. Instead of the white ball of energy that normally gathered in the center of the sphere, a dark rift appeared in the air and slowly widened. Through it, Amon saw a dark ripple fill the rift. Through the ripple, as if it was a reflection on dark water, Amon thought he could make out a star-filled night and the tops of the trees.

"How…?" Amon said. "It can't be—"

Lucas sprinted to the holodeck and pressed the abort key. Amon would have gone to help him, but the mercenaries still stood over him, and despite the unusual rift, they held their ground, although now their rifles were pointed at the rift instead of at Amon. This was his chance…

Before he could make a move, the rift stopped widening, and a metal orb passed through, hovering by its own power in the air. Amon had seen this once before, so his body filled with a cold dread even before he had arrived.

A large man stepped into the lab behind the orb,

dressed head-to-foot in a reflective helmet and a suit of seamless black so dark it seemed to swallow the fluorescent lights in the Translocator lab.

And this time, Amon didn't think it was a hologram.

22

SEARCHING FOR THE MARK

Rakulo scrabbled in the leaves, clawing at the earth as his mouth worked for air. After a moment, his breath came rushing back, choking him with its sudden return. The sphere-shaped demon, buzzing like a rattlesnake, darted off toward another target. Rakulo coughed, trying to ignore the hollow ringing in his left ear, and managed two shallow gasps before someone grabbed his arm and yanked him roughly to his feet.

"Raid!" Quen bellowed in his deep baritone.

Rakulo stumbled forward, pushing the startled Yeli in front of him. She fell in beside him and began to run. Their pace picked up until the trees were rushing by them. The others all seemed to be moving now, some ahead and some behind in a ragged line.

A man with a black-painted face stepped out

from behind a tree and swung a club at Quen. He ducked and stepped inside the man's guard from the side, dealing two vicious jabs to his ribs. While he was distracted, Yeli swept a leg out and tripped the attacker. Rakulo grabbed his club and dealt a solid blow to the man's head. His body went limp.

Then they were running again, darting between bushes and jumping over the thick roots of the big trees in this part of the forest.

Rakulo shouted ahead to Quen. "Where are Citlali and Thevanah? Did they get them?"

"Not sure. They were still in the trees last I saw!"

Rakulo gritted his teeth. That was bad. They were stranded up there.

A spear cut the air in front of his face and thudded as it sank into the soft bark of a tree to his right, its shaft vibrating with the impact. Someone howled, and shoved Rakulo down. Quen and Yeli jumped on top of Rakulo's assailant, hauling the man off—and this time Rakulo recognized him through the face paint. One of Maatiaak's men, an old farmer with long gray hair tied back in a braid who went by the name of Uli.

Rakulo jerked the spear out of the tree and stepped up to the man.

He stared back at Rakulo with an expression of outright disgust and then spat on the ground.

Rakulo thought about taking the spear tip and jabbing it in his stomach and leaving Uli to bleed out while he tried to hold his guts in. But Rakulo couldn't do it. Instead, he dragged the sharpened stone tip along the man's chest and down his cheeks, leaving long red gashes. Uli hissed, thrashed while Quen and Yeli held him.

"I won't kill you," Rakulo said, "but I will mark you as a traitor. What kind of man sneaks up and tries to stab his own kin?"

"You're going to get us all killed with your foolishness!"

Rakulo flipped the spear around and jabbed him in the gut with the blunt end. Uli doubled over, and Yeli and Quen released him. He scrabbled up, then backed away.

"Let him go," Rakulo said. "Let's move."

As they turned away, he pulled Quen down and whispered in his ear. "Lead the way back to the caves. Maatiaak's men will follow you. I'm going back for Citlali and Thevanah."

Quen led the others away. As their footsteps faded, Rakulo found a low branch and climbed up quickly, hiding around the trunk. A few more of Maatiaak's men came running from the direction of the large trees up which Citlali and Thevanah had climbed, in pursuit of Quen and the others. When their footsteps faded, Rakulo cocked his head and listened with his good ear for the telltale buzzing sound that would give away the position of Xucha's demon.

He finally located it and worked his way down the tree with the spear gripped uncomfortably in his teeth. Staying low, he padded back toward the location where Citlali and Thevanah had ascended. Rakulo scanned the canopy for Citlali or Thevanah, but didn't spot them. Good. If they were smart they would stay well out of sight.

Two orb-shaped demons circled slowly around the tree trunk, at a height of three houses stacked on top of each other. They hovered and circled well over his head, but apparently they couldn't go any higher. He looked down and saw the leaves shift beneath the path in which the spheres circled.

That's interesting, he thought, *like something in the demons leashed them to the ground.* Maybe they couldn't get higher because they were limited by how far they could push off the ground, like how Rakulo knew he could only jump so high. Xucha himself did not seem to be here. He'd just sent his demons to help Maatiaak and his men surprise Rakulo's warriors. Rakulo didn't think for a minute that the dark god wasn't watching.

Quietly, Rakulo found another tree, this one medium sized, with low branches. He worked his way up the trunk until he was just above the level the demons now hovered.

From his vantage point, he watched as the demons stopped. What were they doing now? A mouth spiraled open in each of their hulls, and red fans of light crept out and swept toward the tree. In a moment, smoke began to curl up from where the light hit the wood on either side of the tree.

A realization struck Rakulo like a blow. *So that's how they cut down the trees!*

But Citlali and Thevanah were still up there. He couldn't let the demons take down this ancient tree if it might result in danger to his warriors. Plus, he still thought this tree might be their ticket over the walls.

"You!" Rakulo shouted. The shaft of the spear slipped in his sweaty palms. He adjusted his grip. What if they came this way?

The orbs spun in place, the red fans of light snapping back into their circular mouths. They seemed to watch the woods with their featureless smooth faces.

He had suspected this from his previous encounters with the demons that they were not all-knowing or all-seeing, but it was a relief to have it confirmed. Like him, they navigated the world with their senses, whatever that meant for them. Rakulo pushed himself close to the tree in which he now hid, up under the shade of a thick leafy branch so they couldn't spy him. He brought the spear up, vertically, holding it out in front of him.

He'd have one chance. Better make it count.

"Over here!" he shouted again. The humming sound increased in one ear. It was disconcerting not to be able to rely on his left ear, but Rakulo closed his eyes and relied on the hearing of his good right ear as the demons approached.

The first one came around on his left side and buzzed right underneath him, inches below the branch on which he stood. Too late to get that one. *Patience.* The other was coming around…

Now!

Rakulo stepped off the branch and let himself fall through the air as if he were standing. The soles of his feet slipped on the hull of the second demon, but he bore down, using his toes like grips to hold the thing between his feet. He thrust the spear down hard. The stone tip glanced off the demon's hull, leaving a slight dent and a long scratch.

The sphere began to tilt left. Something was holding it up, holding them both up in the air—pushing off the ground with some kind of invisible force. Rakulo brought the spear up and aimed at the dent one more time. This blow put the spearhead through the hull and found its home with a satisfying crunch and crackle in the middle of the demon. A bright spark shot up out of the crack, searing the skin near his knee. Rakulo jerked his face away. And then the force holding up the demon up suddenly gave way.

Rakulo fell. The spear slipped from his hands. He windmilled his arms and let his knees buckle beneath him as he hit the soft leaf-covered forest floor. He tumbled away from the trunk of the tree.

Rakulo rolled, sprang up quick, and looked around. The spear was lost among the leaves. But the buzzing sound remained. Rakulo ducked as the other demon darted at his head. It missed by a hair's breadth. He hit the leaves and felt something long and hard beneath his hands. The spear! The demon swung around and came back, and this time Rakulo got the spear up in time to deflect its blow. The spear snapped in his hands. Rakulo staggered. And the demon wobbled and slammed into a nearby tree.

Rakulo pitched down the broken spear and then he was running flat out, open hands pumping at his sides, legs weaving between tree trunks. He dared to glance back once and saw the orb following his meandering path, a red light sweeping ahead of it.

Rakulo ran faster. He'd seen what these demons could do. At least he bought Citlali and Thevanah some time to get down. Hopefully Xucha would stay away. Hopefully Maatiaak's men had all followed Quen and the others. That was a lot to hope for, but he had to focus to get himself out of harm's way now.

He abandoned his weaving between the trees and chose the straightest path. Rakulo was like the wind. He'd never run so fast in his life. And he slowly gained a lead on the remaining demon, which seemed injured after being struck with the spear.

When the ground beneath the leafy floor grew more firm, Rakulo knew he was getting close to the limestone outcropping. He slowed and placed his feet carefully so as not to twist his ankles.

A group of men was crowded at the mouth of the cave. Rakulo whistled, a shrill sound, and suddenly the crowd was pushed apart as Quen and Yeli shoved through Maatiaak and his men. Rakulo barreled through the gap, the demon hot on his heels.

Maatiaak yelled and shoved, pushing the others to get himself out of harm's way like the coward he was.

Rakulo skidded and came to a stop inside the cave, next to one of the canoes he'd had Quen retrieve earlier that day. Rakulo picked up a canoe paddle and turned again.

The speeding sphere barreled toward the cave. Tilted down, the fan of red light burned a path through the leaf-covered floor, exposing the pock-marked limestone beneath. Its path was unsteady, wobbling. Rakulo squared his feet and waited for it to come close enough. He steadied his aim...

Maatiaak and his men scattered, vanishing into the woods as they retreated. The demon got confused, turned toward their fleeing figures, spinning and burning everything its red light touched. One of the men screamed as the red fan swept across his calf, leaving a long scorch mark. Someone came back for him and it wasn't Maatiaak.

Rakulo turned toward his own warriors, tense and gathered around him at the mouth of the cave. He held the paddle, waiting for the right moment. Timing was imperative.

When the demon had managed to chase away Maatiaak and his men, it seemed to realize that these men were not Rakulo, not the one it was after. It spun, searching for its mark, for the man who had killed its comrade.

As it was searching, Rakulo stepped lightly through the pockmarked limestone floor he knew so well, snuck up behind the demon, and struck it heavily with the wooden paddle once, twice, until it fell to the stone. It struggled to rise, leaves blowing away from the stone beneath it. Rakulo struck it again, and it went still.

Pulling his obsidian knife from his tunic, Rakulo stabbed a rough gash in the demon's carapace and shoved the thin end of the paddle in there, breaking the parts inside with a satisfying crunch.

His warriors slowly gathered around him. Citlali and Thevanah had still not made it back, but the others were here. They were scraped and scratched, tired and disheveled. Yeli had a black eye, which she tried to hide by staring at her feet. Rakulo reached out and lifted her chin gently with his fingers. She smiled shyly.

"I'm proud of you," Rakulo said. "But the fight is not over. Help me bury and hide Xucha's demons.

I've killed them, and now we must get them out of sight. There's one here, and another near the wall."

"You got it," Quen said, putting his foot territorially on the broken sphere at Rakulo's feet.

"Meanwhile, I need a volunteer to come with me. We tried to go around the Wall and a brave man was taken by the sea monster. We tried to go over top of the Wall, and Xucha's demons came out to stop us. That's how we know we're getting close. After a year of searching, we are finally coming up against violent resistance, as expected—as we trained for. I think Citlali and Thevanah are still up there, in the trees, looking for a way over. We shall know more when they return. But for now, we must keep searching. And there is one last attempt we must make."

"I'll go," Quen said.

"Without knowing what I'm going to ask you to do?"

He nodded.

The others stated their agreement and nodded bravely.

"When the demons came through the Wall, I saw cracked earth on the other side, and in the cracks, green glowing water like the kind that fills the Well of Sacrifices. I think that means the waterways connect—underground. There's a river at the back of Gehro's cave. If we can't go around or over the Wall, we'll have to try going under it."

23

DREAMING AND DREADING

Eliana was sick of airplanes. She typed and retyped six drafts of a long message to Amon before deleting it while she waited for the plane to depart. As the plane lifted into the air, she noticed the woman seated next to her in the pantsuit and fancy hat was leaning away from Eliana, holding her sleeve to her nose. Eliana lifted her shirt and sniffed quietly, inhaling a perfume of musky sweat mixed with loamy earth. She smelled like a rancid jungle.

Eliana chuckled bitterly then reached down and shifted the bag holding the new set of soil and rock samples under the seat in front of her, trying to ignore the woman's wrinkled nose and disgusted expression.

A proper shower had been elusive these past few weeks. Enough time in the jungle and you forget you need to do anything more than wash the dirt from your skin with a wet washcloth, only to be soaked in sweat again immediately. Perhaps she should shower before she went to confront Amon. He would probably be more receptive to her ideas if she didn't smell like something a dog would want to roll in.

The flight passed quickly as she considered what angle to take with him. Would he be receptive to her after the prolonged silent treatment? It wasn't like him to hold a grudge, but this was different. Maybe she should have sent that message after all. She checked the wifi fees and scoffed. Twenty-five dollars for an hour of wifi on the plane was robbery. Forget it.

Eliana had always had a rebellious streak. If he didn't want to help her, if he continued to be unreasonable, she would do what needed to be done on her own. Go behind his back if it came to that. One of his engineers would help her. Reuben, or maybe Jeanine.

She hoped it didn't come to that. Her options now felt so limited. Eliana *had* to go back to Kakul. It was the only way to confirm her discoveries. Once Lakshmi and Talia and Tanner had seen the full carving that Eliana had found with Ross, they all agreed with that assessment.

"And we're coming with you," Lakshmi had said.

"That's right," Talia chimed in. Tanner and Ross

both nodded, one like a bobblehead, the other stone-faced and serious. They planned to follow her back to Austin tomorrow, after they finished labeling and photographing the new site in detail. That would give Eliana a chance to work on Amon, and arrange a time for them all to go through the machine together, to continue their search.

The air in Austin was blessedly cool, if you could believe that for central Texas; eighty degrees felt like standing in a walk-in cooler compared to the jungles of central Mexico most of the year.

Eliana drove her car home and unlocked her front door around 11 PM. She felt her shoulders and neck bunch up involuntarily as she entered her home.

"Amon?" she called, her voice echoing in the empty foyer. No one responded. She went upstairs to their bedroom—it was neat, clean, the bed made and apparently unused. "Of course," she said. Amon had been sleeping in the lounge at work again.

Well, she could surprise him there. That kind of surprise always lit up his face after she'd been on the road for a while. Eliana had to drop the new set of samples off at Audrey's lab for carbon-dating anyway. She would do that first and then go see him.

After a long hot shower with lots of soap, Eliana climbed into a fresh change of clothes, feeling like a new person. She buttoned jeans, laced up comfortable sneakers, and donned a cotton t-shirt followed by a spring-weight black jacket. Then she got into her car and drove southeast toward the Fisk Industries campus.

The headquarters building was dark, but Eliana didn't let that fool her. Where Amon worked wasn't visible from the parking lot, so she wouldn't be able to tell if he was here until she got past security to the sub-basement level. Would the guards let her in? Likely not. She hoped someone was in the lobby to call down for her. She walked quickly, gripping the canvas bag of samples in her sweaty hands. Eliana used the fob attached to her keychain to let herself in through the broad glass front door.

She still had access to most buildings because she was still technically on the Fisk Industries employee roster. Amon had thought that would be easier for her than having to sign in as a guest every time she wanted to find him at the office. There was a brief moment of relief as she waved the fob in front of the electronic reader, dispelling the notion that Amon might have removed her access after their last conversation. The light flashed green and the door opened.

Why would she think that? He wasn't given to petty revenges. Still, the fear was present. And more than the fear, the guilt. She must apologize. She should have written. She really should have called.

It was in this state of mind that Eliana first entered the soaring lobby next to the waterfall, thrumming with tension and sick with worry. She immediately decided to go down to find Amon first, rather than drop the samples off first like she had intended. She was procrastinating, and she knew it. She was prepared to face the music now, and it was best to get it over with.

She was walking by the front desk when she heard footsteps clatter loudly down the metal stairs through the open-air of the lobby.

She glanced down the hall and saw a proud man wearing a well-groomed beard and a well-pressed suit, walking down the stairs behind the security checkpoint with his back to her. He held two hands out in front of him, and in his hands was a clear plastic box with a black rock inside of it. When Eliana caught a view of the two big men walking behind him with rifles in their hands, she stifled a gasp and jumped behind the front desk, cramming the bag with the vials and her purse underneath, and folding her long legs in close to her body.

"Kill the old man if he causes any trouble," Lucas said. "Amon relies on him."

A chill raced down Eliana's spine. The elevator door opened, then closed, and took the three men down.

Where were the security guards? She crept out

from under the desk, and tiptoed toward the check-point. Sure enough, the two guards were on the floor, unconscious, though they seemed to be breathing. Eliana hurried back to the front desk and located the desk phone there.

She paused with the receiver halfway to her ear. Would someone get hurt if she called the police? If they were in danger, not calling could be worse. If she set off any alarms, Lucas would know someone else was here, and come looking for her.

Eliana decided that the safest route was not to piss off the men with the rifles. No alarms. No frantic phone calls. She dialed Audrey's number instead.

"Hello?"

"Audrey, listen to me carefully."

"Eliana? Is that you? Why are you calling from Fisk Industries?"

"*Just listen.* Lucas is here. Men with rifles are with him and the two security guards at the checkpoint are unconscious or…or maybe hurt. I think Amon and Reuben are in danger. Call the police. Tell them to send reinforcements. Now!"

"What! I—well, okay, I'll do it, but—"

"Good." Eliana went to set the phone down, then remembered something. "Audrey, there are new samples for carbon-dating under the front desk. I've got to go."

She didn't wait for a response. Eliana hung the phone up and jogged to the back stairwell down which Lucas had disappeared. She slipped around the metal detector and crept down the stairs as quietly as she could, staying low.

Despite her caution, she met no one in the stairwell. They must have been in a hurry, because she descended to the lowest level unseen. No one was in the long hallway that lead to the Translocator lab, either. But as she approached, she saw the base of the Translocator, the sphere of rings around the platform and the massive arch, through the open door.

The air seemed to thrum with electricity. The walls and floor vibrated, sending a shiver through her body. Her heart slammed against her breast, and her mouth dried out. Even the thought of the Translocator was enough to frighten her since she returned, but hearing it active was a more visceral reminder.

As she came around the corner, all the people in the room were staring at the sphere, which spun madly at the back of the room. No one noticed her as she stepped into the room and slipped through the door that led to the lounge.

They were all too busy staring at a kind of window that had opened in the air. Through it, as if looking through a thin sheen of moisture, Eliana saw the black night sky she'd spent the last year dreaming about and dreading in equal measure.

She caught her breath as the dark God of Kakul stepped through the air, the bronze orb floating through behind him.

Xucha.

24

RENDERED INOPERABLE

The man in black turned his head toward Amon and the mercenaries standing over him. The being's face was concealed behind a sleek, reflective helmet that was curved at the front. It was narrow, jutting out slightly where the mouth should be. No face could be seen in the reflection, but Amon had the distinct spine-crawling sensation that it was looking directly at him.

And then the helmeted head snapped with snake-like reflexes to Lucas. Or, more specifically, to the carbonado within the transparent plastic containment unit Lucas held.

The man in black made a sharp gesture with his hand and the metal orb floated forward. A hole opened in the orb's smooth metal face, and a fan of red light formed a blade in the air.

"Down!" Amon yelled, throwing himself sideways into Wes and Reuben, forcing them to the floor. They tumbled to the side as a wide red laser shot out and took the heads off all six mercenaries who stood nearby. A few shots fired from the rifles before the dead men dropped. Bullets clanged off the metallic side of the orb and ricocheted against the wall. The red laser finally cut into the control panel and holodeck, slicing off a backup monitor and clipping a corner of the machine in a flash of sparks and a hot orange glow of metal that liquefied and then reformed in a molten puddle. The bodies of the mercenaries crumpled to the floor with meaty thuds.

Amon gasped and scrambled to his feet, yanking Reuben up with him. Someone gestured from inside the lounge, and the CERN hostages darted toward that room for cover.

Eliana? What is she doing here?

The man in black rushed toward Lucas and the two remaining mercenaries, who now flanked him at the back of the room. The mercenaries shot their rifles and the bullets ripped holes in the floating orb's hull, but didn't seem to damage its motor or do much to stop it. The laser changed to a blue light. It shot at Lucas, and missed him by a hair's breadth— but then the plastic box unit containing the carbonado was rising through the air in the grip of the blue beam. Lucas cried out, his face twisting in a hate-filled snarl, and lunged for the box. The box lifted out of his reach and came to rest in the palm of the man in black.

Amon pushed Reuben and Wes toward the dubious cover of the bank of computer equipment and control panels. The holodeck still responded to his commands, despite the damage done to it by the red laser. The carbonado solution canister sat nearby where Lucas had left it when he went to retrieve the large carbonado from Audrey's lab. Amon watched fearfully out of the corner of his eye while he and Reuben attempted to wrest control of the Translocator back from this powerful creature's black rift. They issued shutdown commands, override passwords, you name it. The black rift remained, the rings still spinning madly. Reuben's white hair stood on end from all the latent electricity buzzing through the air.

Amon continued to gesture and jab at the screen. He plugged the carbonado solution canister back into the power source. Still no response from the Translocator.

The two remaining mercenaries raised their rifles and fired at the man in black. The bullets struck an invisible wall six inches away from the dark suit and clinked harmlessly to the floor.

The orb returned to the offensive, the red light reappearing and slashing out again, driving the mercenaries and Lucas back. Reuben, Wes, and Amon ducked behind the base of the holodeck, and

Amon peered around to get a better angle on the machine. The man in black stepped toward Lucas and his cronies, the metal orb floating in the air in front of him. They cornered Lucas and the mercenaries in the corner, leaving the black rift open behind them.

A slight, dark-haired figure in jeans and a black jacket sprinted from the door of the lounge and crossed the room toward the black rift. Was that—

Eliana slowed just before the rift, and looked back at Amon. She held her cell phone in one hand. Her brow furrowed, and she frowned as their eyes met.

"No!" Amon cried. He got up to run toward the rift, but the orb's red laser swerved toward him and he was driven back down, forced to take cover behind the workstations near the holodeck.

"Eliana, don't!" Reuben shouted.

Under the workstations, Amon saw her hop through the rift.

"I think I can reach her," Reuben said. "Keep the lasers off me!"

Mercenaries dodged and juked away from the lasers, shooting their rifles in bursts at the orbs, which moved in rapid strafing patterns. A few bullets cut gashes into the orb's metal plating. The one that kept Amon pinned down kept swiping it's laser around him. When he tried to peer out, a 3D printer was knocked, in pieces, off a nearby desk. "Okay, go!"

Lifting the wooden lid of a fabricator crate as a flimsy shield, Rueben began to move in a crouch toward the rift.

Through the chaos, the man in black had managed to crack open the plastic case and lift out the carbonado. Though he could only catch glimpses, Amon could see how the stone glowed fiercely in his hand. Bullets fired at the man in black careened wide or clattered harmlessly at his feet, but the constant barrage seemed to keep him pinned down. Rueben made quick progress.

In the other direction, Lucas had fled from the gunfire of the mercenaries toward the warehouse end of the facility. He dug in his coat pocket and pulled out a round object out of his pocket. He looked at it uneasily. The blood drained from his face. He closed his eyes and mumbled something under his breath. A prayer?

Amon had to duck back under the desk as the red lasers cut a piece of the large glass monitor down. It crashed onto his fingers. Amon hissed in pain, and craned his neck around the other side of the desk to see that Reuben had made it unnoticed to the base of the ramp.

"You'll need this!" Amon picked up one of the modern transponder bracelets they had built and threw it toward him. It bounced along the floor.

Reuben picked it up, and kept moving toward the Hopper.

Lucas's angry cussing pulled Amon's attention back in his direction. He tapped on the watch device and glared at Amon with deep resentment evident on his face.

They locked eyes across the room until the firing stopped and the mercenaries rifles began to click on empty.

Reuben had reached the ramp. He sprinted up it and jumped through the rift after Eliana. This time the man in black saw the old engineer go through, and hissed a horrible, snake-like sound. But he didn't follow.

His hearing echoing in the absence of gunfire, Amon peered through a hole in the desk as a back-hand from the man in black opened the throat of a mercenary.

Bodies littered the floor. There was only one mercenary left standing. He frantically clicked his spent rifle's trigger, then tossed it away and pulled out a knife from his belt. A large black hand darted out and gripped him by the neck. A snapping noise split the air and the man fell heavily to the floor.

Amon's skin crawled. The orb was still there, but if he went quickly he could make it across the gap behind the cover of the boxes where Reuben had gone. The sound of the orb's engines receded.

He was about to make the move when Lucas

began to groan. A second later, he screamed. The sound pulled the man in black's attention, too. A faint haze seemed to surround Lucas. His limbs disappeared one at a time until he was gone.

His scream seemed to linger in the air for a long moment. Amon shuddered.

Now or never. He got up to run, but the man in black darted in front of him, impossibly fast.

He gripped Amon by the shoulders.

"How?" The voice was impossibly human, but with a metallic undertone.

"He has a Translocator." Who was this being in the sleek armor? Certainly not a god. But not of this world, either. Amon couldn't help but notice the incredible texture of the suit, like carbon fiber crossed with snakeskin. It seemed to be more than just armor and was remarkably unscathed after the firefight.

"Like this machine?"

He nodded.

"Your machine?"

Amon swallowed the lump in his throat and nodded.

The strange being tossed Amon into the stack of wooden boxes, cracking the frame of one and knocking the air from Amon's lungs.

The man in black took one last look around, hefted the carbonado in his hand, and gestured at his machines. The orbs dashed through the rift. Then the man in black walked up the ramp and stepped through as well.

Amon forced himself to his feet and staggered forward. Wes tentatively stepped in front of him, apparently concerned. Amon shoved him away and moved toward the rift, determined to get through and go after Eliana.

It was shrinking now. He hurried, running with an uneven limp. By the time he reached it, the rift had shrunk to a black ball the size of a fist in the middle of the platform.

It looked like a tiny black hole suspended in the air. Way too small to go through. Dread knotted his stomach.

"God damnit!" he said, bending over and clutching his left knee, which was throbbing with pain from where he'd struck the wooden crate when he was thrown.

He limped back over to the holodeck of the Translocator. The machine was still operable, despite the damage. The monitor was dead, and the power unit partially melted, but the hologram controls worked, and he brought the projectors online now. An array of images appeared in the air around him.

He tried to turn the Hopper back on, but it kept giving Amon an error that told him the magnetic field inside the sphere was unstable.

Translocation cannot be initiated.

Who wrote these damned error messages? Oh, that's right. He did.

Amon hung his head as the surviving hostages, including Agent Moreno, his hands still bound at the wrist, slowly began to trickle out of the lounge in which they'd been hiding.

They watched as Amon swore and gesticulated at the holodeck. No matter what he told the computer to do, the tiny black hole remained suspended in the air in the middle of the stabilization sphere.

It had rendered his Translocator inoperable.

25

SOUL HARVEST

"Easy," Gehro called out. "Careful of the stalactites! They're good luck and have been here for centuries."

Rakulo said nothing. His attention was consumed with wading forward through cold water that reached up to his chin. It was deeper than it seemed from the back of the cave. He reached with his toes for some purchase in the slow-moving river. His hands lay on the canoe, which he and Quen were guiding on a careful path through the low-hanging stalactites at the back of Gehro's coveted cave. It turned out he was very protective of the arrangement of spiky stones that hung from the ceiling.

"Be careful, boys."

"I am, Gehro," Rakulo said.

Quen was taller than Rakulo, so his feet were able to touch the bottom, while Rakulo wasn't. Quen tilted his head to the left to avoid a stalactite, and they pushed the canoe down lower, filling it with more water so that it could fit under the last row of stalactites. They rose up beyond it, lifting and tilting the canoe to empty it of water. Quen reached out and gripped a thick sturdy spike to anchor them. The current moved more quickly here. Above, the cave had opened out into a rounded tunnel winding off in either direction into the darkness.

"Why haven't they come back, Raku?" Quen asked.

"Maatiaak's men and the flying demons are patrolling the jungle around us," Rakulo reminded him. "Citlali and Thevanah will make it back when it's safe to do so."

Quen nodded. "I went out with Yeli not two hours ago. We heard the drums, Raku. The village is gathering in *Uchben Na* for the first time in a year."

Rakulo had heard the drums as well, though only in his good ear. He was growing used to the new handicap. His left ear still throbbed and occasionally a high-pitched squeal accompanied by a sharp pain flashed. It had the power to bring him to his knees with its suddenness. He needed Quen's help *and* his hearing now. Relying on others felt like weakness. That's what Rakulo had always been taught. He did his best to hide his handicap from the others.

"That's why we have to see if this leads

anywhere," Rakulo said. "While we still have the opportunity."

Yeli had stayed behind with perhaps a dozen others. The rest had been taken by Maatiaak's men in the skirmish at the wall and the subsequent retreat, and two had simply gotten tired of living in the cave and defected in the night.

Rakulo told them they could go if they were worried about their families. It was not his job to coerce anyone into helping him against their will.

It was enough that these fifteen—plus Citlali and Thevanah, of course—had stood by him. He didn't know what it proved yet, but it proved something. Maatiaak had, for all intents and purposes, delivered the village back to Xucha, back to the old ways. But they had not taken *his* warriors, the men and women who had fought and searched with him. Men and women who believed there was hope–a very small, very faint hope—that their people could make a life beyond the Wall that had kept them trapped for as long as their people could remember.

"Thank you for coming, Quen," Rakulo said. "Now, we must be careful."

"Of course. Rakulo—" He hesitated. "We have known each other many years. I'll admit, when your father was honored by the water that night after he named you chief, I hated the idea. I thought you were too weak. But now I see that your father was right to pick you. I don't know if what we've done is good or bad, but things are different now. People know, even if they're not rising up against Maatiaak, that the world is changing. I'm sure my mom and dad are scared as anything, but they want to know the truth about Xucha and what's beyond the Wall as much as anyone."

Rakulo absorbed the backhanded compliment slowly, and puzzled through the end of Quen's short speech. That many words from the mouth of quiet Quen was not something to be glossed over lightly.

"Thank you for your faith in me, Quen."

The big man nodded.

"And I think you're right," Rakulo said. "About all of it. I don't know if what we've done is good or bad either. And I grieve for those we've lost. But as long as I'm moving and breathing, I'm not going to quit looking for a way out—*for all our people*. Not while that Wall still stands. We weren't meant to be kept in a cage, Quen. We're free people!"

"Aye!" Gehro said from the other side of the stalactites. "Free people!"

Rakulo blushed, realizing how worked up he'd gotten while he was talking. But Quen gripped his shoulder under the water with one hand and nodded as he locked eyes with Rakulo.

"Good. Let's do this. You get in first while I hold the canoe."

Rakulo nodded, gripped the side of the canoe with both hands, and hopped up into it. He used a clay bowl they'd brought to bail out the rest of the water, then leaned over and gripped Quen's forearm.

"One, two, three!" he said, and hauled the bigger man into the boat, rocking the wooden craft into the middle of the tunnel as Quen steadied himself and found a seat. Quen, being heavier, took the back of the canoe. He reasoned that the heavier man would have a better chance of slowing their advance. The current swiftly began to carry them to the left and around the corner.

"Safe journey, boys!" Gehro's voice came softly as they drifted away on the current, into the darkness.

It was already dim, but the tunnel narrowed their vision to an inky darkness almost immediately. Rakulo strained to see two feet in front of him. The sound of Quen's breathing and the soft rushing noise of moving water was all he heard.

Seconds later, Rakulo shouted, "Left!" and they were both clawing the wooden oars deep into the water, pushing back hard toward the wall to avoid being smashed against a sharp outcropping of rock. Their boat jolted as they clipped it, near Quen's hip.

The river leveled out after that. It was clear and fast, then carried on slowly for a stretch as the water leveled out, spreading under the walls in both directions. Then the tunnel narrowed again and the river suddenly deepened. Rakulo let out a little yelp as his stomach fell out from under him. He glanced back at Quen, whose face was pinched.

"Hold on," Rakulo said.

Rakulo felt his hips rising from his seat and then slam back into the canoe. Foam sprayed into his eyes. His feet flopped up and he pitched backward. Icy water washed over him, he thrashed in the water, and held his breath while up sorted itself from down. A moment later, gasping for air, his head broke the surface.

The fight seemed to have gone out of the water. The tunnel had broadened, the water seeping back under the walls and forming a pool ahead. Raindrops sent cascades of ripples on the water—it was not just a pool, but a sinkhole, a *cenote*, one of the many openings in the ground where water gathered in this jungle. The low-hanging vines and vegetation would make it difficult to spot them from any angle above, but Rakulo could see from his seat where a second fork of the river fed into the pool from left, and a third fork directly across the pond. Three rivers feeding this pool, all connected underground.

Where are we? Rakulo wondered. There were six or eight options, but how many *cenotes* were this big? It was difficult to tell because all the landmarks he used to locate them from the ground were unavailable from this angle. The pool seemed to radiate light, a very slight greenish hue. Or was that the moonlight reflecting off the water, mixing with it in the green vegetation around the opening? Rakulo had never known before tonight that an underground river connected the systems. But it made a sort of sense.

His thoughts were distracted when he finally strained his good ear and made out a rhythmic pulse that seeped through the tunnel walls—the drums.

His jaw hung open when the realization struck him.

"Quen!" Rakulo whispered. "Where are you?"

"Over here."

Rakulo steadied himself and turned toward Quen's voice in the dark. It was easy to locate him by the glowing outline of his broad frame atop the canoe, like a statue in the darkness. This time, Quen hauled him, soaking wet, up into the boat by his arms.

As Rakulo straightened in the canoe, he finally located the source of the glowing light—a bulbous, bushy plant that protruded from the wall, submerged and blocking the mouth of the second branch of the river. The iridescent green glow was faint, but unmistakably coming from the plant.

The drums grew louder. Rakulo guided their canoe nearer to the glow.

"Close enough, Raku," Quen said.

"I need to see."

"You remember what happened to Tolen?"

Rakulo paled, and swallowed past a lump in his throat. Then he paddled back toward the fork they'd taken down the rapids to get here. They sat in the placid water, gazing through the low-hanging vines —thick walls of interwoven tendrils threading through the mossy earth. It completely veiled these rivers from ground level above, and also veiled the surface above from their sight.

They waited a while. Eventually the drums stopped, and a dark shadow fell from ground level into the mouth of the cenote, down, down, like an X in the air, to splash in the water by the mouth of the second river.

Rakulo and Quen, both gripping their paddles, were unprepared for the sudden rush of current that propelled them toward the open pool. Rakulo had the impression that a giant had taken a sudden breath inward, if the rivers were the air he breathed. As a result, the object that had fallen into the water was pulled into the root system of the bulbous plant.

"Get back, get back," Quen said, rowing against the water with his paddle to push their boat back again. Rakulo eagerly joined him.

That wasn't just any object, that was a sacrifice to Xucha, and this was about to get—

A burst of bright green light ignited the plant as the body of the sacrifice was eviscerated. The gods rejoiced, suffusing the water with a brighter green glow to show their thanks. The glow subsided, and seemed to be pulled off down the second fork of the river.

"Gods of the Sky and Sea," Quen murmured.

"I've seen it a hundred times," Rakulo said. "But never like that."

"We've got to get back."

"Wait," Rakulo said. "Where do you think that fork goes?"

"Are you crazy? I don't want to find out."

"I think it leads to the other side of the Wall, Quen. When Xucha's demon came through the Wall, I saw a green glow in the cracks of the dry land on the other side. That fork must leads on the other side of the Wall, Quen. To Xucha's tower."

"Why didn't you say anything before?"

"I didn't realize that it might be connected until now. The tower must be where Xucha lives. He needs our sacrifices for some reason. It's almost like…"

Quen was nodding eagerly, a somber, serious, and quite dangerous expression on his face, more dangerous than Rakulo had ever seen the big man. "Like their life energy gets sucked out of them."

"Xucha is harvesting their souls."

"That's why he needs us. Not just our souls, but our bodies. There are no bodies left after that." Quen gestured to the rooted plant, which still pulsed with a faint green aura.

"We have to get back," Quen said. "To tell the others."

They laboriously began to make their way back up stream, keeping to the walls where the current ran less swiftly, and hauling the heavy load of the canoe up behind them by long straps they had attached for this purpose.

26

PALAVER

Eliana ran through the black rift in the air and barely stopped herself before she launched off the top of the great stone pyramid that towered over the ruined city of *Uchben Na*.

Well that *was unexpected,* she thought.

She surveyed her options. Strangely, the city spread below her was empty. There were drumbeats coming from somewhere, but they were off in the distance, muffled by the jungle and the thick air.

She felt something sticky beneath her feet, glanced down and saw fresh blood on the stones. She sucked in a deep breath, shoving away thoughts of what that implied.

Dear God, what am I doing?

Speaking of Gods, Xucha wouldn't be far behind her. She could either go back home *right now,* or get moving—fast.

Her mind was still reeling at the sudden shift in environment. She turned back to look at the rift one more time—on this end, the window in the air was not jagged at the edges or suspended in the air, but evenly spread in a doorway of stone built in the room on top of the pyramid.

She grimaced as she gazed closer and saw that the rift did not edge up against the doorway of stone, but was instead framed by thick, intertwining tentacles that seemed to be alive, pulsing with energy.

What in the hell?

There was no time to consider this strange discovery—Eliana knew that it wasn't natural, and that was enough for her.

Part of her wanted to go back, but she was so *close* now. She had her phone in her pocket. If she found the carving she needed to verify the connection between the jungles of Mexico and Kakul, she could take photos with her phone.

Which civilization had been there first? Were these stones older than the ones they had found in Mexico? Hell, who *cared?* A clear connection between the two locations would send new theories and rumors reverberating across the anthropology community. If humans made it to this planet, where else had our species traveled? Was Earth even our original home?

She stared at the black rift in the air, through

which she could see the shadow of Amon's lab beyond, like a reflection in deep water. The rift answered one question, yet raised so many others.

Eliana was standing, rooted to the spot, paralyzed by her inability to make a decision, when Reuben suddenly barreled through the rift. Eliana grabbed him and pulled him aside before he could make the same mistake she almost did and tumble them *both* down the pyramid steps.

"Eliana!" he whispered, clutching at her arms. "We shouldn't be here."

She felt at his wrist. "Is this a transponder? To send messages to Amon?"

"Coordinates, not messages. But yes. Eliana, what was that…that monster in black. Is it one of the people you met, in some kind of ceremonial dress? Or is it—"

"No time. We have to go."

"Yes, and quickly. What—"

"Come on!"

She yanked him down the stairs as rapidly as her feet would carry her, and sprinted across the courtyard. Reuben raced along behind her. The old man would be sore, no doubt. But as she looked back she saw a look of elation on his face. He glanced around the vast stone city with an expression of sheer, childlike wonder.

They passed through a stone archway out of the city to the north. She wanted to stop, but with

Xucha close behind them it wasn't safe. She knew the arch was richly carved and decorated, so much like the ruins her team had discovered in Mexico.

It seemed to be night in Kakul as well as on Earth —a coincidence if she'd ever known one—but even if she could see by the light of the two moons overhead, she didn't dare stop moving yet. Not here. Not without someone who knew the area to watch her back. Not with Xucha behind them.

Leaves slapped her face as they waded into the jungle. The brush grew thicker and they had to slow their pace. Now that she had spent more time in Mexico, she recognized the plants in Kakul, names that Lakshmi had taught her—tamarind trees, strangler figs, and ferns among much taller, much older trees that rose like watchtowers into the ancient canopy. She had the sense that this jungle was far more ancient than the one in Mexico she had recently been searching. The trees here were huge.

Eliana slowed her pace as she came to a decision. "We have to find my friend Rakulo."

Reuben stopped and braced his hands on his knees as he caught his breath. Eliana waited for him, scanning the area around them for danger.

"He'll be able to help us," she said. "I never saw predators in this jungle, but that doesn't mean it's safe…" Her voice trailed off.

A rustling sound came to her left and then a woman appeared, wearing a brown homespun tunic wrapped around her chest and waist, with ochre-colored skin and dark hair in dreadlocks pulled back into a messy bun on her head.

"Eliana?" the woman said. "Eliana, is that you?"

Only she didn't say "is that you" in English, she spoke in the dialect of Kakul that was so similar to Yucatec Maya and yet so different. She made Eliana's name sound like a birdsong. It had been over a year since Eliana had used the language, so her tongue stumbled as she formed words to respond.

"Citlali," she said. "Hello. Nice to meet you…No, nice to see you again."

Citlali glanced uneasily at Reuben, then back at Eliana.

"What are you doing here?" Citlali asked.

"I…"

And then she remembered.

"Xucha came to my…" She paused, realizing her Kakuli was very rusty and she couldn't remember the word for "World." Instead, she said. "Xucha came to my home. He hurt people. I came here to make sure you were unharmed."

That's a lie, but a banal one. She hadn't come here to check on them at all, but to find stone carvings for her research. A wave of guilt washed over her.

Citlali didn't seem to notice. "Come," she said. "You are lucky that most people are at the ceremony. The old men have been patrolling this area nonstop for several days. We were using this opportunity to make our way back to find Rakulo and the other warriors."

"Where's Rakulo? Who are the old men?"

"Later," Citlali said.

Eliana remembered how strong and confident this young woman was. She seemed even stronger now, leaner, harder, like she'd been training. Her cheeks were gaunt and she seemed tired. Yet her eyes remained alert, darting to the jungle around them.

"Lead the way," Eliana said.

Citlali nodded. She gestured and another young woman Eliana didn't know appeared out of the jungle. The new woman took up the front, Citlali the rear, and off into the jungle they went.

"What did they say?" Reuben whispered as they walked.

"They're friends. They're going to take us to Rakulo. I'll fill you in on the details when we get somewhere safe."

"Shh," the woman in front hissed.

Eliana shut her mouth and focused on walking.

Eventually they approached a low stone wall like a spine in the earth. The ground was treacherous, uneven stone concealed underfoot by a bed of leaves. Citlali took the lead and told them to only step where she was stepping. They walked until one of the cutouts went deep into the Earth and became a cave. The cave's opening been carefully covered with cut branches, the edges of the opening shored up with heavy boulders and fallen trees.

"It's like a bunker," Reuben said to her as they approached. "No one's getting in here without a fight."

"Why the decorations?" Eliana asked Citlali.

Citlali snorted a small laugh. "Decorations, like for your home? No. Not decorations. These are—" She used a word with a harsh fricative that Eliana didn't know, but which she interpreted as "defenses."

"I see," Eliana said.

Citlali gave a soft call, and someone responded. Then the branches were parted, and they were let in with a subdued cheer from the dozen or so people inside.

Eliana did not see Rakulo among them. She and Reuben stood to one side as the young women were welcomed. Reuben fiddled with the transponder bracelet on his wrist.

"Everything okay?" she asked.

"I think so," he said.

The transponder showed the time—Earth time— and a set of coordinates. A four-way directional pad and two buttons controlled the numbers and the transmission. Simple and compact, no bigger than a small watch. "We should make contact soon to let Amon know we're okay."

"I'm not ready to go back yet," Eliana said.

"Okay. But soon. I'm worried about him."

"Me, too," she said. She knew how dangerous Xucha was. "Soon."

After exchanging greetings with her comrades, Citlali came over to where they waited. "They tell me that Rakulo and Quen have gone down the river. Have some onion and mushroom stew while we wait for them to return."

So they ate and waited. And waited more. Eliana drifted off for a while, and when she woke, Rakulo was standing over her, dripping wet, and grinning from ear to ear.

She stood and he embraced her warmly.

"What are you doing here?" he asked. "I thought I would never see you again."

"Here I am," she said.

"Who is this? Not your husband, is it?"

"No, this is Reuben."

Reuben held out his hand, and Rakulo gripped it firmly. They sat around the fire while Rakulo and the big warrior Quen ate as well. Between bites, Rakulo filled her in about how he had convinced the villages to stop the sacrifices for a year after he became chief, and all about his warriors, their training, and the search for a way beyond the Wall. He had mentioned the Wall before, but she sensed a new determination to get beyond it. The youthful hopefulness he used to exude had been replaced by a very adult determination.

"And today we found a plant in the Well of Sacrifices, where the green glow seems to originate. It devours the bodies of the sacrifices that are thrown into the Well. I think that Xucha put it there, and if we remove it we will hamper his ability to control our people through sacrifice."

Eliana translated for Reuben.

"Is it a machine?" he asked. "If it is, maybe I can help them destroy it."

"He said it was a plant… but if it's glowing like that, maybe it is some kind of biotechnology. You've seen Xucha's black suit, and the orbs that follow him around."

She had also seen those tentacles around the edge of the rift on the Kakul side. Even now, it was unsettling to think about.

"Could be," Reuben admitted. "That orb seems more advanced than any weapon we've ever built. Whatever engine makes it hover would be worth billions on Earth."

Eliana translated Reuben's offer of help back to Rakulo, keeping it simple with her basic command of the language. He nodded his appreciation. Then Eliana finally told him about Xucha's appearance in Amon's lab.

"Really?" he said. "I thought only *you* could travel between worlds. If Xucha can as well…" He shook his head, obviously overwhelmed by what he was up against.

"It's scary, I know," Eliana said. "Xucha came to get the carbonado."

Rakulo cocked his head at the English word *carbonado*.

"What my ring was made out of," she explained.

His whole body sagged, crestfallen. Then he nodded in understanding. "Xucha took my ring, a few days ago, after Maatiaak and his men ambushed me."

"Maybe that's how he opened the rift," Reuben suggested after she translated this new information. "With the stone from the ring. The carbonado is clearly a power source or amplifier of some kind. That's how Amon has been using it to interface with the Hopper, too. There's so much still that we don't know about the material."

They hadn't told Rakulo about the rift, and most of what Reuben said didn't translate, so Eliana simply said, "My friend says that now Xucha is going to be an even more dangerous enemy."

"No one ever said fighting a God would be easy," Rakulo responded. He leaned forward in the fire-light. "Can you use your magic to take me on the other side of the wall?"

She nodded. "Probably."

Amon wouldn't like it…but would he be able to refuse? After all this talk of Xucha, she was worried for him now. She wanted to make sure Amon was all right. "Can you contact Amon now?"

Reuben adjusted the transponder on his wrist and pressed a button while Rakulo watched him intently. The light blinked red, then green for several long minutes. It probably took longer here because of the distance from Earth. But after a minute, the device switched back to solid red.

Reuben groaned.

"What does that mean?" Eliana said, panic suffusing her body, accompanied by a sudden cold sweat.

"I don't know. Something's wrong on Amon's end. Do you think that rift is still open? Whatever it is, it seems like we're stuck here for now."

Not again.

Eliana sighed. At least this time she was here by choice.

ONE PROBLEM AT A TIME

Amon turned to Wes, surveying the destruction and death that littered his lab, and threw his anger like a glass full of acid in Wes's direction.

"You're in charge of security! You let this happen!"

The hostages stood near the blast door huddled close together like scared animals. Only Agent Moreno seemed to have gathered his wits. He was talking with the secretary from CERN, who was cutting his hands free from the plastic zip ties with a knife from the lounge.

"My fault?" Wes said. "Is it *my fault* that Lucas stole the plans to your Translocator and built his own, fucked up version? Is it my fault that—that—that thing stole the carbonado and killed anyone who pointed a gun at it?"

Wes, gazing down and apparently realizing he

was standing in the nexus where six severed heads and the well-muscled bodies they belonged to had fallen, paled and swallowed. He took two steps closer to Amon. There was no blood near the fallen bodies, but the smell of singed flesh hung thick in the air.

Amon raised his chin and stared a challenge at Wes, who returned it. Then he sniffed as if Wes wasn't worth his time, and turned away.

Amon still didn't know if Wes was the mole. Probably it was that guard Roger. But it didn't matter right now.

He eyed the fist of darkness that hung in the air near his Translocator. The computer said it gave off a strong magnetic field. Amon reached out a finger to touch it, then jerked his hand away. Who knew what that thing would do if he touched it. Shock his hand? Freeze it? Rip it off?

Eliana and Reuben were counting on him. Amon needed to take care—and he needed help. Immediately.

"I've seen that thing before—the man in black," Amon said. "I saw it when I rescued Eliana from that hellhole she disappeared to. She told me the people who live there think it's their God. They call him Xucha."

"Don't tell me she's still holding on to *that* theory," Wes scoffed.

"Shut up." Amon pointed a finger at Wes. "If you

say anything else about my wife, I will fire you. If you do anything but be helpful here, you're done at Fisk Industries. Fuck what the board says. I will destroy you if you get in my way now."

Amon held Wes's gaze. Wes finally nodded.

"What is that?" Wes asked, pointing toward the ball of blackness.

"Nothing known to modern physics, that's for sure. We need backup. Fortunately, the brightest minds are at our disposal."

Wes and Amon both turned to the CERN scientists who were stuck here. Agent Moreno had managed to free his hands and now stood over Agent Wiley's eviscerated body.

"But first, we have to clean this up. Do me a favor and don't let anyone near this thing until I get backup."

Wes nodded, positioning his body so he could see both the black fist suspended in the air, the door, and all the bodies between. He dug his cell phone out of his pocket. "All right. I'll make some calls. We'll close down the lab, inform the LTA, and get backup security in here. Tell your FBI friend to keep the local police out of this. We don't need any more bad press."

"I'm on it," Amon said.

Agent Moreno was still staring at the body of Agent Monica Wiley, his former partner. Amon put a hand gently on the man's rounded shoulder and thought about Eliana. With any luck, the distraction of Lucas and the short and painful scuffle with Amon had granted her and Reuben enough time to get clear before that monster got to them.

Reuben had taken a transponder with him, but a fat lot of good that would do with the Hopper frozen up by that...that...wormhole Xucha had left behind.

Amon didn't think the sick feeling in his stomach could get any worse. But it did. He wanted to puke.

"The whole thing was a trap," Agent Moreno said. "They knew we were coming."

Amon reminded himself to breathe. One problem at a time, right, isn't that what Eliana would have told him? *Focus, honey,* he could hear her voice in his mind. *Deal with one problem at a time.*

"It had to have been Lucas," Amon said. "He pulled me away, too, with the diversion on the lunar base. But with that wormhole thing, I can't use the Translocator to send them any more aid. They've had to resort to life-support systems while they fix the damage."

"You went to the moon? Jesus. That's still hard to wrap my mind around. What happened?"

"Not sure. An explosion of some kind? Or sabotage. Do you think the mole is on the lunar base?"

"With another Translocator out there, we can't be sure of anything. I need to call backup."

"No local cops, please. This needs to stay under wraps. If the media gets wind of this—"

"Lucas would love that, I'm sure," Agent Moreno said dryly.

"You only just met the man, and yet you know him so well."

"I know the type—the polished appearance hides an ego the size of your Translocator."

Amon pretended not to notice the slight.

"Most of my career was in white collar crime. Trust me, I know the type. I've been chasing them a long time," Agent Moreno went on. "I agree with you, though—no local cops. But I have to report back to the Bureau Chief. And get an FBI medical examiner out here, pronto."

"I understand. Thanks."

Agent Moreno's chest rose and fell heavily. As he held his phone to his ear and turned away, Amon's own phone rang in his pocket. It was Audrey.

"Audrey, hey."

"What is going on, Amon? Eliana called me freaking out, and now her phone is out of service. Are you okay? She said there were men with guns there!"

"Deep breaths, Audrey. I'm okay. Eliana is gone. She went back to Kakul."

"What? And you let her?"

"Well, no—" He could feel his temper rising. "She didn't exactly ask me."

But she had, hadn't she? Why had he been so stubborn? She was undoubtedly in more danger now than she ever would have been had Amon offered to assist her. He could have sent protection with her, trained security guards, FBI agents, LTA scientists, a paramedic…

Now she was back on that blasted planet alone with only Reuben to help her, and he was stuck here. Again. And it was all his fault.

Deal with one problem at a time.

"Audrey, can you come in? I know it's late, but there's more bad news. Your carbonado is gone, too."

"WHAT?"

"I'm sorry. I'll tell you what happened when you get here."

"I'm parking now. Eliana left me samples and I need to get them and take them up to my lab. Um, I should also say that Eliana wanted me to call the cops. They beat me here."

"Oh no. Audrey, do not let them inside! I'll be right there."

Amon disconnected the call and pocketed his phone. "Agent Moreno! I need you. Now!"

Moreno nodded, spoke a hasty goodbye to whatever FBI official was on the other end of his phone call. Amon heard Moreno's shoes striking the floor as he hurried to catch up. He was already preparing lies to stall the police until Wes warned the LTA and Moreno's FBI people had time to get there.

28

FIBER OF BEING

The magical device Eliana and her odd white-haired friend brought with them was broken. Rakulo had Quen fetch woven blankets for them.

"Rest," he told them. "We'll keep watch."

They stretched out in a corner and fell asleep.

Yeli and Quen took the first watch, and Rakulo also lay down to rest. But sleep didn't come quickly. His mind spun with thoughts of the green-glowing water, with visions of the plant that had eviscerated and absorbed the body of the sacrifice that fell into the water.

Was that what had happened to old Ekel? Had Maatiaak cut his throat and tossed him into the Well?

The experience had made a strong impression upon him. Rakulo had seen sacrifices from the top of the *cenote* many times. Up there, the sacrifice seemed like mysterious ritual magic, the inner workings of which were only visible to the minds of the gods.

Being on the level with it, seeing the plant devour a body with his own eyes—that was different. It changed how he saw things. Xucha was bound to the plant somehow. It was his mouth, and the river his stomach. What would happen if Rakulo destroyed the mouth, as the old man, Reuben, had suggested? Would it stop feeding the stomach?

Could it really be that simple?

He worried for his mother. He worried for the children. He worried for all the people of his little village. What chance of survival would they have if a faction of loyalists among them insisted on continuing the bloody tradition of sacrifice out of fear? Would they continue to feed Xucha for the rest of time? Would there ever be an end?

Sleep finally came, but it was restless and filled with dreams of falling.

Rakulo woke early and took the last watch.

He stoked the fire and was now inspecting the canoe for damage, the one he and Quen had hauled painstakingly back upstream to the cave. It had a few chips and dents in the hull, and one thin crack where the wood had begun to split. The crack hadn't penetrated through the body of the boat, however, so it would continue to function as intended.

Eliana stirred. She sat up as the first rays of dawn filtered into the dark cave. Her eyes were swollen with sleep, and she rubbed at them with the back of her hand.

"There's water if you want to wash," Rakulo told her.

The man called Reuben awoke next, yawning and stretching. When he stood, he cranked at his back muscles with knotted fists. Eliana returned a moment later.

"You were wet last night when you came in," she said. "Did you come through *that*?" She pointed to the back of the cave.

"It's an underground river. Quen and I were looking for a way under the Wall."

"Did you find one?"

He nodded. "Maybe."

The old man said something Rakulo didn't understand. Their language was quick, and the old man spoke like he had rocks in his mouth, mumbling and blending his words into a string of unintelligible sentences. The old man seemed even odder than Gehro did some days, his eyes wild with excitement when he spoke. Maybe these pale, tall people weren't so different from them after all, except for their clothes made of strange, tightly-woven cloth, and the colorful shoes they wore.

"What's he saying?" Rakulo asked.

"He wants to see this thing," Eliana said, "the plant you found in the water. He said he might be able to help you find out how to destroy it, or at least learn more about it. He's good at taking things apart, especially…" She grimaced as if searching for a word. She took a reflective rectangle out of her pocket and tapped it with one finger. "Especially tools. He is a…builder."

"Can he help me fix this crack in the canoe?"

"Not that kind of builder."

Reuben bared his teeth.

If this man really could help them destroy the plant and strike a blow at Xucha, then Rakulo had a responsibility to humor him. At least to see what he might have to offer.

"Yes," he said. "You'll both need to come. I can't understand him without you. Can he swim?"

She told Reuben the news. Reuben reached down, took Rakulo's hand, and shook it vigorously.

"We can leave soon," Reuben said as he withdrew his hand, bemused.

"One thing, Rakulo," Eliana said. "When we get back, I need to go look for something in *Uchben Na*."

He shook his head in a firm denial.

"Yes. I *have* to go."

"It's not safe. Xucha is still out there. As is Maatiaak."

Eliana's face darkened. "I'm going, Rakulo."

"Maatiaak's men are still patrolling the jungle. They control the village, and the city of stones."

"Rakulo, I have to go. It's the whole reason I came back."

He cocked his head at that. "Why?"

Eliana's tongue darted out, wetting her lips. "I'm looking for some carvings on the buildings. I need to know more about their history. They look like buildings in my world. The only place to find the answers I seek is in *Uchben Na*. Maybe I can find out more about your history, too, like how you came to be here."

Rakulo didn't care how they came to be here. All he cared about was how they got out of Xucha's domain, outside the Wall, to freedom. But how could he explain this to an outsider? She came and went as she pleased. It infuriated him, made him feel even more powerless and trapped than he normally did. When her magic was working, she could be gone again in a moment, back to her own world. She didn't know what it was like to be stuck here.

Rakulo fought down his temper. He took three deep breaths through his nose. He closed his eyes and counted to ten.

Eliana had shown him kindness in the past. He should return it now.

"I'll take you to *Uchben Na* myself—as soon as it is safe," Rakulo said. "Not until then. But I promise I will take you when it is safe."

"Okay," Eliana said, pursing her lips. "Thank you."

He hoped she would not try to go behind his back, but he knew better than to try to force her to do anything. She was one of the strongest, most willful women he had ever met, and that included Citlali and his mother. She had earned his respect standing up to his father, despite how things had turned out in the end.

Rakulo woke Quen, and together he, Eliana, and Reuben carried the canoe to the back to the cave. Rakulo woke Citlali and pulled her aside as well.

"We're taking Eliana through the river to the Well, where Quen and I went yesterday. Her friend thinks he knows how to help us destroy it."

Citlali grunted. "If it works, Xucha will bring his wrath down upon us."

"Maybe," Rakulo said.

"He has before, and we've never tried to destroy the Well before."

"I know."

"That doesn't bother you?"

"Of course it does! I don't want to see anyone else get hurt. But we pay the price either way—slowly, in sacrifices, or quickly, in retribution. There is no path out of this situation that doesn't involve blood and death. At least this way, *we're* in control—we get to make the next move. And what if it works? If we destroy the Well…"

"It could make things better. Or it could make them worse."

"It is not about best or worst. It is what we have to do. I'm done waiting."

"I know. I just hope you're right."

"Me, too."

Citlali wrapped her arms around his neck and pulled Rakulo close. Rakulo froze with surprise, but after a moment wrapped his own arms around her as well.

"One more thing," Rakulo whispered. "I need you to keep an eye on Eliana. She wants to go to *Uchben Na*. Knowing her, she will try to sneak out when we're not looking. It might endanger us all. I need you to keep her from going, if she tries."

Citlali pulled away and gave Rakulo a withering look. "You want me to babysit her? There are only seventeen of us left. Do we not have enough to think about?"

"If you keep her from danger, you will keep her from bringing danger back to *us*."

Citlali regarded him for a long moment before nodding. "Fine, I will do it. But only because you asked."

"Thank you."

"For now, I am going back to sleep. I barely slept at all while Thevanah and I were hiding in the trees. Wake me when you get back."

Rakulo returned to the back of the cave, where he found Quen, Eliana, and Reuben. He made Reuben and Eliana strip off their heavy clothing. Then he and Quen guided them underneath the stalactites, and helped them both into the canoe. Eliana went up lightly. Reuben was heavier, and it took both warriors to hoist him up.

Rakulo hoped Eliana was right about Reuben. He was not fat, but close, and he was already breathing heavily after such a slight exertion. Quen had the same thought, and discreetly raised an eyebrow at Rakulo.

Quen and Rakulo finally climbed into the canoe as well. It was tight with all of them, but they made it work.

The canoe was heavier, too, but that just helped slow them down. This time, the journey was less surprising, and while it was harder to turn the canoe with a heavier load, working together with Quen and a better knowledge of the river's turns and rapids, they managed to avoid the bigger rocks and float smoothly down to the placid, shallow stream that led to the Well of Sacrifices.

This time, they paddled through the curtain of hanging vines. No drumbeats echoed, nor did any bodies fall. The morning sunlight angled into the airy *cenote*, illuminating dust-motes and insects and diving birds with a golden aura.

It was stunning. Absolutely beautiful. They stared for a long minute.

Quen finally broke the silence, turning back to Eliana. "Can you see it?"

"Oh!" Eliana said. She pointed and Reuben followed her gaze to the green iridescence under the surface of the water near the fork of the river to their left. His eyes widened. He gestured and spoke rapidly to Eliana in their language.

"Can we get closer?" Eliana asked.

"Yes. Keep your hands in the canoe. Do not touch the water under any circumstances."

"Okay," Eliana said. She told Reuben, who folded his hands in his lap and watched attentively. The wild look had vanished. His intelligent eyes were clear and focused.

Their boat drifted closer. The green glow coloring the water was faint but present. The light purple water was still except for the ripples caused by their boat's passage. As they got closer, they had no trouble seeing the root system of the bulbous plant branching out into the tranquil water. Rakulo tensed, waiting for a tentacle to lash out like that sea monster had done. He called a halt, and Quen back paddled to stop the boat.

Reuben said something. "He says we need to get closer," Eliana translated.

Rakulo pressed his lips together and nodded. Carefully, they pulled the canoe close to the wall and inched toward the nearest visible piece of the bulbous plant.

"What happens if we touch the water?" Eliana asked.

Rakulo looked up into the air. A large beetle was buzzing around their head, one of hundreds of tiny insects. Rakulo snatched one. He crushed its tiny body in his fist then tossed it into the water.

A small, green surge of light emanated from the bulbous underwater plant system. A tentacle reached out and snatched away the beetle, tearing it to pieces in the space of a breath. The green glow receded a moment later.

"Wow," Reuben breathed.

The old man's eyes were darting along the plant, following the green glow that moved down the root system and away into the river, hugging close to the wall.

He mumbled something else that Rakulo didn't follow. But he did understand the finger the old man pointed at the earthen wall of the cenote.

Reuben reached out a hand.

"Careful!" Rakulo whispered.

Reuben showed him his palms in a placating gesture. Rakulo remained tense as Reuben felt along the wall, and ripped out a couple small root systems from other plants, vines growing up out of the water into the wall. Clod of dirt fell of, stirring up more of the glowing root system as Reuben continued to dig. He finally stuck a hand in all the way up to his forearm, and came out with a root the thickness of a finger clutched in his hand.

Rakulo held the root in the middle, so no end was visible. On one side, the root plunged into the earthen wall, headed parallel to the river. The other end climbed down, into the water, and seemed to lead to the bulbous plant itself.

Rakulo grabbed around in the air until he managed to snatch another beetle. This time, when the plant sucked in the beetle's body, A faint green pulse flashed along the length of the root Rakulo held in his hand.

Reuben spoke again, and Eliana translated. "Are you sure you want to destroy it, Rakulo?"

"With every fiber of my being."

"Hold out your knife," she said.

Rakulo took the obsidian knife from his tunic and held the blade out in the golden sunlight. Reuben held out the root between both fingers, and brought it down fast.

The knife sliced into the root, and severed it.

A greenish ichor leaked through the split root into the placid water below. The root system of the bulbous plant beneath the water twitched—and Rakulo was nearly certain it was not a trick of the light.

Reuben found another vein lower in the wall, which he pulled out. Rakulo cut that one as well. More of the green ichor dripped into the water.

Was it blood? More like sap.

Rakulo and Quen paddled their canoe around to the other side of the bulbous plant, careful to give the dangerous root system a wide berth. Rakulo sliced three more veins on this side. He felt them buck and harden in his hand, but Rakulo cut without mercy.

He reached into the dirt and found yet another vein. How many of these things were there?

The severed lengths shrank and pulled back into the wall, as if they were protecting themselves.

Rakulo reached out and snatched a third beetle from the air. He crushed it, and let its body drift to the water.

The root system reached out and greedily took its life. But it lasted longer, and the glow was undeniably softer.

They found and severed a dozen veins in all, running through either side of the earthen wall just over this fork of the underground stream.

They paddled back to observe their work. Green ichor dripped thickly down both walls on either side of the plant.

"Is that all of them?" Eliana asked.

Rakulo shook his head. "I don't think so. They have to lead somewhere. But it's a start. Let's go, before Xucha realizes what we've done and comes looking for someone to punish."

29

GEHRO'S WILD MUSHROOMS

They worked their way slowly back up river—it took a couple of hours and wore Eliana's stamina down. She was more tired now than she had been when she woke up, and she had not even made it back to *Uchben Na* to search those ancient stones for the carving she needed yet.

"I've never seen anything like that," Reuben was saying as they waded through the water, still babbling and excited despite the exertion. "Living technology. We've never even come close to something like that. Those veins reminded me of power cables. They ran through the wall back to somewhere, like Rakulo said. But why? And what was powering them? That green pus leaking out of the veins, I wonder if that's what powered them. No metal or plastic in them at all. Incredible. Do you think they were built like that, or did they grow over time? How long would it take to grow a plant like that? I should have taken a sample to take back with us to show Amon. Oh!"

He checked the bracelet at his wrist. The light went from blinking green to solid red again, and his face fell. "Nothing. Maybe it's because we're still underground," he said. It didn't sound like he was convinced that being underground was the real source of the problem.

"Don't worry," Eliana said. "Amon will fix it."

But Eliana would not be going back through the transponder before she had a chance to explore. If those carvings existed in *Uchben Na*, she would track them down first. She had to. Her career and her reputation depended upon it.

They finally reached the stalactites again. Rakulo and Quen motioned for her to go through first. Eliana swam ahead, and lifted herself out of the river and onto the cold stone floor at the back of the cave.

Dripping wet and feeling exposed in her underwear, she retrieved her jeans and shirt where she had folded them next to the wall. She dried herself off with her jacket, and put the jeans and shirt back on. It was way too hot for the light black jacket anyway. She wrung it out, then folded it beneath her and used it as a thin pillow. Reuben flopped out of the water a moment later. She rested against the wall, and eventually Reuben's babbling about the plant tapered off. She smiled when she turned toward him and saw that he was sleeping with his head leaning back against the wall of the cave. Faint snores emanated from his nose.

Quen and Rakulo went out of the cave without an explanation. Eliana was tired, but not tired enough to sleep. Thoughts of the carvings kept her alert. After a while, she stood and paced around the cave. How would she ever get out of here? The opening was blocked by brush and stones, and guarded by at least two of the warriors at all times. She couldn't leave without several people noticing, if Rakulo would let her go out at all.

The whistling signal that Rakulo had given the night before sounded outside. She thought it would be Rakulo and Quen returning. Instead, an old man with a long grey beard and a wrinkled face came into the cave and emptied a bag full of big mushrooms into a woven basket half full of the things. He noticed her watching him.

"You must be Eliana."

"Hello," she said. "That's right. What's your name?"

"I'm Gehro. Welcome to my house."

"Your…house? You live here?"

"It had been my home for many years now."

"Ah," she said.

Eliana had no idea that anyone lived in Kakul outside of the villages. This revelation put her back on her heels. How did he relate to the rest of their society? "Interesting. You don't live in the village?"

"Indeed, no."

The old man turned to the mushrooms and began sorting through them. He rubbed off the excess dirt, picked out leaves, and threw them into the fire.

Curiosity overcame her reticence. "Can I help?" Eliana asked.

Gehro smiled broadly at her. "Why, yes. I'd appreciate that."

She reached into the basket and picked a clod of dirt off a large cap. They worked in silence for a while, until a thought occurred to Eliana. She paused, twisting a leaf in her fingers.

"Gehro, you know the forests well, don't you?"

"Yes."

"How familiar are you with the carvings on the buildings in *Uchben Na*?"

"Is that why you came here? To look at carvings?"

Eliana lifted her chin, determined not to let some old hermit talk down to her. "Is that a problem?"

Gehro shrugged. "It is no business of mine—just curiosity. What are you hoping to find?"

"Back on my world, I found some carvings that no one has seen in over a thousand years. It showed two moons—your moons—and a pyramid that I think was meant to depict the pyramid in *Uchben Na*. We have pyramids on my world, too, but not there. I need to know if the carvings I found are the same or different than the ones in *Uchben Na*, and if the carving I found actually shows your moons…or something else entirely."

"And you think finding these carvings will give you the answers you seek?"

"I think it's a step in the right direction. The only way I can be sure is to see for myself."

He shrugged. "So go."

"I would if I could," Eliana said, dropping the leaf she had been tearing into tiny pieces into the fire. "Rakulo said he would take me there when it was safe. But he doesn't think it's safe yet. It seems like everyone I know is trying to keep me away from that place."

A smirk spread on the old man's face. "Is the jungle ever really safe? Gods hide in the trees. They always have."

Eliana cocked her head at the wild-eyed old man as he stood, lifting the mushroom basket. As he twirled around, she noticed the others all eyeballing the basket. Had they been watching them clean mushrooms the whole time? Had she spoken loudly enough for them to overhear her?

She really needed to pay better attention to what was going on around her.

"The food is ready!" Gehro said, swinging the basket around and drawing the attention of all of the warriors. Even Reuben stirred. "Who is hungry? Eat your fill now, and I will roast what is left."

The warriors all came away from the entrance to the cave immediately, crowding around Gehro and his basket of mushrooms.

The realization hit her: he was distracting them so that she could get away. She didn't dare waste the opportunity. Her phone was in the pocket of her jeans. She stepped back toward the opening and casually slipped outside while the others stuffed their faces with Gehro's wild mushrooms.

She hurried away, watching her footing on the uneven limestone and slick leaf-cover. She was a half mile closer to her destination when a fit, dark-haired girl stepped out from behind a tree in front of her.

Eliana let out a little shriek, and her hand flew to her mouth. "Citlali! You scared me."

"You shouldn't have left the cave," Citlali said. "It's not safe."

Eliana heaved a sigh, and walked onward, stepping around the fierce young woman. Citlali followed.

"This is important," Eliana said. "It won't take me long, and I promise I'll be careful."

"Careful? You crash through the forest like a drunk child who has never been taught the meaning of silence."

"Ah, silence, yes. I forgot how much your people treasure that quality in a person."

"In a warrior."

"Well, I am no warrior. I am an archaeologist." She used the English word for her job, there being no equivalent that she knew of in their language.

"The stones have always been there. They are not going anywhere. What's the rush?"

Citlali didn't inquire further. Neither did she seem intent on stopping Eliana. Perhaps she sensed Eliana's determination and figured it would be better to let her have her way. They walked together for a time in silence until, ahead, the stepped slope of the pyramid and the lichen-covered curved walls of an arch loomed up between the trees.

Citlali clamped her hand around Eliana's mouth, and yanked her down behind a thick clump of bushes. She tried to yell, she kicked, and she squirmed. But the young woman held her tight.

Citlali whispered softly in her ear. "Sssssshhhhhh."

A minute later, Eliana heard footsteps crunching leaves. Then two pairs of feet passed by, very quietly, not three feet from where they crouched. When the footsteps had faded, Citlali released her hold on Eliana's mouth.

"See? You should have listened to Rakulo. The jungle is not safe."

"The jungle is never safe," Eliana replied, throwing Gehro's words at Citlali. "Gods hide in the trees. They always have."

Citlali said nothing, but looked worried.

That's when it hit Eliana. "Rakulo told you to follow me."

"He did. Though I would have done so on my own. I know you, remember? I know how stubborn you are. And you don't know who we are fighting. You could have put all of us in danger with your carelessness."

Eliana was embarrassed. "I'm sorry."

Citlali regarded her for a long moment. "I forgive you. Fortunately, I was prepared for it. I spent much time in the treetops last week, where Thevanah and I observed the patrol patterns of Maatiaak and his men. Now that I know how they move, the paths they take are very predictable."

"Are you saying that those men who just passed us, you knew they were coming?"

She nodded.

"Huh."

"We should keep moving," Citlali said. "We must be back before dark."

Eliana nodded and stepped into the shadow of the arched gate into the city. She didn't know if this was the same arch she had met Chief Dambu under a year ago, but it could have been. The entire thing was covered over with carved reliefs, their edges softened by time and grown over with moss and vines.

She pulled back some vines, and there it was, just as she remembered—the man-like figure she had seen once before. Two hands, a set of legs, a sandaled pair of feet. Instead of a face, the figure's head was covered in a circular mask...or maybe a helmet. A moon hovered just over his shoulder.

Eliana's eyes widened. That wasn't a moon—that was one of those orb-like machines.

She knew what she was looking at now. It was a depiction of Xucha, their dark god, immortalized in stone. He was wearing robes like a priest, rather than his black armor, but his face was still covered.

Eliana immediately began tearing down the vines.

"What are you doing?" Citlali asked.

"I need to see the rest of it."

Citlali glanced around, then shrugged and began to help Eliana rip out the vegetation. They made a pile of leaves and vines at their feet.

On the side opposite the wall, Eliana finally found what she had been looking for—the two moons, Ky and Kal, just like the carvings she had seen on Earth. They were larger, and carved with more detail here, down to the dark craters in the surface. Below the moons was the pyramid, and below that the head of Kukulkan—which looked eerily similar to the face drawn on the figure of Xucha. Finally, below the head of the feathered serpent was a skull.

The next row down near her feet showed a series of frames—a man being taken by other men in masks; that man being painted purple and smoked with incense; the decorated sacrifice being stretched across two rocks; and finally, the dead man with his heart cut out thrown off the outcropping of rock and tumbling into the hole in the ground—into the *cenote*.

"Oh my Gods!" Citlali said.

"Telling me," Eliana mumbled in English.

"I didn't know this was here."

"How do your people teach the sacrifice ceremony?"

She shrugged. "I never thought about it. I guess the old shamans pass their knowledge to the younger ones. We all witness the ceremony our whole lives, so if you think about it, the only new thing is who holds the knife."

Citlali glanced left, and her face paled as she noticed something out of Eliana's line of sight inside the stone city.

She grabbed Eliana's arm and pulled her away, back into the forest. Eliana stumbled after her.

"What's the matter?" she said as she began to run.

Citlali didn't answer.

"Wait! I didn't take any pictures!" She dug her phone out of her pocket and wrenched her arm out of Citlali's grasp as she turned to go back.

As she turned, Eliana came face to face with a tall, dark figure that towered over her. He wore black from head to foot, and his face was covered in a reflective helmet.

Xucha himself.

Her limbs froze. She tried to move her legs backward but she couldn't. A faint humming sound came to her ears, and Eliana realized she was paralyzed by a stasis beam emanating from the shining orb hovering over his shoulder.

Citlali screamed and attacked the god with her bare hands. He drove a fist into her chest, and Citlali flew through the air and clipped the edge of the stone arch.

Xucha closed the distance between he and Eliana. She watched Citlali out of the corner of her eye. She struggled to her feet and stumbled around a tree. Xucha watched her go, and actually seemed to sigh when she was gone—his shoulder heaved up, then fell, and an exhaling sound came from beneath his helmet.

Finally, he turned to Eliana.

"I have been waiting for you," Xucha said in a voice that echoed and seemed slightly metallic. He spoke, remarkably, in English.

Who was this man, and how did he know how to speak her language?

"We have much to discuss," he said. "Starting with where your people found this stone. I want to know everything."

Eliana shifted her eyes. Her ring with the round

black carbonado glinted in the light. It was mounted in some kind of purplish-black object that fit in his hand.

Xucha lifted her paralyzed body, holding her lightly in front of him. Her head lolled back as he walked under the arch, turned left, and headed toward the pyramid. At the top of the steps, the black rift in the air was there again, just like the one she had gone through to get back here.

Was he taking her back to Earth? No. What she saw through the watery black veil of the arch was nothing like Earth.

Never in her life had Eliana regretted an impulse decision so completely. She had been a fool.

Amon, she thought. Paralyzed, she was unable to form the words on her lips.

How will I ever get back home now?

They stepped through the rift into inky black darkness.

30

NON

"It's not even a possibility," the CERN nuclear physicist said in French-accented English. "No one is using the Large Hadron Collider to power anything of the sort. No batteries, and certainly not this...thing."

The man turned his nose up at the stabilization arch that rose to the vaulted ceiling. He swallowed and looked back at Amon before continuing.

"Our particle accelerator is old now, though it had been updated recently. The LHC was designed for—and is still used for—particle physics *experiments*, not nuclear fission on a large scale, like you're suggesting. But you know this already." He shook his hand to emphasize this fact.

Amon smiled patiently. "Your facility underwent construction six months ago, a temporary closure—"

"Routine maintenance. The equipment is getting old. We needed to make repairs."

Amon pursed his lips and shook his head again. "What if your particle accelerator was modified to work both ways? Were you present during all of the maintenance? Did you personally oversee the work?"

The man huffed out an angry breath and gave Amon a hate-filled look, as if he'd sucker-punched his grandmother.

Amon had forgotten his name. Dr. Emil something or other. The skinny Swiss man pushed wire-frame glasses up on his sweaty nose. He'd been visibly pale and shaken when Amon had first began to question him about his work at CERN—a sensible reaction to the violence strewn around them in the lab, and the black wormhole that hung like an existential dilemma in the air.

The physicist spoke confidently on the subject of his work. Amon wanted to believe what this intelligent man said. But he had to be certain, absolutely certain. So he pressed him again. "Do me a favor and just look into it."

"Believe me." Scorn-laced chuckles broke the Swiss man's words. "I would know if anyone modified the Large Hadron Collider."

"What if someone diverted energy from the experiments over time? The particle accelerator here doesn't produce the energy we need for even a single translocation on demand. Like nuclear power plants of other kinds, we store energy continuously, and feed the power into the Translocator when it's needed. A lot of energy can be siphoned off—"

The Swiss man threw up his hands. "*Merde! Non.* No, sir, is not possible. Trust me, if the LHC was being used as a nuclear reactor or storing energy in any way, *I* would know."

"All right." Agent Moreno held up his hands. "Thank you for your cooperation, Dr. Dirac. I just received word from to my superiors—you and your team are booked on the first flight tomorrow. We've got hotel rooms for you."

"Finally," he said. "Good. Thank you, agent."

Moreno put his arm around Amon's shoulders and gently pried him away from the CERN physicist. Two other FBI agents led the scientists out of the Translocator lab and down the long hallway toward the exit. Taxis would take them away, and with any luck Dr. Emil Dirac would double-check his particle accelerator and assure them that Lucas had not commandeered it for nefarious translocation experiments.

Agent Moreno put his hand over his face and rubbed his temples. The man was holding it together, but barely. He and Amon had managed to fend off the local cops and keep them on ground level, far from the carnage in the lab. The FBI showed up an hour later and began tagging and bagging bodies.

"We knew it was a long shot," Agent Moreno said.

"I can't understand what else could be powering the Translocator that Lucas has been using if it's not the Large Hadron Collider. And where the hell is it? Where did you say they took you?"

"When we realized they weren't Interpol agents, one of them sucker punched me. They tied us up, blindfolded us, and shoved us in a helicopter. It was a short flight, but I don't know which direction."

Amon nodded.

"Somewhere in the Alps, then?"

"That's my guess."

"The plans he stole from Fisk Industries require a particle accelerator as a power source, and he hasn't had time to build one of his own—it took us five years to build this, and that was only because we had funding from the LTA."

"Hawkwood has money," Agent Moreno said. "They were fined 3 million for impersonating FBI agents last year and still reported a 20% profit in the same quarter. And their firm is still growing internationally, where they didn't get the bad press they got here."

"So either Lucas built a particle accelerator in secret, or..." He thought about the clever plastic containment unit Lucas had brought with him to steal the carbonado, and his gut twisted with sharp stabs of anxiety.

"Or what?" Agent Moreno asked.

"I don't know what," Amon snapped. "I have no idea how he's doing it."

A spark shot up into air, and several scientists clustered on the ramp near the base of the Translocator yelped and stepped back.

"I think you have more important things to worry about right now," Moreno said.

Amon nodded and hurried over to the Translocator. His scientists and engineers were gathered around the black wormhole suspended in the air near the sphere of rings. The whole team had been called in for this "emergency"—everyone had arrived within the hour, except Jeanine who was still missing.

"Hank," Amon said. The junior physicist turned toward him. "Where is Jeanine? Call her, would you? Her thesis at Stanford was on black holes. I want to get her opinion."

Amon was aware of Agent Moreno joining the group. The FBI agent stood in his blind spot, and all the scientists fidgeted and averted their eyes, nervous in his presence. Amon's neck itched but he forced himself not to look at Agent Moreno. He hadn't told the team about the mole yet, and didn't want to give away that particular intention.

Jake nodded and went toward the lounge to make the phone call.

"I've never seen anything like this," Audrey said.

"What was that spark?"

"Audrey poked it with a magnet," Christine said. She was another engineer, middle-aged and brunette with a heart-shaped face. "Bad reaction."

Audrey sheepishly held up a magnet duct-taped onto the end of a rubber-coated rod.

"Are you serious?" Amon said.

"No one else would touch it."

"For a good reason! No one touches it, hear me? No one."

He slowly circled the rift. The light bent and disappeared around a point the size of a softball. Or maybe it was more like a knot of air, bent around itself. The sphere of rings, seen through it, appeared as a mirror image, as if reflecting off water. But there was no surface of water there, just a dark spot in the air.

He didn't dare touch it.

"Magnets?" Amon asked again, bewildered.

"Everything else we tried was pulled into it. Wood, iron filings, Jake's ballpoint pen. But the magnets…"

"Is this how you test your meteorites?"

Audrey shrugged. "Subtlety is not my virtue. Better we know how it reacts to things before it becomes an emergency, right? Maybe if we find something that bends it we can at least try to make something to contain it. Or maybe you can just translocate that spot of air somewhere else."

Amon grunted. Jake returned a moment later.

"No answer from Jeanine," he said. "She must be sound asleep still."

"Wasn't her mother sick yesterday?" someone else asked.

"That's a morbid thought."

"Just saying. You never know. Give her the benefit of the doubt."

This time Amon met Moreno's eyes, briefly. Audrey frowned.

Wes McManis stomped down the hall, his cowboy boots striking the hard floor and echoing in the Translocator lab.

"Amon," Wes said. "Amon!"

Amon heaved a deep sigh.

"You should all hear this, I guess."

"What is it?" Amon asked.

"Listen for yourself." Wes held out his phone and tapped the screen. Reagan Gruber's nasally voice came through the speakers.

"What did I tell you? Just a matter of time. The police were at Fisk Industries for several hours last night, called in response to a suspected armed robbery. No suspects were found on site when they arrived. And what's there to steal? That's what I want to know. You can't just walk away with a Translocator. And that happened *just after* the lunar base reported—and I'm reading from the Lunar Terraform Alliance's own press release, published at 7am this morning—an 'unexpected dome depressurization event' shut down the whole facility."

The co-host chimed in like a chorus. "And we thought these kind of incidents were behind us."

"That's not all. According to a source of my own, the police only left Fisk Industries *after* the FBI showed up and claimed jurisdiction. You ask me, this is exactly what's wrong with the situation—it's only a matter of time before Amon Fisk and the LTA make a fatal error. Aren't there enough problems on Earth for these scientists to solve? Why do they have to go inventing new, astronomically expensive problems to solve on the moon? And why do they have to use *our* tax dollars to do it? Wouldn't it be better if the US pulled out of this arrangement and put your money to work protecting your real interests at home? What about the borders, through which immigrants are now flowing freely? What about the jobs those immigrants are taking from hard-working Americans? What about our country's rampant illegal voting problem? What about the global and increasing threat of radical Islamic terrorism?"

"Uh," Amon said. "Did he just conflate our work with radical Islamic terrorism?"

"What a nutjob," Audrey said.

"Hang on a second," Reagan Gruber said. "I'm getting reports of breaking news from my producer. What?" Reagan seemed momentarily distracted.

"Really? Yeah? Wow. Okay people, listen up. One of our long-term anonymous sources in military intelligence, someone I trust, is reporting that a cache of weapons—we don't know what kind, exactly—was stolen from an Army base outside of San Antonio, TX."

Agent Moreno swore and pulled out his cell phone.

"I repeat, this is breaking news. A military supply depot near San Antonio, TX, was robbed today. That's all we know right now, folks. We're going to go to a commercial break while we try to sort out the details. We'll be back in just a moment."

Amon swore. The scientists and engineers arrayed around him in a semi-circle watched him with frightened looks in their eyes. Jake swallowed and rubbed his neck. Audrey twisted a lock of hair in her fingers.

Amon stepped up to the wormhole. The hair on his neck stood on end. He held one hand out and passed it carefully above the rift by a foot. Then he did the same thing on either side, and below it, passing his hands around it on all sides but not touching it. He nodded once and turned back to his team.

"Forget trying to figure out what this thing does. It's too dangerous to leave in the open. As long as it's active, we can't use the Translocator, but neither can Lucas send anyone else in here with his. Build a secure barrier around the wormhole—a very thick, very secure barrier. If anyone else—or any*thing*—comes through it, I want them trapped in an indestructible prison that *we* control. If it were Superman we were after, this would be his kryptonite cage. Understood?"

The scientists and engineers were nodding enthusiastically now. That was within their grasp. Amon was skeptical about how well it would work, but at least they would have something to do with their hands. In the meantime, he could work with Agent Moreno to chase down their other leads.

"All right," Amon said. "Let's get to it!"

31

WHAT KIND OF TRAITOR

Rakulo launched to his feet from the crouching position he had been waiting in. The whistle came again, but weakly, breathless and unfinished. Was it Yeli, back early from their turn at perimeter lookout? He peered out through the bushy branches they had dragged over to help further disguise the cave's opening from the woods beyond.

The camouflage might work for Maatiaak's men and the others who hadn't spent much time at the cave, but Rakulo's warriors all knew exactly where to find it.

A figure limped through the forest in the distance, caught a foot on the uneven ground, and stumbled.

Rakulo was already moving. He was at Citlali's side in an instant, like a swift wind. He caught her as she fell, put his shoulder under her arm, and helped her toward the cave. Her chest heaved and he noticed a large purplish bruise on her exposed ribs beneath her tunic. She took low, shallow breaths.

"I tried—" she said.

"Shh," he said. "Wait until we're inside."

Quen and Thevanah helped Rakulo lay her down. Gehro coached her to breathe through her stomach, and her breathing calmed somewhat after she got the hang of it. Every time her chest expanded she hissed air out through her teeth in pain.

"She's got two broken ribs," Gehro explained, prodding her side gently with his fingers.

Reuben was there, hovering behind the group, rubbing his hands together, a worried expression deepening the crevices in his wrinkled forehead. White strands of hair on his head stood out wildly. He babbled something that Rakulo couldn't understand until he heard Eliana's name.

"Easy," Rakulo said. "Let me speak to Citlali first. Then, I'll do what I can to help Eliana. Yes, yes, I will help her. I promise. Please, old man. Give us a minute."

He hoped he sounded more reassuring than he felt. In truth, a nervous tightness had settled in around Rakulo's throat.

Reuben sighed heavily and sank down with his back against the wall. He began fidgeting with the device at his wrist again.

Rakulo turned back to Citlali. Her face was drawn and pale.

"I've never seen him in the daylight," she said. "Xucha took her, Rakulo. She's as good as dead."

"Did you see him kill her?" he asked.

Citlali shook her head. "He froze her. Knocked me away. Then carried her off. No one the dark god takes has ever come back. You know this."

"We've had many firsts lately, haven't we? Do not despair. If Xucha had wanted her dead, he would have killed her on the spot."

"Rakulo, no—"

"Yes," he said. "I am certain of it. Still, I'm glad you're safe, and that you came back to bring us this news."

Rakulo stood. Citlali let her head fall back. She groaned and clutched her side where the broken ribs gouged at torn muscles.

Rakulo gestured Quen over. "It's time we put an end to this infighting," he said. "I want you to search out Maatiaak. When you find him, tell him I want to parlay at—"

Quen's head snapped toward the woods. Rakulo strained his good and his bad ear. Something rustled in the woods outside the cave. Rakulo crept up to look out. Men bearing spears and staves and bows stepped out from behind tree trunks and into the daylight.

"I guess you can tell him yourself," Quen said.

Rakulo cursed. "They must have followed Citlali back."

Maatiaak stepped forward, holding Yeli before him, her hands bound roughly with coarse rope. He shoved her on the ground in front of him.

A shadow passed across the floor at the mouth of the cave. Rakulo glanced up. Someone had climbed the wall from behind and was now moving overhead.

"We've got you surrounded, Rakulo," Maatiaak called. "Your only sensible choice is to surrender."

Rakulo thought about taking the canoe into the river at the back of the cave and disappearing underground—but only briefly. He could no more turn his back on Maatiaak or leave his warriors to fight in his stead than he could change his height, or choose who his father was. Some things were up to fate. Others, the gods and men decided.

Yeli was a warrior. She held her head high even though she was bound and held hostage. Rakulo said nothing in response to Maatiaak's ultimatum.

"I thought you might respond that way," Maatiaak said as the moment of silence stretched out. "I brought someone else you know, in case you needed more convincing."

Another man stepped forward, pushing Rakulo's mother, Ixchel, before him. She was dirty and had scratches on her face. Her left eye was black and purple. Her wrists were caked with blood where she had strained against the restraints trying to escape.

She had not let them take her easily. Rakulo's throat tightened even more. A high-pitched ringing rose in his bad ear.

Ixchel stepped forward, took a ragged breath, and shouted "Don't do it, Raku! He's—"

Maatiaak swung the wooden end of his spear and struck Ixchel across the back. The old woman stumbled forward, caught her ankle in one of the depressions in the limestone floor, and pitched to the ground beside Yeli.

"You bastard!" Rakulo shouted. His voice whip-cracked out of the cave.

Why did he have to bring her into this? Rakulo thrust the branches of their feeble camouflage aside and stepped into the open. Maatiaak grabbed Ixchel's arm and hauled her back to her feet. Rakulo could see how it hurt her, and how her pain brought a vicious smile to Maatiaak's face.

"Enough," Rakulo said, more softly this time. He forced his concern from his face, and fought to keep his expression neutral. It would not serve him to show Maatiaak how afraid he was for his mother. Yeli was a warrior, but his mother was innocent in this fight.

"What do you want, Maatiaak?"

"That's *Chief* Maatiaak, you insolent brat. Lay down your weapons. Xucha demands many sacrifices to make up for our negligence during your time as chief. No one turns from the dark god and gets away with it. If you come with us, I will let your mother live."

He extended his spear so it was pointed at Ixchel's back, who stood with one hip cocked, favoring her sprained ankle. She shook her head slightly. Tears ran down her face.

"Xucha has no right to demand anything," Rakulo said. "He can't put you in charge, and he certainly can't force us to sacrifice more of our own people. That is our decision alone. Why do you help him? What has he ever done but bring more death to our people?"

"Xucha protects us! The gods give us this gift of bountiful land and sea. Is that not enough for you?"

"He keeps us trapped here, like penned animals! You've seen the Wall. How can this small patch of land be enough for you? Don't you want to see what's beyond the Wall? Don't you want to know what else is out there in the world?"

"Xucha has shown me what is beyond the Wall— nothing but devastation. He guards us from it. He keeps us safe."

"He lies to you, and you believe him," Rakulo said. "Does Xucha tell you where to build your hut, or where to fish? Does he tell you what to name your children? Your own daughter is in that cave right now with two broken ribs—an injury dealt by

Xucha himself. Is that how he thanks his loyal followers?"

Rakulo could tell that this was new information for Maatiaak. The man licked his lips and hesitated. He still cared deeply for his daughter.

But he seemed to come to a decision, and spat in Rakulo's direction.

"If that happened, then she did something to earn it. What kind of traitor fights her own people? Eh?"

Now it was Rakulo's turn to show Maatiaak a vicious smile. "What kind of traitor, indeed."

"We outnumber you three to one," Maatiaak said. "Your refusal will only end in bloodshed."

More needless death, Rakulo thought.

He wanted nothing more than to claw Maatiaak's shortsighted eyes out, but what would that solve? Citlali lay helpless in the cave. His warriors were good for any two men, but three to one? They were outnumbered. And Reuben, who had obviously never been in a real fight in his life, would be slaughtered. Rakulo knew how sharp those obsidian spear tips were, how easily they sank into soft flesh.

Rakulo took a deep breath and held up one finger. Then, he went inside and found Quen and Reuben.

"Go in the canoe through the river to the Well of Sacrifices. Make *certain* that the plant there has been destroyed."

Reuben's eyebrows scrunched down in confusion. Rakulo pointed at the canoe and mimed cutting the veins they found in the earthen wall at the Well of Sacrifices.

"Ahh," Reuben said, understanding shining in his eyes. "Yes. Yes!"

"I don't want to leave you," said Quen. "What if he's lying?"

"Of course he's lying. But you must do as I say. There's only one way out of this. Maatiaak simply advanced our timetable. Please, you have to trust me. Destroy that thing. Make certain of it."

Finally, Quen nodded. He and Reuben picked up the canoe and hurried to the low back of the cave, where it led down to the stalactites and the river below.

Relieved, Rakulo went back outside. Maatiaak still waited there with his hostages.

"Okay, Maatiaak," Rakulo said. "Here's our offer. If you let my mother and Yeli go, then I'll jump into the Well of Sacrifices myself. If the gods take me, then you get what you want anyway."

Maatiaak's smile spread into a grin. To Rakulo, he looked like one of the skulls carved on the stone buildings in *Uchben Na*.

"But I want a promise from you in return," Rakulo said. "If Xucha *fails* to take me, then you must lay down *your* weapons and agree to a truce. No more fighting amongst ourselves. Can I have your word on that? Or are you no longer good for your word?"

Maatiaak's grin turned into a snarl.

"Those are our terms. Accept them, or fight us here and now."

Maatiaak looked around at his men. They shifted their grips on their spears. A few nodded, encouraging him. Most simply waited for his decision.

They must think I'm a fool.

Rakulo's confidence waned rapidly. His knife grew heavy at his belt but he forced his hands to remain open and empty at his sides. Seven men would be on him as soon as he lifted the knife. He might get one or two, but not all of them.

Someone walked up to stand beside him—it was Citlali. She stood proudly, her shoulders thrown back, more fierce than ever. In the sunlight, the bruise on her ribs spread spiderlike across her side and chest. No human could possibly have caused that wound—only one with godly strength.

"Do as he says, father," Citlali said. "Or would you have your men kill your own daughter to satisfy your ego, too?"

Maatiaak looked away from his daughter. He couldn't meet her eyes. At last, he hefted his spear and used the sharpened tip to cut Ixchel and Yeli's bound hands free.

He shoved the women forward. They embraced Rakulo for a long minute.

"Let's go," Maatiaak said.

Rakulo gently separated himself from his mother's tight grip, and walked over to Maatiaak. Men bound Rakulo's hands tight enough to make him wince—but he did not cry out.

Like Citlali, Rakulo stood tall.

The others were led out of the cave and herded together, then directed into the woods away from the cave at spear point, surrounded by the older warriors loyal to Maatiaak.

All except Quen and Reuben.

32

STAR SHARDS

Eliana was carried through the dark rift and into a dim chamber filled with the smell of ozone. She couldn't move her limbs on her own, couldn't do more than take a small breath and hold it as they stepped into that strangely cold and heavy darkness.

Her body shivered involuntarily. She couldn't clutch herself to warm her skin. She still felt the hard armored arms of Xucha and that suit he wore holding her up. Only her eyeballs moved. He took two steps, and paused. Panic rose to her throat like a choking ball of ice.

Shapes and angles began to resolve themselves into objects in the dimness. Ambient light glowed in the semi-circular chamber from a few sources, but very faintly, a tenth of the light of a normal room at home.

Her eyes darted about. As she took in the strange

place—what she could see of it—her panic slowly subsided.

A green glow seeped under a doorway set into the far, flat wall. Another faint shine bled through the translucent skin of a mound on the floor to her left, at the edge of her peripheral vision. A chair? A couch?

Above that and across the wall, a bank of controls made a little alcove. The control unit reminded her of Amon's holodeck for the Translocator but...very different at the same time. It was not made of plastic or metal, but of a living plant-like material. Bulbous growths emerged from the wall seemingly at random. She slowly came to understand that these growths were controls—nodes and levers and dials and buttons, but of a kind that she had never seen on Earth.

This was not a cave, or even a prison cell. It looked more like a shop. A lab.

Again she thought of Amon. *Amon.*

Being angry at him seemed, now, like a frivolous luxury. Would she ever see him again? Would she ever have a chance to apologize?

From the right, a crystal of some kind set into the ceiling emitted light. It shone down on three round metallic orbs lined up on a shelf—the devices that Rakulo called "Xucha's demons," arranged like basketballs on display in the fancy office of an NBA executive...only, no, that wasn't it. Executive was the wrong description. Those things were weaponized robots. Lined up on a low shelf, the orbs were covered in oily black stains and scorch marks. Metal-handled instruments lay haphazardly among dirty and stained rags on a shelf below. One of the orbs had a huge gash in the top. A second orb was pocked with bullet-holes.

Several indentations, like spots for more of the machines, sat empty.

The final source of faint light came from the middle of the chamber, where the large carbonado that Xucha had taken from Lucas in the Translocator lab hung suspended in a beam of blue light.

Blue light sounds weird, but that was the best way she could think of to describe it, for the vertical beam seemed to both swallow the light and give it back in equal parts. The chamber was big enough that the area around the suspended meteorite was separated from the other equipment by thirty feet in every direction.

She absorbed this in the time it took for Xucha to cross the room and set her down, surprisingly gently, on the mound on the floor.

The mound reformed to her figure and seemed to move beneath her until it supported her whole body, like a beanbag chair—if a beanbag chair could move and seemed to *breathe*, expanding and contracting ever-so-slightly...

When the metallic orb hovering over Xucha's

shoulder floated away and set itself down on that shelf with the others, her temporary paralysis was released.

She shook her head reactively, hard enough that her neck twinged. Her whole body shuddered then, and her hands pressed down on the mound supporting her—its surface felt oily, but not wet, like the skin of some jungle reptile she had encountered in Mexico.

"Ugh." The involuntary noise of disgust spilled out through her lips. She immediately regretted it, clamped her mouth shut, and held still.

Xucha watched her, waiting.

Eliana wanted to get up and sprint away. Every fiber of her being shouted at her to run. But when she turned her now-free head to look around the room, there was no rift, only the chamber shaped like a circle cut in half, with a single door that had no handle. The round walls were made of the same material as everything else in here—like tiny inter-locking scales, slimy, but not wet, and undeniably alive.

She had the impression of being inside a massive lung. There were no windows. As she gazed around, the whole room seemed to expand and contract by millimeters—like the walls themselves were breath-ing. Xucha watched her, saying nothing. He cocked his head, and Eliana stared back at him.

"What do you want with me?" she said.

She swallowed and thought of her mentor, Renee, and of Amon. How would they act in this situation? She forced more steel into her voice.

"Tell me why you brought me here. I have a right to know."

The form of Xucha, clad head to toe in seamless black, turned from her and held his hands out toward the column of light in which the meteorite hung suspended. His gloved fingers flicked through the light and caused the rock to rotate slowly, dancing in suspension. The beam of transparent blue light glowed brighter and seemed to bend around his fingers where they came into contact.

"That doesn't belong to you," Eliana said. "You stole it."

What does that thing even do?

Xucha dropped his hands from the spinning rock and turned back to her. Eliana pushed off the mound, which hardened when she pressed into it, and stood.

"My people," Xucha said, "learned how to harness the power of star shards millions of years before your species crawled out of the ocean." His metallic voice resonated clearly in the chamber, coming not from him but from the walls themselves.

Eliana couldn't help a wary glance around the chamber. "Star shards?"

"A rough translation. That is what we call them." He gestured to the meteorite. "Forged by intense heat at the center of a star when it explodes, the shards are cast outward into the universe. My people have been using them to travel between galaxies for aeons. This is quite a small one."

Star shards...what Audrey and Amon would give to hear that!

It seemed clear by this point that Xucha didn't intend to hurt her—if he wanted her dead, he never would have brought her here. She had seen those men he killed in the Translocator lab, six mercenaries beheaded by a single sweep of the orb's lasers. That didn't mean she was safe, but it did mean she had some time to figure out what he wanted.

You have to keep him talking.

"Why did you bring me here?" she asked again.

"Because you have made an impression upon me," he said. "I've been watching you since you first arrived with this little shard." He held up the object where her ring was now embedded. It was made of the same material as the walls—it had been grown around the ring. He had not even bothered to remove the carbonado—the star shard—from the gold ring in which it was mounted. The object must allow him to control the shard somehow. Could Eliana use it?

I bet he never lets that thing out of his sight.

"I knew you couldn't have come here on your own. When you first arrived, I decided to wait and see what happened. My patience paid off. When you departed last time, I traced your path to that other machine. What do you call it?"

There was no sense in lying about it if he knew. "It's called a Translocator."

He nodded. "A primitive version of our starpaths." His hand reached out to touch the shard in the light beam once again, caressing it lightly.

"Is that so?" she said. She took a casual step closer to him. He turned away to look at the meteorite. Apparently, he thought she was no threat at all.

The metallic voice coming from the walls took on a musing tone. "It surprises me, how your species has evolved. You were always been highly susceptible to disease, weak of flesh, and short of life span. Evolution has not been kind to you. But instead of going extinct, like I suspected you would when I first encountered humanity, you seem to have thrived. To develop this kind of technology… How many of your species are living on that planet?"

Your species?

Eliana had suspected he wasn't human, but this confirmed it. So what was he? He had two legs and five fingers on his hands, didn't he? Was she wrong in thinking about him like a male? She had just assumed his gender, from the bipedal structure and flat chest and narrow hips…

Eliana looked at Xucha's hands more closely. Actually, his hands had four fingers, she saw now. Again, that sense of unnatural revulsion returned, like she'd seen a particularly creepy spider. She never had reason—nor opportunity—to look at Xucha's hands before. Her encounters with him had always been brief and violent, and usually at night. Did he keep this place dim because he was a nocturnal creature?

She had so many questions.

"Who are you?" Eliana asked. "How did you learn to speak my language?"

He tapped the side of his reflective black helmet. "My armor translates for me. Your fragile vessel would not be accustomed to the speech of my species."

That made some sense. It must be how he spoke the native language of Kakul, as well. Her anthropological curiosity kicked into high gear.

Where did Xucha come from? What kind of society did his people create? And what did he want with the Kakuli people?

Xucha interrupted her racing thoughts. In the blink of an eye, he'd darted across the room to loom over her, his night-black suit glimmering from the reflection of the many ambient lights in the chamber.

"As for your other question…"

He shoved her back onto the mound, which reformed to her body and caught her. Xucha gestured, and it spun her around to face the wall. At another gesture, the swirling patterns on the wall began to glow. Three tentacles, like the ones that Rakulo and Reuben had found and severed at the sinkhole, but thinner, lighter, with split ends, whipped out from the wall and wrapped themselves around her wrists, her ankles, her throat.

When she was tied down securely, two tiny, wire-thin tendrils slithered out of the wall and tickled her cheeks.

Their cold lengths plunged into both ears at once.

She gasped as visions began to gallop across her mind's eye.

33

HIT THE MARK

The wormhole still hung in the air, bending the light all the way around it. It felt wrong, hanging there in the middle of the platform, like a fracture in the fabric of reality. A blemish. A fault.

Yet there it was.

"I don't trust it," Amon said.

"Can we neutralize it?" Audrey asked.

"How?"

Audrey arced her hand forward and tossed another paperclip below the wormhole. The paperclip was drawn toward the fault at an unnatural upward angle. When the metallic object came into contact with the corner of bent light, a small blue spark sent the paperclip careening through the rings, to bounce off the wall some fifteen feet away.

"What did you throw at it the first time?" Amon asked. "To make those sparks?"

Audrey glanced at him. "A wrench."

Amon laughed. "Very subtle."

"I figure the…wormhole? The wormhole wasn't left here to destroy anything. If it was a bomb, it would have gone off already, right? So it must have been placed here simply to interfere with the Translocator. And, as such, there was a high probability that it had some kind of self-defense mechanism."

"Since we can't neutralize it…"

They both glanced back to the warehouse side of the Translocator lab, where the scientists were searching and sorting through the equipment at their disposal. Jeanine had finally arrived, claiming she had missed their phone calls because she had forgotten her phone at home while she visited her boyfriend. Amon wanted to believe her, but he saw how Agent Moreno watched her out of the corner of his eye when he thought she wasn't paying attention.

Jeanine took the lead in the organizational effort, however. The boxes earmarked for the lunar base contained all sorts of supplies suited to their purpose, as the research buildings and basic infrastructure of the base were still heavily under construction. Audrey and Amon had scoured the warehouse with the team, then come back in here to sort out what, precisely, to do.

"We could build a glass prison around it, like in a superhero movie," Amon said.

"You ever notice how the bad guys always escape from those?" Audrey said. "As soon as you call something inescapable—"

"Good thing we're fresh out of giant glass prisons. Here's what we do have: metal sheeting, plexiglass, a box of white t-shirts, nylon webbing, and four kinds of rope."

"Well it can't be sealed off completely," Audrey said. "No metal sheeting—it's too brittle. And I want to be able to see the thing."

"It has to be big enough, too, and strong enough to contain a threat in case the rift is opened again from the other side and the man in black comes back for seconds."

"Did I see steel rebar in the warehouse?" Audrey said.

"What are you thinking?"

The design came together quickly after that.

With the whole team's help, they managed to weld a six by six foot cage of two-inch steel rebar around the wormhole. It took the better part of a day to complete. Then they wrapped the cage in a net of heavy-duty nylon webbing, the kind used to tie down awkwardly-shaped gear on stormy trans-pacific voyages—sturdy stuff. They had enough mesh to secure it tightly around the cage on all sides.

Easy enough to cut a hole and reach an arm in— or pull someone out if you had to. But sturdy enough to contain a threat—or at least slow them down.

Amon was helping rivet the edges of the mesh to the metal deck of the platform when Agent Moreno came hurrying across the room, his phone clutched in his hand, followed closely by a frowning Wes McManis and the angular and thin Dr. Badeux, who had arrived that morning from France, and had been acting as a tireless buffer between the FBIs demands and the immediate problem of the wormhole Amon was trying to mitigate.

"Amon, the president is asking to speak to you," Agent Moreno said.

Amon's gut clenched. That was new. He glanced at Dr. Badeux, who shrugged.

"President Roscoe?" Amon said, stupidly.

Agent Moreno thrust the phone into Amon's hand. He took it and raised it to his ear.

"Amon Fisk, is that you?" The man's southern accent was unmistakable. It was the president himself.

"Hello, Mr. President," Amon said, after a drawn out pause. He rubbed his one sweaty palm against the seam of a pants pocket several times, and then pulled at his collar even though it was loose—his old nervous tics coming back to him.

"I'm glad we met at that Christmas gala in DC two years ago, because I'm afraid I have the unfortunate responsibility of informing you that your

Translocator has become an issue of national security. The NSA are now overseeing this matter on my behalf."

"Yes, sir," Amon said. What else could he say?

"You're still in charge of the machine, because we need you."

It seemed to Amon that a silent *for now* was implied in the President's orders.

"Yes, sir," Amon said.

"You should know that the NSA has secured the area under my direct orders."

Amon winced. "Pardon me for asking, sir, but don't you think that will just draw needless attention? What if the media gets wind of it?"

"They already know, Amon. The news broke an hour ago."

Amon forced himself not to glance at the people gathered around him, staring with rapt attention. Was it the loudmouth, Wes, breaking under the same business pressures to which Lucas had been susceptible? Or was it Jeanine? She had arrived later than everyone else had; did she really stay at her boyfriend's house, or did she leak the information to a journalist?

"I've already talked to authorities in the city of Austin. They're preparing for a city-wide evacuation, if the need arises. I'll take care of all that. What I need to know right now is this. Are you fully committed to the safety of this country, Mr. Fisk?"

Amon swallowed. "Yes, sir."

"And can you contain it?"

"Honestly, sir? I don't know. I've never seen anything like this before." Amon didn't know what the president had been told—or who was listening who couldn't be trusted—so he didn't go into detail. "But I'll try."

"You do that. You have every possible resource at your disposal. Just ask Agent Moreno. He knows how to contact me."

"Thank you, sir."

The call ended. He thought he heard the president harrumph, but that could have been the sound of a finger brushing against the receiver.

Amon looked between the FBI agent and Wes, who frowned. "Did you hear all of that?" Amon asked.

"There's something else," Agent Moreno said. "Two more places were raided—a firearms manufacturer in Boise, Idaho, and a cache of supplies bound for the middle east at MacDill Air Force Base in Tampa."

"Damn," Amon said. "Lucas is always a step ahead of us."

"What's his game plan?"

"I don't know, but trust me, he has something specific in mind. He's not the type of person to do anything randomly."

Jeanine and Audrey bolted the last rivet into the floor.

"We're done here, for now. I need to walk and think for a minute. Enzo, can you fill me in on what's happening at the lunar base?"

Dr. Badeux pushed his square glasses up on his nose, clasped his hands behind his back, and fell into step beside Amon as he strode from the room. Agent Moreno and Wes trailed behind them.

"Wes?" Amon said, turning back for a second. "Would you mind cataloging the parts we used for the cage?"

"Aw, come on now."

"It's important. I want to make sure we keep track of everything and pay the LTA back later, in full." Amon stepped closer to Wes and lowered his voice. "Besides, I need someone to keep an eye on them."

Wes's nostrils flared, but he nodded reluctantly and hung back. Amon didn't really need anyone to babysit his scientists and engineers, but he wanted Wes to think he was needed—and get him out of earshot.

Amon, Agent Moreno, and Dr. Enzo Badeux walked down the long hall.

As the elevator carried them up, Amon said, "I trust both of you. You can't be the mole, Agent Moreno, because you're trying to find and stop the mole. And it can't be you, Enzo, because you didn't know the guard rotation or where in the building Audrey's lab was, since your office is in D.C. now. But as for the rest… Does the press know about the wormhole?" Amon said.

"Thankfully, they don't," Dr. Badeux said.

"That Reagan Gruber knows something is up," Agent Moreno said. "I had my men keeping an eye on his online updates. He posted about the police showing up at Fisk Industries. He has a lot of wild theories, but none of them have quite hit the mark yet."

"That's something, at least."

The elevator doors opened on the lobby.

The level of activity stunned Amon. He had expected an empty lobby. Instead, FBI agents crowded around mobile communication stations and talked quietly amongst themselves. They glanced at the trio of men as they arrived, but didn't stop to greet them.

Sunlight streamed in through the jauntily slanted glass wall, and Amon felt himself sway unsteadily. He blinked his heavy eyes. He needed sleep, but he couldn't afford to sleep yet. Several unmarked white vans were parked in the otherwise empty lot visible across the quad. He had no doubt that similar vehicles surrounded the entire campus. That would be the NSA people.

Which meant Fisk Industries was now on lockdown.

Except for holidays, Fisk Industries had been shut down only once before. This time, Eliana had gone through voluntarily. Though how she had gone was unsettling, it was not an accident. Amon wasn't in the habit of lying to himself in the face of the facts: he had lost her again. Not lost her through a technical accident, not even lost her in the confrontation with that that black-armored god-pretender.

No, Amon had lost his wife several weeks ago, when he refused to help her return to Kakul and search for archaeological clues to continue her research in the one place she needed to go. He might as well have pushed her through that black rift, that wormhole, with his own two hands.

God, what a fool I was. Amon clutched his temples and covered his tired eyes with one hand.

"You should rest," Enzo said. "Is there a place you can sleep?"

"Back in the Translocator lab, in the lounge."

"It's not safe," Agent Moreno said. "Somewhere else. I'll post men to guard you while you sleep. Just for a little while."

Amon nodded. Moreno was right. He trudged to his office at the back of the first floor.

Amon thought he could keep Eliana safe by keeping her away. In the red morning light streaming in through the glass windows, it seemed so painfully obvious that he had been guarding the wrong thing—hedging against his own desires and fears, rather than thinking of what Eliana wanted and needed. She must have felt like she had no choice but to take the opportunity to get back to Kakul when it presented itself. If Amon wouldn't let her use the Translocator, what other choice did she have?

He should have tried harder to have more empathy with her situation, to see past his own misgivings. She had always said he could be inconsiderate about other people's feelings when he was focused on a project.

Still, Amon felt that if he could just talk to her, maybe he could explain…

Amon's thoughts ran over and over on this loop as he stumbled into his office. He kicked his shoes off and fell onto the leather couch under the framed hi-definition photographs of the historic rocket launches that had inspired his passion for most of his life. That led to thoughts of the wormhole, that bizarre corner of light hanging suspended in the air four floors below him, looming like a loose screw ready to cause the long-anticipated explosion of this metaphorical rocket launch.

Stern, muffled words came through the door as Agent Moreno gave orders to the FBI agents stationed outside.

Amon tossed and turned until a restless, fear-haunted sleep took him.

34

THE WAY OF THINGS

Maatiaak's men surrounded Rakulo. Together, they passed under the stone arch. Rakulo saw the ripped and scattered foliage and the exposed carvings that they used to hide. This must have been where Eliana had come to look at the stones.

She had found something. Or, rather, Xucha had found her.

One problem at a time.

He would only be able to help her if he got Maatiaak to agree to a truce. His one saving grace was that if Xucha was occupied with Eliana, there was a good chance he wouldn't interfere with what was about to happen.

Maatiaak led the group of warriors, old and young, across the overgrown stone plaza of *Uchben Na*. The city had not aged well. Facades had chipped, steps had crumbled, statues had fallen over and broken into pieces. Weeds and tree roots grew between the paving stones. A row of grinning skulls carved across the roofline of a tired old temple to Rakulo's left had somehow survived the wreckage of time. Black eyeholes stared out over the group as they passed, vacant and hungry—a reminder of what the gods desired.

Blood. Flesh. Death.

This Rakulo had known since he was a child. It was an unavoidable fact of life. No wonder Maatiaak had laughed at him when he suggested throwing himself into the Well of Sacrifices. No one had ever made that leap and survived, not in his lifetime, not in the lifetime of his father, not in the lifetime of his grandfather's father.

Citlali walked uneasily at his side, wincing and drawing painful breath through her teeth in pain. Occasionally, if she began to lag behind, one of Maatiaak's men would push her gently forward. They were not mean about it, merely firm. Rakulo would have reached out to support her as she walked, but his hands remained bound. He leaned close and let her put her hand on his shoulder to steady herself. Maatiaak looked like he might object, but swallowed his words.

Maatiaak tried to look nonchalant, but Rakulo saw how he kept Citlali in his line of sight, and set the pace at an easy walk. It was good he still cared for his daughter, or they might be in a worse situation than they already were.

They found the path of white stone on the far side of the plaza, and began to follow it into the forest. After several long minutes of walking, the path opened up into a clearing, in the center of which lay the sinkhole his people called the Well of Sacrifices. A flat outcropping of stone on the near side jutted over the edge of the opening. Sacrifices were thrown from there, so they had a clear fall into the green-tinted waters below.

"Here we are," Maatiaak said. He untied Rakulo's restraints and pushed him out onto the jutting stone. "Time to see what you're made of, boy."

Rakulo glanced down at the water a hundred feet below, then around him at the jungle. Everything was vivid and bright. It was bizarre to be here in the daylight, as the sacrifices were usually cast into the water under the light of the full moons. In the daytime, the sinkhole seemed…innocuous. Exposed. Like how shadows and creaking noises might frighten a child at night, and in the morning light turn out to be nothing more than a tree branch knocking against the side of a hut. In the daylight, the Well of Sacrifices was not a holy place filled with death, but a clearing in the forest where a sinkhole filled with rainwater fed an underground river that couldn't be seen from this vantage point. When the child sees the tree branch in the morning light, he laughs at his own fear from the night before. So Rakulo felt his hysteria bubbling up now, as he looked around him.

Peering over the edge into the water, he spotted a canoe, just visible at the near edge. He suppressed a sigh of relief. Reuben and Quen were making their way along the wall to the river fork to where the hungry plant roots waited to devour Rakulo, body and soul. He hoped they managed to disable it in time.

Maatiaak approached to gaze over the side. Rakulo must not let him see Reuben and Quen, lest he get suspicious. He had to believe that what was about to happen was the god's choice, not Rakulo's doing, or the result of Quen and Reuben's blades.

Rakulo put his body in front of Maatiaak. "Xucha wants us all dead, you know. He doesn't care for our lives. We only exist to feed the gods. They are always thirsty, and it is only the blood of our people that quenches their thirst. Is that how you would have our people live for the rest of time? Beholden to a dark master? A cup from which the night god drinks endlessly, for eternity?"

"It is the way of things, Rakulo. You cannot change what has been for a thousand years. That is how our people continue to thrive."

"Thrive? We've been killing our own children for a thousand years. How many huts lie empty in the village? Dozens. When was the last time a new hut was built? Years ago. People don't want to have children because they're afraid Xucha will punish them and strike down their children, like what happened to my little brother. Does that seem like thriving to you? Our people are not thriving, they're dying."

"You're as short-sighted as your father was. If it wasn't for *my* interference, Xucha would have punished our people after you became Chief!"

Rakulo's blood chilled instantly. He had thought that Xucha's power had weakened after his father's body had been sacrificed. He had believed that his resistance was working, that their willingness to stand together had given Xucha pause. If they didn't sacrifice their own, then the sacrifices must end.

How naive he had been. This was the truth that Ixchel had unwittingly discovered after Ekel's disappearance—while Rakulo was training his young warriors and scouring the wall looking for a way out of this trap, and carving canoes, and tying ropes, Maatiaak had been running interference.

Maatiaak laughed. "Did you really think that Xucha would just sit back and let you *disobey him?* He is a powerful GOD! No, you foolish boy. *I* convinced him to wait. *I* offered my own life to appease him— but he didn't want it. He was patient. I took him my chickens and my fish. When he tired of those, I captured two of the old hermits hiding out in the woods. Did you ever wonder why so many men left Kakul to live in the caves? Cowards, all of them. I caught them, and offered their lives, as unwilling as they were—except for Gehro. He was too sneaky to be caught. So then I convinced old Ekel to sacrifice himself for the good of the village, to die a noble death and go to join his wife in the afterlife."

Rakulo shook his head when Maatiaak began talking. And then he went still. His face burned with shame. *How could I have been so foolish?*

Maatiaak stepped around him and glanced down into the water. Rakulo followed his gaze—the green glow seemed to have disappeared. But it was hard to see in the daylight, and from so far up. The canoe was nowhere in sight.

Either they had done it, or they had given up. There was only one way to be certain. Rakulo had to jump now.

But first he had to make sure Maatiaak would hold up his end of the bargain.

"We had a deal, Maatiaak."

"How dare you question me?" Maatiaak said. "Do you think Xucha would have trusted me if I didn't keep my word? Do you think these men would trust me?"

The others had gathered around—sixteen young men and women loyal to Rakulo, plus his mother, surrounded by forty older men his father's age loyal to Maatiaak.

"I've kept our people safe despite your foolishness, Rakulo. But go ahead. Jump in and see what the gods decide. They will decide to devour you, just like they devoured those hermits I threw into the Well. Just like they devoured Ekel when he jumped." Maatiaak leaned close and lowered his voice so that only Rakulo could hear him whisper. "Just like the gods will take your mother after you're gone. Gladly."

Rakulo stared at Maatiaak until the man backed up and crossed his arms, waiting. Then he met the eyes of his mother, of Citlali and Yeli, and each of the warriors in turn—the ones loyal to him, and the ones loyal to Maatiaak now, and to his father, formerly. They were good men and women. This was not their fault. It was the fault of a system of sacrifice that had forced them into a position where they were obligated to kill their own people, unless they wanted to be killed themselves.

That was no way to live. But what they were about to see would change everything.

"This is not goodbye," he said.

His mother gasped and raised her hand to cover her mouth. Citlali clenched her jaw and nodded, lowering her center of gravity and adjusting her feet in case there was a fight. Yeli did the same, tensing automatically.

All eyes were on Rakulo. He turned, and stepped off the edge.

35

SUCH A FRAGILE VESSEL

Aeons of alien culture flashed before her eyes.

The chamber, the mound, the tentacled interface that was somehow injecting these visions directly into her cerebral cortex, came back into focus again. Eliana's chest heaved. She pulled gasping lungfuls of ozone-scented air as sweat poured down her body.

"What is this?" she said. "Make it stop. Please."

"Such a fragile vessel," Xucha said. "But the worst is nearly over, child."

"Please, no. Oh, god. No, no, please."

The tiny tendrils stiffened in her ear, and once again, Eliana's spine arched, her muscles knotted, and the next vision slammed into her like a truck, taking her breath away—consuming her mind and pushing out all other senses.

In the space of a single breath, Eliana witnessed the evolution of a species of intelligent, four-fingered bipedal animals. The first two walked out of the ocean countless billions of years ago, on a planet much like her Earth, and took a similar path to her species' own. Small relative to the predators of their home world, they were forced to rely on their brains and tools they created to survive. They traveled over long distances to track down swift game. They explored the farthest reaches of their planet, pushing themselves to find better foraging spots that would support their growing tribes.

This traveling and foraging eventually led to farming, when a knowledge gathered over generations finally hit a breaking point. After that—again, much like her own people—a long settling down period came, a period of incredible growth. The next leap forward came with a kind of industrial technology that helped them break the bonds of their farming communities. Their population expanded rapidly, until they took over their world.

It took longer—much longer—for these People to evolve than it took humanity, because they lived longer. With longer memories, traditions were easier to enforce, and change came slower. They had a central spine like humans, but were cold-blooded. Part of their longevity was owed to their reptilian heritage. They developed a carapace to protect themselves from the violent moods of their planet's climate, and from the dangers of war. They, too, fought their way to dominance by killing off the cousins of their own species. When they ran out of cousins to kill, they turned to the large predators on their planet, until they were rendered extinct.

Eliana blinked.

Like humanity, minute variations among their species had far-reaching implications throughout the social hierarchy of their culture. Their mastery of technology developed, was wiped out by a natural disaster, and developed again. She witnessed the People's journey off world to explore among the stars in their breathing generation ships. Their lifespans stretched out again as they introduced stasis pods to help them travel farther, this time by determined and slow manipulation of their genetics. As a result, their birth rate decreased. The sadness this caused among the People went deep, but it was not enough to overcome their hunger for exploration.

Eliana inhaled.

A great civil war rent their relatively peaceful intergalactic society of star explorers asunder. Once united by the desire to conquer space, they were now fighting for control over it, much like they had vied for dominance against their cousins on their home planet. At the same time, the star voyagers continued to make great discoveries. They found the star shards, and learned how to make more of them using the stars as a sort of galactic furnace. And then, perhaps by accident, someone discovered the rift travel technology and its terrible power.

Eliana exhaled.

She absorbed the story with a heavy heart, tears now coursing down her cheeks, as the civil war tore their home planet apart. It had become easier to make war than peace, easier to fight than find common ground among opposition parties. The only outcome of an all-consuming war was total annihilation. The planet that gave the People life was finally destroyed by the People themselves. Great generation ships carrying the survivors drifted off into the galaxy in a dozen different directions.

Eliana blinked.

The visions faded and the dim chamber came back. The tendrils snaked away from her ears, wrists, and ankles. Eliana was left physically exhausted and breathing hard on the mound, which cushioned her body and seemed to rise and fall in time with her heaving chest, as if it was conscious of her breathing patterns.

Disgusted by the thought, she rolled off the mound and came to her feet as Xucha turned and began to walk slowly away, his head hanging. He must have been standing over her the whole time she had been plugged into that…that…brain thing. Had he experienced the visions with her? Certainly he had directed them. He had *wanted* her to see. Had the thoughts of his people's long history and eventual self-destruction put him in a despondent mood?

She reached out a hand to touch his armored

shoulder. Xucha spun around. She raised her fingers slowly to his helmet, that smooth, sleek reflective mask that sometimes showed nothing, and other times a hissing snake. Was that his true form? When her hands were on the sides of the helmet, she thought he might slap her hands away. He raised his own hands, but slowly, and helped Eliana turn the helmet slightly to the left so it unlatched.

He let her lift it off his head.

Eliana let the helmet fall to her side, held by one hand, and walked slowly around until her back was to the meteorite suspended in the beam of blue light. The glow from the blue beam illuminated Xucha's face.

It was an ancient face, but not unkind. Deep, almond-colored eyes flecked with gold, like huge orbs, took up most of the face. The nose was only slightly raised from the skull, with a single slit where the nostrils would be in a human. The lips were made of tiny, hard scales, but formed a full half-moon mouth. The rest of the face was covered with small feathers, a thin band of forehead above the eyes, and then longer feathers that stretched back into a full feathery mane of…hair?

Eliana raised her hand and brushed the feathers lightly. They bristled, Xucha shivered, and the feathers raised up into a beautiful turquoise and orange fan that extended back from the head.

"Your feathers are beautiful," Eliana said.

The bird-lizard creature inclined its head.

"Is Xucha your real name?" Eliana asked.

He shook his head, and his mouth did not move when he next spoke. The big eyes seemed to go into a distant focus, and the voice came from the walls of the chamber like it had before, the source unclear.

"No. My name is Remethiakara Aba Carna Tualina."

"That's a beautiful name. It sounds almost feminine. Do males and females both have the crown of feathers?"

Xucha nodded. "Both do. Technically, in your terms, I am a male. But distinctions between the sexes of my species became unimportant millennia ago. Our children are hatched, not born, and both share in the child-rearing duties."

"Oh," Eliana said. "We share child-rearing duties as well."

The alien grimaced and shook his head. Eliana nearly laughed at how human the gesture seemed.

"Did that happen when the birthrate slowed?" she asked.

"It has always been…but yes, the birthrate slowed when we began to modify our genes. Since we began to elongate our lifespans to explore the stars more fully, it has become nearly impossible for one of my people to fertilize an egg without the aid of our science."

Eliana felt within herself a deep well of empathy

for this bird-lizard creature. She now understood the tragedy it had been living with. Eliana saw no signs of others here. He was one of a dying species, and he was all alone. Is this what Xucha—Remethiakara—wanted Eliana to feel? Was that why it showed her his history? Or had he just wanted to share it with someone?

Eventually, her training overcame her personal feelings. She may never get a chance to ask these questions again. She must ask them now.

"But why are you here? And how did the Kakuli people get here?"

"I will show you." Remethiakara turned and gestured back to the mound where Eliana had been secured by the tentacles just a few minutes before.

Eliana forced a smile onto her face and nodded. The alien turned his back to her, walking toward the mound and gesturing with his fingers so that the tentacles emerged again from the wall. The mound dimpled and bent in the middle like a recliner.

Instead of following him or sinking into the seat, Eliana seized the opportunity when his back was turned to cross to the center of the room, toward the glowing beam of blue light where the star shard was suspended. Eliana clenched her teeth and thrust her hand out, into the light, to grab the rock—

She hissed when the light singed her hand. Puffy white welts stood up on her fingers immediately.

Eliana looked down. The black helmet was still

seized in one hand. She had seen the alien's gloved fingers go into the light—the helmet was made of the same material.

Eliana hauled back on the helmet—and was stopped by Xucha's hand where he grabbed the helmet.

She spit into his big brown and yellow eyes. He released the helmet with a snake-like hiss that made Eliana wince. The noise was high and piercing. But she was already swinging the helmet around in a full arc. The light of the beam flared up where the helmet came into contact with it. It struck the star shard and knocked it to the floor on the other side. The beam of light went out.

When Eliana turned back, Remethiakara loomed over her, his half-moon mouth open and baring two rows of sharpened, tearing teeth. The hissing sound came louder now. Eliana dropped the helmet, clutched her ears, and fell to her knees.

36

ANONYMOUS TIPSTER

A text message alert on his phone startled Amon off the couch. He checked the phone in a frantic half-sleep, his heart pounding.

"Amon, this is Lakshmi," the message read. "Eliana gave me your number for emergencies. She's not answering my messages or calls. Is everything okay?"

Amon swallowed and closed the message as he fought down a wave of guilt. Better not to respond than try to explain. He left his office and greeted the FBI agents outside his room with an inhospitable grunt.

He found Audrey in her own lab on the third floor, and by that time he was almost fully awake. The agents followed him closely. Normally he would have objected to their presence, but having them around reassured him now. They began to post up outside the door of Audrey's lab when he went in, but Amon beckoned them inside with him.

The floor of the lab had been swept clear of debris. The marks made by the bullet holes were still visible. Amon's new bodyguards glanced at them, raised their eyebrows, but didn't ask any questions.

"Audrey, do you have any coffee?"

"Instant coffee in that cabinet." Audrey pointed, without looking, over her shoulder.

Amon heated water in an electric kettle and shoveled three heaping scoops of instant coffee grounds into a battered mug. The bodyguards declined coffee and took up stations on opposite sides of the room. When the water boiled a minute later, Amon poured it over the brown powder and took the steaming mug with him to peek over Audrey's shoulder. She was working with several soil samples and other fragments made of bone, clay, and wood, split out into clearly labeled groups—A2, B2, C2, and D2.

"What are you working on?" Amon asked.

"Samples that Eliana left here for me from her trip to Mexico. This is the first chance I've had to carbon-date this new set."

"Aren't you worried about the wormhole?"

"Of course I am. Why do you think I'm working?"

Amon nodded. He understood the desire to cover over the fear with work. If he hadn't needed sleep so badly, he'd be doing the same thing.

"Anything interesting?"

"I'm not sure what she's looking for, to be honest. These ones date to the same time period as the previous set of samples she gave me—they're from 800 AD to 1500 AD."

"That's the Late Classic Maya era that she studied for her master's degree. Do you think she found something? Is that why she's having you date the samples?"

"She must have. She said she wanted me to be discreet."

Amon sighed. "One of the women that's been working with her in Mexico texted me while I was sleeping."

Audrey winced. "I bet she's worried about Eliana."

His phone buzzed again. This time the message read, "Tell Eliana that we found another ruin. Have her call me."

Amon put the phone back in his pocket. "I know. I am, too. But I can't risk telling them much at this point."

One of the FBI agents touched his ear and spoke softly into the cuff of his suit jacket. "Mr. Fisk? Agent Moreno is asking for you."

"Okay," Amon said. "Tell him I'll be down to the lobby in a minute."

"He says it's urgent, sir."

"Everything is urgent right now," Amon

muttered, but he said goodbye to Audrey and followed the two men out the lab and into the elevator.

As the elevator lowered, a worry that something had happened to the wormhole or the Translocator built up in his mind. But that wasn't it, because Agent Moreno's voice echoed from the Translocator lab as Amon picked up his pace down the long hall. His voice was raised, and he was definitely arguing with someone with a Texan accent. He walked past the armed guards and FBI agents at the entrance, who were all listening surreptitiously.

Amon crossed the Translocator lab. The scientists were still there, but work had obviously slowed now that the cage was built around the wormhole. They worked on laptops and were digging through detailed graphs on the holodeck, but had paused to watch Wes and the FBI agents argue.

"You have no right to do this!" Wes McManis said as an FBI agent cuffed his hands behind his back in the doorway that led to the warehouse side.

"I have every right."

"I want my lawyer."

"What's going on?" Amon demanded, walking up to them. Wes McManis, red-faced and fuming, looked down when Amon approached.

"We subpoenaed phone and email records for your employees, and found that Wes McManis has been sending 'anonymous tips' to Reagan Gruber."

"That ain't illegal!" Wes said. "And you got no right to go through my emails."

"The judge who issued the warrant says otherwise," Agent Moreno said.

"Wes, is this true?" Amon said.

Wes lifted his chin. "Controversy makes good press. It's good for business."

No wonder Wes was always the first to hear when Reagan Gruber began to spout off at the mouth.

"If that jerk had his way, The Auriga Project would have been shut down years ago!" Amon said.

"He doesn't have that kind of power," Wes sneered, his tone dripping with condescension. "But the Fisk Industries name on the radio sells the rest of our products. Sales have been up since I took over. I'm just trying to do my job, Amon."

Amon crossed his arms. "Were you feeding Lucas information, too?"

"No," Wes said, shaking his head. "You have to believe me, Amon, I would never."

"We'll see about that," Agent Moreno said. "Take him upstairs and keep a close eye on him."

The FBI agents hauled the unwilling Wes McManis down the long hall. He cussed at the agents all the way to the elevator.

"We don't have enough evidence to charge him with anything yet," Agent Moreno said. "But we can hold him for forty-eight hours."

"How did you figure out it was him?" Amon asked.

"I already had people looking through phone and email records of your employees, searching for the mole. It could have been anyone. After Wes found that news report on Reagan Gruber's radio show, it gave me the idea to check him out a bit more—they have a phone number for anonymous tips listed on their website. Call records show that Wes has contacted that number several times in the last few weeks."

"Wow," Amon said. "But…you know, he could be telling the truth. And Gruber is only right half the time when he's talking about Fisk Industries and the Translocator. Wes could easily have been feeding him misinformation."

"We'll get to the bottom of it. There could be another mole. I still don't know how Lucas found the information. None of the numbers on Wes's phone records point back to Lucas, at least that we can tell."

Startled gasps from the scientists gathered at the holodeck drew Amon's attention. He and Agent Moreno ran across the room.

"The wormhole, it's gone," Jeanine said.

"What did you do?"

"Nothing. I—we didn't do anything. We were just measuring the magnetic field, and then it was gone."

He didn't understand it, but Amon wasn't one to

disregard a lucky break. "Spin it up. If the test runs pass muster, first we have to send some extra supplies to the lunar base, and then I'm going after Eliana."

"I'm going with you," Agent Moreno said. "You don't have any field training."

"I have more than you think," Amon said.

A beeping sound came from the holodeck.

"Incoming coordinates!" Jeanine shouted.

Amon and Agent Moreno exchanged glances. The scientists closed their laptops and moved away from the Translocator platform, where the now-empty cage they'd constructed stood on the platform among the sphere of still rings.

Agent Moreno drew his gun and adjusted his grip as Amon approached the holodeck.

37

THE WELL AND THE WALL

Rakulo plummeted through the air like a rock.

Out of the corner of his eye, he saw the canoe, hidden under the hanging vines. Reuben and Quen stared with expressions of dismay as he fell.

Green ichor tinted the normally purple water rising to meet him. He pulled in a deep gulp of air and held it.

His feet hit the surface. It parted and cold water rushed over his body. Rakulo kicked both legs, and a moment later his head broke the surface. He expelled his held breath and pulled in air. His hands parted the green ichor on the surface of the water.

But it was not the glowing green of a sacrifice being accepted by the gods. It was the sickly green ichor from a dozen severed veins, dripping where they had been ripped from the earthen wall and chopped up—dozens of lengths. They had found more after all.

The bulbous plant beneath Rakulo reached out its roots weakly. It burned where the ends brushed against his legs. He kicked away, windmilling his arms backward, and bumped into something hard. Quen and Reuben pulled him into the canoe.

He looked down at his legs. Where the roots had brushed him, white welts marred his brown skin like burns. But he was alive, and in one piece.

The tentacles of the bulbous plant went limp under the water again.

Rakulo grinned at Quen and Reuben, then glanced up. Maatiaak was staring down over the rim of the sinkhole.

"The gods decided not to take me today, Maatiaak!" Rakulo shouted, and laughed. He couldn't help himself. The brush with death had made him giddy, so that even the burning, searing sensation on his legs could not foul his reaction. It felt like his smile filled his whole face.

"Xucha!" Maatiaak cried, spinning around and screaming at the forest. "Xucha! Take this traitor!"

But the god did not come. Rakulo didn't know why, but it was a stroke of luck he was glad to have. It reinforced his point that Xucha was not in control.

Ixchel was crying now. Tears streamed down her cheeks. "Rakulo! My brave son! My only son!"

The other warriors, old and young alike, peered

down over the lip of the sinkhole to see Rakulo in the canoe with Reuben and Quen. Seeing he was alive, and well, and laughing, they glanced around, looking for the black-clad figure in the forest, and straining their ears for the insect-like buzzing sound that usually announced his presence. When they found none of these things, they began talking amongst themselves. Several lowered their spears. Dozens turned to Maatiaak and squinted, their distrust of him evident.

"We had a deal, Maatiaak," Rakulo shouted.

The group stepped back from the lip, and Rakulo heard arguing, but could no longer see them. He searched for a sturdy vine he could climb to get back up. It would take too long to go around.

Suddenly, Maatiaak and Citlali appeared again. They were arguing. Maatiaak struck out at Citlali, but she was faster than her father and ducked under his hand, which caused Maatiaak to spin. At the same time, Yeli jumped forward and shoved the old man over the edge. Everyone paused while he fell. He toppled head over heels through the air and hit the water with a painful slapping sound, then came up spluttering and shouting a moment later.

"See!" Rakulo said. "The gods are gone. We have banished them from the water."

Maatiaak's warriors stepped forward, but Citlali and Yeli had recovered and stood back to back with their spears raised threateningly.

"Lower your weapons!" Citlali said. "We had an agreement. You gave Rakulo your word!"

Although they were outnumbered, Maatiaak's men were apparently bewildered enough by Rakulo's ability to disable the Well of Sacrifices that after a tense moment, one man set his weapons down, and then another, until the situation had been defused. Citlali gathered the spears and blades and bows.

These people didn't really want to hurt their kinsmen. They were just doing what they thought was right—and that illusion had been shattered by Rakulo.

"Oh!" Reuben said at his side, a stream of unintelligible words pouring from his mouth. He grinned and pointed at the bracelet on his wrist. The dot that had been red before was now green. Reuben pointed up to the surface of the Well of Sacrifices. Rakulo took that to mean that he wanted to go up.

One of Maatiaak's men had a long rope with him. Citlali tied it to the trunk of a nearby tree and threw the other end down. With a boost from Quen and the help of several people at the top, they hauled Rakulo up first, then Reuben. Quen came last and took a dozen people to pull up.

Maatiaak remained treading water nearby. He swam frantically for the canoe as soon as Quen was lifted out of it. Even if he realized that the Well was no longer dangerous, years of training had instilled a deep fear of the water here in him.

Ixchel embraced Rakulo, and then Citlali and the others did as well. Maatiaak's warriors each came up to him one by one and asked for his forgiveness.

"I'll forgive you all if you agree to stop fighting with each other."

Eventually, they all agreed. Any remaining tension leaked out of the gathering. No one enjoyed fighting their own people. They had done it out of necessity, and now that necessity was gone. The identity of the enemy was no longer clear. All they knew was that the time of Xucha, the time of sacrificing generations of their people at the Well was over. If Xucha couldn't be defeated, then at least his source of power could be neutralized.

"Leave Maatiaak in the water for a while," Rakulo told the others. "He needs to consider what he's done. Maybe if he sees how we destroyed the carnivorous plant that has been devouring our sacrifices for a thousand years, that will change his perspective. Maatiaak made his choice, as you have made yours by agreeing to this new truce."

Reuben had stepped away from the others and was pressing buttons on his bracelet. Rakulo had seen this before—next a bright light would appear to consume him, and then he would be gone.

Reuben gestured Rakulo over, and asked him something. Rakulo couldn't follow the man's excited gestures, and he didn't know his words. But then Rakulo remembered his thought about getting on the other side of the Wall using their strange abilities.

When Reuben held out his hand, Rakulo understood.

This was much scarier than jumping in the sink-hole. When he had jumped, he knew exactly what he was getting into. Where Reuben wanted him to go, Rakulo couldn't see.

He held up a finger to Reuben and stepped over to his people for a moment. He embraced his mother, who sniffled, and Citlali and the others who had been able to trust him.

"Citlali," Rakulo said. "I must go with him. Eliana said that their magic could take us to the other side of the wall. You're in charge while I'm gone. Quen, mother, you must help her. Keep the peace, and make sure Maatiaak doesn't get any more ideas. I'll return as soon as I can."

He walked back over to stand by Reuben.

Reuben pressed a final button, and the green light began to blink. The old man with the wild grey hair pulled Rakulo close to him and watched him with a smirk on his face. Rakulo felt at his side for his obsidian knife, but realized that Maatiaak's men had taken it from him at the cave. The forest and the others vanished as the brightness swallowed him.

Rakulo's stomach twisted and turned upside down, like he'd felt when he fell over the lip of the *cenote* into the water, but a hundred times worse.

The ground seemed to tilt under his feet, and he stumbled forward—into hard bars and a netting of some kind, like you might use to catch fish, but tougher and thicker, and a bright orange in color.

When the light faded, Rakulo realized that he and Reuben were standing inside a cage. Through the bars, through the netting, he could see dozens of men pointing some kind of strange objects at them. The men were dressed all the same, but in no clothes Rakulo had ever seen before. And the objects they pointed seemed dangerous, but if they were bows or spears they were strange things, small enough to hold in one hand, almost delicate.

Rakulo glanced up and got dizzy at the height of the ceiling, and the great arch, which rose up nearly to the top, the height of a small tree.

Reuben called out. A man came forward—a confident, tall, sandy-haired man that Rakulo recognized. Reuben said something, gestured to Rakulo, and spoke some more.

Who was this man he spoke to? Why did he spark some sense of familiarity in Rakulo?

Ahh, Rakulo realized, *it's Eliana's husband.* Rakulo would not have recognized him, as they'd only met once, if it were not for the concern on his face when he said Eliana's name.

What was he called? Rakulo had forgotten…but that wasn't important right now.

"Xucha took her," Rakulo said.

Both men stopped talking and looked at him. Rakulo repeated himself, and Reuben nodded before barreling into another long and wordy explanation to Eliana's husband.

"Send me beyond the wall," Rakulo said, interrupting them again. "If Xucha has her, I'll find her. Send me there now. Now!"

The men's eyebrows drew down as they watched Rakulo, struggling to understand his words. The others beyond the cage of bars in which Rakulo and Reuben found themselves trapped had relaxed by now, and lowered their weapons, apparently realizing there was no threat. While Reuben and Eliana's husband spoke, Rakulo looked around the room, at the walls, made of smooth seamless material like the Wall on his own world.

Finally, Eliana's husband seemed to come to a decision. He went over to a broad display of flashing lights and images that hung magically in the air, and motioned at it. The machine responded, and then Reuben was gone. He reappeared a half-second later outside of the bars. Only Rakulo was left in there now. Fear began to constrict his throat until Reuben came up to the outside of the cage, grasped the netting, and muttered something. Rakulo understood the tone if not the words, and felt his gut tighten.

"My knife," he said, feeling at his waist where his

weapon was missing. "I need a weapon." He made a slashing motion with his hand.

Reuben said, "Ahh," and spoke to some of the other men. He left and came back a moment later with a big blade, and a passed it through the bars. The molded handle felt cool in Rakulo's palm. The blade sharp and bright. It, too, was made out of the same shining, smooth material that the Wall was made of.

Who were these people? How could they make things like Xucha?

But there was no time to ask, and no way to communicate his question. Rakulo held the blade at his side.

"I'm ready," he said.

Eliana's husband waved at the machine that made the air images, and seemed to control it somehow. The light grew around Rakulo, and then he was standing on hard, cracked earth, the ground dusty and dry beneath his sandals, in the shade of great tree.

His stomach lurched and settled. The men and the cage of bars were gone as fast as they had appeared, and now Rakulo was alone back on his own world. He looked up, and felt a chill.

He was standing in shade, but not cast by a tree— it was cast instead by the great Wall, which curved, for the first time in his life, away from him.

His people were on the other side of that Wall.

He approached it and laid his hands on the cool surface. Then, deeply satisfied that he had finally made it beyond the Wall, he turned toward his purpose.

Opposite the Wall stood the tower he had first glimpsed over a year ago. It was a dark color, almost black, and seemed more like a tree, that grew out of the ground, than a building that had been constructed on top of it. It was made out of some material that reminded Rakulo both of Xucha's black armor and the tentacles that the water-plants' tentacles were made of. Not the same, precisely, but of the same family.

He began to make his way quickly toward the tower. As he approached, the cracks in the ground widened, and Rakulo could see water flowing through them. The base of the tower sprawled like a hand, great purple-black roots extending down into the cracks, into the water and earth.

The water was a natural light purple, but many thick roots ran through the cracks. Rakulo reached down into the softer earth bank and pulled out a root—it was thick, the size of his forearm. He lay his new, bright blade along it horizontally, and with a single downward stroke cut it in half. The two ends fell to the ground and began to seep green ichor.

They were one in the same, this plant and the one in the Well of Sacrifices. Perhaps this is where the roots led.

Rakulo walked up and down both sides of that crack in the earth, pulling out roots and cutting them, working quickly and quietly. He kept looking over his shoulder the whole time, worried that Xucha would appear and take him like he had taken Eliana. When all the roots in this crack were cut, Rakulo gripped the blade in his teeth and lowered himself slowly into the water.

That's when the dark god appeared. A black rift opened in the air near the base of the tower, and Xucha walked out of it—without a helmet to cover his head. Rakulo caught one glimpse of that vicious birdlike face, stifled an intake of breath, and lowered himself deep into the crevice.

The figure walked along the edge above Rakulo's head, his footsteps sounding softly. Xucha's shadow passed over him, and then was gone.

Rakulo squirmed up the crack, into a dark tunnel of some kind that led toward the base of the tower. Rakulo followed it until it ended at a circular chamber where all the roots from all sides seemed to collect. But the tunnel didn't end there, it curved—up.

Rakulo gazed up through the tower like the inside of some great hollow tree. Striated muscle-like walls here were wet and practically oozing with that green ichor. There was a tiny vertical shaft, barely big enough to squeeze his shoulders through.

He reached up, found a large striation, gripped it, and hauled himself upward.

Rakulo took the knife out of his teeth and secured it in his tunic. Then he began to climb slowly, holding back his nausea as the green gunk coated his body.

38

THE ALIEN ELEMENT

The horrible hissing that came from the angry alien's maw cut off. Eliana braced herself for an incoming kick to the ribs while her ears rang in the abrupt silence. She kept her hands clutched over her ears, and her body in the fetal position on the ground.

But the next punishment didn't come. Eliana tentatively uncovered her ears and uncurled her body to peek up.

Remethiakara had turned away, distracted by something, his four-fingered fists clenched at his sides. He focused on an invisible point beyond the walls of the chamber, on something in the distance. Almost as if he was listening. Feeling…

She hadn't believed him when he said that her "fragile vessel" couldn't handle the sound of his speech, but now she believed him. She wouldn't make that mistake twice. Human ears weren't built for that kind of range. It was horrible, like rusty nails being dragged across a chalkboard. Even now, her inner ears ached from the brief experience.

The helmet still lay on the floor where she'd dropped it. What other powers did that armor grant him? She wanted to pick it up, but he was right there, standing still, not breathing, just listening.

What did this alien want with her? What did he need with any of them? If he was so powerful, why did he tether himself to her and the Kakuli people?

The millennia-spanning history Eliana had witnessed had neglected to provide answers to these questions. It gave her some context, but now she was more lost than ever.

Remethiakara sprang into action all of a sudden, striding over toward that mound in the corner. As he approached, it squeezed up into the form of…she didn't know what. A pedestal? Its edges hardened and it became a rectangular thing, standing at the height of the alien's armored hands. He punched Eliana's ring into the top of the pedestal, and the whole chamber lit up with a phosphorescent flash.

Eliana squinted as a dozen tentacles emerged from the nearby wall, entwining and forming a rough oval eight feet tall and four feet wide. The tentacles intertwined like strands of rope, and pulsed.

Three seconds later, the center of the oval grew

dark and then solidified, filling with what seemed like a thin sheet of black water.

The rift, Eliana thought. *Just like the one at the top of the pyramid I came through to get here.*

When Eliana stared into the inky blackness, she began to make out shapes of the landscape on the other side. She saw massive roots plunging into thick fissures in the ground, and beyond the cracks, a sheer metal wall curving away from her.

Remethiakara stepped through the rift with a faint ripple. The darkness parted and then came together behind him. The black ripple disappeared a moment later, and the tentacles slithered back into the wall as if they had never been.

Eliana found herself alone in the chamber for the first time. The big meteorite of deep black and rough steel grey stone that the alien called a star shard sat on the floor near the helmet. She was hoping for a more explosive result when she knocked the star shard out of the light beam.

And then what—had Remethiakara noticed something?

It chilled Eliana that he'd left her behind without an explanation. She was just a plaything to him. How old was he? In his perspective, she was an insect. A brief flame of life that flickered and died in a few decades.

What a perspective shift.

Eliana stood. She blinked several times to clear

her aching head, and walked around the chamber, searching, circling. The only thing resembling a door or exit was a rectangular crack set into the flat wall. It had no handle or doorknob that she could find. A green glow seemed to shine through the crack, but the line was too fine to see through it to what lay on the other side.

Eliana turned back to explore the rest of the chamber and smacked her parched, dry mouth. There was no obvious bathroom or place to get water, either. The part about bodily functions hadn't been included in the historical visions. That set her to wondering what else had been held back…and what Remethiakara had twisted to suit his own nefarious purpose.

Would more details about Remethiakara be in that vision-machine? Would it be able to tell her how Rakulo's tribe came to be involved? And could she access them, like a computer?

The mound remained in that podium-like form with the small star shard and her ring set into it. She grasped it between two fingers and tried to pry the ring up. It wouldn't budge. It was stuck, the carapace-like material holding it fast.

She stopped trying to lift it, and instead, lay both hands on either side of the ring. She focused, concentrating, and a thrum of electricity—like putting your hand on the rubber-coated outside of a live wire, or holding one of those shock stick games at a carnival—buzzed into her hands and forearms, numbing them.

The wall in front of her twitched and undulated.

Eliana gasped and withdrew her hands. The wall instantly smoothed out again. She drew several shallow, quick breaths. What would happen? It was like using a computer for the first time when you were a kid. Except this computer had pipe-thin tentacles that jabbed into your ears without asking.

Well, she had come out of that experience unscathed, hadn't she? Eliana inhaled and let out a shaky breath, then placed both her hands back on the pedestal.

The walls rippled again, but nothing happened. She concentrated harder, and slowly the wall pinched together and began to grow out toward her. Distinct forms began to take shape, and Eliana thought one bulge looked a lot like her own laptop at home. She concentrated harder.

The chamber lit up with another phosphorescent flash. An invisible force shoved Eliana back from the pedestal.

Remethiakara stood over her. He squinted his big orb-like eyes at her, then crossed the room and picked up his helmet. He fitted it onto his head again.

"I have killed men for less than that," he said through the walls. "You would do well to mind yourself."

Eliana licked her lips, her thoughts racing. Should she apologize? Did an apology show weakness? What was the best move here?

Clearly whatever had drawn his attention outside had distracted him from his anger at Eliana for knocking the big shard to the ground. Eliana glanced toward the wall where the rift had formed. "Did you find something out there? What happened?"

"Nothing you need to concern yourself with."

"Okay. Um…" Eliana glanced back at podium-like object where the ring was still mounted.

"That star shard is too weak now to make another trip back to your world, if that's what you were thinking," Remethiakara said.

He crossed the room and picked up the star shard in both hands.

"This one, however…"

Eliana thought she sensed some emotion in his voice. Desire? Nostalgia? Maybe if she could get him talking…

"When did you first go?" Eliana asked. "To my world? To Earth."

"Long ago."

"What happened?" She licked her lips. "Please. Among my own people, I'm an anthropologist. I'm a good listener."

His face was hidden now, so she gazed into the inscrutable reflective mask. Eliana had the predatory impression that he was wondering at which temper-ature she would cook best, or how long she could bleed before she stopped breathing.

She forced herself to stare into the blank black face of the helmet with an expression as neutral as she could manage, digging deep into herself. She thought about open air green spaces, about curious children, about the turtle that crawled to the edge of the log, reaching…

"I depleted my last star shard," Remethiakara finally said, "trying to fix an anomaly that has plagued my people for millennia."

Eliana inhaled sharply through her nose. *The star shards…*

"But I have found more, thanks to you. I owe you for that kindness…"

"Oh," Eliana whispered under her breath. "Oh, no."

It's all my fault. Eliana had led him to the star shard. That's why he was keeping her alive. That's why he tolerated her insolence.

Could she play this to her advantage?

"Those people out there," Eliana said. "The Kakuli people, the humans. What do they have to do with you? Or the star shards?"

"I brought them here," Remethiakara said.

Eliana blinked. "From my planet? You brought them from Earth?

He nodded.

"But why?"

He reached a black hand toward the podium and removed the ring. It had been immobile a second before, impossibly stuck when Eliana tried to lift it, but Remethiakara's gloved fingers plucked it out effortlessly. The podium fell back into its mound shape, and dimpled back into the soft chair-like shape.

"I can show you," Remethiakara said.

"I'd really rather not."

"No harm will come to you."

Eliana thought for a long moment. There seemed to be no way out of this place unless this strange alien wanted her to leave. She needed him to trust her. Or at least keep her alive long enough to find another way out.

And in truth, she desperately wanted to know more about Rakulo's people. Why were those carvings of Kakul's moons in the Mexican jungle marking nothing? That was why she came to Kakul, to search for clues. Archaeological evidence was one thing, but this was a direct line of sight into history itself. Or, at least, into one interpretation of it.

Eliana cooperated, lowering herself into the cavity that was shaped to cradle her body. She was expecting the way it moved ever so slightly beneath her now, breathing. Not accustomed to it, but at least she knew what to expect.

Remethiakara stepped up next to her, casting his shadow over her.

He gestured with the ring in his hand, and the tentacles came out from the wall again. They curved around Eliana's wrists and ankles, but this time she didn't resist. Their touch was gentle, slightly ticklish. They wrapped around her ankles and wrists, supporting her gently, no longer squeezing.

She only stiffened slightly as the smaller tendrils went into her ears.

Eliana breathed in.

A thousand years after the great war obliterated their home planet, Remethiakara and two of his kin found a small, green marble in an unexplored spiral galaxy. It was a bountiful land filled with primitive creatures who called themselves People. They welcomed the aliens with open arms, threw gold at their feet, and fed them sweet fruits and smoked meats. Remethiakara's stomach was not used to these strangely rich foods, but they smelled incredible. Nor did his people have any use for gold. They thought it garishly bright. But he withstood their attention patiently, curious and open.

It was not for several days that Remethiakara and his kinsmen realized that these People, strange furry creatures, so like them in structure and yet so different, had the mistaken impression that Remethiakara and his kin were some kind of gods.

These people were intelligent beyond their primitive means. They had the concept of the number zero, and built great temples to honor the gods they believed in—gods which did not exist. But they had strange customs, too. They lived in a dry country, and often resorted to sacrifice of living creatures and their rivals in an attempt to bring the rains, a sort of request to the gods.

Remethiakara's people had seen other species sacrifice animals in their travels among the stars. It didn't bother them, but they deeply loathed the waste and inefficiency. So Remethiakara lent the shamans a star shard, and showed them how to capture the life energy of a sacrificial victim and use it to feed their crops, similar to how his people used the star shards to build and repair their breathing generation ships and build the complex technological mechanisms through which Remethiakara's people incubated and nourish their young.

Humanity was overjoyed with the gift. To honor their generous gods, they held an enormous celebration.

But eventually Remethiakara and his kin had to move on. This was a wonderful planet, but his kind had evolved to travel the galaxy. They were not content to stay in one place. Being apart from their living ships for so long, an emptiness had begun to grow in their hearts.

Eliana blinked and another thousand years passed.

Remethiakara and his kin descended to explore a desert in another galaxy, a long way from Earth. There they found a dangerous, terrible virus deep underground while they were mining for star shards they thought had fallen here. One by one, Remethiakara's companions began to grow sick. Their feathers fell out, they began to bleed from all orifices of their bodies. It was a terrible wasting virus. Remethiakara depleted the vast majority of their star shards trying to devise a way to save his suffering companions' lives.

Eventually, he too grew sick. He was not able to reverse the effects of the virus for his companions in time. Unable to keep down any food or water, they each died from dehydration, one by one. When Remethiakara was the only one left, he finally managed to construct an anti-virus and save himself.

He survived, but he was left heartbroken and alone. And as the last member of his species in this sector of the galaxy, it was now Remethiakara's responsibility to sire children. This was a difficult task. Due to the purposeful manipulation of their life span, it was remarkably difficult to sire children. The process took a great many years and was fraught with failure. Yet Remethiakara took this responsibility on himself.

Eliana blinked.

An unknown time passed while Remethiakara considered his options. It would be easier to accomplish his new mission with more star shards. But he had used up his reserves saving his own life. There was only one place where he was certain a star shard could be found.

He used the rest of his energy reserves to take his ship back to Earth. When he arrived, the people seemed to have some distant memory of him, in stories passed down through the generations. Yet their greeting was subdued. They had become beaten down and tired in the thousand years he had been absent. Constantly embroiled in tribal warfare with their neighbors, fighting amongst themselves, and in the middle of the longest drought they had ever experienced, the tribe he had once taught had lost the star shard.

Remethiakara wanted to teach them again. He could help these People, and in return for saving them from self-destruction, they could help him.

It would take a long time—capturing the minute amount of life energy released through human sacrifice was tedious in comparison to infusing shards with the energy of a star. But he couldn't make more star shards with the power his ship had left. He could, however, help this human tribe end the drought, and then use the leftover energy to create and power an incubation chamber that would allow him to sire healthy children.

But not here. Not on Earth, where these people were constantly under threat and fighting amongst each other. It was too dangerous. In just a few days, Remethiakara hatched a new plan…

Eliana blinked a final time, and she was suddenly looking out at a vast rift. Remethiakara stood among a gathering of a dozen shamans at the top of a great stone pyramid. A line of hundreds of people extended down the pyramid steps and zigzagged across the plaza.

One by one, the people walked up to the top of the temple and offered themselves to Remethiakara. It had taken some convincing, but once the shamans were on board, it had been easy enough.

When the blood of thousands washed the courtyard, the stone city with all its temples and offices and observatories and market squares and ball courts was transported through the rift, to an uninhabited planet Remethiakara had prepared on the opposite end of Earth's spiral galaxy.

Eliana blinked again.

The tendrils slithered out of her ears. She stood slowly, as if in a dream. The power of the visions was that they felt more real than reality. Remethiakara waited near the far wall. She walked over to him.

He pressed a hand against a small section on the wall by the door, a flat panel she hadn't noticed before. The door slid into the wall. Green light from the other chamber flooded into this one, and the alien gestured for Eliana to enter ahead of him.

She walked into a chamber that was, in size and shape, the mirror image of the one from which they had just come. The whole structure made a circle, with the flat wall bisecting the two chambers. Beyond that, the similarities between the chambers ended.

Lined up along the curved outside wall of this new chamber were twenty massive eggs made out of the dark purplish black carapace or scale-like material. In the floor in the center of the room was a hole like a drain, from which hundreds of tendrils snaked out. Ten or more tendrils led to each egg, pumping that glowing green fluid into them.

When Eliana thought of the tendrils that had just been in her ears, her gorge rose. She fought down the urge to vomit as Remethiakara came into the room.

He hissed under the helmet when he saw that a handful of the tendrils at the left of the room had been severed. Two of the eggs were no longer connected. Green fluid leaked out onto the floor.

The helmet muffled the horrible hissing sound, but it came out harsh and obviously full of pain. The alien darted forward and bent down, lifting the tendrils gingerly in his hand.

And that was when another figure, sticky and dripping with clumps of the green fluid, stood up from cover behind the incubation equipment and kicked an egg with his foot.

39

POWER HUNGRY

The man in the loincloth gripping the big knife became obscured by the sphere of spinning steel rings. Amon focused his eyes back on the holograms displaying the power levels and molecular stability of the translocation. He had the focus area switched to manual, and was trying to keep the disassembly keyed in on the young man's body, and not send any rebar or mesh netting with him. The bright light finally consumed the man's form, and then he was gone. Jeanine, Reuben and the others approached up the ramp.

"Remove that cage!" Amon called to them. "Clear the area."

"You got it," Reuben said, giving Amon a thumbs up.

"I'll get a saw," Jeanine said.

Amon sagged with relief. He didn't know what

had removed the wormhole, but he said a silent prayer of thanks to whoever it was.

Amon confirmed Rakulo's reassembly, and then switched the Translocator back to automatic focus. The cage of rebar and mesh they spent hours building needed to go. His team unhooked the mesh netting, cut the rebar where it had been welded to the floor, and carried the cage into the hall.

"I should have gone with him." Amon checked his own transponder bracelet to make sure it was working. It blinked back a confirmation. "Eliana might need my help."

"There's some freaky shit going on over there, Amon." The look on Reuben's face told Amon all he needed to know.

"Tell me about it."

Reuben just shook his head. "That thing they call Xucha—it's powerful. Rakulo looked like he was about to face death itself, but at least he knows what he's getting into. What if he's walking into a trap?"

"What if he's already dead?" Amon turned to the FBI man. "Agent Moreno, can I borrow a sidearm? Yours or someone else's, I don't care."

"Do you even know how to use a gun?" Moreno asked.

Amon looked at him, his expression deadpan. "I've had some experience recently."

"Well, it's not exactly protocol—"

An alert whooped from the holodeck. Dr. Badeux

rushed to the control panel and gazed over Reuben's shoulder at the message.

"What is it?" Amon demanded.

Dr. Badeux's face paled and his eyes widened. He looked at Amon. "Amon, it's Stanis Rachmaninoff. He's saying that the MegaPower reactor has been breached."

"What happened?" Amon demanded. "I thought they fixed the access tunnel. I was there when they were doing it! The reactor was untouched."

Enzo shook his head. "He says they did. He says…" He swallowed. "He says that someone came through the Translocator platform. They thought it was Fisk Industries sending supplies. Three people went to retrieve the supplies…but it wasn't supplies. The three astronauts who went looking for supplies were killed."

"Oh god." Amon put his head in his hands.

"Son of a bitch," Agent Moreno said. "It's Lucas, isn't it?"

"He must have granted his own Translocator access when he was here."

Amon was torn. He thought about Eliana. What if that black-armored being got to her? What was Lucas planning to do with a MegaPower reactor? A horrible revulsion filled his whole being with nausea as he was split at cross purposes.

Reuben came up to Amon and put one hand on his shoulder. "Take a deep breath."

Amon complied, exhaling shakily.

Eliana had gone through the rift on her own two feet. She knew the risks. Thinking about it now, it had been foolish to send that other man through armed with nothing but a knife. That black-armored being had decapitated six armed mercenaries with a laser. Amon had seen it with his own two eyes. What was a cave man with a knife going to do against something with that kind of power?

What would Lucas do with a reactor? Given his track record, it was certainly nothing good. It wasn't just Eliana who would suffer if he didn't act, either. Lucas was a threat to the whole world. How many had he already experimented on and killed? How many more must suffer?

"Ok," Amon finally said. "We deal with Lucas first. Then I'll go after Eliana. Reuben, you send me to the lunar platform. Moreno, come with me."

"Don't we need space suits?" Agent Moreno asked.

"A suit isn't necessary. There's no breach in the domes this time."

Half a dozen FBI agents crowded onto the translocation platform with Amon and Agent Moreno.

"Ready?"

"Here," Moreno said, handing Amon a pistol. "Just in case."

"We're ready," Amon said.

"Stand still."

Amon closed his eyes against the light, his stomach flipped, and they found themselves in the lunar base in Dome 2, on the platform.

A domed ceiling rose above them. In front of them, a ramp led down into the insulated plastic tube that served as a walkway to connect the primary domes of the lunar base and the underground MegaPower reactor.

White sheets covered three lumps on the floor—the astronauts, where they had been gunned down by Lucas's mercenaries.

The FBI agents drew their weapons when they spotted the bodies. Yet all of them still gazed around, looking at their surroundings in wonder.

"This way." Amon started off at a brisk walk down the hall. At the second intersection, he opened the airlock and turned into a tunnel that moved left. Once in the tunnel, Agent Moreno gestured, and his men fanned out in front and behind them.

"Keep your hands off the trigger unless you don't have any other choice," Amon said. "The domes are made of a strong plastic, but a few stray bullets could breach the atmosphere. A stray bullet to the reactor could breach the core and irradiate us all."

After a few sections of hallway, they finally approached the last segment that led to the door of the reactor. The airlock let them through, and then they were looking at the open door to the reactor—

the locks had been drilled through with powerful lasers.

A ten-foot thick concrete structure insulated and protected the MegaPower core in the center of the reactor—a huge section of the wall had been cut away, exposing the metal core. Wires connecting the klaxon alarm had been cut at the communications panel on the wall, but a red light still spun on the ceiling, illuminating the reactor room in rotating shades of red.

Inside the main room, Amon saw movement. Beyond the big fans and pumps designed to bleed residual heat out to the surface, Amon could make out a few people walking around on the far end near the reactor itself. Two big blond men lifted and carried a Stirling engine—the piece of equipment that transformed the heat from the nuclear reactor into electricity—between them. That meant they must have detached the engine from the nuclear fission reactor already.

"Ahh, Amon." Lucas stepped out from behind the cement heat shield surrounding the core at the center of the large dome. "I was wondering when you'd get here."

"What are you doing?"

"What does it look like I'm doing?" Lucas stepped past the rolling cart.

When Agent Moreno saw him, he and the other agents drew their guns.

"Careful, boys! There be radioactive elements."

"Easy," Amon said.

Agent Moreno adjusted his grip on his pistol. "This bastard killed my partner."

"I know." As he approached, Amon saw that Lucas's face was drooping down on one side. "What happened to you?"

Lucas held one arm close to his side, and even seemed to walk with a slight limp. "None of your concern."

"Ah, I see what happened. When you translocated out of my lab without the aid of a platform or the carbonado, you were maimed by your own Translocator."

Lucas smiled, but it looked more like a grimace now. The left side of his face was paralyzed and didn't move when he smiled. His suit, however, was still immaculately pressed, his black wingtips polished and clean. Even the tri-folded handkerchief in his pocket was perfectly creased.

"I'll admit," Lucas said, "that my deformity is unfortunate. But it is not irreversible. Now that we have a more reliable power source, nothing can stop us."

A wash of sweat prickled to the surface of Amon's skin as he realized how Lucas was powering his Translocator.

"You're using a nuclear reactor as a power source, aren't you?" Amon said.

Lucas clapped slowly, the sound echoing hollowly. The second large Stirling engine was carried across the room behind him.

"Took you long enough," Lucas smirked.

"That's why you were having issues with the translocations. Not a lack of a platform to focus the reassembly—you don't care if those people get hurt —but you don't have enough power. You need the plutonium."

"Something like that," Lucas said. "Now that we have the nuclear fission reactor, we won't need any more plutonium."

"You can't take that with you."

Several big men lifted the nuclear core and set it on the cart between the Stirling engines.

Lucas limped up to Amon until he was standing face to face with him. The deformity of his face was more obvious from here. It looked like a heat source had melted half his face.

Agent Moreno had followed Lucas with his gun. "I'm warning you."

"What? You're going to shoot me? My men have guns, too, you know."

To show him they were telling the truth, the blond men each drew pistols from holsters on their belts.

"If you shoot, they'll shoot back. And if one of you misses, you'll breach the dome and we'll all get sucked out into the cold vacuum of space."

The men rolled the cart forward until they were right behind Lucas. Amon and the FBI men blocked they doorway. The two groups stared at each other for a long minute.

"He's right," Amon said. "Let them go."

Amon stepped aside.

"God damnit, Amon!" Moreno shouted. He kept his gun trained on Lucas.

"Either shoot me or move, man." Lucas stepped up until the barrel of Moreno's gun was pressed against his chest. "You're wasting your time. The clock is ticking."

"What did you say?" Amon ran around the back of the cement heat shield that housed the reactor core. Several brick-shaped objects wrapped in plastic and a small clock had been left on the floor there.

"Agent Moreno! We have a big problem!"

"Damnit!" Moreno said. The FBI agents finally stepped aside. Lucas and his men wheeled the rolling cart quickly down the hall. And then they were running, to get to the platform no doubt.

They slipped through the first airlock and were gone a moment later.

"Agent Moreno," Amon said. "You better get over here!"

"You two, follow them," Agent Moreno ordered. Then he found Amon at the back of the reactor dome.

The red letters on the clock currently read, 19:51, and counted backward. It made a small, barely audible beeping sound with each second that ticked by.

19:50...
19:49...
19:48...

40

BEHIND THE BLACK CURTAIN

Rakulo felt a vicious, animal satisfaction deep in his core as the egg cracked under his sandaled heel. He slipped as his foot came down, and he staggered back. The phlegmy fluid coating his body was something between blood and mud, slick and sticky. It got in his mouth and tasted sour and salty at the same time.

The big egg struck the floor and cracked a second time. Fluid spilled out of it and pooled in a lopsided puddle.

Xucha roared, a horrible angry sound muffled by his helmet, and bent over the broken egg briefly. Rakulo seized his chance, leaping forward and bringing the knife down on Xucha's head, going for the killing blow that would destroy his God.

His aim was true—the blade struck the helmet

square in the middle—and glanced off. The tip of the knife sank into the spongy floor.

Xucha stood up lightning fast and kicked Rakulo in the ribs, knocking the air from his lungs. The knife stayed stuck in the floor.

Rakulo landed on his wrist, which bent awkwardly. He cried out. Then Xucha let a black-armored fist fall. It struck Rakulo in the jaw. He splayed to the floor.

Xucha staggered to the side all of a sudden. He used the wall to brace himself. Someone else was on him, hanging from around his neck—Eliana! So she was here after all!

She gripped her white arms around Xucha's black-armored head, and twisted. The helmet came off, and Eliana fell backward. She landed on the floor and rolled away, the helmet in her arms.

Rakulo took advantage of the distraction to take off the bracelet that the old man had given him.

"Eliana!" he shouted, and threw it in her direc-tion. She caught it in the black helmet, and then lifted it, pressing the button at the same time. The green light went solid. A second later and she was gone in a flash of bright light.

Rakulo was left facing Xucha across the chamber at the top of his tower, the knife in the floor between them. Beneath his helmet, the God had a snake-like face with big yellowish-brown eyes. His skin was scaly and alien, but covered with delicate colorful feathers like a bird. Where a nose should have been was a vertical slit. But the mouth was wide, and twisted with anger.

Xucha lunged, and Rakulo dove to avoid him. He was so fast! Rakulo rolled across the floor and came back up to his feet with the knife in his hand once again. He twirled it effortlessly, like an extension of his body.

"Come on!" he said, turning to kick at another of the eggs near him.

Xucha's mouth fell open and he screamed again. Without the helmet to muffle it, the screeching noise reverberated off the walls and made Rakulo's head ring…except, only on the right side, where his good ear was. He couldn't hear anything on the left side. That ear had gone bad, and for once, it was an advantage.

Xucha darted across the room. Rakulo ran the opposite way, shoving another egg off its perch as he went.

Xucha bent toward the egg and stretched his hands out. But he just missed it. The egg hit the floor, and cracked. Xucha's shoulders rose and fell once, twice.

The God was clearly distressed, more worried about protecting the eggs than about stopping Rakulo. It was almost as if Rakulo was nothing more than an irritating insect, a frustrating distraction, but not a real danger—except to the eggs.

Rakulo took the opportunity to reach down and quickly cut a thin strip of fabric from his tunic. He balled it up, and stuffed it into his good right ear. It stayed in thanks to the sticky ichor coating his body.

The next time Xucha let out a cry, it was loud, but nothing he couldn't bear.

His cries were still cries of horrible pain, like the kind Rakulo had heard his mother make when Rakulo's younger brother, Tilak, died. The kind of pain only a parent can possibly understand.

Xucha finished securing the cracked—but not broken—egg back in its spot, then turned slowly back to Rakulo. A twisted, hate-filled snarl split his strange snake-face. He stepped slowly across the room toward Rakulo. Frightened at the sudden focus and slowness of Xucha's movements, Rakulo backed out of the egg room and into the other chamber from which Eliana and Xucha had first come.

Out of the corner of his eye, he saw three round demons on a shelf to his right. Xucha gestured at them, but they didn't rise.

He made a fist in his frustration.

He can't control them without the helmet, Rakulo thought. This was his chance. Xucha made his way over to the opposite wall, keeping Rakulo in his sight the whole time. At his touch, the wall lit up and shifted, a hundred shapes coming to life and dazzling Rakulo with their twisting forms.

One of the orbs finally rose from its perch behind him. It wobbled unsteadily, and Rakulo now saw the tools below the half-empty shelf, the blackened, dirty rags. Nonetheless, a blue light spread out from the orb, encompassing Rakulo in its light, and freezing him in place.

Xucha crossed the room. He took Rakulo's knife from his paralyzed hand, aimed the point at a spot between his ribs, and slid it deep into his body. Rakulo could only move enough to gasp slightly as his whole body went cold. With his eyes, he glanced down and saw that the blade had sunk up to the handle in his gut.

Rakulo flinched when Xucha's feathered head darted in close, but he couldn't turn away. He was cold, so very cold. And the pain had begun to burn as well.

Whatever Xucha was, he was not Rakulo's god. The creature's breath was hot on his neck. "You're coming with me," he whispered.

Xucha set Rakulo's paralyzed body on the floor in the center of the chamber near a night-black stone twice as big as his head. Rakulo gritted his teeth when Xucha set him down. The demon continued to hover nearby, the paralyzing beam of light immobilizing Rakulo.

Xucha touched that wall again, and a dozen tentacles twined together to form a doorway. A rippling black curtain appeared in the doorway.

Rakulo thought he could see a similar-looking chamber to the one they were in through the black ripples. Was there another tower? Or somewhere else Xucha could hide?

Xucha stepped through the black curtain and was gone. In his frozen position he could only watch the open doorway. Xucha returned a minute later, retrieved an egg from the chamber in which Rakulo had arrived, and carried it through the doorway.

Several long minutes later, Xucha returned empty-handed and went back into the room with the eggs. He gingerly carried a second egg—the one that Rakulo had cracked but not broken—across the room in front of Rakulo, and disappeared through the doorway again.

All the while, unable to move his limbs or anything more than his eyes, Rakulo bled onto the floor, the knife up to the hilt in his side, and watched as Xucha transported his little godlings to safety.

41

TWO DANGERS

Eliana stumbled forward and nearly crashed into a steel ring that sliced down in front of her face.

She gasped, then darted through the gap in the rings before they had fully come to a stop.

"Eliana, is that you?" Audrey called from across the lab. The dozen or so men pointing pistols at her waited.

"For the love of god, lower your guns," Audrey said. "I've just had about enough of guns for a lifetime." She hurried over to Eliana's side and guided her to a nearby chair.

Eliana glanced down at the helmet in her hands. She worked her lips a few times but no words came out. It was always jarring coming through the Translocator, but this was another level of contrast entirely.

"Audrey," she finally said. "He's in danger. I have to help him."

"Who is in danger?"

"Rakulo."

"Is that the man that they sent back to look for you?"

"Yes! He found me. Remethiakara…I mean, Xucha was there. They were fighting, and Rakulo threw the transponder to me. I panicked, pressed the button, and then I was here. But I have to go back. I have to help him."

"We'll do what we can, I promise. But first…"

She glanced toward Reuben and Jeanine and the other scientists, who were now crowding around the holodeck. Eliana felt a moment of relief, seeing Reuben, to know that he had made it home safe. When had he returned?

Faint voices came from the middle of the gathering, from a speaker near the holodeck itself.

"Agent Moreno," Amon's voice shouted. "You better get over here!"

But Amon wasn't here. He was somewhere else.

"What's happening?" Eliana said.

Audrey just shook her head.

"*Oy gevalt*…" Reuben said with a groan. "That little *pisha*."

42

ONE EMERGENCY AT A TIME

When Agent Moreno finally caught sight of the bomb, his skin went pale and waxy.

Amon looked from the FBI agent's face to the red-lettered digital clock facing up on the top of it. Exposed wires ran from the back of the clock to the wrapped packages stacked below.

Nothing fancy about it. Just good old fashioned plastic explosives, arranged in a brick about two feet tall by two feet thick. Enough, Amon figured, to blow the top off the auxiliary dome housing the nuclear facility—inflatable interior, radiation shield, and all.

They'd be picking up the pieces for months.

"We need to go," Amon said. He grabbed Agent Moreno and pulled him away from the bomb.

"We need a bomb squad," Agent Moreno said. "I have some basic training on how to defuse bombs, but…" He reached out his shaking hands and began to fiddle with the colorful wires. The other FBI agents shifted nervously. Agent Moreno dropped his hands to his sides and sighed. "Not enough."

"Reuben, did you get that?" Amon said.

Reuben's voice came after the normal delay. "Loud and clear."

"What do you mean, bomb squad?" someone else said, the voice faint but distinctly female. Amon gasped. He knew that voice.

"Let's get out of here while we can," he said.

Wasting no time, Amon sprinted down the access tunnel the way that Lucas and his men had gone a moment before. He slapped his hand against the button that would open the airlock, ran through the adjacent segment, and slammed his hand into the button for the next airlock. By this time he was panting hard. Ahead, he saw a flash of light as the platform disassembled Lucas and the nuclear equipment.

In the Translocator platform, a dozen or so scientists who worked on the lunar base were gathered around Stanis, who clutched his bleeding head. "I tried to stop them—" he said.

"We have a bigger problem," Amon said. "There's a bomb. We all have to go, right now."

Amon got them all to gather closely on the platform. The lurching feeling began in his gut. They reassembled on Earth a moment later.

Amon put his hands on his knees as he fought to keep the contents of his stomach on the inside. He'd been using the Translocator a lot. Apparently too many reassemblies in a short time period still made one quite nauseous. He squeezed his lips shut and dry heaved once, twice, as the others moved off the platform and spread out into the crowded Translocator lab.

Fortunately, Agent Moreno was less affected.

"We need a bomb squad, stat!" the detective shouted.

"Already on it, boss," an FBI agent said. He spoke into a headset. "HQ says they can get a bomb squad here in 10 minutes."

"Not soon enough!" Agent Moreno said. "There's only about fifteen minutes left on the clock. By the time they get down here it will be too late. Who else knows their way around plastic explosives?"

"What about the NSA?" Eliana suggested. "Audrey just told me they were outside."

Amon lifted his head. He staggered into one of the metal rings, steadying himself against the metal, still warm from the reassembly. "Eliana! When did you get here?"

"Hey, babe," she said. "Are you okay?"

"I am now," Amon said.

He stepped off the platform and walked down the ramp to meet her. He pulled her into his arms with a sigh, then held her out at arm's length. He inspected her dirty face. She directed her gaze away from him, but didn't pull her body away. Amon pulled her back to him again and buried his face in her neck. Her hair smelled like...ozone?

"Is it really you?"

"Yes."

"I'm so glad you're okay."

Agent Moreno was on the phone now. "Do you guys have a bomb squad on premises?" He heaved an audible sigh of relief.

"Yeah?" Amon said.

"The president insisted on assigning a bomb squad. He wanted to be ready for every eventuality. They're coming inside now."

It was Amon's turn to sigh. "Remind me to send that man a very expensive gift basket."

Eliana pulled away from Amon.

"What happened there?" he asked. "I was so scared for you."

"I'm okay. Or, I will be." Her eyes darkened all of a sudden, and she clenched her jaw. "My friend Rakulo is in danger."

Amon blinked. He looked down and saw the transponder bracelet on her wrist. Rakulo must have given her his transponder. Well, that was good. At least if she did another crazy thing, she could contact him through the device this time.

"Don't you care?" Eliana demanded.

"I do," he said quickly. "I—" He glanced down the

hall. "I've just been so worried about you. One emergency at a time, okay?"

Eliana twisted her mouth. She did that thing she always did when she was mad, and pressed her tongue against her lower teeth.

Amon felt the guilt return like a gut punch. *How do I always manage to say the wrong things?*

Eliana finally nodded and walked over to stand by Audrey and Reuben. The whole room shifted restlessly, waiting in silence for the bomb squad to arrive.

A man in a big bulky dark green blast-resistant suit, followed by two other agents carrying radios and laptops, sprinted into the room.

The man stopped just inside the door. He looked around. "Where's the bomb?" he said.

"In there," Amon said, pointing at the sphere of rings.

The bomb tech paled, but hurried forward nonetheless. The others went with him.

"Stand inside the rings," Amon said, directing him.

"I'll show them where it is," Agent Moreno said.

Reuben raised his hands at the holodeck and all four men vanished. Amon guessed they had about 5 minutes left now.

"All right, we're here," Agent Moreno said through the radio a few minutes later. He was breathing heavily. "Looks pretty straightforward…"

"How much time is left?" Amon asked.

"Three minutes," Agent Moreno said.

Silence on the line for over a minute. The seconds seemed to drag on. Reuben stepped up between Eliana and Amon. He put one arm around each of their necks and held them close. Jeanine came over and joined them a moment later, and then Enzo as well.

They all stood, arms interlocked, their collective fingers crossed, in the silence.

Agent Moreno finally sighed into the radio. "He got it. The clock stopped at seventeen seconds."

"Oh, thank God," Reuben said, sagging forward.

"Crisis averted," Amon said. He chuckled nervously. The laughter spread through the others. They all grinned.

While Amon waited tensely for the disabled bomb to arrive back in his lab, Eliana turned to face him.

"Amon," Eliana said. "Rakulo is in danger. He needs our help. The others would go to his aid, but they can't reach him. There's a Wall blocking their way."

"A wall?"

Eliana nodded calmly. "A huge Wall built by Xucha to trap Rakulo's people there. So that he can exploit their sacrifices."

"How do you know that?" Amon asked, incredulous.

"He told me," she said. "Sort of."

Amon felt his eyebrows raising. Standing nearby, Reuben's rose, too.

"What if we send that bomb to Kakul, and use it to blast a hole in the Wall?" Eliana said. "We do that, then his friends will be able to get through the Wall."

"It worked then, sending Rakulo on the other side of the Wall?"

Eliana met the old man's eyes. "He saved my life, Reuben."

The old man pulled Eliana to him. "I'm glad you're safe, dear."

"I don't know," Amon said. "If it were up to me, I'd do it, but…"

Eliana stared at him with an unblinking gaze. Amon inhaled through his nose. Even Reuben scowled at him.

Amon licked his lips, chagrined. He turned. "Agent Moreno?"

Eliana explained the situation a second time to the FBI and bomb tech guys.

To Amon's surprise, Agent Moreno shrugged. "Sure," he said. "Why not?"

"I'll go with her," Amon said, stepping forward almost automatically.

"Send the bomb tech instead," Eliana said, her eyes burning with something akin to passion. "Someone who actually knows what he's doing."

Amon sagged. "Of course. But, why do *you* need to go back then?"

"So that someone can explain what's happening. The people there have never seen a bomb before."

"They won't freak out, will they?" the bomb tech asked.

"No," she said. "They're no strangers to powerful magic. They've just never seen this kind of magic before."

The husky, bald FBI bomb tech that disarmed the device at the reactor went up the ramp to join Eliana in the Translocator platform.

Amon didn't take his eyes off his wife. Reuben activated the machine, using the carbonado this time. The rings spun and the bright light given off by the transfer burned his retinas. The red outline of her form remained in the air for several seconds after she was gone.

He looked down. Had she really just been in his arms a second ago? He couldn't hold on to her.

43

BLAST RADIUS

She and the bomb tech reassembled in the jungle of Kakul a few hundred yards south of the wall.

Eliana looked around. Forest, forest, forest... *there*.

"So, uh," the bomb guy said. "Where do you want it? Didn't you say there was a—" His mouth fell open as he followed Eliana's gaze into the jungle toward the setting sun.

Eliana said nothing. She just stared up. Even from a hundred yards away, the metal Wall towered over them, casting a shadow as long as the coming night.

Eliana had never seen such a Wall. The closest thing it could be compared to standing at the foot of the Dallas Cowboys football stadium. Except this Wall was constructed of a single sheer, unmarked, and slightly concave bronze face.

The wall was a structure of such singular alien construction that any doubts Eliana harbored about Remethiakara's origin fled from her head. At the same time, she knew he must have left many things out of his vision-stories. The wall was a clear sign that the Kakuli people's presence here—and, therefore, their service to Xucha—was anything but voluntary.

The bushes around them rustled, and suddenly Eliana and the bomb guy were surrounded by pointed spears.

"Whoa, whoa, whoa!" the bomb tech said.

"Easy."

When Citlali saw Eliana, she barked an order and the spears lowered.

Eliana recognized Quen and Thevanah and a few of the younger warriors from the cave. The others were older men, mostly. Were these older men from the other faction they had been fighting?

She could ask questions later. For now, there was an urgent matter to attend to.

"Rakulo is in trouble. He's in Xucha's tower on the other side of the Wall."

Citlali's face fell. "Then he is lost."

Eliana shook her head, and grinned. "No. We brought something that will allow us to go through the Wall to find him. I hope."

The bomb tech carried the charges the last hundred yards through the forest. The natives stood by, watching uneasily as the bomb guy attached the plastic explosives to the Wall, positioning them against the base.

He finished and stepped away from the Wall. "Get everyone to move back. We need to be out of the blast radius."

Eliana translated, and they moved back by a few yards. The tech found a large tree to shelter behind.

"Way farther back!" he said.

Eliana ushered the warriors back another fifty yards. The bomb guy stuck his fingers in his ears.

Eliana cupped her hands over her ears as a ball of fire flared at the base of the Wall. Smoke rose from where the bombs had been planted a moment before.

They approached slowly. The hole made by the explosives was a thin, ragged tear. The metal had held up remarkably well.

But the warriors were not to be held back. Using the ends of their spears on the hot metal, they pushed the torn edges back until the gap was wide enough to squeeze through.

Through they went. They ran across the cracked, dry ground, heading for the tower where the roots, like a great tree, meandered down into the cracks in the ground.

Citlali walked slower than the rest, breathing painfully. Eliana slipped through the Wall, and put her arm under Citlali to support her as they walked.

They watched the others explore the base of the tower, gazing into the cracks at the green water and pointing.

"That's how he got in," Eliana said to Citlali. "Rakulo was covered in that green slime when I saw him."

But the other warriors had already figured it out. Quen, the big man, was the first to slip his broad shoulders into the widest crack.

44

MOVING HOUSE

Rakulo's vision faded to black at the edges as Xucha carted eggs and other supplies out of the chamber.

Funny, that a so-called God should have to move house like this. Apparently, all sorts of supplies had to be stowed and carried through that black doorway. Where was he planning to go? Rakulo watched as well as he could with limited motion as Xucha carried a case full of the long tubes that ran from the trunk of the tower to the eggs across the room. Some blood seeped around the side of the blade in his gut—he could feel the liquid dripping down his abdomen—but for the most part the weapon blocked the wound, and kept him alive.

That scared Rakulo far more than the possibility of death. He had already accepted the possibility of death. He wouldn't have been able to jump into the

Well of Sacrifices if he hadn't. But to be kept alive, and used for who knows what nefarious purpose?

Rakulo had never been so frightened in his life.

Yet, even this he would be willing to endure, if it meant that Xucha would leave his people alone.

Rakulo winced when an explosion rocked the chamber. The tower itself seemed to sway. Xucha hurried with the eggs, moving faster now from the far chamber through the dark doorway, snarling and hissing in agitation.

The next time Xucha went through the doorway, Rakulo thought he saw something moving in the egg chamber. There were whispers, and then a heavy thud, and Rakulo gasped and groaned. He could move his limbs again! The demon rolled on the floor of the chamber by his head.

Quen knelt in front of him, the man's broad shoulders dripping with that green ichor. He mouthed the words, "Are you okay?"

"Quen!" Rakulo said, his voice barely audible to himself. "Xucha is coming back. Block your ears with cloth!"

"Shhhh," Quen whispered. Rakulo clamped his mouth shut when he realized he was yelling. He couldn't hear a damned thing.

Rakulo pointed to the doorway, then pointed to the cloth stuffed in his ear.

Quen nodded, then said something over his

shoulders. Others were trickling in—Thevanah, Yeli, and even Maatiaak's warriors! Quen cut two strips of fabric from his tunic and stuffed them both in his ears. The others followed suit.

When Xucha stepped through the door a moment later and screamed, his warriors flinched, but held their ground. Thevanah darted forward, shoving a spear at Xucha. He parried the jab, then struck her. But then another warrior was there, beating him down, and another, and another.

Each time the god threw one warrior against the wall, another took his place. They backed him into a corner with sheer numbers and the ferocity of their attack.

Xucha threw Quen off him for a second time, then tried to dart toward the egg chamber. He wanted to get back there, but there was no way he could with all the others blocking the way. He couldn't get to the wall to control his demons, either. There was only one way out.

As the black-clad god backed into the black doorway, Xucha opened his fang-lined mouth and stared at Rakulo across the chamber. And then the tentacles that made up the frame began to unwind, and the doorway disappeared, taking Xucha with it.

Rakulo's vision had continued to fade this whole time, as the pain increased. By the time Xucha was gone, a moaning sound came from somewhere, and

Rakulo realized it was him moaning. As Xucha disappeared, the adrenaline rush subsided, and Rakulo lost consciousness.

45

DARKNESS STARES BACK

Nearly four hours after Amon sent Eliana through with the NSA bomb tech, a commotion on the ground floor sent Agent Moreno running to rescue Eliana's archaeological team, who had shown up unannounced and were presently being accosted by the irascible combination of NSA and FBI agents and private security personnel set to guard the perimeter.

"Oh no," Audrey said, standing. "They must be worried sick about Eliana."

Amon sighed and glanced back at the Holodeck —no incoming coordinates shone on the display, which had him wondering where Eliana was and what was taking her so long. Amon squeezed his eyes shut and buried his face in his hands.

His heart fretted for his wife, and his mind

darted from the classified compound his once-peaceful office had become to his obligation to inform the president about Lucas's nuclear ambitions. The delays caused by the stolen nuclear fission reactor would cost the LTA billions. Even with their engineers working round the clock, it would take another 3 months—minimum—to construct a new nuclear fission reactor, and get the base back online.

"I'll go," Audrey said, standing. "You've got enough to worry about."

Amon smiled weakly. "Thanks, Audrey."

She hurried after Moreno, edging nervously past Reuben, Dr. Enzo Badeux, and the guards. Together, they reviewed the new guard's 24-hour rotation schedule.

Amon stared at the holodeck. He twirled a finger to refresh the display. Still no signal from Eliana.

Reuben and Enzo had set the place to rights in the past few hours, with almost no direction from Amon. He felt a deep appreciation being surrounded by such capable people, and a deeper fear that he couldn't trust anyone completely ever again, not after the betrayal by both Lucas and Wes.

Enzo arranged for the cage of rebar and netting to be disassembled, and cleared any unneeded personnel out of the Translocator lab, including finding hotels for the rattled lunar base scientists and astronauts to spend the night. Then Reuben got the idea in his head that they needed motion detection installed on the premises in the wake of the breaches, and Enzo authorized funds for it from the LTA. FBI spies showed up and Reuben supervised the new installation. Additional security was a top priority with another Translocator loose in the world.

Meanwhile, Jeanine began making phone calls to LTA. They started arranging a way to use satellites to track down any large amounts of radiation being given off around the world, in the hopes that they could track down Lucas and his Translocator. Their theory was that once he managed to set up the fission reactor, they would be able to track him down by the heat signature.

Amon no longer had any doubt about Lucas's ability to get a functional Translocator online. He'd obviously made some errors with it, but he'd managed to make it run, albeit with varied and often disastrous results. With a MegaPower fission reactor at his disposal for energy needs, he would be extremely dangerous.

While they worked, Amon brooded near the holodeck. Over time, an idea began to develop in his mind.

Enzo finally came back to Amon. "How are you holding up?"

Amon made a noncommittal sound in his throat. "It could have been worse. I hate the idea of setbacks.

It will take another three months, minimum, to build a new nuclear fission reactor."

Enzo shook his head. "A few weeks, tops."

Amon raised his eyebrows. The doctor shrugged. "A team at the LTA came up with a new 3D printer that can handle the types of strengthened metal alloys needed to build new reactors if we need them. It's just a matter of mining enough helium-3 from the moon in that time frame to make it viable."

"That's great," Amon said, before remembering his other problems and sighing deeply. "At least it's a step in the right direction."

"You'll find Lucas," Enzo said. "I promise."

Amon nodded. "Enzo, I've been thinking. How would the LTA like to buy me out of the Translocator contractor?"

Enzo pursed his lips and stared through his thick square-rimmed glasses. "Why? It's your brainchild."

Early on in his work with the LTA, Amon had insisted on patenting his molecular reassembly designs under his own name. It had been a long discussion, but Amon eventually brought Enzo around to his way of seeing things. Amon fought hard for that. Amon understood if it was hard for Enzo to see why he wanted to give that up now.

"I'll keep working on the project, but I'm an inventor. I need freedom of movement. But having it here under the same roof as the rest of Fisk Industries is like working in a military compound. It's bad for business. And, frankly, it's starting to cause problems in my marriage."

"Ahh," Enzo said. "I see."

"The Auriga Project is over, Enzo. I want to split the business. You buy the Translocator from me, and I'll take the rest of Fisk Industries somewhere else."

"Who's going to run the project if you go?"

Amon gazed across the room at Reuben, who was pointing at floor plans as the FBI spies nearby nodded and listened attentively.

"Reuben can do it. He's been my second-in-command long enough. Time for him to pilot the ship."

"Hm," Enzo said. "I like the idea. But why don't you think about it, eh?"

"Nothing to think about," Amon said. "Now that Lucas has his own Translocator, I have to focus on finding and stopping him. I don't know what his plans are, but I can't imagine they're good after what he went through to get that reactor. Maiming himself like that? I can't let him use something I built to further his own dark purpose."

"And you think chasing a madman around the world will help your marriage?"

Amon blushed. "No, but—"

Enzo held up a hand. "I'm sorry. That was unkind."

"No. You're right. It won't. But what choice do I

have? I feel it's my responsibility to prevent or reverse any harm he may cause."

"When you stare into the darkness long enough, the darkness stares back."

Amon wrinkled his nose. "Are you really quoting Nietzsche to me?"

"Just because he went mad at the end doesn't make his lucid thoughts any less true. If you're going to stop Lucas, you need access to the Translocator. You will continue to work on the Translocator. But perhaps it would be good to give Reuben some more responsibility. And Jeanine." The doctor nodded at Jeanine, who sat nearby working on her laptop.

"We'll see," Amon said. "In any case, I'm happy for you to make those calls. I've had some bad luck picking trustworthy people lately."

"Don't blame yourself. And don't listen to what the press says, eh?"

Amon groaned. He'd forgotten all about Reagan Gruber until now. Well, one problem at a time.

"Ahh," Jeanine said, the relief evident in her voice. "Here she is, Amon."

Amon turned back to the holodeck, and activated the Translocator. Eliana appeared on the platform as the spinning rings came to a halt. The bald bomb tech and Eliana stood on either side of the young man in the loincloth, supporting his weight. The knife Reuben had given him was now buried in his gut.

"Paramedic!" Eliana shouted. "We need a paramedic!"

Amon rushed forward to help carry the young man down the long hall and up the elevator. Reuben had called ahead and EMTs met them outside. He was rushed off to the hospital.

When Eliana had wiped her hands, she came out and faced Amon.

"I'm sorry," he said for the second time.

She looked at him and took a deep breath. Her mouth was a thin line of worry. "Thank you for saying that. But it's my fault he got hurt."

"I wasn't talking about Rakulo. I was apologizing for my own behavior."

She nodded.

"I'll understand if you can't forgive me right away."

"Just give me some time."

Amon nodded as he felt his heart break. "Also, your archaeologists have arrived," he managed to say.

When Eliana's eyes lit up at that news, Amon felt his broken heart fall into a dark hole.

"Have they really?"

Amon nodded. "Audrey probably took them to her lab. I heard she had some other samples you left her."

Eliana took a step closer to him, and reflexively leaned in…but stopped herself. She squeezed his arm instead. "I should go check on them. And apologize to Audrey for the way I left. I…We'll talk soon, okay?"

Amon nodded, and forced a smile that fell as he watched his wife walk away.

46

THE SAME ERA

"Easy, girl," Eliana said weakly.

Lakshmi had wrapped her arms around Eliana's neck as soon as she walked in the door, and the taller woman was now crushing her in her embrace.

"Oh, I'm so glad you're okay," Lakshmi said.

"We didn't know *what* to think when I saw all those vans outside," Talia said.

"And the security guards," said Tanner.

"Good to see you in one piece, boss," said Ross.

Eliana separated from Lakshmi and hugged the others each in turn, including Audrey, who wiped tears from her cheeks. Framed in her bright red hair, her watery blue eyes sparkled.

"Are you okay?" Eliana said.

"Still adjusting," Audrey said. "I'm just this scientist, you know?"

They all laughed.

"I'll be fine," Audrey added.

Eliana gazed around at her friends' grinning faces. "How did you figure out I was here, Lakshmi?" Eliana asked. "You couldn't have seen my car from the perimeter where the guards are stationed now, could you?"

"We didn't," Lakshmi said. "Your phone was off. Your car wasn't parked at your house, and the house lights were all off. So we came to see Audrey, instead." Lakshmi shrugged. "We wanted to know about the radiocarbon dating on the second monolith samples. And show her the pictures, of course, so she knew what she was working with."

"I'm dying to know, too," Eliana said.

"I can tell you with some certainty," Audrey said, "that the second set of samples dates to the same era as the first. They may have been built less than a few years apart."

"I'm glad to hear it," Eliana said. "But the real test is ahead of us."

"What do you mean?" Audrey asked.

The others listened in rapt silence as Eliana explained how she had gone through the rift to Kakul. She told them how Reuben had followed, what happened when they encountered Rakulo and the others, who were fighting amongst themselves. At last, she came to the part where she had visited the stone city, in search of carvings...and been taken captive by Xucha, the alien being impersonating a god.

At first, her words were hesitant. She faltered and stuttered. But her voice gained confidence and power as she went on. Telling the story seemed to diminish the alien's hold over her.

"He said his name was Remethiakara," Eliana said. "And that your carbonado, Audrey…he called it a star shard. He told me that the stones were forged by intense heat at the center of a star when it explodes. The shards are cast outward into the universe. I guess that's how one landed here. He seemed to be able to draw energy from it somehow like…electricity that he could control. That's the best way I can describe it."

Audrey's eyes widened as her mouth fell open. "Wow," she finally managed to say. "Does he still have it?"

"I'm not sure we'll ever know. Rakulo's friends brought him back from the tower. I asked one of the girls if the shard was still up there, but she said they looked all over and there was no black rock or anything like it."

"Damn," Audrey said. "The only other piece of that meteorite is buried under hundreds of feet of Antarctic ice."

47

FOR HIS PEOPLE

Rakulo woke in a small white room full of so much sunlight that it made him squint. Except, it wasn't sunlight, it was a brightness that came from rectangles set into the ceiling.

Eliana, Reuben, Amon, and several other people he had never met before, light-skinned people mostly, but one brown woman too, taller than any woman he'd ever seen, stood at his bedside.

"Hello," Eliana said in his language. "How are you feeling?"

Rakulo patted gently at his ribs. A thick padding of white bandages were wrapped around his ribcage.

"Alive," he said. "Where am I?"

"On my world."

"Your world is very bright."

Eliana chuckled. "Not all of it."

She spoke to the others in her own language and they laughed. It made him feel very uncomfortable.

"Thank you for healing me," he said.

"I was worried you wouldn't make it for a while," Eliana said. "But the doctors have cleared you to leave. Do you want to go home now?"

"Yes. Very much. I need to be there for my people."

48

WHAT SHE WAS LOOKING FOR

Lakshmi seemed surprised when Amon agreed to let Eliana and her team go back through the Translocator with Rakulo.

Eliana wasn't surprised. The hangdog look Amon gave her made his motives transparently obvious.

It would take more than that to make it up to her for the way he'd acted. She wanted to forgive him. She really did. She had been inches away from saying, "I forgive you," several times, but the words wouldn't come out. It was like her tongue had been tied in a knot.

Amon had given the rest of the team their safety brief, proper protocols for using the transponder bracelets he made them all wear. But he wasn't at the office the day they went back to Kakul. She thought that might have been intentional. Reuben and Jeanine operated the Translocator. They both hugged her before she went through. They didn't mention Amon once.

Her team arrived in the village to a riotous, chaotic greeting. Once people had settled down, Rakulo asked a few warriors to take Eliana and her friends where they wanted to go. A sizable escort of young warriors gathered and led them to the ruined city of *Uchben Na*. The protection turned out to be truly unnecessary. Nothing bothered their visit except for the ever-present tickle of mosquitoes at their sweaty necks. The humidity had ratcheted up again as well, she noticed.

Soon, they crossed under the archway into the main courtyard.

"This is incredible!" Turner whispered.

"I've never seen a ruin so well preserved," Lakshmi said.

"If the city was only recently abandoned—as in, the past few hundred years—what do you think happened?"

"They took care of the city for a long time," Eliana said. "And then one day they didn't." She had slowed to look at the carvings underneath the arch one more time. This would be the first thing she recorded. She would give the rest of them a tour first...

But as Eliana walked under the arch and saw the courtyard in the daylight, she gasped and put her hand to her mouth.

Where the great central pyramid had once been —a pyramid as big as Chichen Itza's famous wonder —a pile of rubble now stood. The pyramid had collapsed to the ground since her last visit only a few days ago.

"What's the matter?" Lakshmi asked.

"The pyramid collapsed," Eliana said. "It was standing just a few days ago. How…"

"Oh," was all Lakshmi could say. "What happened to it?

"Why don't we ask their Chief?" Eliana said.

Rakulo entered the city behind them. Though he walked slow and carefully, his hand at his side, he crossed toward them, tall in the sunlight. His chest had filled out and he seemed to have lost much of the adolescent awkwardness that Eliana had seen in him when they first met almost two years ago. He looked so much like Chief Dambu that Eliana felt uncomfortable for a moment…until he smiled. Rakulo's smile filled his whole face and wrinkled the brown skin at his eyes.

"Rakulo," Eliana said. "What happened to the pyramid?"

"I don't know," Rakulo said. "The others said there was an earthquake. The ground shook for several minutes. When people came here to investigate, it was like this. The earthquake must have taken it down."

Eliana translated Rakulo's explanation to her team.

"They say the pyramid at Chichen Itza was built on top of a *cenote*," Lakshmi said. "Maybe this one was, too, and the earthquake took it down."

"Maybe," Eliana said.

Rakulo interrupted her reverie. "Did you find what you were looking for?" he asked.

Eliana saw Lakshmi's eyes light up, and her lips murmur something under her breath. She was still in awe of the natives—and maybe a little bit in lust, too, Eliana thought.

"We will," Eliana said in the Kakuli language. "We just need to take some samples and pictures and we'll be on our way."

"Dirt?" Rakulo said. "What do you need with dirt?"

"It will tell us how old this place is."

Rakulo regarded the city for a long time, gazing among the stones, and then shrugged. "If you want to, go ahead. I don't care how old it is. I am happy to see the pyramid destroyed. People are saying that Xucha destroyed his temple in anger because we have turned away. But it has been peaceful ever since. These stones could sink into the sea for all I care."

"Don't you want to use the stones to rebuild?"

"This is the past," Rakulo said. "Our future is in the village, not among these cold stones."

"Now that you can go beyond the Wall, will you always stay in the village?"

"We'll stay for now," Rakulo said. "There are crops to harvest still. If we leave, we will need time to prepare. There is no danger now except to protect what we have left."

Eliana nodded. She guessed, based on what the alien had told her, that their population had been slowly declining for centuries.

"I have a favor to ask," Rakulo said. "Can you get me more of those"—he expanded his hands and made a rumbling noise with his mouth—"things you used to punch through the Wall?"

"I can ask," Eliana said. "Although there are probably more practical ways. I'll work something out."

"Thank you," Rakulo said.

Eliana and her team took several soil core samples from different spots all around the stone city in the week they spent there. Then they went home.

49

A PARTICULAR KIND OF JUSTICE

The old man, Reuben, was the one who brought the new tools back with Eliana. Rakulo was astonished the first time he watched Reuben use the light-cutter describe a circle in the sheer, unmarked Wall. The circle could then be battered out, leaving a gaping hole with a sharp, curving edge.

They couldn't take down the Wall, so Rakulo did the next best thing. He and Citlali used the light-cutter to make dozens of exits, each about a thirty minute walk apart. No matter where you were, there was always a way through the Wall.

Rakulo felt this served a particular kind of justice. Even if there turned out to be nothing for them beyond the desert on that side of the Wall, his people would never be trapped here again.

It was only once this had been done that he was able to sleep at night.

Eliana left behind one of those bracelets with him. Rakulo kept it tied and hidden in the thatch roof of his hut like he had with her ring for so many months. She said that if he ever wanted to visit their world again, or reach them, all he had to do was hold the button to send them a "signal."

Strange word, "signal." But having the object also brought him some peace.

They held a big memorial with a bonfire for all those they had lost. At midnight, when no one else could see, Rakulo threw the obsidian knife that had once belonged to his father, and before that to generations of shamans, into the ocean, as far as he could hurl it.

It had served him well, but he didn't want to carry a symbol of the old ways on his person any more.

Instead, he armed himself with the other object he had acquired that came from Eliana's world, the big knife that Reuben told him was made of "metal." Another new word for him.

Carrying the thing that had brought him closest to death reminded him how precious life was. How fragile. And what he had done to rescue hope for his people.

"Good news, Raku!" Citlali said as she came up to him at the cliff's edge. "Yeli thinks she is with child."

"So soon?"

"She says it is Quen's."

Rakulo grinned. Their tribe would begin to grow once again.

50

THE HALF OF IT

Eliana kicked off her sandals and sat cross-legged on the shore of the turtle pond at the University of Texas at Austin. She placed the blue folder thick with loose pages on the grass next to her. The summer air was dry and hot, but her skin felt thirsty for the sun. She didn't mind sweating a little as long as her hair was pulled up off her neck. She watched the turtles battle for the sunny dry spot on the end of the log while she waited for Renee to arrive.

The fall semester was still several weeks away, so the campus was sparsely populated. Only two people shared the pond with her—a old lady power-walking across the campus, and a young woman with her headphones in, strolling along the opposite bank.

Eliana had refused an invitation to return for more guest lectures during the fall semester. Since the last trip to Kakul, her mind filled with thoughts of her research, and what they had discovered.

Things with Amon remained in a kind of synchronous orbit, repeating the same motions but staying more or less the same distance apart. He was currently overseeing the removal of Fisk Industries renewables business to a new facility further outside of town. Given recent events, she could hardly blame him wanting to separate the two businesses.

She did hear that Reuben was getting a raise in all the change. That was something she could be glad for. He deserved it.

Eliana closed her eyes and lay back. She was only laying that way for a few minutes when she heard footsteps crunch through the crushed sandstone path. Someone cast a refreshingly cool shadow over her face.

"Hello," Eliana said.

"You look relaxed."

"I am."

Renee sat cross-legged next to Eliana, picked up the folder, and began to scan through the numbered pages, her fingers ruffling the corners and her eyes flicking down through the bold sub-headers.

"Eliana, is this what I think it is?" Renee said. She read for a few more minutes, mouthing silent words as she read. "Incredible!"

You don't know the half of it, Eliana thought. For each piece of evidence she had included, she had left a thousand speculations out. That's part of the reason the article had taken her so long to write.

"What about those people you met there? I don't see anything about them in here. What can you tell me?"

"They don't keep written records, and haven't lived in the site of the ruins we carbon-dated for centuries. Besides, I'd rather leave them out of it. They just want to live their lives. Isn't this enough without them?"

"Well, yes, I think that finding stone ruins on two different planets of the same age is certainly 'enough.'"

"I believe the stones may even have been mined from the same quarry, too. We need to do a few more tests, but I think the results will prove my theory."

Renee's mouth fell open. "Amazing." She glanced down at the title page.

"Who is Audrey Larson?"

"The world's first astrogeologist. Can you believe that?"

"Have I met her?"

"No. She works with Amon. She's the scientist who dated everything—the limestone and the soil samples."

"Well, I'm certainly impressed. What's your theory as to how the stones got there?"

Would you believe me if I told you? Eliana thought.

She considered the question for a long minute before saying, in the end, "I'm sure of what's in there. No more than that. Let others look at the evidence and draw their own conclusions."

51

SOLARPULSE-1 ONLINE

Amon was impressed. When the President of the United States signed off on a project that was deemed a matter of national security, things got done fast.

The US military rolled in two days after events had come to a head. They built twenty-foot tall cement walls topped with a curl of barbed wire around what had formerly been the Fisk Industries main campus and now belonged to the Lunar Terraform Alliance.

With Dr. Badeux and Reuben's help, Amon split his company in half. While he kept a large stake, ownership of the particle accelerator and the Hopper itself was signed over to the LTA. Fisk Industries now focused exclusively on photovoltaic systems, with research focused on developing more efficient solar cell production.

It turned out well in the end—Amon got some cash back in return for his company's investment in the Hopper, and he was still able to keep a voting share. He would be involved—though in a slightly different role—with the lunar base and supply transport projects.

And he still had unlimited access to the Translocator—although now the LTA handled it directly, rather than Amon. The extra money from the deal he used to buy Wes out of his original investment and remove him from the board of Fisk Industries. These two things combined were an enormous weight off his shoulders.

When Agent Moreno looked back through Wes's communications, they discovered that Wes was, in fact, the mole they had been looking for. Emails on a private account registered under a fake name were discovered by Agent Moreno. Wes had foolishly secured the new email via two factor authentication with his Fisk Industries' email account. Wes had been feeding Reagan Gruber "anonymous tips" for months.

Among other grandiose fabrications, all the information that Lucas needed was sprinkled throughout the emails—the info about how NASA had moved some of their meteorites to a new lab in Fisk Industries, that the construction on the lunar base was moving ahead, and which dome the nuclear reactor was located in. Amon remembered Wes typing with focus on his phone as they toured the lunar base, probably taking sneaky silent photographs when no one else was looking.

The question of how this information had made its way to Lucas was summarily resolved as well. Regan Gruber, who seemed obsessed with Fisk Industries and the Translocator, had published all of the info Wes sent him on his blog, albeit buried among rambling diatribes against modern science and stacked with overblown, click-baity headlines. Most of it got shunted into the conspiracy theory section of the website, but it was all there for a diligent reader who was aware of Reagan Gruber's obsession—a person like Lucas—to find, given a little patience and time.

The nuclear reactor on the lunar base meant to replace the one Lucas had stolen was still being built. Engineers on the lunar base managed to get power back to most of the important research facilities using smaller radioisotope reactors and additional solar-charged batteries that Fisk Industries supplied.

This enabled them to continue moving forward on the SOLARPulse-1 detection array, which went online today.

Dr. Badeux and Amon traveled through the Translocator to the lunar base in the early afternoon.

They made their way through the switch-backing access tunnels to the upper lip of the Tycho crater, to see the detection array come online for the first time.

"Any luck locating Lucas or his Translocator?" Enzo said as they walked.

"Agent Moreno and the FBI are still searching," Amon said. "They've more or less given up on finding Lucas's Translocator by tracking heat signals."

"Maybe we can turn SOLARPulse-1 toward earth for a little help?"

Amon smiled wryly. "If Lucas is smart—and I know he is—the reactors will be well shielded, or deep underground, or both. And if that's the case, then we'll have to wait for some other activity with the Translocator to find him. Any kind of long-term, reliable translocation still requires a platform at the other end."

"Unless you don't care for the quality of the reassembly on the receiving end."

"True enough. I don't know what he's up to."

"Can you come up with another way to detect a molecular disassembly?"

"At this point, I have no idea how. But if anyone is going to find him, it will be Agent Moreno. I'm going to do everything I can to help, too."

"You'll find him, and he'll get arrested and

brought to justice. It's just a matter of time. You have my full support, too, of course. The Nazis showed us the kind of horrors that people with the right funding and strange ideas can conjure. The world doesn't need a repeat of that experience."

"Indeed, it does not."

They turned another corner and followed the slope of the floor up. The tunnel finally terminated next to that broad window that looked out over the Tycho crater and the lunar base below. The air was clear this time because the fabricators didn't have enough power to run yet. But they would run again soon.

Amon turned from the window and entered the door that led to the SOLARPulse-1 detection array.

In the room, half a dozen scientists were seated at their own computer stations, arranged in a half circle around a hologram replica of the solar system.

Stanis Rachmaninoff greeted them and gave a short tour that ended with the blue-green hologram of the solar system.

"The diagram of the system is to scale. And you can zoom in and out, like this."

He held out his hands and brought them slowly apart to zoom in on the Tycho crater.

"We're here," he said.

Then Stanis brought his hands together. The scale of the hologram changed until the sun was but a speck among a hundred thousand other stars in the Milky Way.

"Would you like to try?"

Amon nodded. "Thank you."

The controls were different than his own machine, but Amon quickly adjusted to the nuances of this system, a newer build with lower latency and a more advanced visualization engine. Then he got lost in the beauty of what he was seeing. To be able to explore most of the Milky Way and see it in 3-D spacetime was remarkable. Amon located the sun around the world where Eliana's Kakul was located, a small planet with two moons.

The pain of Eliana's distance had receded slightly, but it still felt like a numb ache in his gut. He was trying to be patient, to give her the space she needed. If he did that, she would eventually come back to him, find a way to forgive him. It hadn't happened yet.

A rapid beeping sound came from one of the computers nearby.

"Another?" Stanis Rachmaninoff asked the scientist seated there, pleasant surprise filling his voice.

"NEO entering the system."

Stanis turned to Amon and Dr. Badeux to explain.

"The SOLARPulse-1 is programmed to detect any objects entering our system if they meet certain velocity, mass, or composition requirements. We want to know well in advance if any asteroids are heading on a path toward Earth, so we can take action. We've found several new meteorites since SOLARPulse-1 came online. This is probably another one."

The beeping stopped as suddenly as it had begun.

Stanis glanced back at the scientist again, who cocked his head and leaned toward his monitor, confused.

"It stopped," he said.

"What?"

"It just stopped moving."

Stanis shooed Amon away from the hologram of the universe, and gestured until the solar system came back into tight focus.

He located the meteorite that had been detected. It was currently edging past Pluto. He zoomed in again.

What Amon saw looked, at first, like any other meteorite, round or oval with irregular edges.

But as he studied it, Amon noticed that it was perfectly symmetrical lengthwise. And the back of it had a kind of…fin sticking up.

Suddenly, it picked up speed and began moving again. The computers' warning blared.

Stanis locked the hologram on the moving object and stared, aghast, as the blood drained from his face.

"That's no meteorite," Dr. Badeux said.

"It's a spacecraft," Amon said. "And it's headed straight toward us."

<hr>

Thank you for reading *The Alien Element*!

The third book in the series, *The Ares Initiative*, is available now! Turn the page for an excerpt...

THE ARES INITIATIVE (EXCERPT)

Chapter 1 - Shift

Remethiakara nearly ripped the mothership to pieces as he shifted into hyperspace.

The massive living spacecraft heaved, quaked, and hurled him to the floor of the bridge. His head cracked against a hard edge—the armrest of the pilot's chair, most likely. The impact would have been enough to break his skull, but he was spared a life-threatening injury by the thin but durable fabric of his armorsuit. It was still enough to split the outer shell of the helmet and send him tumbling backward, end over end, until he struck against a circular doorframe.

Air was driven from all four of Remethiakara's lungs as his body impacted the shapeshifting carapace that made up the walls of the mothership. He focused on trying to regain his breath even as blood filled his mouth from a cut on his tongue. The ship continued to rattle around. He couldn't make out anything but blurry shapes, streaks of brownish-purple, an azure luminescence flecked with black. Red spots crowded his vision as the multiplied gravity of the ship's acceleration flattened him against the wall with such force that his organs lurched inside him.

He managed to choke down one ragged breath. Then another. It felt like breathing with weights on his chest, but it kept him conscious. A ghoulish sound like flesh being rent from bone suddenly crowded out the other sensations. His whole body tensed.

At first, he thought it was one of his own limbs breaking. Then he realized it was happening not to him, but to the mothership that carried him. Due to their truethought connection, her autonomous neural system screamed in his mind—a sharp sound that he felt as much as heard, a small needle being gouged straight into his eardrum. He closed his eyes and held on as an aft compartment was torn away from the tail of the ship, shredded as it passed through the hyperspace continuum, and scattered through a billion miles of space.

He felt the ship's pain as his own pain, but muted, distant. The purpose of the pain was to allow the pilot—in this case, him—to identify the breach and respond quickly. A nanosecond after the aft compartment was torn away, Remethiakara hurled a sharp mental command at the mothership's receptors. The living vessel's vascular system clotted to seal the breach, preventing the rest of the atmosphere from bleeding out.

He did not need to see it to know it happened. He felt it as a flash of physical knowledge—similar to the way it felt when one of his servitor bots stitched up a deep cut in the soft flesh at the small of his back.

The pain faded to a dull throbbing as the breach was finally sealed. The sense of panic and urgency that had been transmitted to him with the sensation subsided. And the mothership finally achieved equilibrium with the hyperspace continuum into which he'd thrust her.

When the quaking rumbled down to a low vibration, and the artificial gravity returned to normal levels, Remethiakara sagged to the floor. There had been a high probability that forcing the ancient mothership into hyperspace would tear him and the spacecraft to pieces. Getting away with a lost limb was perfectly acceptable—even to be expected. But he also knew that were he to try the maneuver a second time, he would certainly not make it through alive.

Not that there was enough juice left in the star shard to make another shift.

He only had one chance to get this right.

Remethiakara pushed himself to his feet and surveyed the rest of the damage the shift had caused.

One of the fragile eggs containing his precious offspring had jostled free of the stasis pods where he'd put them for safekeeping. He hadn't been sure how much of the ship would hold up in flight, and decided to keep them close. But they were too large and awkward at this point in their gestation for the stasis pod lids to close, and the straps he'd used to secure them had come loose in the turbulence.

The eggs shouldn't be anywhere near the low gravity of space travel this late in their development. But what choice did he have? After the savages had swarmed through the Wall and overwhelmed his defenses with the help of more advanced Earthlings and their quantum teleportation device, he'd been forced to discard the old plan to ensure the preservation of his race.

Remethiakara bent down and gingerly ran his hand along the broken shell of the cracked egg— then jerked his hand up to his helmet, now gashed in a similar way. He swallowed his panic, jerked the busted helmet off over his head, and took deep draughts of air through his slitted nostrils and thin, lipless mouth.

Another of his children had been killed, this time by his own actions. That knowledge caused an inescapable feeling of guilt to clawed its way up from deep in his lower stomach. Globs of half-formed flesh were visible through the crack in the egg, floating in a thick amniotic fluid. He could see the curve of what might have been a neck. What a terrible waste. What a tragic loss.

He closed his eyes and looked away.

The young leader of the savages had destroyed four eggs. His own carelessness had ended the life of another. There were only four left.

With shaking hands, Remethiakara checked the remaining straps. Coming out of hyperspace might be rockier than going into it, and he couldn't take any chances. These four eggs were his last chance to uphold his duty, his last chance to ensure the survival of his race, a nomadic species who had wandered the stars since the destruction of their native world.

Remethiakara rose to his feet abruptly and strode back to the center of the bridge, where a column of blue light in front of the pilot's chair held a large chunk of meteorite suspended in its beam. The sable geode was so black that, from a certain angle, it looked like a hole in the light rather than an object suspended within it.

In reality, it was an ancient source of power called a star shard. Wrought by the intense heat of exploding stars, his race had been using their concentrated energy to power their motherships as they made way from planet to planet for aeons.

This particular star shard Remethiakara had recovered by tracking a human woman who had shown up on the planet where he'd been living. He used the star shard she brought with her to create a singularity that took him back to Earth.

There he learned that a group of intelligent Earthlings had managed to harness the shard's energy with their own transport technology...but that they didn't seem to grasp the true extent of the shard's power. Their tech was inefficient, their defenses thin. Eventually, Remethiakara's long patience had been rewarded. He cut through them easily and reclaimed the star shard as his own.

But then they had killed his children and destroyed the place he had called home for the last thousand years.

They would pay for that.

Remethiakara tossed the busted helmet aside and reached out with his gauntleted hands. The blue light bent and crackled, shooting sparks into his fingertips. He manipulated the beam. The display inside the helmet would normally show energy readouts. Without it, he cast the readouts directly into his cornea. An array of numbers and symbols no Earthling would be capable of comprehending superimposed themselves on his vision. After spending a moment tweaking the complex mathematical formula in his mind, he clenched his jaw.

It was as he suspected. The ship was just too

large to expect anything else. Raising the mother-ship from what was meant to be the living vessel's final resting place on Kakul, traveling through the planet's atmosphere, and shifting into hyperspace had taxed the star shard to such an extent that its power was already nearly depleted.

If he was lucky, there would be enough energy left to complete his journey and little, if any, leftover. Was it enough to construct an incubator for the eggs until he could establish a more permanent settlement? He hoped so.

Remethiakara thrust his hands back into the blue-white beam of light and checked on the course of the jump. Noting that the two planets had moved away from each other more than the ship's systems had predicted since the last time this ancient mothership had journeyed between the stars, he made some adjustments which took the unexpected orbital drift into account.

All Remethiakara could do after that was wait. He passed the time by monitoring the energy drain on the shard, and carefully feeding the eggs through a complicated manual link with the living mothership, using what little power the shard could spare to sustain them.

The end of the jump felt like it would never come.

Then it seemed to come abruptly.

He prepared better this time, strapping himself in beside his eggs.

The mothership quaked and lurched, throwing the metallic sphere of his last servitor bot across the bridge and smashing it to uselessness against the doorway.

The floor rumbled and there was a change of speed, like stepping off a fast-moving vehicle onto solid ground.

Remethiakara braced, then slowly relaxed as nothing happened for a moment. *Was that it?*

He unbuckled himself and thrust his gauntlets into the beam of light. The walls of the mothership turned transparent—or rather, they simply transmitted through the vascular systems what the outer membrane was experiencing visually, so that it seemed as if he could see directly into the black emptiness of space from deep within the heart of the mothership.

The velocity shifted abruptly again. This time he was expecting it, and it merely hurled his body back into the pilot's chair, piling seven or eight gravities of force upon his chest. He fought to remain conscious as a cold blue planet blurred past on the starboard wall, followed by a massive orange one with an enormous ring system.

Then the spacecraft went completely still as the vessel exited hyperspace.

He slumped down, his chest heaving.

And felt his slitted nostrils and lipless mouth expand into a helpless grin.

Despite the hiccup in the landing, the ship had ended up not only in the right system, but almost exactly on target. Off by only a few hundred thousand miles. Not bad for a derelict mothership that was six thousand or so years past its prime.

Now the starboard wall was filled with the great red curve of a desert planet receding behind him.

Meanwhile, directly ahead, a tiny green and blue speck was just becoming visible in the distance.

He stood there for a long time, smiling, as the planet known as Earth slowly grew larger in his viewframe.

After another day it was the size of his fist.

It wouldn't be much longer now.

If his brief encounters with modern Earthlings were any indication, they had already made note of his ship and were now making their own preparations.

He suspected that his arrival would not be taken lightly.

Get *The Ares Initiative* now.

A GUIDE TO THE PRONUNCIATION OF NAMES

Though ample evidence suggests there existed a wide variety of languages and dialects among the ancient people of Central America, the author based the language of the *Kakuli* people on Yucatec Maya, the most commonly spoken—and well documented—Mayan language today.

Words, when borrowed, were taken from modern Yucatec Maya dictionaries and archaeological texts. Where English transliterations varied, spelling was chosen for consistency and simplicity. The sounds of the Mayan language are poorly expressed by English letters, so a rough pronunciation guide follows.

NAMES

Citlali

[kit-LA-li]

Dambu
[DAHM-boo]

Ixchel
[EESH-chel]

Kakul
[KAH-cool]

Maatiaak
[MAH-tee-ahk]

Rakulo
[Rah-KU-lo]

Tilak
[Tee-LAHK]

Uchben Na
[OOCH-ben Nah]

Watiya
[Wah-TEE-yuh]

Xucha
[SHOO-cha]

ABOUT THE AUTHOR

M.G. Herron writes science fiction and fantasy for adrenaline junkies.

His books explore new worlds, futuristic technologies, ancient mysteries, various apocalypses, and the vagaries of the human experience.

His characters have a sense of humor (except for the ones who don't). They stand up to strange alien monsters from other worlds... unless they slept through their alarm again.

Like ordinary people, Herron's heroes try to make the world a better place, and sometimes screw things up.